A Dance Through Time
Lynn Kurland

A romance writer falls asleep in Gramercy Park, and wakes up in fourteenth century Scotland—in the arms of the man of her dreams . . .

This Time Together
Susan Leslie Liepitz

An entertainment lawyer dreams of a simpler life—and finds herself in an 1890s cabin, with a handsome mountain man . . .

Remember Love
Susan Plunkett

A bolt of lightning transports the soul of a scientist to 1866—and into the body of a beautiful Alaskan woman. But her new life comes with a price: a maddeningly arrogant—and seductive—husband . . .

Lost Yesterday
Jenny Lykins

A curator from Pierce mansion is sent back in time—and falls in love with a man whose face she knows from century-old photographs—Hunter Pierce himself!

$\mathscr{S}$ILVER
$\mathscr{T}$OMORROWS

Susan Plunkett

JOVE BOOKS, NEW YORK

SILVER TOMORROWS

A Jove Book / published by arrangement with
the author

PRINTING HISTORY
Jove edition / April 1997

The Putnam Berkley World Wide Web site address is
http://www.berkley.com/berkley

ISBN: 0-515-12047-2

A JOVE BOOK®
Jove Books are published by The Berkley Publishing Group,
200 Madison Avenue, New York, New York 10016.
JOVE and the "J" design are trademarks
belonging to Jove Publications, Inc.

PRINTED IN THE UNITED STATES OF AMERICA

10 9 8 7 6 5 4 3 2 1

For Darlin' Dan.
Thank you for the treasure of
your love,
your friendship,
and your encouragement.

Chapter 1

DURANGO, COLORADO, 1997

"D<small>ON'T DISAPPOINT ME</small>, Emily."

Emily Fergeson's grip tightened on the telephone receiver. The fangs of reproach bit into her heart. The familiar rush of acid bubbled in her stomach. "This is the first vacation I've taken—"

"I'm aware of that. Some things are more important than a vacation. You're the only one I can count on." Ronald Warner's voice lowered into a warning tone that anyone who had denied his wishes recognized as dangerous. "If I can't rely on my family—"

"We aren't exactly a family, Ron."

"You're my daughter. You owe me."

Emily bit her bottom lip. What did she owe him? Love? There had never been a hint of love between them. Ron had made it clear he wanted no emotional ties with her.

"Emily?"

"Yes?"

"Let's start again. I wouldn't interrupt your vacation if this wasn't critical. You are the only one I can rely on to bring the fine points together. I have a great deal riding on the outcome of this engagement. The candidates for both parties will be attending. Do you realize how much arm-twisting I had to do to get them to agree?"

Battling the dread churning fresh waves of stomach acid into a froth, she made a noncommittal sound.

"Craig Lyman specifically requested your presence. He's interested in you, Emily, and I approve of him. Considering that he owns the lion's share of ARB Circuits, Craig would make an excellent financial ally for both of us. All you have to do is lead him to the altar."

Emily closed her eyes and sagged against the wall. Her head began throbbing. "Mr. Lyman is interested in my financial assets. He's only a few years older than I am, and he's been married as many times as you have." After the words tumbled free, she wished for them back. Any discussion of Ron's four failed marriages, or his youthful summer of rebellion with Lorena Fergeson, was taboo.

Emily rubbed her temples. Her pulse pounded in Ron's silence. The last thing she wanted to do was cut her vacation short after Laura's wedding tomorrow and race back to San Francisco. How many soirées and political events had she hosted for Ron? She had lost count years ago. She wished he would marry again and give her a reprieve. *Soon,* she told herself. *He never stays single for more than two years.*

"We can discuss Craig at a more convenient time. All I'm asking of you now is to place the family's best interests ahead of your vacation. Will you do your part for the family?"

"My part. . . . Does that mean you've changed your mind and I may address you as Dad or Father?"

"Sarcasm is unbecoming and unacceptable. Since my request for your help comes at an inconvenient time, I'll overlook it."

"I wasn't being sarcastic, merely inquiring at what point you become my father other than when you want something bad enough to acknowledge that I'm your daughter."

Ron's harsh intake of breath filled a brief, tense silence. "You're being childish, which you rarely are, Emily. Are you finished wounding me and ready to give me an answer?" Ron asked, in a tone that conjured images of crosses, nails, and a Roman centurion with a whip.

"I'll be there."

"Good." The relief in his voice flowed across the mountains separating him from Durango, Colorado. "I told the caterers to contact you on Wednesday."

He had known when he called that she would oblige him, regardless of the personal cost. He had counted on it. "Call them back. I'll hostess the party, but you'll have to get someone else to oversee the final preparations."

"Emily. . . ."

Something snapped inside her. "Don't push me. You got your way. I'll be back in time to act as your hostess. That's all, Ron. As you've often reminded me, I'm your accidental daughter. I am not your secretary, your personal slave, or a professional party-giver. I will conduct myself as your hostess for the evening. Nothing more. As for Craig Lyman, if you don't quit trying to force that lecherous Neanderthal on me, I'll make a scene you both will find hard to live down."

"Emily, your organizational skills are the best. I need—"

Head shaking, she lowered the phone from her ear. "I need, too. But you're incapable of giving me the consideration you'd give a stranger." She dropped the receiver into the cradle. For a long minute she stared at it before realizing she had hung up on him.

Good grief, had she actually threatened a scene?

In her wildest dreams, she was not brave enough to stand her ground in front of Ronald Warner. A public debacle drew attention. She winced at the absurdity of the empty threat. Notice on a personal level by anyone in the elite social circle they traveled was the last thing she wanted. Over the years, the unspoken pact of superficial camaraderie she had forged suited her fine.

In the bathroom, Emily swallowed two headache pills and chased them down with a tall glass of water laced with antacid. She applied lipstick and tucked a stray lock of dark brown hair into the elaborate crown piled on her head.

"So much for my vacation," she mumbled at the woman in the mirror, blotting her lipstick on a piece of tissue.

Gazing at the reflection, she dropped the tissue into the trash. Braced on her palms, she leaned toward the mirror. "I can't believe you spoke up." Awed, she bent closer. Nothing had changed in her outward appearance. However, she *felt* different. For the first time since her mother's death thirteen years earlier, she had dared to speak out and hold her ground.

Emily turned away from the mirror.

She had not held her ground. Nor had she stood up for herself. For three years she'd planned a vacation. One crisis after another postponed her departure. If not for Laura Sawyer's request that Emily be her maid of honor, the vacation might never have happened. Now that she was away from San Francisco, Emily longed for an island of time unfettered by business and Ron Warner's demands. The taste of capitulation soured the brief sweetness of freedom.

Emily wondered if her lips would ever form the word *no* when Ron demanded a slice of her life. Was he her Achilles' heel? Did she crave his approval beyond all else? She found herself asking those questions more frequently. In the dark moments when the clock read three in the morning, her motives surfaced with a bitter clarity.

Since the day they met at her mother's funeral, she had tried to earn her father's love. When that failed, she had sought acceptance and respect as suitable alternatives. But there was no substitute for paternal love, nor could any power on earth make Ron cherish her as a daughter. He was incapable of loving anyone longer than the time it took to fall in, then out, of love.

Perhaps that realization was why she had been able to give him only part of what he demanded.

"Let him find someone else to organize it," she muttered. It was time to apply what Ron called her "excellent organizational skills" to restructuring her personal life.

She smoothed the sleeves of the unadorned mauve dress she had donned for dinner. Relegating the telephone call to the back of her mind, she turned her attention toward the evening's festivities.

The phone call from Laura Sawyer three months earlier had decided the timing of her ill-fated vacation. Old friends from their days at Stanford, years and distance had eroded the camaraderie they had once shared. Emily had not thought that Laura considered her a close enough friend to bestow the privilege of being maid of honor. However, not one to refuse a friend, Emily had launched her vacation by spending three days in Durango for the wedding.

Emily descended the stairs with trepidation. In the foyer, Laura's mother, Lucy, paused and waited for Emily to join her. Not a single blond hair dared stray from Lucy's perfect Dutchboy style. A skillful application of makeup enhanced the artistry of Lucy's plastic surgeon. She took Emily's arm when she alighted from the bottom stair.

"We're so pleased you adjusted your busy schedule for Laura's wedding. It means a great deal to her father and me, and of course, to Laura."

"Well, we were friends." The lame response was all that came to mind.

"It isn't often someone of your social caliber goes so far out of her way to help another rise." Lucy led her into the parlor, where the rest of the family had gathered.

"My social caliber?" Emily's churning stomach tightened. Was that why Laura had asked her to be maid of honor? Because of her connections with the power brokers in the Bay Area?

Lucy had the grace to blush. "What I mean is, you have a thriving software development and documentation business and you're involved in your father's busy social life. We're thankful that you hold your friendship with Laura in such high esteem. I do thank you for being Laura's friend, Emily." Lucy's dulcet laugh softened the tension. "I'm afraid I'm not doing a very good job of expressing my gratitude for your arranging to attend Laura on her wedding day."

Disappointment rendered the aspirin Emily had taken useless. Like the wanna-bes pandering to Ron's powerful associates, the Sawyers coveted her social connections. "You're doing an excellent job of expressing yourself, Mrs. Sawyer."

Visibly relieved, Lucy allowed her smile to assume a genuine sense of pleasure. "Please, call me Lucy. We're going to be such good friends, too."

Emily bit back the response welling from the pit of disillusionment and changed the subject. "I take it you're pleased with Laura's choice of a husband."

"Oh, very. Leo is the epitome of what every mother desires for her daughter. Just look at him."

Emily saw the groom at the same time he saw them and lifted a wine glass in their direction.

"Laura could not have done better. The Kramer family is an old, prestigious Colorado family. Why, the Kramer men have populated the government and judicial halls in Denver and Durango for decades. Their ranch is one of the largest in the state. Leo, being an only child, has a great deal of responsibility and tradition to uphold. Laura is the perfect woman to help him advance in the political arena."

Lucy Sawyer beamed at Leo Kramer as though Emily didn't exist. "Laura's modeling classes have served her well." She glanced at Emily. A tinge of guilt marred her perfect hostess smile. "I mean, my Howard is a wonderful husband and father. But being a successful hardware and ranch supplier isn't exactly an entry card to the levels of society we aspired to for Laura's benefit."

"You want her to have it all," Emily speculated softly. "What does Laura want?"

Lucy's smile dimmed. "Why, what is best, of course. She trusts our judgment implicitly."

"I'm sure she does." Laura would never defy her parents. Like Emily, she craved love and approval. Perhaps that was what had drawn them together years ago. They knew each other's weaknesses and how to close ranks for protection. *The weak leading the weaker.*

Lucy nodded at her husband impatiently pointing at his watch. "I believe it is time we went in for dinner." She patted Emily's hand affectionately. "I'll make sure we have plenty of time to chat tomorrow evening."

Resigned to her role as friend, maid of honor, and society deb, Emily pasted on a smile and took her place at the table.

The food appeared tasty. It may have been, had Emily given it a fair chance. Instead, she picked at it and engaged in light conversation. Meanwhile, she wondered if this was a preview of the rest of her life—meaningless banter, pleasantries, double meanings to each friendship. Somewhere, there had to be someone who liked her for herself. Maybe there was even someone to love her, someone who she could love.

A quick assessment of the august diners promised that she wouldn't find the answer to her dreams here. With a mental sigh that did not touch the dazzling smile lighting her face, she tucked away her disappointment and dreams.

"My knowledge of Colorado politics is limited," she told Randall Crouse, an investment banker seated on her right. "How have recent policy decisions affected the state's financial growth and the business climate?"

Once she got him started, Crouse spoke through dinner. Emily listened, occasionally asking questions and commenting when necessary. With a little eye contact, she drew their dinner companions into the conversation. She had perfected the art of interpersonal dialogue before graduating from high school.

As with the countless dinner and party guests she had spoken with over the last decade, Emily did not contribute anything insightful, controversial, or personal. An inner ear listened with an uncanny perceptiveness that sifted meaning and innuendo. It was an expertise honed to precision over the years.

After dinner, the family and guests gathered in the parlor. The rich furnishings bespoke a tasteful show of wealth not unlike the dozens of homes Emily had frequented in her father's company.

Emily sought refuge from the banal chatter in the far corner of the room. Within minutes, tall, blond Laura had joined her. The two of them were a study of contrasts, Laura with her short, naturally curly hair and Emily with her long, straight tresses pulled away from her face. For the first time, Emily noted the haunted expression in Laura's pale-blue eyes.

"When we were at Stanford, who might have ever guessed I'd marry Leo Kramer?" Laura asked with a false brilliance.

Your mother. "I wouldn't have. You never mentioned him."

The champagne glass twirling in Laura's manicured fingers bespoke her nervousness. "I never set my sights that high."

Emily glanced across the room at Leo. Impeccably dressed in a white dinner jacket and black trousers, he exuded the polish of being raised in a level of society set apart from those who worked for Emily. She preferred to associate with her technical writers and editors and computer programmers. They dealt with life's problems head-on. The only one greasing the way for them was Emily, along with client companies of Fergeson Inc., and the generous benefits she offered.

"Do you love him, Laura?"

"I'm marrying Leo," Laura answered softly. The champagne flute stilled as her fingers closed tightly around it.

Emily stared at the diamond glittering on Laura's finger. There wasn't anything else to say. Laura was marrying a man she didn't love. For position. For prestige. For her mother.

"Make yourself happy, Laura. No one else can."

Obviously uncomfortable, Laura excused herself.

Emily gathered the familiar cloak of imperviousness around her emotions. She wouldn't think about Laura languishing in a marriage void of affection.

"You appear deep in thought. Does our wedding give you ideas about your own?"

Emily glanced up at Leo Kramer. The tan acquired by hours on the ski slopes seemed out of place in early May. Sun and weather had streaked his blond hair almost platinum. The coldness in his blue eyes reminded her of Craig Lyman, and a shiver crawled up her spine. "I have no plans for marriage. I'm content being single." The practiced smile armored her face. "Besides, from what I've seen, a good marriage takes a lot of work and compromise. I'm not ready to give up my independence."

"I like that in a woman."

Unsure what he liked and not caring, she remained silent.

"Independence, that is."

"But not too much, right?"

Leo's sudden laughter forced her to look at him. If only his character was as deep as his pockets, Laura might find a basis for a real relationship. "You show a talent for reading the message behind the words."

Emily shrugged and glanced around for an avenue of escape. In that instant, she decided that she did not like Leo Kramer, nor would she pretend to for Laura's benefit.

Leo's hands closed on her shoulders. Every muscle in her body tensed as his thumbs roamed along the sides of her neck. His bowed head forced her to meet his gaze.

"You're a beautiful woman, Emily. I've been watching you since you arrived yesterday. You strike me as a woman with a great deal to offer a man."

Years of sidestepping sexual advances came to her rescue. "What I have to offer is mine to give when I choose. Please, take your hands off me."

"But that's the point, Emily. I'd like to have my hands all over you, and I think you'd like it too."

Emily dropped all pretense and let her revilement show. "You're marrying my friend tomorrow morning. What's the matter with you?"

"There isn't anything the matter with me that a few hours in bed with you wouldn't cure. Besides, I'm getting mar-

ried, not buried. I'm a man of strong appetites, and I just
bet you're a tasty, satisfying main course."

"Leo?" she queried softly.

"Hmmmm?" he hummed with the smug expression of a
stock speculator who had bought low and unloaded at the
peak of the market.

"Go on a diet!" Without considering appearances, she
slapped his arm away. The depth of her anger sent her striding through the guests. She met Lucy Sawyer's startled
glance with a shake of her head. She didn't stop walking
until locked safely in her room.

For the next hour, she stood in the shower and scrubbed
her shoulders. The depravity of Leo Kramer's overture pervaded the pores of her skin. The lingering sensation defied
the cleansing of soap and the scrub of a washcloth that
turned her skin a fiery red.

Not until she got out of the shower did Emily realize she
had been crying the entire time.

Sleep eluded Emily. The impersonal detachment she used
as a shield to deflect involvement refused her summons.
Twenty-seven years of practiced acceptance and appeasement simmered like an overheated pressure cooker.

Recalling Lucy Sawyer's alarm when she hurried
through the throng of guests, Emily cringed. Lucy had noticed her exchange with Leo. Emily had half-expected a
knock on her door followed by an inquiry. She wondered
who else had noticed her departure. Oddly, she didn't care.

Leo's nefarious proposition haunted her. The man was
void of conscience. The implications for Laura tumbled
through her mind. The skin on her shoulders and neck
crawled with Leo's phantom touch. Revulsion kept her
stomach churning. How could Laura marry him?

"Does she even know he's a womanizer?" she murmured
into her pillow. "Would it matter?"

Uncertainty fed her agitation. It wasn't her business. Her
personal policy of nonintervention in other people's lives
warred with her instincts to protect someone more vulnerable. If Laura was unaware of Leo's debaucheries . . .

Emily sat up. Elbows on knees, she dropped her pounding head into her hands. What if Laura knew about Leo's proclivity for philandering?

"Why would she marry him knowing he'd be unfaithful?"

No sooner did the whispered question escape than an image of Lucy Sawyer popped in her mind's eye. No help there. Lucy's ambition for Laura embodied a selective blindness concerning Leo Kramer's shoddy integrity.

Slowly, prodded by an inner conviction as relentless as the power of lava forging a vent to the surface, Emily climbed out of bed. Anxiety and a lifelong aversion for involvement in the affairs of others warred with the force shoving her feet into slippers and her arms into a robe.

Before fully realizing her intent, she found herself rapping her knuckles on Laura's door. A familiar voice inside Emily begged her not to knock loudly enough to awaken anyone—especially Laura.

"Come in," Laura called softly.

Emily drew a deep breath. There was no retreat. She opened the door. The battle raged between speaking out for friendship's sake and holding her silence. She leaned against the door with no clear tactic in mind.

"I thought I was the one who was supposed to suffer premarital jitters." Laura drew her legs into an Indian-style position. The binding of a well-worn book she had been paging through sank into the cradle of her legs. "Come and sit with me. I was looking at our senior pictures, and remembering."

As though answering a summons issued by a higher power, Emily crossed the room. Gingerly, she perched on the edge of Laura's bed. She glanced at the dog-eared Stanford Quad yearbook and wondered how often Laura looked at it.

"Do you still have yours?"

"My what?" Emily said absently.

"Your yearbook."

"I don't know. Probably."

Laura sighed, then flipped a series of pages to a picture

of the Stanford band. A bright smile lit her eyes when she lifted her head. "I noticed you hung your tassel on the mirror of that cute Thunderbird you drive."

"It matches the paint job." Emily considered it vehicular interior decorating consistent with the period of the classic '56 T-Bird. Ron thought it gauche. Even after she grew tired of the tassel dangling in the middle of the windshield, she kept it. Her small rebellions allowed an illusion of control over her life.

Laura flipped to another well-worn page. "I loved this dress," she murmured wistfully at an elegant evening gown. "These were the best years of our lives."

"Our best times should be ahead of us."

"They're not." Laura flipped half a dozen pages.

Emily snatched the yearbook, slammed it shut, and tossed it aside. "Don't marry him, Laura."

"I have to." Laura turned her head to the wall.

"Why? Are you pregnant?"

"No. It's just too late to do anything else."

"No, it is not too late. Back out of this. Good grief, Laura, he'll make your life hell. Believe me, I've seen how people can tear one another up. That part of my education came gratis from selling tickets to the Ron Warner marriage mill."

Laura's cheeks colored a bright pink. "Did . . . did Leo proposition you, too?"

"Too?" Shocked, Emily stared until Laura turned toward the dark window. "Are you telling me that you know he's a womanizer and you're marrying him anyway? How can you consider saying 'I do' when you know he'll break his vows the first chance he gets? Good grief, Laura, what about AIDS? What about—"

"What about it?" Laura asked sharply as her head whipped around to Emily, her chin tilted in defiance.

In disbelief, Emily searched Laura's face and found nothing but a calm resignation for whatever fate lay ahead. "Why?"

Laura's nervous fingers dragged the yearbook within her grasp. "I'm not a strong person." A small, apologetic smile flickered at the corners of her mouth. "You know that better than anyone else. I could never do what you're doing now. Was there ever a person who avoided confrontation and conflict more than you and I? I know you must have agonized before you came at this hour to talk me out of getting married tomorrow. For your consideration, your caring . . . and your incredible daring, I thank you, Emily. You are a true friend. But the wedding has to take place. If I don't marry Leo, my parents will never live it down."

"How can your mother expect—"

"She can. She does. She's right about where Leo is going with his career. Once he's in the public eye, he's smart enough to know he won't be able to indulge his sexual appetite outside of marriage."

Emily's gaze never wavered. "I see. And has the date been selected for when this leopard is changing his spots?"

Clutching the yearbook, Laura shook her head, her chin balanced on the front rim of the cover. "Don't worry about it. I'll handle it."

"Don't worry about it?" Incredulous, Emily laughed. "No. Your mother pressures you to make me your maid of honor because she thinks of me as an avenue to my father's social connections. What good will they do any of you in Durango? You're asking me to condone a union the groom has no intention of honoring. Good grief, what do you people think I am? Degenerate? Totally void of conviction or belief? I don't think I can do this, Laura. I don't think I can walk down that aisle and watch you condemn yourself to your mother's ambitions and Leo's duplicity."

Laura dropped the yearbook, surged across the bed and grabbed Emily by the shoulders. "You *must*. Oh, Emily, don't . . . don't ruin this for me."

The angst expanding inside her knew no bounds. "It seems to me, I'm saving you from absolute disaster."

"*No!* Disaster is anything that disrupts the wedding. Oh, Emily, you can't do this to me. *Please.* I'm begging. Be my friend. Of all people, you understand how important it is to keep the waters calm. Can't you pretend this is just another

social function? Can't you just be what everyone expects?
Like we were at Stanford? I've admired your ability to be
whatever was called for . . . to say the right thing without
thinking . . . to create the illusion of involvement. But you
weren't involved. Ever. Do it one more time. Remove our
friendship from tomorrow morning. Be the socialite.
Please. I know you can do it. . . . For me?"

Emily studied her friend. Without a doubt she knew
Laura would marry Leo Kramer in the morning whether
she attended or drove away tonight. Could she do it? Wrap
herself in emotional insulation and play the expected role
one more time? "Tonight, I'm involved. You and I always
feared the day when something would force us to take a
genuine stand. For me, it's here. Now." A subtle shift
closed the door on detachment. The sensation of being alive
permeated every grating, tingling nerve in her body.

"You would hurt me that much?"

"Hurt you?" Emily stiffened in disbelief. "Laura, I want
to help you. You can leave Durango—"

"Leave? Let my parents face the debacle of their ungrateful daughter jilting the county's most prized bachelor
at the altar?"

Emily gazed sadly into her friend's blue eyes. Fear of
disaster robbed the color from Laura's face. "Stay or go, it
will pass. Follow your good sense and call it off. What's
the worst thing that could happen?"

Laura's pale-blue eyes widened with speculation. "If
your mother worked hard to provide an opportunity for
you, would you break her heart at the last minute and
refuse?"

Emily touched the necklace she had inherited from her
mother. Lorena had never removed it while alive; Emily
had worn it every day since her mother's death. An acrylic
oval encased the fine craftsmanship of a free-floating rose.
Her parents' initials sat on the leaves like dew instead of
gold. The pendant was a reminder of free-spirited Lorena
Fergeson. As a mother, she had demanded little and loved
without expectation.

"I have to do this. I'll deal with Leo's roaming eye in my

own way, in my own time. Be my friend and stand with me at the altar. I need your strength. Your support."

Emily rose from the edge of the bed, her heart as heavy as one of the nearby granite mountains. The consequences of taking a stand on someone else's actions were too new. If Emily quit the wedding party, Laura faced disgrace and turmoil. If she stood beside her, Laura delayed and compounded the misery. Either way, she hurt Laura.

Emily walked to the door and turned the knob.

"Do you love him, Laura?" she asked without turning around.

"No, but he makes me laugh."

"Don't make the mistake of thinking he loves you, either. It will destroy you."

"Can I count on you in the morning, Emily?"

"I'll do it your way." Heavy-hearted, Emily slipped into the hall and shut the door.

Dear God in heaven. What have I done?

Chapter 2

SIX HOURS WITHOUT anesthetic in the dentist's chair would have been more enjoyable than yesterday's wedding. Irrepressible anger and deep sorrow were Emily's only companions as she sped away from Durango, Colorado.

"How could you marry him, Laura? How could you go through with it?" she shouted, taking a curve on the highway between Silverton and Ouray fast enough to screech the tires. The grand scenery she had hoped would soothe the tumult passed unnoticed outside the car windows. The mountain rose straight up on the passenger side. Across the oncoming lane, the same mountain plunged into a valley that seemed bottomless.

"Leo Kramer is a creep. A philanderer. Oh, Laura, no amount of money or social prestige is worth the price you'll pay for marrying him."

Emily shivered at the memory of Leo's proposition. Recalling the vile sensation of his hands on her shoulders sent fresh revulsion rippling over her skin.

"I should have walked out," she murmured. "I should have done *something* more than what I did."

Emily tapped the brake. The tires squealed around another curve.

"If I don't stand my ground, Ron will maneuver me into the same thing with the same kind of man," she seethed, leaning into the next curve. Recalling the numerous dinners and cocktail parties her father hosted for his prestigious friends, her anger found a new direction. "He wants something from Craig Lyman and is willing to trade me in the bargain. No doubt playing the role of devoted daughter and fill-in hostess when he's between wives will be part of the deal, too."

The classic '56 Thunderbird sped around another sharp curve. Rocks littered the road ahead. A wave of fear swept over her with a flood of perspiration.

Emily swore, slammed on the brakes, and did her best to avoid the hazards. Her damp palms slipped on the steering wheel. Gripping tighter, she jerked the steering wheel back and forth. The rocks seemed to grow out of the pavement. She missed the largest obstacles; those she struck battered the underside of the car like golf ball–sized hail on a tin roof.

An adrenaline rush introduced caution to her driving. Barely breathing, she slowed the car further. Ahead, dark clouds roiled across the slice of sky exposed between the peaks of the majestic San Juan Mountains.

A clear highway stretched a short distance before her. The thunder of her heart and frenzy of her nerves made her skin feel too tight. Her breathing quickened as she realized how dangerous the rocks had been. As her chest heaved, visions of the car crashing into the great valley below summoned fresh waves of anxiety dampened by the relief of escaping certain death.

The car lurched, straining the slim grip she held on the urge to panic. Something in the engine clunked like a dropped coffee can full of bolts. Emily swore and slammed her foot on the brakes. Nothing. She pumped the brake pedal and prayed.

The car barely responded.

She downshifted into second. The car shivered, slowed, then something under the floorboard snapped. "Please don't," she muttered, eyeing the uphill grade ahead gratefully. Near the top, the sheer cliff dimpled into a small space of ground beside the road.

Using every driving skill she possessed, Emily maneuvered the car toward the tiny recess. The cliff face absorbed the impact of the front bumper. The headlamp shattered. The screech of metal crunching against the rock vibrated around her. Perspiring, she banked the wheels, then plopped back in the seat. Harsh, rapid breathing dried her mouth into a desert.

Fear rattled her entire body. It had been her second close call in as many minutes. Once over the hill, the car would have gained speed on the twisting downgrade until she went over the side.

How could she have been so stupid? A road like this demanded respect and caution. She had given it neither.

Gripping the top of the steering wheel in both hands, she rested her forehead on her knuckles. After a while, the queasiness abated. Her slow, deep breathing gained a steady rhythm. The first tears slipped down her cheeks and dripped from her jaw onto her leg.

The emotional overload crumbled the last of her defenses. She cried for Laura, and she cried for herself, for not taking a firm stand. All she had ever wanted to do was get along. She had given and given and changed with each new circumstance life had thrust upon her. Adaptation avoided conflict and diverted unwanted attention. It had been her catechism. Words never uttered had proven easier to swallow than those that could not be retracted. She had spoken out this time and it hadn't been sufficient. She should have shouted to anyone who would listen when Laura begged her to continue with the wedding. Instead, bowing to Laura's wishes, she had sunk into familiar si-

lence. In so doing, she had let them both down at the most
critical time in her friend's life.

Emotion bottled up for years gushed forth in wracking,
tormented sobs. When the worst of the maelstrom ebbed,
she exhaled hard and collected her wits.

No, Emily thought, opening her teary eyes. She couldn't
be what everyone expected. Not anymore. She wouldn't.
Never again. Determined, she yanked the black tassel from
the rearview mirror and tossed it at the dress lying on the
passenger-side floorboard, next to the Stanford yearbook
Laura had given her to "remember the good times." From
now on, there would be nothing subtle in the way she controlled her life. No more petty, private rebellions.

Judging from the sky, she would have to hurry to reach
Silverton before the storm broke and added to her misery.
She stuffed a change of clothes and a few personal items
into her backpack, grabbed her jacket and purse, then abandoned the car. With a backward glance, she decided to
leave it unlocked. Maybe someone would steal the elegant
maid-of-honor gown, the yearbook, and the tassel. She was
finished with them all.

The sign across the highway proclaimed Silverton ten
miles behind her. Ten miles. Maybe by the time she back-
tracked to the little pocket of civilization nestled against the
high mountains, her angst-ridden state would have played
itself out.

Storm clouds rumbled in the mountain peaks. Emily hurried, glad she had worn jeans and running shoes for the
drive. Downhill was easy walking. After rounding the
curve, the road angled up and to the left. She hunched into
the steep incline and bent her head against the gusting
wind.

The next rumble sounded like thunder, but deeper. Emily
stumbled, then stopped, her feet braced apart. The ground
shuddered. Frantic, she glanced around. A Californian, she
knew an earthquake when she felt one. Splinter faults rid-
dled these mountains.

"Great. Make my day," she muttered, hearing the first

onslaught of rocks tumbling down the mountain. She raced for the cliff face and found the deepest recess.

Small rocks arced over her shelter from the high cliff above. They fell like uncertain drizzle, then gained in volume. The noise increased to a roar that shook her entire world. Boulders careened down the mountain with an explosive velocity. Some bounced on the pavement and continued into the great chasm below. Others fragmented on impact and bounced in all directions.

Emily cowered against the cliff face, then crouched into a ball behind the shield of her backpack. Fear froze her in place. Dust filled her nostrils, forcing her to breathe through her sweatshirt. The endless roar mingled with the staccato of her heart and echoed in her head for what seemed an eternity.

Curled against the cold, unyielding belly of the mountain, Emily tried to shrink into the ground as she awaited the blow that would take her life. Anticipating death alternately increased and quelled her terror. The roar of a mountain crashing down on her drowned the hysterical laughter filling her head. Through the cacophony, a small voice promised that next time around, if there was such a thing as reincarnation, she would belong wherever she was born.

"Mama? Am I dying?" she wailed into the sweatshirt. *Will I see you? Is that the reason for this?*

Some time later, an unnatural silence descended. Emily thought she had become as deaf as the stone sheltering her. Terror lingered with the uncertainty of whether she was dead or alive.

Time stood still while she determined that she had survived. The realization made her giddy with disbelief. She was alive. She drew a shaky breath through the dust-encrusted sweatshirt. The air carried a new sweetness. The sensation of blood rushing through her veins surged with a new appreciation of each rapid pulse of her heart. A dull buzzing lingered in her ears.

One by one, she checked body parts without raising her head. Toes. They wiggled. Hands. Flexible. Knees. Shoulders.

Slowly, Emily opened her eyes. The light had faded to near darkness. The first flickers of panic charged through her.

A wall of rocks surrounded her. Overhead, clouds raced across a dust-riddled sky. A car-sized boulder rested inches from her toes.

I should be dead, she realized, awed by her good fortune. Doubt rose to darken her amazement. *Maybe I am dead.*

Brushing away the morbid thought, she groped the boulders and stood. Her fingers twitched as she pulled on her backpack. Anxious for open space, she scrambled out of the shelter as fast as her shaky legs could move.

Gazing into the small abyss she had vacated, she trembled harder. Not one rock had bounced her way. Instead they had piled around her and formed a stone shield. "How—" She bit off the question. Although her mother had constantly assured her that nothing in the universe happened without a reason, Emily knew that some things, like death, seriously challenged that axiom.

With effort, she dragged her gaze from the coffin-sized sanctuary. In either direction nothing remained of the road. To her left, the mountain had slid over the pavement, giant trees and all. The scar cut by the road no longer existed. To her right, an enormous rock scree created a precarious path that obliterated any sign of man's encroachment on the pristine mountain wilderness.

She eyed the scree. Crossing the steep, loose rock was dangerous.

She drew a steadying breath and weighed her options. Staying in place was foolish; with the road closed, no one would find her. Given the storm brewing, it might be tomorrow before the wind died down enough for an air search.

"Okay. Move forward. One foot in front of the other." The tremor in her voice faded. She had hiked more trails in the Santa Cruz Mountains than most knew existed.

"Thanks, Mom," she breathed, grateful for her first thirteen years spent in a commune deep in the Santa Cruz

Mountains. Absently, she fingered the pendant hanging from her neck.

As Emily climbed toward the meld of rock and grassy slope, the mountain sounds replaced the buzzing in her ears. The wind whipped through the pines and sang with the birds. High overhead, an eagle cried out and caught a new current.

She murmured a prayer of thanks for being alive. Whatever life hurled at her in the future, she would openly embrace it and wring out every ounce of sweetness it contained.

No more playing hostess for her father. Ron would have to find wife number five to fill the void. God help her, she cared about Ron and had expressed her gratitude to him for overseeing her education. However, she did not love him. She was his child—never his daughter. His legitimate offspring, the ones for whom he had paid child support, were his acknowledged daughters and sons. The days when free love and peace flowed in Golden Gate Park had not included marriage with Lorena.

And no more visits to the commune. All they wanted was a hunk of her mother's money they hadn't known about until Emily inherited it.

In the epiphany of the moment, Emily resolved to build a new life away from California. Maybe in Silverton. She was pointed in that direction. Her days of being a chameleon and appeasing those around her were over. Life had her attention now. Perhaps there was a reason for her close calls today. She could build a future without the trappings of the past. Couldn't she?

Emily's brow knit thoughtfully. Why not? In the electronic age with the information highway, she could work anywhere. Her step lightened as she climbed toward a different life she welcomed with open arms and an eager heart.

SAN JUAN MOUNTAINS
NEAR SILVERTON, COLORADO, 1882

"How much longer is that fancy woman and her family going to wait for you?" Teigue Jackson asked his nephew.

Royle Tremaine wiped his face on a stained towel. "She is not a fancy woman. Rebecca is a debutante from one of Virginia's finest families." He had thought Teigue's silence on the volatile subject too good to last. His uncle had to be bursting from the month-long containment.

Teigue scowled and worried the biscuit pan from the fire. "Debutante? That's just another name for a fancy woman. Seems to me that any woman who'd marry a man she never met is either a fancy woman or a slave. Her daddy's selling her to you. Nothing more. Nothing less. We fought a war over slavery. It's illegal now. That means she must be a fancy woman, and he's her broker."

Royle tugged his shirt on and did not bother fastening the three remaining buttons, each dangling by a thread. They had had this conversation a hundred times. Tonight, Teigue wanted to rile him, but Royle refused to bite. "Have it your way."

"It isn't a matter of having it my way. That's the way it is. How do you know you'll like her? Hell, she may be so damn revolting you'd rather gnaw off your arm than put it around her." Teigue shook the biscuits onto the center of the table.

"I'll take my chances." Royle dished up two plates of beans and bacon.

" 'Course it's been so damn long since either one of us was in the company of a woman outside a saloon, you probably won't know how to act. Maybe she'll change her mind once she gets a gander of you."

"I'm sure my parlor manners will come back to me." The faster summer approached, the harder Teigue harped on the subject. "You're welcome to accompany me and see for yourself."

"Whoa! Not me. I'm not going back to Virginia. Ever. The past is dead, Royle." Teigue sat and curled his hands into fists on top of the table. "And you damn well better bury it, because it isn't coming back. What was, was. You can't change it. Not by marrying a fancy woman with a heritage not half as good as your own. Not by buying all the pieces that're left or trying to rebuild it. It's gone, son. You're gonna rip your guts out if you don't give up this foolish notion."

Royle shook his head, determined. "They're my guts to rip out. I have to do this, whether you understand or not." He met Teigue's concerned brown eyes with the resolve burning in his soul glowing brightly. "I am going to do this, so let's drop the subject and eat."

"Goddamn, I always thought you were smart. You show such promise of having good sense, then you piss it down a snake hole. All the money we've damn near killed ourselves making isn't gonna buy you happiness."

"I never said it would."

"Then why are we doing this? Why are you so dead set on wrecking your life?"

"Drop it, Teigue."

"What're you after, if not happiness? There isn't much else that's worth this kind of effort."

The sincerity etching the roads of hard living in Teigue's face forced Royle's softly spoken answer. "Peace."

Teigue shook his head, his soulful brown eyes never faltering from Royle's tolerant gaze. "It isn't in Virginia, Royle. It's in here." A callused finger thumped Teigue's chest over his heart.

"I'm done talking about this," Royle told him evenly. "Dinner is getting cold." He reached for a biscuit. Teigue had asked nothing of him in their eighteen years as partners. During that time, Teigue had been a friend, father, and mentor. They agreed on most things and found compromise on everything else, except returning to Virginia.

"Yeah," Teigue grumbled. "Colder than a carpetbagger's heart."

Royle ignored the bait. That can of worms had been writhing since his return from England at age sixteen. Getting into a discussion about Southern Reformists and carpetbaggers would double back on the subject he wished to avoid.

They ate in silence. Royle stole glimpses at Teigue, who attacked his food as though angry at it.

"Answer me something," Teigue demanded.

Royle's fork paused midway between his mouth and plate. He lifted his shoulders in a shrug.

Teigue set his fork aside and pushed away his plate, scraped clean with a biscuit. "Suppose, just suppose now, you met a sweet little darling that stole your heart. One who made every bad day seem better than good. Suppose you fell in love with her and found yourself needing her more than silver. More than going to Virginia." Teigue's voice dropped. "More than your next breath of air. What would you do?"

"Are we supposing this epitome of femininity is going to hunt me down before or after Rebecca and I are married?" A wry smile curled his lips. Teigue was damned good at the *supposing* game.

"Take it both ways."

"Sure. The answer is the same. I would walk away. If I was married, I would have to walk away or be unfaithful, which I doubt I could stomach, regardless of the temptation. If I was not married, I would have a little more time for a dalliance. In the end, I would continue down the road I'm on." Royle nodded solemnly. He meant every word and had the determination to carry forth.

"You're a Goddamn ignorant fool, Royle. You've never been in love or you wouldn't be blowing wind out your mouth. I'm telling you, you couldn't walk away. Not and find the peace you're searching for."

"Yes, Teigue, I could and I would." To lighten the mood, he grinned. "Are you expecting some angel to knock on the door of this ramshackle cabin for me to fall in love with?"

"I suppose it could happen."

Royle's laughter boomed in the cabin.

Indignant, Teigue stiffened. "We've had some strange luck lately. Like that earthquake shaking down the back wall of the mine and showing us a new silver streak. Saved us months of digging, if we'd have thought to dig there."

Royle sobered. "We would have gotten around to digging or blasting there. Eventually. Our real luck was not being killed when the tunnel collapsed."

"No argument there." Teigue rose and poured coffee for them. "But you haven't answered my question. What if you can't walk away?"

Royle settled his weight on his forearms and held the steaming cup in both hands. "You still miss Aunt Madeline, don't you?"

"Now and then she grabs hold of my heart and won't let go. I reckon thinking of her is a habit I'm not particularly interested in breaking."

Royle sipped the hot coffee, then gazed at Teigue through the steam. "Tell you what. Any little darlings that knock on the door are yours."

Teigue shook his head and chuckled sadly. "It isn't that simple."

"And no one is coming, so it's a moot point."

A soft tapping sound punctuated the silence. Royle met Teigue's puzzled expression with uncertainty.

It sounded again.

"Someone's at the door," Teigue whispered, color draining from his face.

"Then they must be looking for you." Instinctively, Royle snagged the Winchester propped against the wall behind him.

Teigue rose slowly, glancing back at Royle. "Nobody comes up here, let alone knocks so faint you can't hardly hear it over important conversation."

"I suppose not." Royle set the rifle on the tabletop with his finger resting on the trigger.

Teigue opened the door partway, then stiffened as straight as a board.

"Hi. I'm Emily Fergeson. I'm afraid the earthquake that shook down the mountainside left me stranded. You did feel the earthquake, didn't you? Man, it was a doozy. Not quite as bad as the Loma Prieta quake, but much scarier for me. I thought I was going to die."

She paused for an audible breath. "Sorry for rambling. The truth is, I'm lost. I can't find Silverton. And I can't even find the highway. Do you have a phone I could use?"

The feminine voice sent chills up Royle's spine. He and Teigue had finally agreed on something tonight and both were wrong. A female stood at the door. A female.

An awkward silence settled over the cabin.

"I'm sorry. Maybe I've caught you at a bad time. I can understand you wanting your privacy, living out here like this and all. But if you'd be so good as to call a cab for me so I can get to Silverton. . . ."

A female. Her words floated past him. The lilt of her expressive voice carried an uneasiness he shared. Her pause forced Royle into action. "Teigue. Invite your lady friend in. Where are your manners?"

"Thanks anyway, but if you'll call a cab, that will be fine. I don't want to intrude, so I'll just wait out here until it arrives."

"Fergeson? *Miss* Fergeson?" Teigue asked with a note of interest Royle didn't like.

"Yes, sir. Emily to my friends. And you are?"

"Teigue Jackson at your service." He executed a formal bow that Robert E. Lee would have admired, then took her hand and brought it to his lips. "Please, won't you accept what little hospitality we can offer."

"Well, I . . ."

"I won't take no for an answer. Besides, it's a long way to Silverton and there's no other shelter for miles. It looks like the storm caught you. Come in and warm yourself before you catch a chill." Teigue stepped aside and glanced at Royle, his eyes dancing with mischief. "Miss Fergeson, may I present my nephew, Royle Tremaine."

She glowed. No angel shone as brightly as the vision in the doorway.

Shoulder-high to Teigue, she held herself with a poise that belied the tentativeness evident in her hazel-green eyes. Even dripping wet, she radiated a sensuality that spoke to the part of him he preferred to ignore until his next trip to Silverton.

Staring at her expressive mouth, he rose from behind the table. A soft flush of color crept up her slender neck and spread across her delicate jaw before settling in her high, well-defined cheekbones. Tendrils of rain-dampened dark brown hair clung to her neck. A braid so thick it appeared made of heavy ropes hung over her left shoulder and disappeared under the colorful bag she clutched.

"Mr. Tremaine," she said, extending her hand like a man. "I'm Emily Fergeson."

For a heartbeat, his throat locked. The strange men's clothing she wore didn't obscure the feminine allure of her delicious curves.

He took her hand, then swore under his breath.

Chapter 3

EMILY HAD NEVER met a man who seemed to possess the qualities of a biblical dark angel more than Royle Tremaine. Even seated, she could tell he was a tall man, perhaps even taller than the pleasant older man beside her. She didn't want to stare at Royle, but could not drag her eyes away. Hair so black it reflected the cabin light matched his eyebrows and the thick veil of lashes most women she knew would kill to possess.

When Royle Tremaine stood, her gaze dropped and her heart quickened. A well-worn plaid shirt hung open from the wedge of his wide shoulders. It gaped wider across whorls of silken chest hair and hung free at the taper of his waist. Even without touching him, she knew the contours were as hard as the floor beneath her feet.

Shaking his hand was a mistake. A big one. Heat intense enough to boil steel shot up her arm. Had she been able to move, she would have pulled away. But the heat paralyzed every cell in her body, set her heart hammering, parched her mouth, and weakened her knees.

Although not a complete stranger to desire, she had no idea that the potency of a sudden assault could be so volatile. Her gaze flew to his.

A subtle softening of the faint lines running away from the corners of his eyes unmasked a hunger lurking in the navy blue depths. Royle Tremaine knew the effect he had on women and obviously enjoyed seeing it at work. He was the kind of man Laura's mother had warned them about when visiting them at Stanford.

What did Laura's mother know about men? She had virtually forced Laura to marry Leo Kramer. Emily did not need an echo from the past to warn her of Royle Tremaine's lethal qualities. She felt them in every nerve. The way his gaze slid leisurely across her body hardened her nipples and shot another thousand pounds of jet fuel over the pyre leaping inside her.

"Miss Fergeson." He released her hand.

"Would you mind if I sit down for a moment?" If she didn't, she would fall.

Teigue offered his chair. "Make yourself comfortable and get warm. That rain is damn cold. How about some coffee?"

"Yes, please, if it isn't too much trouble." Her gaze fixed on the rifle pointing straight at her. Whatever they had expected when Teigue answered the door, it had not been a woman lost in the mountains with no food or water.

With her thumb and forefinger, she gingerly scooted the barrel away from her.

"What are you doing up here?" Royle removed the Winchester from the table and tucked it behind him within easy reach. "Who is with you?"

"What makes you think anyone is with me? I'm alone." The admission was out before she considered the consequences. She *was* alone. So were they. A fresh heat crawled along the surface of her skin. Anxiety.

"I'm looking for Silverton. The road sign said ten miles. The landslides from the earthquake covered the road, so I had to climb the mountain and . . . I never did find where the road cut back in. It's gone." Head shaking, she could not believe that her keen sense of direction had failed.

Emily accepted the steaming coffee from Teigue with trembling fingers. Her eyes roamed the cabin as she alternately blew and sipped the strong brew. Primitive. That was the only way to describe the rough-hewn table and chairs and the makeshift counters. No running water. Probably no indoor plumbing of any kind. Central to the cabin was a large hearth used for heating and cooking.

Survivalists. Mentally, she groaned. Most of the groups she had read about epitomized everything she stood against. They plundered the forests and hunted for their own purposes without regard to posterity. A proponent of gun control, Emily frowned at the rack of antique rifles and shotguns on the wall behind Royle.

"How did you get out here?" Royle's head cocked slightly to the left as his eyes narrowed.

"I drove," she answered, then met his suspicious gaze.

"You mean you rode all the way here? How many horses?"

Men and their odd interests. How was she supposed to know how many horsepower the engine was? The speedometer reflected the horsepower, didn't it? She shrugged lightly. If not, undoubtedly Mr. Tremaine would inform her posthaste. "About a hundred and fifty," she answered.

"And they're gone?" Teigue whispered, dragging a stool up to the table. "All gone?"

"The whole mountain came down. There's nothing left."

Royle swore. "A hundred and fifty horses? And you were alone?"

Why didn't the man believe her? It wasn't as if she was the only woman who traveled the scenic highways alone, for heaven's sake. "Would you like me to show you where I was? You could dig down and—"

"Easy, Miss Fergeson." Teigue touched her arm lightly. "Royle gets a bit short at times, but he doesn't mean anything by it. It's such a damn shame to lose that much pulling power in these mountains."

"Well how do you think I feel? I'm the one whose left with nothing except what I've got on my back and in my pack. I had a major investment wiped out in less than a minute. If I had stayed with it, I'd have been buried, too. As it was, I came very close." She shivered at the memory.

Three times today she had escaped disaster by fractions of a second, only to wind up in a mountain cabin with two big, strange men. What had she been thinking when she knocked on the door? Chagrined, she recalled the promise of warmth, safety, and a way into Silverton. All things considered, the odds of dodging a fourth disaster in one day were stacked against her.

"If I could use your phone, I'll be out of your hair in no time." Scanning the room, she did not see a phone. For that matter, there had not been any lines outside running to the cabin. A sense of foreboding weighted her wet, chilled body.

"A phone?" Teigue asked, turning on the stool at the end of the table. "What's a phone?"

The question stunned her. She blinked several times, not believing he didn't know what a phone was. "You know. A telephone. Punch in a number. . . ."

The way his brow knit forced her to look at Royle. He shook his head and gazed back like she had lost her mind.

"How long have you two been up here?"

"Better than five years," Teigue answered.

"Whatever a phone is, we don't have it. And we don't want it, either," Royle said, leaning on his forearms and cradling his cold coffee. "We have everything we need here."

Come to think of it, she had not seen a car or truck either, only a few horses and at least twelve mules. "Oh," she exclaimed, realizing her error. They were not survivalists. They were part of a religious sect. "Are you Amish?"

"Are we what?" The lines in Teigue's brow deepened with uncertainty.

"Amish." She glanced at Teigue. Too late, she realized

their attire wasn't even similar to the black coats, pants, and white shirts shown on television.

Teigue puffed up and straightened his proud shoulders. "Hell no. We're Americans—miners working our claim."

The deep chuckle rumbling in Royle's chest fascinated her, yet set her nerves on edge. The man had a winning smile that made him interesting, but not quite handsome. Not that he was unattractive. He possessed the kind of raw looks she preferred; even features without the artificial polish of a men's fashion magazine.

Shaken, she wondered how they kept in touch with the rest of the world. "Okay. No phone. No car." She paused, watching the men exchange puzzled glances. "How do I get to Silverton?"

"The way I see it, you have two choices." Royle's voice pinned her with an electric intensity as he shoved his hands into his trouser pockets. His shirt slithered across his ribs and dangled from his shoulders. The full expanse of his chest and abdomen rose and fell with his breathing.

"And those are?" she pressed, dragging her gaze away from his exposed flesh. Under different circumstances, if he kept his mouth shut, she would enjoy staring at him until her eyes grew tired.

"I'll draw a map for you to follow into Silverton. This is rough country." His eyes narrowed as though trying to see inside her. "You do know how to read a map, don't you, Miss Fergeson?"

"Emily," she amended softly, trying to figure out his game. "Of course I can read a map, provided it's accurate and marginally to scale."

"The chances for a man alone, on foot, are not good. Yours are less. But if you want to try it, we can help you with a canteen and food. I'll draw a map—with good directions."

"Enough. No more games, Royle. No map." The sudden harshness Teigue directed at Royle melted when he regarded her. "I can't let you do that, Miss Emily. It'd be suicide. I won't be a party to anyone getting themselves killed in these mountains."

She studied him for a moment and found sincerity before turning back to Royle, whose confidence in her ineptitude went a long way toward neutralizing the physical effects of his presence. "And my other option?"

Royle fetched the coffeepot and poured a round. "Wait. Go into Silverton with us."

Optimism cast away the weight pressing her cold body onto the chair. "Oh, that would be splendid. When can we leave?"

"Six weeks or so," Royle answered, with a quick glance in her direction.

The chilly rain and altitude must have affected her. Either that, or she had not walked away from the avalanche with her hearing unscathed. "How long did you say?"

"Six weeks." Royle cocked his head at Teigue and got agreement.

"Six weeks!" Emily started out of her chair. "Are you out of your mind? I can't wait around here for six weeks." Six weeks in this tiny cabin with two men who hadn't seen civilization for—how long?

Royle dipped his head and shrugged one shoulder. "Want a map? I'll make it for you now."

"Damn right I do. It had better be accurate, too." She settled at the table, then rummaged through her backpack for a pencil and tablet.

"No, no map. You can't make it alone, Miss Fergeson," Teigue said, so matter-of-factly that she paused.

"How far is it?"

"About fifteen miles. Hard miles. Impossible miles, if you don't know where you're going." Teigue's brown and gray mane shimmered as he shook his head. "Even if I lent you a rifle—"

"A gun?" Distaste wrinkled her brow.

Teigue touched her damp arm. "You can't go into that country without a gun. What we can't spare is a horse. We'll need every animal we've got to get us into Silverton when the time's right."

Icy dread turned the blood in her veins to lead. He was serious. His intensity and Royle's cavalier encouragement

frightened her. "A gun?" The thought of handling a weapon
revolted her. They were instruments of war. Death, maim-
ing, and destruction were the only purposes of a bullet. No,
she would not pick up a gun.

"You can shoot, can't you?"

She resented the amusement dripping from Royle's question. "No, I can't shoot a gun. Nor do I have any desire to
so much as touch a gun."

"You have some strange notions, Miss Fergeson."

"Emily," she insisted, lost in thought of finding her way
to Silverton.

"Miss Emily," Teigue implored gently, his brown eyes
filled with concern. "If you stay in this part of the world,
you will have to learn how to defend yourself."

"I do fine. Thank you."

Royle snorted in disbelief. "What do you do? Say pretty
please Mr. Bad Man don't eat me?"

A growing impatience at his taunts shone in her eyes.
She pasted a sugary smile on her lips and batted her lashes.
"The first time, yes."

"There are no second chances up here."

"Thanks for the warning. I'll park my manners at the
door when I leave." Agitation clawed at her typically placid
disposition.

"Let's say you *can* stall a two-legged enemy with a smile
for a couple of minutes. What will happen when what's
after you has four legs and sharp claws strong enough to
shred the bark from a tree? Do you think such a predator
will succumb to your smile and prettily spoken words?"
Disgust curled Royle's mouth into a harsh frown. "It's in-
sane to wander these mountains without a good rifle, Miss
Fergeson. For your own safety, you had better overcome
your squeamishness and learn how to shoot or go back east
where you can fend off predators with a scream."

Anger colored her neck a warm pink. "I'm from California, not the East Coast. All I want to do is get to Silverton.
That's not unreasonable, is it?" She hated the sarcasm dripping from her words.

With a sigh, she forced herself to relax and fingered the

dented coffee cup in front of her. She pushed away the
damp tendrils of hair from her face, then rested her chin in
her hand as her gaze flickered over Royle. Seeking neutrality, she stared at an upside-down biscuit in the center of the
table. "Look, I'm really having a bad day. A bad two days.
If you can't help me out, say so, and I'll be on my way."

Royle pushed his empty cup toward her, forcing her to
look. Gone were the disdain and arrogance. Curiosity
coaxed his features into an almost kind expression with a
half-smile that made her stare.

"We know all about bad days. We've had our share
lately. We can't leave to take you into Silverton." He
straightened and regarded her with new interest that made
her suspicious. "Tell you what. Since Teigue is dead set
against turning you out on your own, maybe you can be of
assistance in getting us into Silverton in, say, four weeks.
Five at the most."

Emily glanced at Teigue, then stared hard at Royle. Five
weeks. So much could happen. What about her clients? She
wondered whether Gil and Mary could keep the business
running. Of course they could. The skilled programmers
and publications specialist of Fergeson Inc. made it the
most sought after development house in the Bay Area. She
had trained the management team well and at the last
minute had given Mary Edwards complete signature authority. At least the employees and the monthly creditors
would be paid.

Satisfied that no one would suffer from her forced hiatus,
her concerns ebbed. In their wake, she felt no anxiety for
the business she had built with long hours and more tenacity than she'd thought herself capable of mustering. Other
than Gil and Mary, no one would look for her. When she
missed the dinner slated for the Warner mansion, Ron
would find someone else, maybe wife number five, to hostess his future parties. Laura . . . well, it would be a while
before Laura realized she had never made it home.

Five weeks. Maybe she could sort things out in her head
and find a new direction for her future. A laugh that never
reached her lips filled her head. Maybe for five weeks she

could pretend the rest of the world had disappeared or that she lived in a simpler time. For five weeks she would not play the chameleon she had been since her mother's death. How scary, yet liberating the temptation was. When would the opportunity come along again to learn exactly who she was without the layers of polished armor reflecting what the watcher wanted to see? Maybe never. She wanted to discover what lay under the camouflage forged by years of self-defense.

Maybe the men at the table wanted something, too. Something she would not tolerate for five seconds, let alone five weeks. "Exactly what sort of help do you think I can provide, Mr. Tremaine?"

"Suppose you go to work for us."

Cautious, Emily glanced from Teigue to Royle, then back. "What sort of work?"

The movement of Teigue's callused fingers over his stiff whiskers made a rasping sound. "Brilliant idea, Royle. We could sure use some help around here." He gave Emily his full attention with such ebullience that she almost smiled.

"Royle and I aren't the worst housekeepers, but we sure aren't the best, either. Even if you've never cooked before, you couldn't do much to hurt the food." His eyes narrowed. "You can cook though, can't you?"

"I create my best cuisine with a Jenn-Air and a microwave, but I can handle an open fire, too." She glanced at the fireplace. "It won't be five-star gourmet fare, but it will be edible." As the skeptical side of her overtook her enthusiasm, her chin lifted. "You want me to cook in exchange for a roof over my head, meals, and a guided trip to Silverton. Is that it?"

"Keep this place clean," Royle added, then glanced down at his shirt. "Do the washing, too."

"Anything else?" she asked, jotting down the tasks on the tablet she had taken from her pack.

"Yeah. Can you sew on a button?"

"Of course."

"Then we'd like you to do the mending." He glanced at the sorry state of his shirt buttons.

"And?" she coaxed, wanting to hear the full list.

"Feed the mules and horses in the morning. Rotate them in the pastures when I tell you." Royle relaxed against the back of the chair. The longer the list grew, the more pleased he appeared. "Of course, they will need a bit of grooming now and then. Can you handle animals?"

"Yes." *Keep going.*

"Are you any good with a hammer and pliers?"

"I can change a light bulb," she muttered.

"Is that a no?"

"I'm familiar with the pounding end of a hammer and which end of the pliers to grip. Why? Do you need a new roof?"

Royle grinned as though he liked the idea. "Not yet. But occasionally you may need to fix a fence post or something. The tools are in the corner over there." He pointed across the room at a wooden box the size of a footlocker.

"We get our water from the spring that runs beside the cabin." He inclined his head toward a water barrel laid on its side with a spigot tapped into the end. "It fills from the top. Best not to let it get too far down. We drink a lot of coffee before we leave in the morning and when we return at night."

"What time do you leave?"

"Before dawn. Around five. Of course, we'll want breakfast before that."

"Of course." *Keep digging, Mr. Tremaine.*

"Maybe after you catch up on some of the things we've let go, we will expect you to bring lunch over to the mine."

"Certainly. Auntie Em's lunch wagon at your service." She gave Royle a friendly smile and finished a quick calculation. "What about stall mucking? Do the animals remain outside? What do you do for hay? Oats?"

"We bring the mules and horses into the shelter when the weather turns foul. As for hay, there is plenty in the shelter. Same with oats. Just don't leave the gates open so they can get at it. I'll show you how much to feed them."

"That's it?"

"Jeezus, Miss Emily, he's given you a full day's work

from before sunup until bedtime. Isn't that enough?"
Teigue demanded.

"I have found that a complete job description avoids mis-
understanding. So far, it doesn't sound like anything requir-
ing a great deal of brainpower. How much would you
charge me for room and board for the next five weeks?"

Stunned, obviously never considering that aspect, Royle
turned his head toward Teigue, who shrugged. Slowly,
Royle swiveled his head back and met Emily's gaze. "Five
dollars a day. You still have to cook the evening meal."

"Okay. I estimate that you've given me a list that takes
an average of twelve hours a day. Are we figuring a five-,
six-, or seven-day workweek?"

"We work every day."

Nodding, she changed the calculation. "Okay. I'm figuring twelve hours a day, seven days a week, at minimum
wage." She circled the amount. "I expect to be paid
weekly." With a flourish, she spun the tablet around for
Royle to see.

He glanced at the number, at her, then back. Color
drained from his tanned cheeks before his neck and face
filled with a reddish hue. The outrage stemmed from his
toes and turned his chest the same shade of crimson. "You
are out of your mind."

"I am being very reasonable. When I work for a corpora-
tion and have to use my brain, I make that much in less
than a few hours. You're getting off cheap." Arms folded
across her chest, she sat back. "Besides, I didn't see a line
of applicants for this job. Maybe the commute from Silverton is a little rough."

"Lemme see." Teigue drew the tablet away from Royle.
He read the list and glanced at various items around the
cabin as he went. "Looks right to me. You're hired."

"Now wait a damn minute, Teigue. We're doing her a
favor, not the other way around."

"Nope. Sounded to me like you asked her to go to work
for us and she accepted. Now you want to quibble about
paying her. Would you do all that work for this amount?"

"You know damn well working in the mine does not—"

"And since she's going to do our chores, how much more silver do you think we'll pull out by working the longer hours?"

Emily marveled at the way Teigue handled his nephew. He circled the issue, then struck the heart of it with a single piece of logic. She would take a lesson from him. It might come in handy later.

Royle slapped the table with both hands. "All right, damn it. You're hired."

"And you will pay me weekly."

"Yeah."

"Not so fast." Emily leaned forward on the table. "Am I safe here?"

"As safe as we are," Royle snapped.

She leaned closer. "Am I safe here, Mr. Tremaine? Will I sleep undisturbed? Will I be treated with the same distance and respect you'd give a third man?"

Royle nodded slowly. "Most assuredly you are where *I'm* concerned. I had already promised Teigue that he could have all the little darlings who knocked on our door." Royle inclined his head at Teigue. "Is she safe from you ravishing her, Teigue?"

Teigue ignored him. "You have my word you won't be pestered, Miss Emily."

Gazing into his warm, coffee-colored eyes, she believed him. "Thank you. We have a deal."

Royle snorted, his head hanging and shaking in blatant disbelief. "Now that you have ensured your virtue, which was never threatened, you can start earning your exorbitant wages by cleaning up dinner."

Emily drew a deep breath and exhaled slowly. "I don't think so. I believe I'll accept your hospitality and have dinner, then you can show me what you want done with the animals before I go to bed." She glanced around. "Where do you plan for me to sleep?"

"I'll fix you a spot in the supply loft. It's warm and comfortable there. And it's private," Teigue assured her with a wink.

"Where do . . ." She caught sight of two beds around the

far side of the hearth. Royle Tremaine would be sleeping close enough for her to hear him breathe. For a split second, she considered running out of the cabin and not stopping.

As though reading her thoughts, Teigue laid a fatherly hand on her arm. "You're going to be dry and warm and safe here, Miss Emily." He waited until she looked at him before adding, "I promise."

She believed him, and did not question why. Every grain of logic she possessed screamed that she was crazy to settle in with two strange men for the next five weeks. Yet, it did not feel crazy. The internal alarms she expected remained silent.

A slow smile formed as she nodded at Teigue. "Mind if I eat a couple of these biscuits?"

"I'll get some beans for you." Teigue left the table.

She glanced at Royle. Although he sat still enough to become part of the wooden chair, the masculinity he radiated made him the most intriguing man she had ever encountered.

No, she was not crazy to stay. Her brush with death had buried her common sense along with her car and the road to sanity.

Chapter 4

"MISS FERGESON, I'D like breakfast before sunup."

At Royle's strident demand, her eyes flew open. After a moment of disorientation, she collected her bearings. "I'm coming," she called. The best night's sleep she'd enjoyed in years had been in a strange cabin with two men she didn't know a short distance away. She dressed in the faint light pouring into the loft.

With a few practiced strokes, she plaited her hair into a braid, wrapped it around itself, and clipped it into place with a barrette. Later, she would sort out her predicament. Now that she was rested, things might become clear enough for her to appreciate the silver lining bound to exist with the right perspective. What was the worst thing that could happen?

Rape. She shivered in revulsion. *No,* she assured herself. They'd given their word on her personal safety. Beneath their unkempt appearances she perceived an integrity more precious than the ore they mined.

Her sense of people had been a lifesaver more times than she could count. Teigue liked her. She was as certain of that as she was that the regard was mutual.

And Royle? What of him? She didn't know what to make of him or the sensations he created with a touch. All her instincts warned that he was dangerous. However, he seemed more the type to seduce, rather than rape, his intended victim.

She descended the ladder with a resolve not to be anyone's willing victim for the rest of her life. She was in charge of her destiny now. Confident, she glanced around her new domain.

Royle busied himself by fixing a pot of coffee. The same shirt he had worn the previous evening hung open from his shoulders. It looked like he had slept in it. She averted her gaze, not ready for that much exposed masculinity or the tingling way it affected her before sunrise.

Teigue sat on the stool and pulled on his boots.

Emily put on her best smile. "What'll it be for breakfast this morning, gentlemen? Eggs Benedict?" The abrupt stillness warned that neither man had a sense of humor this early in the morning. "Okay, how about oatmeal?"

She glanced from Teigue to Royle. Both gazed at her as though she had just stepped off a spaceship. "All right. What do you eat for breakfast?"

"Beans. Bacon. Rice. Meat, when I have time to hunt," Royle answered. "That's about it."

Beans? For breakfast? "Okay, then that's what we'll have. How about biscuits? They won't take long and you can take what you don't eat with you."

"Sounds good," Teigue answered, buttoning his shirt cuffs.

Emily went to work. Soon, the aroma of biscuits baking in the fire and simmering beans filled the cabin. Keeping busy held the crush of thoughts she needed to sort through at bay. Once the men left, she would figure out if she had lost her mind or found the path to a new way of living.

Emily fished the biscuit pan from the fire with a poker. "How long are you gone during the day?" She snatched up

a rag pocked with burn marks beside the hearth and used it
as a hot pad.

"It varies. Today, we won't be back until late." Royle
poured coffee for the three of them.

"Okay." She had all day to organize and launch the monumental task of cleaning the cabin. That meant plenty of
time to think, too.

"Why?" Royle took a menacing step toward her. A dark
scowl drew his mouth down with suspicion. "Are you planning on taking one of the horses and going somewhere?"

The accusation glittering in his eyes spoke louder than
his voice. Emily dropped the biscuits into the center of the
table and faced Royle with an undisguised resentment.
"Are you insinuating that I'd steal from you?"

Confidence underscored the challenge reflected in the
stern set of his jaw. "If you did, I'd track you down. We
hang horse thieves in this part of the world. No questions
asked."

"What the hell is the matter with you, Royle?" Teigue
dished up a plate of beans. "Miss Emily'll do exactly what
she said she'll do. Besides, where the deuce would she go?
The closest town is Silverton, and we both know it isn't an
easy trek even if you know which trails to take." Teigue sat
at the table. "Eat and let's get going."

Emily watched Royle dish up a plate of beans.

From the first, she and Royle had clashed. She wished
she knew what it was about her that bothered him. While
his rancor wounded her, his hostility cauterized her
wounded feelings.

Out of habit, she considered how to appease him.

Resolve firmed her backbone. She wasn't falling into
that comfortable trap again. How easily she lost herself
switching from one character in the play called life to another with a change of scene. From now on, she was the
star of her production. At the moment, the cabin offered the
only stage available.

"Mr. Tremaine, I have no idea why you have such a low
opinion of me. However, I'm sure if you think about your

accusation, you'll realize that you owe me an apology. I'll
expect to hear it before dinner."

Blue eyes flashed at her. Two days ago, she would have
backed down and apologized for offending him. Not today,
though. Empowered by the rush of satisfaction standing up
for herself unleashed, Emily pressed on. "You don't seem
the type of man who would wish to be judged with the
speed, and in the same light, that you have judged me. But
then, perhaps I've misassessed you, and you aren't a fair
man of strong character. If that's the case, we'd all be better off if you drew a map for me, and I took my chances in
the mountains. I have no desire to work for anyone who
does not respect my integrity to the same degree that he demands respect for his own."

In the sudden silence, Emily's heart pounded in her temples. Free-flowing endorphins made her more giddy than
afraid. Even if he threw her out on her ear and she wandered the mountains for days, it was worth the feeling of
self-reclamation surging through her. Having stood up to
Royle Tremaine, on his ground, she felt confident she could
hold her own against anyone, anywhere.

Royle continued to eat in the uncomfortable quiet
marked only by the sounds of forks on metal plates and an
occasional pop from wood splitting in the fire.

Old doubts crept across Emily's newfound assertiveness
like spiders in the night. She had overstepped. The longer
the silence lasted, the more tightly those spiders spun their
webs around the fledgling prey of her self-confidence.

Abruptly, Royle stood and snatched a sheepskin jacket
and gun belt from the pegs near the door. "I'll saddle the
horses."

Teigue sighed and gathered the empty plates. "You're
making an ass out of yourself. Don't bother with mine. I'm
walking—as usual."

The biscuit Emily had eaten formed a lump in her stomach. Royle really thought she would steal his horse. Of all
the things she had been accused of in her life, being a thief
had never been considered.

"Ignore him," Teigue suggested. "He's been up here too long and can't think straight lately."

Her eyes stung as she met Teigue's paternal gaze. "I'm not a thief." She had never so much as taken a free pen from a hotel room.

"I know." Teigue carried the plates to the worktable against the far wall.

Emily wrapped the remaining biscuits in the cleanest flour-sack towel she could find and handed them to Teigue.

"Don't worry about Royle. He works damn hard at doing things that'll make him miserable. He'll come around," he assured her. "Just hold your ground the way you did this morning."

To her astonishment, Teigue chuckled. He was still grinning when he closed the cabin door behind him.

"Oh, Lord, how am I going to make this work?" Emily sagged into her chair. In the muted light of the sooty lamps, she took stock of the enormous task before her. She did not need to think about Royle Tremaine for the rest of the day. Chin in hand, head shaking, she knew that was impossible. She would think about him whether he was here or at the mine. Escape seemed impossible.

Besides, Teigue had called it right. She had no way to go where she did not know how to go. *One thing at a time,* she told herself. *The universe has a logical reason for everything. Everything has a purpose and a place.*

She finished her coffee and pushed to her feet. "May as well make the best of it." A firm resolve softened her frown. Anything she did to the cabin would be an improvement.

"Are you ready to tell me what's eating you?" Shortly after noon, Teigue leaned his pick against the tunnel wall and mopped his brow. Dust filtered through the lamp-lit air.

Royle loaded another shovelful of silver-rich ore into the wooden cart. He didn't know where to start counting the things that bothered him about Emily Fergeson. "For starters, her story lacks credibility." Exasperated, he glanced at Teigue. "One hundred and fifty horses? Buried by the mountain? And her traveling alone? Teigue . . . Even you cannot believe that. Hell, she could win the liars' competition at the rankest saloon in Silverton with that straight face of hers and those big innocent eyes."

Teigue shrugged. "She said she's alone now. She didn't say she was alone when the mountain came down. So what? Maybe she figures how she got here isn't any of our business."

"And maybe she has a passel of friends waiting to jump us, too." Expecting trouble, he had worn his sidearm today. He did not trust Emily Fergeson. Hell, he did not want to trust her. At the first sight of her, things stirred inside him that he had not suspected existed. If he had not been without a woman for so long, the instant arousal of his body might have concerned him more.

"I don't believe it. There's something special about her. I feel it in here." Teigue tapped his chest.

"Damnit, Teigue, that's probably a case of dyspepsia. I didn't think you were the kind of man who was blinded by a comely face and big green eyes. Maybe I was wrong."

"You aren't wrong, except about her eyes. They're hazel," Teigue corrected, chuckling. "And I'm not blinded. You are."

"The hell you say." He released the brake and started pushing the ore cart down the tunnel. "Her eyes are green."

"Hazel. She doesn't have a mean bone in her body. All she is, is lost and looking for a way home."

Royle paused at a wide spot in the tunnel for Teigue to skirt the cart and take the lead with the lantern. "Or a way into our silver and that little strike of gold we uncovered last year. More than one man's downfall was caused by a lying tongue in a sweet face."

"She isn't my downfall." Teigue laughed. "Yours, maybe."

"Only if she has friends waiting to bushwhack us."

"She doesn't."

"How the hell can you be so certain?" Royle vented a stream of curses under his breath. "You are losing your brains, Teigue. Old age is scattering your good sense."

"Old age my foot. I can get it on with you any day, and you damn well know it."

Royle did know it. That was the crux of what troubled him. Never before had the two of them disagreed about an individual's character, male or female. This afternoon, they were on the flip sides of a coin bearing Emily Fergeson's profile.

Teigue grabbed the leather harness at the front of the cart. "I've been walking this earth for better than fifty-two years. I've been rich, poor, and in between. I've rubbed elbows with the wealthy and powerful and been courted and shunned by the same. Of all the benefits of being rich, I liked the ladies the most. Until Madeline. She was all I needed, and it didn't matter to her if I had a dime or a dollar."

"What does Aunt Madeline have to do with this?" The tunnel bent sharply to the right. The steep incline sent Royle bracing his weight against the ore-laden cart.

Teigue hunched under the strain of the leather harness. Together, they muscled the load forward. "By the time I met Madeline, I reckon I'd met every kind of woman there was. You learn quickly what they want. It isn't always what they say they want. Knowing the difference can save you a lot of heartache."

"Come to the point." With palms braced against the back of the cart, Royle pushed with his legs. Perspiration beaded his face and ran down his chest and back.

"That little lady at the cabin doesn't want anything from us, Royle. Leastwise nothing we can't give her. I don't think anyone has given her much. I can see it in her eyes and the way she views everything around her with a wary sort of innocence."

"Or she's looking for our ore."

"How the hell would she know about the pure vein we struck? We haven't even taken a load into town."

The floor leveled out. Royle wiped away the sweat dripping into his eyes on each of his extended upper arms.

He had no answer, nor did he need one to foster his suspicions. He and Teigue could not both be right about Emily

Fergeson. In every fiber of his being he knew she posed a threat.

Teigue was wrong about her. Royle knew he had to be very careful. Every instinct he possessed warned that this woman could ruin them.

Emily hung wet laundry on the line strung between the corner of the house and the fence post. The slant made little difference since she had to tie each article over the rope. Any clothespins they owned were still buried among the heirloom treasures stashed in wooden boxes. Late as it was, she would let the laundry hang outside overnight. She tied off the last shirt and set aside the wooden crate that doubled as a laundry basket.

Satisfied with the day's progress, she stood back and assessed the stately evergreens at the fringes of the alpine meadow. Above, the trees marched up to bare rock. The steep, high peaks scraped puffy white clouds from a sky so blue it reminded her of Royle Tremaine's eyes.

The mountain wilderness had always made her feel insignificant and very contented. The possibility of escaping notice by a force as formidable as nature carried an odd power of its own. Among the trees, Emily felt a kinship with the small lizards that changed color to match their surroundings, and the timid rabbits that turned white to hide in the snow during the winter. If those slight creatures found ways of surviving the austere environs of moody wind, extreme weather, and fierce predators, so could she.

Sporadic clusters of wildflowers dotted the green grasses blanketing the clearing that surrounded the little homestead on three sides. Delighted by the colors and textures, she gathered the closest flowers. In the cabin, she found a jar that the antique shops in Los Gatos would have paid dearly for and filled it with water and flowers.

The sturdy log cabin was her home for a while. The flowers at the center of the table put a finishing touch on her decision. The swaying factor had been the admission that a woman alone in these rugged, unfamiliar mountains ran unacceptable risks. So long as the perils of the outdoors exceeded those in the cabin, she would remain. Besides, she wasn't ready to try out her new way of dealing with the world. She needed to hone it on Royle Tremaine. What a perfect foil to practice against.

All things considered, she had done a full day's work and then some. A fresh batch of beans simmered on the low fire. The cinnamon aroma of a dried-apple pie hung in the rafters.

Satisfied, she plundered the newspapers stacked in a crate near the fireplace. After selecting the top bundle, she poured a fresh cup of coffee and settled at the table. "Good grief," she whispered, stunned.

Charged with excitement, she flipped through the pages and found the papers were antiques from Silverton and Denver. "1882. Way over a century old. These belong in a museum, not a crate where they'll molder or be used to start a fire."

Intrigued, she perused the history on the pages in front of her. A niggling sensation created an itch in the middle of her brain. Nothing relieved it, and it grew stronger.

After a while, she settled back and assessed her surroundings. Everything in the cabin originated from before the turn of the century.

A small wave of goose bumps rippled over her skin.

"Coincidence," she murmured. Her vivid imagination had been overtaxed by her earlier decision to remain until Teigue and Royle went into Silverton. While it might be fun pretending the calendar had leaped back more than a century, she knew better.

She turned the page and continued reading, but couldn't help noticing the white crispness of the paper. Age had yellowed the old, brittle newspapers she recalled from museums. This newspaper did not feel like the local paper from home. The stiff yet flexible paper felt fresh—new, or at least relatively new.

Head shaking, she carefully returned the papers to the crate in which she had found them. An elusive thought she preferred not to acknowledge made her restless.

Eager for the distraction of motion, she retrieved the

bucket from the wall and visited the stream to top off the barrel. To gain an edge on the night's chores, she made two more trips and filled the big pot beside the fire. By supper, they would have warm water.

The sun had dipped below the saw-toothed mountain peaks when she entered the animal shelter. She set out hay for the mules and the two remaining horses. Royle could feed and groom his own horse.

A wince that passed for a smile crossed her face. "Take your horse, Royle Tremaine. I don't want him. I don't want anything you've got that I can't pay for," she muttered, closing the heavy gate guarding the hay in the shelter.

"Is that so?"

Emily spun on her heel and nearly fell. Red-faced, she lifted her chin in defiance. He was not going to intimidate her. She would not allow it. "Yes, Mr. Tremaine, that's so. It must be incredibly lonely living in a world dominated by mistrust and suspicion. A world like that doesn't allow much room for laughter or enjoying the unexpected gifts life offers if we but open our eyes and see them."

"Are you one of my unexpected gifts?" The last strains of evening outlined him in the wide doorway. The velvet darkness muted his features. Only his eyes glittered with a secret laugh that entranced more than angered her.

"Not hardly," she whispered, then latched the gate and skirted him on the way to the cabin. "Precious as your horse is to you, I'm sure *you'll* want to give him his ration of hay. That way, you'll know he's properly taken care of by competent hands."

She kept walking to the cabin porch. All the way she felt the burn of his glare on her back.

Stripped down to his long-john top and heavy pants, Teigue stood on the side of the porch and washed in a basin. "You've got it so nice inside, I can't come to the table looking and smelling like the hard-rock miner I've become."

She smiled, amazed by the power and youth evident in his muscular build. "It's your home, Teigue. You come in any way you want. I'd feel terrible if I did anything that made you uncomfortable."

Teigue adjusted the lamp, then squinted at the brilliant, clear flame inside the sparkling glass. "Madeline, my late wife, liked me to clean up and shave before dinner. I suspect it's the least I can do to show my appreciation for the work you did today."

He dipped a bristle brush into the washbasin, then swirled it in a soap cup until foam rose above the rim. "I don't think these lamps were this clean when we bought 'em."

Fascinated, Emily watched Teigue spread lather over his face. She had never seen a man shave with a straight razor.

He adjusted the mirror on the shelf above the washstand, then drew the razor to his throat.

Emily thrust her chin forward, lifted, and stretched her throat. She could almost feel the warm steel blade slicing off the coarse stubble. The steady scraping sound enthralled her. With each pass, more of Teigue's face came into view.

"You ever watched a man shave before?" Teigue asked out of the side of his mouth.

"Not with a straight razor," Emily answered from the side of her mouth. "Aren't you worried about cutting yourself?"

"I wouldn't dare. Close as you're watching, you might bleed instead of me."

Emily drew back sharply. Embarrassed, she made her face blank. "Sorry. I'd better make some biscuits."

"Don't leave. Hell, the show's not over." Teigue curled his upper lip down and cleared the foam and whiskers between his lip and nose.

Emily found herself sucking her closed lips between her teeth and stretching the skin for him.

"Your daddy never let you watch him shave when you were a little sprat?" He polished off the plane of his square chin.

"I didn't meet my father until I was fourteen." She drew in her lower lip and dropped her jaw.

"Guess you were a little old then. The war separated a lot of families."

"He was against the war. That's how he met my mother."

Teigue rinsed the razor. "Hell, Emily, most of us were against the war."

The spell shattered. "Yeah, well . . . I better fix those biscuits. You and Royle must be hungry."

"I saw that pie. If it tastes half as good as it looks, I'll give you a raise."

Emily laughed. If Royle overheard Teigue he would fume hot enough to ignite the roof. "Come in when you're ready."

The sound of Teigue splashing water on his face followed her into the cabin. She gathered the ingredients for the biscuits. The baking powder can was a few grains shy of empty.

"Teigue?"

"Yeah?"

"Where do you stash the baking powder? We're out and I didn't find any more today."

"There are a couple of provision boxes up in the loft. Check them."

Emily carried a lamp up the ladder to her sleeping quarters. Several wooden crates sat in the shadows at the foot of her pallet. She worried the tops off, then sorted through the contents.

"You guys have a culinary gold mine up here and don't appreciate it." She examined the tins of canned fruit, spices, syrup, and finally baking powder. "Tomorrow's project. Organizing the larder."

At the worktable near the hearth, she rummaged around for a can opener.

"What do you need?" Teigue asked from the door.

"Can opener."

"I'll do it."

Shrugging, she scooped flour into a bowl. Her gaze caught on the writing emblazoned across the unfamiliar baking powder tin. Below, the image of a smiling woman in a long dress protected by an apron appeared new. The men may have been in the mountains for a long time, but supplies over a hundred years old were out of the question. The niggling thought from earlier burst forth with a jolt. "What's today's date?"

"It's the first of May." He punched the can opener into the lid and began seesawing it around the rim.

"What . . . what year, Teigue?" The awful dread spreading through her forced the question.

Teigue stopped worrying the can open. "Eighty-two."

"Eighty-two?" The question was nearly a whisper. The answer made no sense.

"1882." He set down the can opener and faced her.

Staring into his kind eyes, filled with concern, Emily felt the blood drain from her head. Her vision shimmered as though nothing was real. All the air in her lungs gushed out with the force of a giant fist slamming into her midsection. Out of reflex, she grabbed the table edge as she swayed with a rush of vertigo.

This could not be real. 1882? Impossible. No one traveled through time. No one . . .

Teigue stood in front of her and held her shoulders. "Emily?"

She managed a faint nod. "1882?"

"Something wrong with that?" He held her shoulders straight and braced her against the table edge. "Take a deep breath, and you'll feel better. Sometimes the altitude takes a little getting used to. Hell, you did too much work today."

"1882?" she whispered, dazed by the sound of the year contorting her tongue.

Teigue searched her face. "What'd you expect me to say?"

"Nineteen . . . ninety—" She bit off the rest and squeezed her eyes shut. How often had she wished for a simpler time? What if . . . She opened her eyes and met Teigue's concerned expression. They looked at each other for a long moment while she pulled herself together.

"Goddamn," he murmured. "You really are lost, aren't you?"

Emily blinked slowly, unsure of whether she was as lost

as Teigue perceived or if she had just found her place in the world. Either way, the new life she wanted lay before her. Was that why she was in this time? There had to be a reason. Something had to make sense. Nothing happened without a reason. With an inexplicable certainty, she knew there was no going back and part of her was oddly relieved.

"Why? How . . ."

A sound drew her attention toward the door.

Swathed in hostility, Royle strode into the cabin. All he lacked was the dark wings of the legendary fallen angels to fully epitomize the image he cast. His gaze met hers and narrowed as he stopped in his tracks. "Where's dinner?"

"Oh, damn is right," she murmured to Teigue.

She closed her eyes and prayed. *Please, God, give me a sign that Royle Tremaine is not the reason I am here.*

Chapter 5

Preoccupied, Emily toyed with her dinner. Incredulity dulled her senses. Perhaps shock accounted for her lack of panic or the kind of hysteria appropriate for discovering herself severed from everything familiar. Most disconcerting was a niggling sensation of relief. The crux of her uncertainty lay in whether she failed to comprehend the magnitude of change, or she just did not care.

This place felt solid, comfortable, like an old glove broken in by a trusted friend. "Tell me about Silverton, please," she asked Teigue.

The tremulous smile she managed conveyed her appreciation of his concern. He had watched her closely since revealing the date that had resulted in her weak-kneed reaction. Had she said anything to betray her impossible situation? She could not remember and hoped that she had not. Keeping secrets, especially her own, ranked high on her list of capabilities.

"Not much to tell. There are still more saloons than churches. Silverton's a mining town with a good smelter and lots of men eager to part with their hard-earned money for a few drinks and female company. You'll have to stay close to us when we go, Emily. A little darling like you will attract attention. I don't want anything *else* happening to you." Teigue cut another slice of pie and handed the pan to Royle.

"What will you do when you reach Silverton?" Royle asked, scooping the last piece of pie from the pan.

"I . . . ah . . . I'm not sure anymore. There must be somewhere I can get work." Defensive, she met his gaze for the first time since they sat down for dinner. "Not in a saloon, that's for sure."

What would she do? In this era without electricity or computers, cruising the information highway was a pipe dream. A hollow laugh escaped her. She had wanted a change. She got it, aces up! "I don't have to decide tonight," she said as much to herself as to him.

"Is someone waiting for you in Silverton?" Royle cut into the large piece of pie on his plate.

"No." His casual demeanor did not fool her. He intended to continue probing for something sinister. Suspicion glowed around him like a lighthouse beacon on a clear night. With great delight she relished her latest secret. Not even Sherlock Holmes could divine the bizarre circumstances of time that fate had thrust upon her.

Royle downed most of the pie in front of him before asking, "Do you know anyone in town?"

Presently, she barely knew herself. Emily giggled, then laughed out loud.

"Was that a yes or a no?" Royle lifted his fork. "Good pie. I'm impressed."

Emily shook her head. "Thank you. And no, I don't know anyone, except you two, and I can't say I really know you either."

"You get no argument from me on that," Royle said thoughtfully. "The Denver & Rio Grande Railroad should be through from Durango in a couple of months or so, maybe around the Fourth of July. You can take the train into Denver then and catch the Union Pacific for San Francisco."

Avoiding Royle's heated scrutiny, Emily collected the dishes from the table. "I'm not going back to California." Giving the decision voice reinforced her commitment to change everything in her new life. Such a golden opportunity demanded nothing less.

"Why not?" Royle pushed his empty plate toward her extended hand.

A layer of the numbness slid away from an irritated, raw patch of emotion. "Because I'm moving forward, not backward. Like the country song says, 'there ain't no future livin' in the past.' " She paused, realizing the only future she had was set in a past she had only read about or seen on film.

"Listen to her," Teigue warned. "She's talking smart."

Royle dismissed Teigue's admonition with a shrug. "Just so you move on, Miss Fergeson. Teigue and I are leaving these mountains at the end of the summer."

"You need not worry, Mr. Tremaine. I'm very capable of taking care of myself. I won't be a burden to you or your pocketbook—beyond my wages." She carried the dishes to the pan of warm water near the fire.

"Suppose you two call a truce and we take it one day at a time," Teigue suggested. "Nobody is going anywhere for at least a month. Maybe longer."

Emily nodded, her skin prickling with the heat of Royle's gaze on her back. "Sure. It's easy for me. Unlike Mr. Tremaine, I don't think I'm sharing my house with a thief."

"Excuse me." Royle pushed away from the table and went out to the porch.

Tension had crept into the tendons in her shoulders and coiled them into steel. She consciously tried to relax. "This isn't going to work, Teigue. Suppose I stay the week while you prepare me for what I can expect on the way to Silverton. Meanwhile, I'll get everything cleaned

and organized here. You can draw a map and I'll get out
of your life."

"Don't think about leaving, Emily. You're the first
genuine ray of sunshine to touch this place. If you have
no place to go and no time you have to get there, what's
wrong with staying?"

"Everything." She rinsed the last dish and scrubbed the
utensils. "I've spent most of my life with people who
didn't want me around and did whatever they could to
shuffle me off into a corner. When I had to be home, I
was tolerated as an outsider. I fit in as long as I played
the expected role. Never as myself." She tossed her head
and ducked her shoulder to move her long braid around
to her back.

"I did all the right things, said the right words, and
people liked me. I'm very good at adapting to my envi-
ronment. But adaptation does not equate to belonging,
anymore than being liked for what you can give or do
equates to genuine caring or acceptance."

Emily swirled the utensils in the rinse water and set
them aside. "I'm done living like that. Somewhere in this
world there's a place where I can be who I am. Say what
I want to say. Not have to step into a role of someone
else's design. . . . You probably don't have a clue as to
what I'm talking about, do you?"

When he did not answer, she glanced over her shoulder. A wave of goose bumps rippled up from the tips of
her dishwater-reddened fingers. The understanding of age
cratered the lines on Teigue's smooth-shaven face. His
eyes regarded her without blinking—eyes so sad Emily
thought she saw the misery of a tortured soul in their
depths. "I'll help you find your place, Emily. I'll make
damn sure you do. That's a promise."

How had she come to like and trust him so quickly?
More important, she believed him now. A ball of emotion
formed in her throat. "Oh, Teigue, why would you want
to? You don't know me." Still trying to release the tension gathered in her muscles, she drew a deep breath and
forced a smile. Only one side of her mouth twitched.

"Nor do you owe me anything. Why would you make such a promise when I might be everything Royle thinks I am?"

"You aren't. You need a friend. So do I. How about it?" Anxiety drew his brow down as he approached.

"You tempt me," she murmured. The old yearning for a place and people with open acceptance flared.

"But you won't take me up on it?" He handed a flour-sack towel to her, then captured her dripping hands.

Everything in her wanted to cry out her desperate need for a real friend. Her expression crumbled as she shook her head in denial. "I can't. And I can't stay. I really like you, Teigue. You have a beautiful spirit and a generous soul. The last thing I want for you is dissension, and it seems to be alive and well between Royle and me. The biggest favor I can do for you as a friend is to leave as soon as possible and let you and Royle continue—"

"Royle and I are parting company when we finish what we've set out to do here. He's going to Virginia. I'm not."

Emily felt as well as saw the sorrow behind his revelation. Thinking of Teigue isolated during the long winter twisted her loneliness into compassion. He did not want to be alone any more than she did. "Oh, Teigue. I would hate to think of you living here by yourself. You would be so alone in the winter. Wouldn't you get lonely?"

"I'll miss him. There's no question there. Royle is determined to travel a road I can't go down with him. But being alone and being lonely aren't the same."

A sad smile curled her lips and she lowered her gaze. "I know." Loneliness had been her companion since her mother's death.

"I thought you might. So, how about being my friend and partner?"

Longing dampened the last strains of her tenuous smile. One by one he had destroyed her objections. She truly liked him and for a fleeting moment wished that he had been her father. Had that been the case, she doubted she would have had to wait until her mother's death to meet him. No, Teigue would have never deserted them. With his generous heart, he would have showered his children with love and nurtured them when the world tried to beat them down.

"I would be honored and forever proud to call you my friend and be yours." Emily squeezed the hands holding hers as the care lines softened around his temples and mouth.

Beyond Teigue, Royle leaned against the doorjamb, his tender gaze fixed on Teigue. "I apologize, Miss Fergeson," he said softly, never taking his eyes from his uncle.

"Apology accepted," she murmured, shaken by the love for his uncle shining in Royle's eyes. "Truce?"

"Truce." Royle slipped out into the night.

For how long? she wondered.

Royle remained outside after Teigue and Emily retired for the night. The wind held its breath as though loath to disturb his mood. Over the years, Teigue had reiterated his position on the subject of returning to Virginia more times than Royle cared to recall. Until tonight, Royle had managed to ignore Teigue's vow to avoid anything east of the Mississippi River. The inevitable separation from his friend and last close relative settled with a bone-jarring finality. Given a choice, Royle would remain in the West with Teigue. However, choice had been stripped away the day he returned from London.

Royle bowed his head to the truth he had worked hard to ignore.

When he and Teigue parted at the end of the summer it might be for the last time. Once he embarked on fulfilling his responsibility to his Tremaine heritage, it would be years before he could carve out the time to venture west again. Even if he wanted to, he doubted the three women haunting his dreams would allow it. Nothing in the elusive dreams hinted of menace, only of waiting—for him. They were part of the compelling reason he had to return to Virginia.

Overhearing Teigue and Emily, he knew with bitter

certainty that Teigue had crossed the Mississippi for the last time.

Teigue had taken him under his wing when he had returned home from England. Had it been nearly eighteen years already? The quest for wealth had consumed more than half of Royle's life. It seemed that he and Teigue had been picking or blasting gold or silver out of the mountains forever.

They had done well in South Dakota shortly after the discovery of gold in '74. In spite of the Sioux and the crush of miners that flooded the Badlands, they had worked their claim until the gold disappeared.

By any standards, he and Teigue had left the Badlands wealthy men. But it had not been enough. What Royle needed to do in Virginia required an obscene amount of money. Rather than do it halfway, they had ventured south into the Colorado peaks. Their combined knowledge of geology and prospecting had paid off handsomely. Their efforts had reaped great rewards. And they had chosen well.

Hating the dismal prospect of leaving Teigue at the end of the summer, Royle lit a lantern and headed toward the mine. If he could not sleep, he may as well work. He doubted he would sleep any better tonight than he had last night.

He had lain awake trying to hear Emily breathe over Teigue's snoring. Having her so close had hardened his manhood until it screamed for release loud enough to wake the dead.

It made no sense. In the past, necessity had dictated that he abstain from women for months at a time. In the Badlands, he had gone a year without indulging his sexual needs. Even then, he had not become a slavering maniac with a flagpole straining his trousers at the sight of a woman. Furthermore, he had never lost a moment of sleep over a female, not for any reason. Why this time, after only a few weeks of forced abstinence?

If he admitted Emily's presence caused his uncontrollable condition, he'd have to credit Teigue's assertions that every man was vulnerable to the right woman.

Teigue was wrong.

Royle already had a marriage agreement with the right woman. Rebecca Weston. By this time next year they would be wed and hopefully have a child on the way. The Tremaine line would prosper as his father had intended, and his grandfather before him. He would make sure of it.

At the mine, Royle lit a pair of lanterns and headed into its depths. One thing about silver—it didn't care if the sun shone or the moon hid behind rain clouds. It merely waited for an enterprising miner to free it from the tons of rock holding it prisoner. He grabbed a pick and swung it.

Regardless of how hard he worked, his thoughts wandered to Emily. By the middle of the night, he had equated her to a leaky roof. He either had to avoid the drips or get used to being rained on. She wasn't leaving and neither was he.

Royle mopped his chest with his shirt, then wiped the sweat from his eyes. He had not needed to see Teigue's expression earlier that night. His uncle would move heaven and earth to keep that woman around. Whatever Teigue saw in her, it damn sure wasn't the same things he did. Why the hell couldn't Teigue see how she played on a man's tender side? One look into her big eyes, and Teigue cast his fine sense of people judgment aside. Hell, the woman probably had half a dozen men watching them right now, waiting to kill them and seize the mine.

Royle tossed his shirt aside and hefted the pick.

He wasn't going to succumb to Emily Fergeson's big eyes or her tempting body. Keeping a distance from Miss Fergeson had been easy today. Her wariness of him helped. Something about her had set him on fire during the brief moment they had shaken hands. He pushed the memory away. But within moments it returned with a twist. As he swung the pick, he mentally undressed her. He imagined his callused hands gliding over her long, naked thighs and cupping her smooth, curvy bottom. A sudden shortness of breath and a hard ache in his groin forced him into an unnatural stillness. His body wanted her on a primal level. His mind knew better. She was a liar and a schemer packaged in alluring smiles and seductive dependency.

The walls seemed unusually close and the heat from the lanterns hotter. Royle dropped the pick and adjusted the lanterns to better illuminate the rock he needed to sort. Tossing the rocks veined with high-grade ore into the cart, he found no solace from the sensual effect Emily Fergeson had on him.

He worked faster. Tonight wasn't the first time he'd tried to outrun the devil. However, the demon never wore tight denims and a long braid he ached to undo and spread across her naked shoulders.

"Have you been working all night?" Teigue asked when Royle entered the cabin shortly before dawn.

Royle punched his arms into his soiled shirt damp from the quick wash-up on the porch. "Yeah. Sleep managed to avoid me last night."

"Coffee?" Emily offered a steaming cup and kept her eyes fixed on the rim.

"Thank you." Royle carried the cup to the table and set it down as he took his usual place. He fetched the Winchester and checked the load. "I'm going hunting at first light."

"For—for what?"

"Dinner."

"My god. I hadn't thought about that. You really shoot helpless animals." As Emily stood between the table and the hearth, all color drained from her pert face. The line of her lips drew down in a white frown as she stared at the rifle. The steaming stack of flapjacks balanced on the spatula in front of her lent the only hint of life to her statuesque pose.

"She looks like she's going to swoon, Teigue," he murmured, setting aside the rifle.

Teigue thrust a plate under the flapjacks and turned her hand. "Sit here for a minute."

Emily sank into the chair, then leaned toward Royle over her folded forearms.

Royle leaned an elbow on the table. "Are you sick?"

She shook her head quickly, then drew back. "We've been eating animals you killed. . . ."

A foreboding reached out of his memories from England. Cousin Francine had had unusual lapses that set everyone on edge for a while. One day, everything erupted in a melee of shouts and tears followed by stone silence. A month later, Francine married a stranger. Five months later, she gave birth to a chubby daughter.

The notion of a man making love to Emily's luscious body, then abandoning her, filled him with revilement. "Are you—" He swallowed and tried to phrase the delicate question tactfully. "Are you expecting a child, Miss Fergeson?"

Her eyes grew wide with horror. Her mouth opened and closed in indignation. After an eerie stillness, sound leaked from behind her pressed lips.

In disbelief, Royle watched her erupt into side-splitting laughter accompanied by tears streaming down her cheeks. Each time she stole a glance at him, she laughed harder.

The woman was more than dangerous; she was crazy. Nothing about his question or her uncertain condition merited the feeblest hint of frivolity.

"No, Mr. Tremaine," she managed between gasps for air and wiping her cheeks on her flannel sleeve. "You may rest assured that I am not pregnant."

Relief assuaged his anger and left him confused. Why did it matter to him if she carried a child? He glanced at Teigue's grinning face and knew the answer. Damn, if she had said that she was, Teigue would have found a silver lining in the bleak situation and sunk deeper into his role as the shining knight of a downtrodden damsel.

"What—what are you going hunting for? Please tell me you're looking for herbs? Wild onions?"

He regarded her nervous suggestion with incredulity. Why the hell would he *hunt* for plants? "I will be hunting for food, Miss Fergeson. Deer. A young doe, to be specific."

Her eyes narrowed with a revilement worthy of those guilty of the most heinous crimes. "I can't believe you're going to hunt down Bambi's mother."

The sharp demand sparked a glance at Teigue, who appeared as uninformed as he. Royle shifted uncomfortably beneath the weight of her censure. "Who the hell is Bambi?"

For the next ten minutes he listened spellbound. The animated tale she spun with voice inflections and expressive twists of her face and hands unraveled an entire animal kingdom. The denizens spoke with one another and had names like Thumper and Flower.

Sometime during the telling, Teigue set a stack of flapjacks in front of Royle. He ate without tasting them. The depths of Emily Fergeson's dementia daunted him. What had they opened the door on and brought inside?

A deafening silence descended when she finished the story. Royle stared at her for another long, restless minute before asking, "You do not really believe that tale, do you?" He remained statue-still in hope of her denial.

She shrugged her right shoulder. "It's a fairy tale, but it has a message."

"I must have missed that part." Royle drained the cold coffee from his cup.

"Everything in nature struggles to survive. There is a natural balance and order when man stays out of the way. What kind of sport is there in an uneven playing field?"

"Consider me undereducated, but I have no idea of what you are talking about."

"You're a big, strong man. How much sport is there in hunting down an animal by using a deadly rifle when the animal is unarmed?"

The lack of sleep was catching up with him. Surely, she wasn't suggesting . . . He blinked once, twice, then cleared his throat. "Which are you advocating—that I chase the deer down and wrestle it to the ground with brute strength until I break its neck, or that I give Bambi's mother a rifle?"

Unbelievably, the radiant smile she bestowed on him lit the entire cabin. "Either way would be more equitable—providing that you teach her how to use the rifle."

Teigue erupted in a howl of laughter. The wooden legs of his stool grated against the cabin floor as he scooted away from the table.

Fed up, Royle snatched the Winchester and gathered a handful of shells from the box on the shelf over his bed.

"Oh, God, you're not really going to hunt down—"

Royle turned on Emily with a forced, patient smile both recognized as feigned, but threatening. "No. I am not going to kill Bambi's mother. History would judge me too harshly. I am going straight for Bambi. Next week, I will get Thumper. Flower is the only safe one in the bunch. Furthermore, I have never considered hunting a sport any more than I consider eating a luxury or a hobby I dabble in once a week."

He straightened, enjoying the flow of emotion rippling across her features. "When I return with Bambi, I will expect you to butcher him, then cook him for supper."

Within a few rapid heartbeats, she surged to her feet and knocked the chair over in the process. With her hands balled into fists on her hips, her eyes glittered like icy emeralds from the other side of the table. "For minimum wage, Mr. Tremaine, I don't do windows. I don't do ovens. And I *damn* sure don't butcher baby deer!"

He snagged his jacket and pulled the door open so hard it banged against the wall. "We don't have any Goddamn window glass to wash. Or a stove with an oven you need to clean. And unless I get going, we won't have Bambi, either. I will butcher and cure the venison. All you have to do is cook and eat it."

"I don't eat venison!" she hollered from the doorway.

"In that case, Bambi will feed us another day, and Thumper gets to live a little longer." He whistled for his horse and ducked into the shelter. Tired as he was, he wasn't sure which gave him more satisfaction, the prospect of being away from her for most of the morning or making her angry.

"We damn well better find Bambi," he warned his horse as he reached for the saddle.

Chapter 6

THE WEEK FOLLOWING the assassination of an aging buck tough enough to be Bambi's great-grandfather passed with the frayed truce intact. Each morning Royle brought the day's meat from the underground ice shelter beside the cabin, and Emily prepared it. However, she refrained from eating it—beans and biscuits suited her fine.

Emily fell into a comfortable routine. During occasional breaks, she scoured the newspaper stack. What might be construed as mundane, she found exciting. A hunger to learn more of the world beyond the peaks became an obsession that Teigue indulged.

"I read something in the newspapers I don't understand—about a reference to the Miners Home," Emily said after dinner to Teigue. She ignored Royle's wary scrutiny.

"Ah, the Miners Home," Teigue murmured, then grinned. "Good idea, wrong place."

"Why? Aren't these mountains loaded with miners?"

Royle leaned back in his chair. "Exactly what do you think the Miners Home was?"

"The way the few articles that mention it read, it sounds like a retirement center."

"What is a retirement center?"

She met Royle's narrow gaze. "A place where the residents are taken care of, their needs met by a professional staff, their meals cooked for them. I would suppose the miners pay a monthly rate or negotiate a lump sum for their care after they retire."

Royle grinned. "I suppose they might have negotiated such a thing."

"What don't you understand, Emily?" Teigue asked.

"Why it failed. One of the articles said the Miners Home offered activities and had musical entertainment from traveling players."

"They did. For a week. The people of Silverton apparently did not appreciate them. However, the Miners Home was not the benevolent place you may believe it was." Teigue shifted in his chair.

"Oh, I don't know about that," Royle quipped. "Seems to me it had all the things she mentioned. Good liquor. A wooden dance floor. Plenty of rooms upstairs with a professional staff of ladies waiting to attend a man's needs. I can think of several men who would pay a monthly fee to be taken care of there. But there's more profit in serving a miner's base needs than in variety entertainment."

"Do you really believe that the only needs people have are physical?" she demanded of Royle.

"When you work in a dark mine day after day, month after month, needs become simple and urgent."

"People need more than their physical needs and comforts met. Life can lose its purpose without outside interests," Emily mused.

"Is that why you're here? To provide an outside interest for Teigue and me?"

"I'm here because I lost my way. If my presence enriches your narrowly defined life, then we are all fortunate. At least we're discussing something other than mining and animals." Warming to the edge she perceived, she straightened. "What you said about the Miners Home makes me wonder what happens to miners who become physically disabled."

"They go home, if they have a home and family, and die."

"And if they don't have a home?"

"They keep mining until they die from the cold, or a cave-in, or any one of a dozen reasons." Royle glanced at Teigue, then met Emily's relentless gaze.

"How can you be so callous?"

Royle straightened. "Callous? I'm just answering your questions."

"Aren't you at all concerned what happens to these men? Don't you worry about their welfare? Whether they'll be in pain, hungry, dry, or warm? Whether they'll have the medical attention they need?"

"No."

The simple answer astounded her. "Why not? You have a responsibility as a caring human being to look after those weaker than you."

"No, I don't." He leaned his forearms on the table. "Why should I give any of my stash to someone who drank or gambled his own away?"

"Because they aren't as strong or smart as you. They need—"

"They need to take care of themselves. I don't know how it is where you came from, Emily, but here a man lives, or dies, by his own efforts. The only thing anybody is going to give you is a few ounces of lead if you try taking what isn't yours. I'd think a big reader like you would be familiar with Charles Darwin's theory of natural selection. It isn't a theory here. That's the way it is. You take care of yourself and those you're responsible for. That's it."

"You're the first person I've ever believed has absolutely no social conscience. How can you turn your back on hungry children?"

"Who said anything about children?" Royle pushed away from the table. "Say anything you want. I'm going to bed."

Emily watched him go, and wondered how any social reforms had occurred when men thought like Royle Tremaine. Slowly, she decided, very slowly.

The topic she planned for tonight's after-dinner conversation resulted from her sense of fairness and determination to move forward. Dread for Royle's opposition made her edgy. Adding to her restlessness, the men were later than usual in returning from the mine. When she heard their footfalls on the porch she put the biscuit pan in the embers.

Out of the corner of her eye, Emily watched Royle enter the cabin. Her heart skipped a beat, then accelerated. Cleanshaven, he appeared almost civilized. The familiar heat ignited by his presence blossomed through her. The image she held of him as a dark angel seemed more appropriate than ever. Her mouth went dry when he pulled off his shirt and tossed it into the crate designated as a hamper. Hours in the sun as he worked the slag pile had darkened his back to a gleaming bronze. The liquid flow of muscle for the simple task of selecting his favorite red, white, and black flannel shirt made her overly warm.

Shaken by an erotic fantasy of running her hands over the contours of his powerful shoulders, she dragged her attention away. That would never happen. His polite exterior belied the dislike she knew he harbored for her. It dismayed and fascinated her simultaneously. In her entire life, no one had actively disliked her.

Emily sighed and set the table for dinner. Just by being herself and refusing to assume the roles that had insulated her in the past, she was bound to bump against those who did not like her. So be it. Royle was merely the first. Too bad.

The glitch was that she liked him.

During other pleasant after-dinner conversations she had discovered that she enjoyed his dry humor and quick intelligence. He held some chauvinistic notions about women, but perhaps not out of line with the times, if she interpreted the tone of the *San Juan Herald* articles correctly.

"Do I smell a pie?" Teigue strode into the cabin sniffing the air and grinning.

Emily beamed at him and felt the ever-present tension between her and Royle ebb. "You most certainly do."

"Uh-oh. We are about to be bushwhacked." Royle pushed his shirttails into his waistband as he approached the table.

Guilt stained her cheeks with color. How transparent her actions must be for him to read her intentions so easily. Emily shot a cautious glance at him. The dazzling grin lighting the paler skin where his whiskers had been changed her anxiety to heart-stopping desire. The grin faded. Sensual hunger glittered in his navy blue eyes and held her frozen.

"Is something wrong, Miss Fergeson?"

The soft-spoken question weakened her bones.

"Emily?" Concern tempered the desire focused on her.

"Uh. No, nothing is wrong. This is the first time I've seen you shaven." She straightened and drew her wits around her flagging defenses. Damn, she sounded like the high-school geek she had been her first year at St. Cecilia's. "You're almost as good-looking as Teigue." Well, that polished everything up nicely, she admonished silently.

"Almost?"

The laugh in his voice made her smile. "Yes. Almost. I thought you wore your beard to keep from scaring me." She raised her left shoulder and tipped her head. "But then, I should have known better." She winked at Royle, then grinned at the confusion in his lopsided smile.

"Yes, I guess you should have."

She caught Teigue's eye and raised a questioning eyebrow. He seemed inordinately pleased about something. For the life of her, she couldn't fathom what it might be. "Did you have a good day?"

"Good enough to go back tomorrow." Teigue settled into his place at the table with a smug smile.

Emily dished up dinner and set it on the table. All the while she gathered her courage. As she sat, Royle glanced at the hearth. "Biscuits?"

"Oh." She hurriedly fished the biscuit pan from the embers and checked them. "Perfect."

Royle waited until she sat down before picking up his fork. "What is on your mind, Miss Fergeson?"

"Your pocketbook, Mr. Tremaine." She met his steely gaze with resolve. In truth, she had been suffering tremendous guilt over the amount of money they were paying her for performing simple chores. According to what she had gleaned from the newspaper, entire families lived for more than a month on what they paid her in a day.

"Are the thoughts rolling around your mind going to cost me?"

"On the contrary. I was about to offer a way for you to save money." She split a steaming biscuit.

"You have my complete attention." Royle set down his fork.

"Oh, please. Eat. I doubt I'll forget the idea before dinner is over." Now that she had his attention, she intended to let him mull over the possibilities. Confident that his limited scope of thinking when it came to females wouldn't venture in the direction of her plan, she began eating.

Emily bided her time until Teigue dished out the pie. "I was thinking. . . ."

"Again or still?" Royle goaded.

"Still," she answered pleasantly, not willing to let him go ballistic until she finished her proposition.

Teigue cut into his pie. "What do you have in mind, Emily?"

"I have the mending done, the laundry caught up, and the cabin cleaned. The daily chores of maintaining the place won't consume as much of my time in the future."

"Yes, you may have a cut in your wages," Royle agreed. "No need to thank me."

Emily swallowed. He wasn't going to make it easy, but then she hadn't expected anything else. "I was thinking that I could help at the mine three or four days a week. You know, like every other day. If I left before you did in the evenings, I could get the evening meal prepared without any change in the way we've been doing it."

Astonishment stole across Royle's dark features. "And what do you want in return?"

"Nothing."

"You want to work at the mine for the same wages?"

Emily nodded. "I wouldn't charge you for helping at the mine. Call it payback for helping me get on my feet."

"Absolutely not acceptable," Teigue growled.

Stunned, she gaped at Teigue. He wasn't in favor of her proposal? "Why not?"

"You don't work for nothing, Emily. Not now. Not ever. And not here." He dug into his pie with a vengeance.

"But Teigue, you and Royle work so hard for your money. Look how much you can save by not paying me every other day. Besides, another pair of hands at the mine can help. I can carry tools. You can teach me how to sort rocks. Oh, Teigue, you don't want to spend the rest of your life trying to eke out a living inside that mountain, do you? Let me do this. I'm strong and I'm willing."

"Eke out a living?" Teigue echoed, exchanging glances with Royle.

"Teigue, I read the newspapers. The number of miners who come into these mountains and wind up leaving broke and broken brought tears to my eyes. I want more than that for you. And I can't be a parasite leeching away your hard-earned profits or the nest egg you may have set aside for your retirement."

Very slowly, Teigue set down his fork, then stared at her.

The silence stretched until Emily heard the blood rushing in her temples. How could she make him understand that while she needed the income, the excessiveness of it in this era would haunt her? According to the newspaper articles, the two of them had to be working most of the day to pay what in her time was minimum wage.

"Let me understand this," Royle said slowly. "You want to cut what we pay you by approximately half and still do everything we agreed to?"

"Yes. And I—"

Royle cut her off by raising his hand. "In addition, you want to do hard, dirty, backbreaking work at the mine with us for nothing?"

"Yes. Because—"

This time, he curled his fingers into a white-knuckled fist and pressed it into the narrow expanse of table between them. "Are you stupid or do you think we are?"

Anger surged up from her toes. "Neither! What I'm proposing isn't stupid. It's fair."

"To whom is it fair?" Royle demanded.

"All of us. What possible ulterior motive could I have? And don't give me that bull about having friends hiding in the bushes. I don't and you know it." She drew an audible breath in an effort to calm herself. "You think I don't know that you check on me during the day, Mr. Tremaine? King of the silent Indian scouts, you are not. Even if I was wearing combat boots, I'd be quieter in the woods than you are."

Royle was across the table and gripping her wrist in a heartbeat. "What the hell do you mean, checking on you?"

"I'd call shuffling around the back of the cabin and under the porch window while I'm taking a sponge bath more than checking," she answered through gritted teeth, her nose an inch from his.

"When?"

"You ought to know when. I heard you out there three days ago and again yesterday afternoon. Now let go of me before I punch you in the nose." She balled her free fist.

The stream of expletives pouring from Teigue forced her to turn away from the menace directly in front of her.

"That wasn't me," Royle hissed. "If it had been, you would not have heard a thing."

"Then . . ." All the fight drained out of her. She had assumed the man prowling outside the cabin had been Royle. Given his suspicious nature, his presence hadn't surprised her, nor had it frightened her. "But if it wasn't you . . . who was it?" Meeting the rage in Royle's flashing gaze sparked fear. "I thought it was you," she whispered.

"Why?"

"Because you dislike me so much, and you're so sure I'm out to hurt you in some way."

"Are you?"

"Get real. You're the one breaking my wrist, not the other way around." His grip loosened instantly. "How am I going to hurt you, Royle? Starch your long johns? Sew the buttons on your pants lopsided? Tear up your favorite shirt and use it as a rag? Maybe I'll steal your horse and ride him around the meadow."

Tears stung her eyes. She didn't want his dislike to matter, but it did. Worse, she was frightened and he knew it.

"Tomorrow, you go to the mine with us. And you are going with us every day until we leave you in Silverton. You don't go anywhere without me or Teigue. Not even to the outhouse without telling one of us. Understand?"

"No," she whispered, confused.

"What don't you understand?"

"Why would you go out of your way to protect me? That's what you're doing, isn't it? Trying to protect me?" Lost in the tumult of his blue eyes, she felt nothing made sense.

"Yes, damn it. You matter to Teigue, and he matters to me." He released her wrist and settled back into his chair.

"I've been taking care of myself for most of my life, Royle. You needn't put yourself out. But I thank you for your concern."

Royle stood so abruptly that his chair toppled. "Talk to her, Teigue. No more wages. She can have whatever she pulls out of the mountain instead."

Drained, she watched Royle storm from the cabin. The slamming of the door punctuated the finality of his position.

"I don't understand him, Teigue." She dropped her forehead into her open hand. "I don't understand me, either. Why do I even care what he thinks?"

"Don't worry about it, Sunshine. He doesn't understand himself. Just between us, it's going to get a hell of a lot worse for him before it gets better. And it won't get better unless he pulls his head out of the hole he's digging for himself."

Teigue poured coffee, then scooted his chair closer to her. "Every now and then someone wanders through here, and we don't get too concerned. Stealing the mules or horses and taking them into Silverton to sell would be damn near impossible. Everyone knows they're ours, and we wouldn't be selling until we're ready to pull out. Still, Royle knows best on this. You can't stay here alone anymore. We'll split up the chores and work and live like partners. This is what you wanted, isn't it?"

"Yes and no. I don't want to be a burden you two feel you need to baby-sit out of some noble sense of chivalry. That isn't right, Teigue."

Teigue threw his head back and laughed. "Maybe not. But it's more fair than some of the unexplainable quirks in life you've already experienced, wouldn't you say?"

She slid her palm down to her chin and looked hard at Teigue. "You know, don't you? From what I said earlier."

"I know, and your secret is safe with me. Even if you hadn't said anything when I told you what year it is, the questions you ask and the way you look at things would make me question. I've got a few of my own whenever you're ready to talk about it."

"You'd believe I came from the future?" Skepticism forced her to glance away.

"If you say you did, I believe it. I believe you, Emily." Smiling, he toasted her with his coffee cup. "If Madeline and I had had a daughter, she'd be about your age. Be part of the family Maddy and I wanted, Emily."

Two tears spilled down her cheeks. "Teigue? You're the best friend I've ever had, and the first man I've ever loved. I'm honored to be a part of your family. Really honored that you'd want me." She lifted her cup to his and touched the rims.

"Welcome home, Sunshine."

Fingers of golden orange stretched over the rim of the towering peaks and promised a warm day. The motion of

Emily's backside as she followed Teigue to the mine heated Royle from the inside. He had spent another restless night trying to decide if she was naïve and giving, or an excellent con-woman.

Any doubts he harbored about an intruder had disappeared when he checked the back of the cabin. The footprints in the soft dirt had measured too large for Emily and too small for him or Teigue.

The rich fantasy life his dreams wove around Emily made the trespass an invasion of his private territory. As long as she remained at the cabin, she belonged to him—at least in his imaginary realm. He had accepted the potent physical attraction to her after the second sleepless night he spent working in the mine.

He tried hard to dislike her and even harder to incur her disdain. She had accused him of that after supper last night. Better she believe that than the truth—he liked her too much and wanted both her body and her approval. However, the road of his future allowed no detours. In six months, he'd marry Rebecca Weston. Emily would be nothing more than a frustrating memory.

"How can I help?"

Emily's question pulled his thoughts into the present. "Can you swing a pick?"

"It's been a long time, but yes. However, I'm better with a shovel."

"A shovel it is." Before she reached for the tools propped against the wall just inside the mine, he caught her hands. Calluses still pink with their newness hardened the pads of her strong fingers and palms. His thumbs measured their width with casual slowness. The warmth and softness of her skin conjured an image of those fingers skimming his body until they wrapped around the erection growing in his trousers.

"You need gloves," he murmured, pressing his thumbs more firmly into the center of her palms and drawing her fingers into perfect curls for relieving the ache she created with a look or word.

"Take mine. They may be big, but they'll protect your

hands." He placed the gloves in her palm, then wrapped her fingers around the supple leather.

"What will you use?"

Royle ducked through the entrance and struck a match.

"Mr. Tremaine?"

He stopped short and lit the lantern. Damn it, he wanted her. If she gave any indication of sharing that desire, he'd make love with her every chance he got before they went their separate ways in Silverton.

"Here." Emily took his hand and slapped the gloves into his palm. "Thank you for the offer, but you'll need them more than I will. I'll be careful and tonight I'll see what I can find to make a pair of gloves for myself."

"Look, I . . ." Royle's voice faded as he gazed into Emily's eyes that became greener the longer she looked at him. He saw himself reflected in their emerald depths. The relentless attraction between them confounded her as severely as it confused him. The warmth of her hands cradling his right wrist slithered through his body and stoked the fire raging in his loins. He caught her fingers in his left hand and closed them around the thick, supple leather. "Use the damn gloves. Please."

Fighting the desire, Royle reminded himself that this woman could be his downfall. Her luscious body and beguiling eyes were decoys for duplicity and deceit. Royle turned away. With each practiced motion of preparing for a day of mining, he drew his defenses into place. She was good. Damn good. His only salvation lay in recognizing the pert Miss Fergeson was more than she seemed.

Royle navigated the maze of tunnels inside the mountain without a backward glance. At the back of the offshoot he and Teigue had worked for the past week, he set the lantern down. Without thinking about it, he propped the Winchester against the wall, then removed his gun belt and jacket. Next, he opened his shirt. The cold radiating from the stone did not penetrate the heat suffusing his body.

He lit a second and a third lantern, then examined the streak of silver he wanted separated from the mountain.

The sound of metal on stone reverberated through the

shaft. Royle worked with a rhythm created by a body in tune with the rock. His mind floated freely.

He had to keep sight of his goal. As long as he did so, nothing would deter him. *Obstacles are what you see when you lose sight of your goal.* His father had told them that from the earliest time he could remember until the family put him on a ship to England.

Royle had objected to being sent off to live with a distant cousin by using all the weapons available to an eleven-year-old. He had fought and railed against leaving home. His parents had been immovable on the subject, his father threatening to hog-tie him and put him in the hold of the ship if Royle could not muster the dignity to comply with his parents' wishes. In the end, he had gone on his own two feet, stood on the deck of the ship and waved good-bye.

To honor his father, he had excelled at Eton. Not once had Cousin Stephen found it necessary to chastise his behavior. Royle had made his father proud and looked forward to the end of the travel-and-trade embargo between England and the Confederate States. After the war, Cousin Stephen sent him home with a blessing and an offer of a splendid future should he change his mind and return to England.

Only one family member met the young Virginian at the docks. Everything and everyone else was gone.

Royle swung the pick hard, letting the reverberations travel up his arms, across his shoulders, and down his back into his legs. Years of venting the injustices of life on rocks had not diminished the rage inside him. It had twisted it into a grudging acceptance that molded his resolve.

A distant rumble froze him with the pick high over his left shoulder. It grew louder.

"Teigue!" Royle dropped the pick, snatched up a lantern, and started running.

"Emily! Teigue!"

The rumble swallowed his frantic shouts.

Chapter 7

EMILY HADN'T MEANT to dislodge the beam. She had barely leaned against it for support. The next thing she knew, the tunnel shuddered. Debris rained from the ceiling. One hand over her head, the other clutching a lantern handle, she ran away from the crumbling walls. Thick billows of dust chased her with a roar.

Emily closed her stinging eyes and groped her way down the tunnel. Her trembling fingers skimmed the rough rock until it abruptly fell away. She turned, following the offshoot, then pressed her back against the solid wall as though the danger would pass by. She opened her eyes to a squint.

Away from the main swirl of dust, she ventured a breath through the sleeve of her sweatshirt. The ache in her chest tightened. She was alone in the bowels of a mountain high enough to scrape stardust from the night sky. Fear shot through her, leaving a sheen of perspiration in the chilly depths.

"The walls are not moving," she whispered, then coughed. Billows of dust crept around her with the relentless speed of an ocean tide. As the encroaching curtain threatened to suffocate her, she forced her legs into motion. It didn't seem right that she had been thrust through a wormhole in time only to die alone in an abandoned tunnel.

"I'm not going to die here," she promised the darkness around her. "That can't be the reason I'm here."

Fortified by her hollow-sounding words, the promise of breathable air lured her deeper into the side tunnel.

Teigue had said that most of the tunnels intersected and eventually joined the main tunnel. She fervently hoped the avenue ahead offered escape, not a dead end.

Fighting back the fear hovering on the edge of the shallow sphere of light cast by her lantern, she called Teigue's name. The sound bounced through the tunnel until the darkness swallowed it. The return silence carried an absoluteness that settled eerily into the marrow of her bones.

Speaking softly, she encouraged herself the way she might assist a stranger. In front and behind her, utter blackness reigned.

"Move a little faster. The juice in this lantern won't last all day," she muttered, picking up the pace, yet careful of where she set her feet. Her ragged breathing and the crush of fine rock under her shoes were the only sounds punctuating the frantic thrum of her heart.

What seemed like the world's longest passage ended against a pile of rocky rubble. The lack of dust roiling in the stale air revealed that this collapse had occurred much earlier.

Lifting the lantern high, she examined the barrier and ceiling. This area had been worked hard. Stress fissures formed by the explosive charges Royle had mentioned setting to do the worst of the rock-splintering showed clearly in the granite.

A fresh ripple of fear shot up her spine. Only the strength of the rock kept the mountain overhead from collapsing. Forcing back the wedge of panic caught in the center of her chest, she contemplated her predicament.

Going back the way she had come was impossible until the dust cleared. How long would that take?

If she couldn't go back and couldn't go forward . . .

She quit thinking. The daunting possibilities generated fear, not solutions.

Facing the loose, rocky mound angling from a point just ahead of her toes to the ceiling an easy twelve feet up the slope, she swallowed hard. If she was going to get out of here, she had to dig her way through the minimountain ahead.

She set the lantern aside, then scrambled up the rocky slope. It was narrowest at the ceiling. If she could tunnel through, the other side might lead to a surface corridor.

As she pulled rocks away and pushed them down the slope, she refused to consider the thickness of the rock slide ahead. After a few minutes, she stripped off her sweatshirt and tore up the sleeves. She wrapped the fleece around her gloved knuckles as extra protection from the biting rocks.

To conserve lamp oil, she dimmed the flame to barely a glow and kept working. Showers of dirt and small bits of rock slithered across the area she cleared. Using her fingers, she measured her progress on the ceiling. There was progress. Slow progress.

When at last she climbed down into the company of the lantern, every muscle in her body screamed in protest. Exhausted, she rested her elbows on her knees and dropped her forehead onto her wrists. What she wouldn't give to hear another voice . . . even Royle's acerbic suspicions would be music. Again, she thought of him first. Why?

He lurked on the periphery of her awareness every waking moment, and invaded her dreams at night. Right now, he would be marvelous company. Strong. Invigorating. Sensuous.

A laugh took too much effort. She managed a faint smile, knowing she could find the energy that eluded her now if Royle were digging next to her. No other man had turned her blood into fire and her placid disposition into aggressiveness. Even now, when she should be concentrating on widening the hole to freedom, he dominated her thoughts.

No doubt Royle would have dug through three times the amount of rock she had removed. Head hanging and shaking, she did not know if her hands would last. They had to. To stop was to give up and die. Her eyes focused on her aching hands stained by dirt and blood. They almost looked holy.

A weary snort passed for laughter in the faint light.

Holy.

She stared, feeling for the moment that the tattered sweatshirt wrapped around her battered, gloved knuckles protected someone else's sore, bruise-riddled palms.

A wiggle of her forefinger let her know in no uncertain terms who owned the hand. Pain shot up her aching arms. Stardust glittered in the dim light. She stared for a long time, sure her sight was playing tricks.

When she mustered the resolve to start again, she leaned toward the lantern. Her breath caught in her throat.

All around her the floor glittered. She lifted the lantern. A sparkling trail led straight up the rockfall.

Excitement banished the aches and pains. She turned up the lantern and lit the cavern. She half-scrambled, half-crawled up the golden trail.

In the ceiling, small globs of gold spread into quartz and mottled granite. With bloody, bruised fingertips poking through Royle's worn-out gloves, she touched the treasure.

"Oh, Teigue, you won't have to work in a mine again once we get this out." Invigorated, she resumed digging.

Long after the lantern had burned out, she kept working. The darkness spurred her on. Twice, she laid her head on her arms and dozed soundly. Fickle time no longer mattered. Only the progress of inches held importance.

One more rock. Move one more rock.

Thirsty and hungry, she did not need to see the rocks, just move them. Weary beyond belief, she braced herself against the back of the hole she had created just below the roofline and adjusted her footing. Before she could catch her balance, the rocks under her feet shifted. She cried out, her foot slipping between two rocks tumbling down the slope, dragging her down to the rubble-strewn, black floor.

In frustration, she screamed every curse she knew, then bit off the tirade with a sob. Pain shot up her leg. Already, she felt the flesh around her ankle begin to swell. As much as it hurt, not being able to see it was a strange relief.

Hold it together a little longer. Suck it up and make that hole big enough to climb through. Then you can drink water and rest. Lay down and rest. And drink an ocean of water.

Inch by grueling inch, she crawled up the slope on her hands and knees. At the hole, a thin stream of sweet air teased her nostrils. Greedy for more, she carefully, very carefully, expanded the hole. Without warning, debris slipped down and sealed the fresh air flow. Heart thundering, she barely breathed. Fine grit rained from the top of the escape tunnel she'd carved.

Emily closed her stinging eyes, afraid to move lest the ceiling collapse and bury her from her head to her hips. She imagined herself sealed half-in, half-out of the escape tunnel. Instead of leading to freedom, it would be a crypt. Yet the terror rampaging her thoughts refused to free her from immobility. She remained there, bent at the hips with her torso stretched into the jaws of the tunnel.

The longer she stood anchored to her precarious perch, the more aches settled into her limbs. After a while, the lack of air forced her to move.

Slowly, she inched back on trembling legs. Her swollen ankle buckled, forcing her to grab the very rocks that she wanted to stay in place.

She froze, the blood from her fingers creeping across her palm and trickling a trail across the inside of her wrist. Any second, the ceiling might drop. A few grains of crushed rock sifted down.

One at a time, she relaxed her aching fingers from around the rock protruding from the ceiling. The only sound was her breathing and the grating of her elbow along the escape tunnel floor.

When she emerged, she groped for a rock to sit on. Shaken, she gathered the last shreds of her strength and courage. The only thing she wanted more than not having to go into the hole again was escape. Unfortunately, it lay on the other side of the rockfall. She had smelled sweeter air for a brief moment before the rocks slid down to seal her on this side of freedom.

The longer she sat, the stiffer her legs became and the more her hands hurt. In the total darkness, she felt the pressure of the mountain closing in on her from all sides. The mountain might not fall or the walls move in to crush the life from her; instead, the danger rode on the back of more insidious beasts: thirst, hunger, and oxygen deprivation. All things considered, being crushed by the mountain seemed the least painful option.

At last, she rose and faced her fear. Cautiously, she moved into the escape tunnel. One rock at a time, she expanded the space as though one wrong move would pull down the ceiling.

Her battered fingers groped for holds. Gingerly, she dislodged the rocks and pushed them forward. They clattered down the opposite slope. She held her breath, waiting for the ceiling to collapse and seal the narrow opening. Slowly, she inhaled sweet air that promised freedom and widened the opening.

A flicker of light glowed through the tiny opening. Either someone was at the far end of the long tunnel ahead, or the great white light at the end of life approached.

"I'm here!" Although her mind commanded a scream, the sound died on her thirst-swollen lips. The light winked out. Frantic, she tried again.

"I'm here." This time the cry grated into the darkness. She followed it by pushing frantically on the rocks ahead of her. As they tumbled down the slope leading to freedom and sweet air, she cried out again, "Don't leave me."

When she heard a voice call her name, she replied by pushing more rocks forward. The opening grew with amazing speed. The last of her energy evaporated. All she could do was lie half-in and half-out of the hole carved through the debris.

"Damn." Royle's anger penetrated her exhaustion.

Garnering the last of her strength, she lifted her head.

Anger etched his dirt-smudged features. His eyes bore through her like sapphire lasers.

"Gold. Teigue can retire." Every second of terror and fear, and each muscle wracked with aches and pains was worth the price of ensuring Teigue's future. "When you leave."

Swearing under his breath, he raised the lantern.

"Look," she rasped, her throat dry and sore. She thrust her abused, bloody hands into the warm glow of his lantern.

At first there were no signs of the glittering flakes and she wondered if she had hallucinated the find.

"Forget the damn gold. If you'd had enough sense to stay with one of us, you would not be in this predicament."

"But I—"

"Close your mouth, Emily, and hold still. I need to get you out of there before the ceiling comes down." Royle leaned forward and slipped his hands along her ribs, over her waist, and across the swell of her buttocks. "You're clear. Just barely. Lie still. I'm going to pull you through."

She almost smiled. She didn't think she could help. There was nothing left in her reserves. "I'm so tired, Royle."

"I know you are. You may not be smart, but you have a lot of guts. We had damn near given up on you." He slipped something under her belly.

"So soon?"

"Two days isn't soon. It's forever down here." He braced himself. "Just relax. I'm going to pull you through. Make this easier on both of us—no kicking or helping. We don't want to bring the ceiling down."

"The ceiling . . . It's gold," she whispered, letting her entire body go limp.

"Sure it is." He grabbed her wrists and pulled steadily. "Here we go."

She felt like a fat piece of yarn being pulled through the eye of a needle. Strong hands skimmed down her body, turning and gathering her against his chest, soothing her with every change of grip. By the time her feet dragged across the last rock, she felt stretched to six feet tall.

She curled against his broad chest, not wanting to ever release him. Through her perspiration and lingering stench of fear, she caught his distinct masculine scent. "I'm golden. Look. . . ."

Royle turned her toward the light. Flecks of gold dust and flakes clung to her sweat-saturated shirt and Levi's. Even her running shoes glittered like a New Year's spangled dress.

"Teigue—"

"Does not give a mule's ass about gold. He is damn near out of his mind with worry." Royle set her down as though she was made of fine porcelain. He fetched the canteen beside the lantern and opened it. The tender way he held the water to her swollen, cracked lips belied his gruff demeanor.

Water had never tasted so good. She wanted to drink it all at once.

"We've been digging where the tunnel collapsed. Every time we cleared a section, Teigue expected to see your crushed body."

"I ran," she rasped between gulps. Eagerly, she took the canteen and drank again. Had she ever been this thirsty?

"Sip it slowly. If you go too fast, the water will come back on you and burn your throat like bad whiskey."

When she lowered the canteen, she realized Royle was running his hands over her pain-numbed body.

"Why are . . ." The welling up of water in her throat forced her to swallow repeatedly.

His hands stilled. "Keep swallowing, Emily. That a girl."

If there had been any moisture instead of grit in her eyes, the tenderness of his voice and gentleness of his touch would have made her cry. "I need to check for broken bones."

"My ankle. The rocks gave way." She silenced, feeling the cramps in her stomach ebb under the sensual heat created by his hands running along her legs.

"Too bad you lacked the good sense to bind this ankle." Royle untied her shoe, spread the laces, then supported her ankle as he slipped it off.

"With what? Besides, I couldn't see it." Glancing at the black hole in the rock slide, she shivered. "It was so very, very dark. And quiet."

"The inside of a mountain usually is," he agreed, removing her sock.

Unthinking, she reached out and touched Royle's hair. "As dark in there as your hair and as lonely as walking against the tide." Had she ever been so tired?

He removed his shirt and ripped it into strips. With practiced, gentle hands, he began binding her ankle. "Why do I get the impression that you usually walk against the tide?"

The stone wall cradled her head as exhaustion seeped into her bones. "I promised if I ever heard your voice again, I wouldn't argue with you." Hugging the open canteen to her breasts, she closed her eyes. "Just . . . please, don't leave me alone in the dark. Please don't hate me that much."

He did not hate or even dislike her. However, he was guilty of trying to achieve one or the other, preferably both. The failure frustrated him and shortened his already explosive temper.

Since the cave-in, he and Teigue had moved what felt like half the mountain to the slag heap. Neither had slept more than an exhausted hour or two. The need to find Emily had driven them with a near-frantic obsession.

The shifting lamplight glinted off the creases of her shoes and the weave of her sock. He touched a cluster of flecks, then examined it closely.

By God, she *had* found gold. The woman could slip on horse apples and wind up smelling like apple blossoms.

Gold.

Emily's first thoughts had been of Teigue. He wanted to believe her generosity was a ruse perpetrated by a conniving woman.

Teigue needed more gold like he needed a blister on his backside. The only reason Teigue continued mining was for Royle's sake. The amount of wealth Royle required in Virginia had kept them in these mountains an extra two years.

Teigue had more money than he could spend before he died of old age in another fifty years.

Royle swore under his breath.

Guilt gained a toehold in his conscience.

While he seldom gave a thought to the long hours Teigue spent in the mines, Emily's concern was to make his life easier. The woman thought they were dirt miners with nary a spare dollar between them. She had as much as said so. Neither of them had corrected her erroneous assumption.

Did delivering Teigue from what she perceived as drudgery in the mines for the rest of his life augment her drive to carve a tunnel through the old cave-in? Regardless, Royle was grateful for any incentive that fueled her determination. He and Teigue had been killing themselves by digging in the wrong place. The relief of finding her alive and relatively unhurt expanded until his chest ached. He kept a hand on her, needing the assurance that she was more than an illusion. Since the cave-in, he had lamented every derogatory word uttered in her direction. Fear of death finding an easy victory with Emily had formed a hole in him that had expanded every hour she was missing.

She was alive. He wanted to shout with joy.

Royle wrapped the shirt strips around her heel, over her ankle, then beneath her arch. The swelling and discoloration meant she endured constant pain. She was no delicate flower who wilted at the first hint of a crisis, nor had she waited for rescue.

She commanded his respect and admiration at every turn. Damn few men and none of the women he knew would have survived the absolute darkness and increasingly stale air of the sealed tunnel that had entombed her. Most men would be mindlessly ranting and crawling for sunlight.

Watching her, Royle felt as puzzled as he was proud of her. Instead of screaming or demanding he take her outside, she rested against the rock wall and yielded to weariness.

Her swollen, parched, and scabbed lips parted in sleep. The only clean spot on her face was at the end of her nostrils. He swept away a cluster of gritty hair dangling over her left eye. It demanded all of his fortitude to keep from embracing her. Yielding to the powerful feelings she set burning in him would mean disaster. Rigid with self-denial, he waited for the moment to pass.

Somewhere during the past two days he had lost the ability to paint a suspicious light around her every action. How easily she had dashed his barriers with her concern for Teigue. She had neither claimed the gold nor considered it solely hers.

Watching her caress the open canteen in sleep denied his last attempt at callousness. No one had that kind of tenacious purposefulness after crawling out of a dark coffin lined with gold dust.

He trailed the back of his thumb along her dirty cheek. The chill of her soft skin increased his worry for her beleaguered condition. He removed the canteen and folded her arms around her shoe. After slipping the closed canteen over his shoulder, he scooped her up.

The lantern hung from his hand beneath her knees. The slow pace he set allowed him to relish the feel of her against his chest. Even asleep, she taunted something inside him that defied comprehension.

Soon, they arrived at the camp he and Teigue had set up at the mouth of the mine entrance. Outside, rain pounded the mountain as though some woodland god wept in empathy over Emily's beaten condition.

He carried her to the pallet Teigue had prepared and relinquished his excuse for holding her. He tucked a blanket around her, then simply looked at her. Unaware, he wound the dusty end of her thick braid around his finger and brought it to his lips.

When he realized what he had done, he spread his fingers and let the hair drop onto the blanket. She had consumed damn near all of his waking, and most of his sleeping, thoughts since her arrival. She was becoming an obsession. The only way to purge her from his thoughts was to . . .

To . . . what?

The problem before him had no clear solution. Something about Emily drew him closer each day. He wanted her in his bed. She might succumb to a well-planned seduction. Then what? What if, as Teigue speculated, he could not walk away after they made love?

Honor demanded he leave. Rebecca awaited him in Virginia. Honor also might demand he stay. Would he have the resolve to carry out his duty to his family? Royle understood self-doubt, but had known little fear in his life. He recognized it now.

Angered by the turmoil she incited, Royle turned away. He poked kindling into the campfire embers until a blaze leaped brightly. He added dry wood and fanned it until a hot fire warmed the recess and warded off the damp evening chill.

He heated water in a pot and set the coffee on to boil before washing up in the rainwater collecting in a chipped enamel basin. The nippy water braced him against the warmth of watching Emily.

He found a shirt and pulled it on. Because it had all the buttons, he fastened it. Again, he was forced to give credit to Emily's ability with a needle and thread.

When the water warmed, he lifted the blanket and gingerly withdrew her left hand. Dried blood pasted the layers of fabric and tattered gloves to her palms and knuckles. Gingerly, he unwound the filthy wrapping. Peeling the remnants of his gloves off her scabbed skin made him wince. Dirt crusted beneath her shattered and split nails. Contusions and discolored abrasions covered her dirty, swollen fingers.

He found clean stripping for bandages.

Without warning, Emily sat up, her eyes wide and staring. All color drained beneath the gray mask of dirt.

Instantly, Royle gripped her shoulders, fearing she would bolt. "Emily. I'm here."

Her chest rose and fell as though she had just run a great distance.

Royle shook her, then captured her chin and turned her face toward his. "Emily. You are awake. Look at me. I'll keep you safe." The small hairs on the back of his neck bristled. Her frantic green gaze bore through him. Damn, she must have been afraid in the tunnel. No water. Complete darkness. The mountain pressing in on all sides. Just her and the tunnel she carved with a rare, unfettered tenacity.

He hauled her against his chest and wrapped his arms around her like a shield from the terror trying to reach her. She trembled uncontrollably against him, making him hold her even tighter. "Hold onto me as tightly as you can."

Her hands barely lifted.

"I cannot feel you, Emily. Hold onto me. I need to feel your arms around me. Tighter."

Her arms moved along his ribs in a half-hearted embrace.

"Tighter," he whispered.

He closed his eyes and bowed his head into the crook of her neck and shoulder. Even filthy and sweaty, her intoxicating womanly scent fired his blood with desire. Gradually, her trembling eased and her arms tightened, then fell away.

When he released her, she kept her head down. He curled his finger under her dirty chin. "Are you all right?"

She nodded slightly, but kept her eyes averted. "I'm sorry."

"What are you sorry for?"

A quick shake of her head revealed the tremulous hint of a frown. "I'm just . . . sorry."

He lifted her chin higher, forcing her sad eyes to meet his. "You have not one damn thing to be sorry for, Emily. You've been through a hellish experience that's not going to disappear just because you escaped it. Understand?"

She managed a feeble smile. A chapped spot on her lower lip beaded with rich red blood. The smile disappeared into a wince. He reached over and squeezed water from the bandage cloth. "That has to hurt. Let's get you cleaned up."

"It might be easier if I stood in the rain."

Royle shook his head in disbelief. "And catch your death from a chill? Teigue would shoot me in the head, sure he wouldn't hurt me because there were no brains in my skull to injure."

She pinched her bottom lip to keep it from stretching when she couldn't hold back the smile. "Don't . . ."

"But I do know where I ought to take you."

"Home?"

"Not home. To the hot spring."

Both eyebrows lifted in yearning. "A hot spring? Like in, a hot tub?"

"I guess you could consider it a large tub. The water bubbling from the bottom has formed an irregular stone basin. And I'll take you there soon. For now, I need to find Teigue. Will you be all right if I leave you here alone?"

She glanced toward the mouth of the tunnel as though measuring the distance, then nodded. "Can I have some coffee?"

He poured a cup for her and placed it beside the blankets. "Let me get these wraps off your hands. The last thing you need is to spill hot coffee on yourself."

Painstakingly, he unwrapped her hands. "Let's soak the right one. It looks the worst." He helped her twist around and lean against the rock wall. He adjusted the blankets, then placed the warm water so she could soak her hand.

"Royle?"

"Hmmmm?" He stoked the fire and added another log.

"Would you do me a favor?"

"Is it going to cost me?"

"That's better. No, it won't cost you a thing."

"What?"

"Don't be nice to me. I'm not going to die or turn into a raving lunatic. Either one takes too much effort."

The plea in her voice stopped him cold. When he could move, he tossed the stick he had been using to arrange the fire into the flames and stood. "I was unaware that I was being particularly nice to you, Miss Fergeson."

"It felt like you were."

"Maybe I was. Even I don't like kicking a dog when it's down." Admiration for her bravado sparked an irrepressible grin.

"Arf. Arf." Holding her lip, she managed a smile that shone in her eyes. "That means thanks."

"I should go find Teigue. He has been worried sick."

"I'll be right here." She turned her face toward the cool breeze of gray twilight. "Near outside," she whispered in awe.

Goddamn, why did she have to be so likable, vulnerable, and levelheaded at the same time? The woman was driving him crazy.

Chapter 8

Emily opened her eyes. Directly above her, a strained smile twisted at the corners of Teigue's mouth. Worry lingered in the way his eyes narrowed on her.

"Good morning." A raspy harshness clipped her words.

"How do you feel, Sunshine?" Teigue eased back.

From the vantage of Royle's bed she saw the low fire in the hearth and a pot of beans and the coffeepot in their regular places. "Better. I was so tired." She sat and swung her legs over the edge of the bed. "I'm still tired. And I'm dirty. When did you bring me home?"

"We didn't want you spending the night on the rocks. You scared the wits out of us. You hardly stirred when I lifted you up to Royle on his horse." Teigue raked his fingers through his brown and gray hair. "We didn't know if that was good or bad, but you seemed content enough and kept on sleeping."

Fighting the image of cuddling in Royle's arms, Emily held her bandaged hands in front of her. "I probably thought it was you, or else I was too tired to care."

"Could be." Teigue's brown eyes sparkled with a teasing she loved. "Then again, maybe you knew it was him. He's not as hard as he makes out."

"I'm better off believing that he is." That thought made her more uncomfortable than the hands she examined. When she stayed motionless, the pain hovered at a steady throb. "You bandaged my hands. I thought they would hurt forever before they fell off."

"Royle did. They're cleaned up real good. Now, all we need to do is clean the rest of you."

She pushed off the edge of the bed. Every muscle in her body reminded her of the debilitating ordeal. Her twisted ankle rebelled against further movement.

"Easy. Royle tightened the wrap on your foot, too. You listen to him about that ankle and your hands. He knows what he's talking about. He's patched up my carcass more than a few times—and his own as well." Teigue helped her straighten. "Let's get you over to the table and prop that foot up while you have something to eat."

Emily leaned heavily on Teigue's arm. Each time she put too much weight on her ankle, a sharp pain shot up the inside of her calf and down to the tip of her big toe.

"Royle mentioned a hot spring." She settled into the chair and let Teigue lift her foot onto his stool.

"Yeah. He went up there to check it out. The heat comes and goes. There's no telling how that last earthquake effected it. If the water is warm, he'll take you up there to soak off the dirt. Meanwhile, eat. You need your strength to heal up."

Emily balanced a spoon awkwardly in her right hand and ate everything Teigue placed in front of her. Plain food had never tasted so good. She stared at the steaming coffee cup beside her plate and wished for a straw so she wouldn't have to move her hands. She cradled the cup in the thickest part of her bandaged hands and braced it with her tender fingertips.

"Did Royle tell you what I found?" Excitement eased the aches and brightened her smile.

"He said you were rambling about a gold strike when he found you."

"It is a strike, Teigue." Excitement bubbled into a smile. "I really found gold. I don't know what it's worth, but I think there's enough for you to retire on when Royle goes east. You won't have to mine anymore. You can pick a spot and enjoy your life."

"I can, can I?"

"Yes. I'm sure it's a rich find, though it might not be very big. If you watch your spending, it might be enough. I don't have a very good idea of what things are worth," she mused. In truth, she had no idea of the value of the strike, let alone what Teigue needed to leave the cold darkness of the mines forever.

"Retire, huh? Are you wanting to send me to one of those old folks' homes you were talking about?"

"No, Teigue. I just want you happy and comfortable."

"Tell me, is everyone where you came from so concerned with the welfare of others?"

"No. Caring for those who need it takes money. Taxes."

"Ahhhh," Teigue breathed, nodding. "Who makes those decisions?"

"In a real sense, everyone and no one. It's political."

"I don't want to know about the politics. Are people better off? Have we mended the wounds of the War?"

Emily shrugged. "The war you're referring to, I suppose we have. There is still a fierce pride in the South. I'm sorry, Teigue, the South does not rise again, but there are no more civil wars. However, we've had other wars, two that involved the whole world. With the advance of technology, killing has, shall we say, lost its personal touch. We can press a button and send a missile through the air with the capability to kill hundreds of thousands of people and ruin the land for thousands of years."

"I don't think I'd like where you came from."

She set the cup down and gazed into Teigue's questioning face. Worry deepened the fine lines stretched across his temples and cheekbones. "Sometimes I didn't either. I like it here, Teigue."

"Good. Will you come with me when I retire? We can spend the evenings talking about a future you won't have to see again." A sudden smile lit his face. "I love a good story."

"Is that what you want?"

"Yes. What about you? It damn sure looks like me and Royle are the only sort of family you have, such as we are."

Emily laughed. Considering the thoughts and dreams she entertained concerning Royle, he hardly fell into the fraternal realm. "You, yes. Royle, I seriously don't think so."

The creak of the door hinge announced Royle's return. Without a word, he poured coffee, then perched on the corner of the table. "The hot spring is there. We'd better get going. I don't like the look of the clouds."

"I can live dirty," Emily offered, hating to be hurried when each movement extracted a harsh price with new-found aches.

"I am sure you can, and it would not bother me or Teigue a bit. However, those aches you're trying to ignore would ease up if you soaked in the mineral spring for an hour." He drained his coffee and set the cup in the center of the table. "I have two mules in the harness and the wagon ready. Let's go."

Always pushing. Didn't he ever stop? Recalling the tender way he had held her in the mine made her shiver. If he was nice to her, she would fall in love with him in no time. That complication brought discomfort and heartache. She needed no more of either.

"Okay. I need my backpack."

Teigue retrieved it from the bottom of the ladder leading to the loft. "You're all set."

"You're not coming?" she asked Teigue.

"No. I'll be here when you get back. It doesn't take two of us to get you clean."

Emily glanced down at herself and nodded. "A strong hand with a scouring pad might do it." Taking Royle's arm for support, she started toward the door. The promise of hot water swirling around her aching body sounded too good to pass up.

She cried out in surprise when Royle scooped her up.

"You have no shoes on. All you need now is to cut up your feet to be a total burden on us."

"I think you just like to show me what a wussie I am. You're big and strong and smart, and I'm supposed to cower in awe as the frail, naïve, city girl, right? Think again." On the wagon seat, she took her jacket and back-pack from Teigue. For a moment she could have sworn he was trying not to laugh.

"Here." Teigue shoved what passed as a few towels at her. "You'll need these."

Emily gathered the towels in the same embrace in which she held her backpack. Everything she had in the world rested on her lap.

Royle flicked the traces and spoke to the mules. The wagon lurched forward, forcing her to grab onto the seat and brace her feet for balance. She glanced at Royle. Anger rolled off him in waves.

"Why?" she asked after several moments of uncomfortable silence.

"Why what?"

"Why are you so angry with me?"

"We could be pulling silver out of the mountain."

"Why aren't you?"

Icy blue eyes turned on her without blinking. "Because I'm taking you to the spring."

"No you aren't. Take me home. I don't want you feeling like you're doing me the supreme favor. If there is anything I cannot stand it's a martyr without the affability of graciousness."

"The affability of graciousness? What the hell is that?"

"It means I can feel your anger and resentment, and I don't like it directed at me." She turned away and lifted her hands. "Of course, where else would you direct it? You must have been ready to explode before I came along."

"I seldom had a reason for anger before you came along."

"How boring your life must have been."

"Why? Because I wasn't angry?" Shaking his head, he gave his attention to the mules.

"Not just that. I have the distinct impression you keep your life so regimented and controlled that you wouldn't know a little spontaneous excitement if it stood flat-footed in front of you. All you would do is be angry—like you are now—because it was in your way."

"And you are never angry?"

"Sure. But a lot less since I quit doing things I don't want to do."

"I never said I did not want to take you to the spring. If you recall, I suggested it back at the mine."

"But you'd rather be mining. So turn this wagon around, drop me off, then go do what you want to do."

When he made no move to comply and locked his jaw, Emily sighed. "This isn't a difficult concept, Royle. All you have to do is what you want to do."

"I am doing what I want to do."

"No you're not. You said you'd rather be mining. Go back to the mine."

He kept the mules on course. Several long moments passed before he spoke again. "You scared the hell out of us. I don't think Teigue and I have moved that much rock in a week, let alone damn near two days. I'm angry that it happened in the first place, and you were alone. You should have been with one of us."

"Then what? Two of us would have been locked inside the mountain?" She rested a bandaged hand on Royle's forearm. "You aren't responsible for me. Neither is Teigue. I dug myself out, didn't I?"

Royle studied her wrapped hand. "Yes, you did. You got lucky. Very, very lucky. Teigue and I were digging at the new collapse. We kept expecting to find. . . ."

When his voice trailed, she straightened, knowing what they had expected to find. "I told you, I can take care of myself."

"Right. You told me that before, and you can tell me that again. Just don't expect me to believe it."

Emily shifted, stretching the ribs along her left side with great care. "You'll believe whatever suits you."

"What do you believe?"

Emily let her guard drop. A flash flood of emotion swept through her, then disappeared. In its wake she tasted the tart familiarity of her past and the tangy excitement of her future. "I believe no one is safe."

"Safe? From what?"

"From anything. It's an illusion, like most of the veils we weave around us. You and Teigue can't protect me in the mine or anywhere else." Her wrapped hand lifted lightly from his forearm. "Oh, you can divert a threat or intimidate someone who might want to harm me, if you chose to do so. But my real safety lies within myself. I'm just learning that . . . and how to be myself."

Royle snorted a sarcastic laugh. "You were someone else before?"

"Many someone elses. For years, I was whoever I needed to be at the moment while the real me hid behind the wallpaper of any room I happened to occupy. That was my best guise of self-protection. No one could hurt me. They didn't know who I was. The trouble with that was, I didn't know either." The confession reminded her of the wasted time spent denying herself while trying to please those who would never find her acceptable.

"You're serious," Royle said slowly.

Emily nodded. This, too, was who she was. Her vow of absolute honesty about her thoughts and feelings came to the rescue. "Yes. I became obsessed with pleasing, measuring up, doing what was expected. I thought I'd earn love that way. When that didn't work, I settled for respect. But no one can respect someone without substance. As long as I was being what someone else thought I should be, instead of what *I* thought I should be, I was incomplete. Recently, I've learned that each of us has to find our own way, not what someone else thinks or demands we do. That path leads to disaster, not destiny."

Royle pulled the mules to a halt. "Some of us lack the luxury of a choice."

Emily shook her head and smiled sadly. "A man's gotta do what a man's gotta do. Is that it?"

She felt his gaze burn on her, but did not look to see the anger she felt growing in him again.

"That says it well. Sometimes, it is a matter of honor."

"Sometimes honor is used as an excuse. It is easier and less frightening to follow a path we didn't have to chart ourselves, than forge one of our own," she muttered, inching her way toward the edge of the seat.

"Are we talking about the same thing?"

"Probably not. I was talking about me. What were you talking about?"

Royle hesitated, then got down from the wagon and came around to Emily's side. He carried her up the slope and inside a rock outcrop sheltered on three sides. Without a word, he unwrapped her hands and folded the bandages, then walked away.

"Royle?"

He paused, but kept his back to her.

"What were you speaking of?"

His broad shoulders squared before he answered. "Nothing anyone can change now."

Enthralled by his uncharacteristic wistfulness, Emily watched him go.

With a sigh, she eyed the hot spring, then examined her hands. They looked as sore and raw as they felt.

Before climbing into the hot spring, she laid out her change of clothing, glad she had the foresight to stuff the spares into her backpack before leaving the car. Thinking about the Thunderbird brought a sigh. She had loved that car, but wouldn't trade it to change whatever had brought her to this time and place.

"Are you decent?" Royle called from beyond the rock curtain.

"Yes," she answered, scooting to the edge of the pool.

"I'm coming in there."

She finished unwrapping her ankle and set the cloth strips on the ledge of a rock jut.

"You forgot these." Royle set the towels beside her clean clothing.

"Thanks." Emily slipped into the water.

"I'll wait outside. You don't have to keep your clothes on while you bathe."

"Actually, I thought this might soak out the worst of the dirt. As my muscles loosen up, I'll take them off." The therapeutic warmth of the water seeped into her aching body. She sat on a rock that allowed her to submerge up to her chin, then leaned her head back and slowly rocked from side to side. The gentle sway of hot water sluicing through the long strands of hair felt wonderful. From now on, she'd bathe in this scrumptious hot spring instead of taking sponge baths and rinsing her hair in cold creek water.

She dipped back a little farther to allow the water over her face. The small cuts and scrapes on her face and neck stung. Her hands remained poised just above the surface, not yet willing to take on the assault of another cleansing.

The next thing she knew, a strong hand braced her neck while fingers combed through her hair floating in the water. She lifted slightly to draw a fresh breath.

"Relax. I have you," Royle crooned.

He did have her in the palm of his hand in more than a physical sense. When she set aside his caustic retorts and irritating barbs, his actions painted the picture of a very different man. The hidden Royle Tremaine possessed a rare compassion and a greater share of her affections than she cared to admit. The kindness he tried to hide seeped through in odd gestures and strange moments, like bringing water from the stream or fixing coffee in the morning. Those small acts might have escaped notice if not for the tenderness with which he had held her after pulling her through the tunnel she had bored through the rock fall. Fatigued, drained of fear, she had felt his flood of relief and his need to ensure that she was alive and whole. In his arms, with both of their defenses down, she had felt cherished for the first time. Wanting to experience that rare peace again, she gave herself over to his ministrations.

The way his strong, supple fingers worked the kinks

from her muscles created more pleasure than pain. Again, he had spoken gruffly, then treated her as though he cared. Emily opened her eyes. During the brief instant in which she caught him by surprise, she recognized the same hunger that gnawed at her insides. As his deep blue eyes met hers, his expression resumed the hard, implacable facade he preferred.

Saddened by the charade, Emily closed her eyes. She knew about hiding, about adapting and shielding the secret side of her identity.

"You don't fool me, Royle."

His hands slipped into her armpits. Using the buoyancy of the water, he guided her into a sitting position on a smooth rock. Strong, gentle fingers massaged the kinks around her shoulder blades and loosened the tight balls of muscle along her spine.

Emily turned her head, amazed by the range of mobility her relaxing muscles allowed. Gingerly, she gathered her hair.

Royle took her wrist and moved her hand aside. Slowly, almost reverently, he gathered the streamers of hair bobbing in various layers of water, then draped the silky, dark brown clusters over her left shoulder. Though his touch remained firm and gentle, his words carried a hard edge. "What is it you think I was trying to fool you about?"

"Yourself," she whispered. "And I'm not sure it's me you're trying to deceive."

Royle snorted in disdain. "You speak in riddles."

A faint smile curled Emily's lips. Head down, she was glad Royle could not see her face. "Perhaps. But I know you understand. You're doing it now."

"What?"

"Your touch is soothing, positive, and healing. You know just how to work the knots and kinks out of my muscles without bruising me. You know just how hard to press and where to rub to make it feel good. Your hands have an undeniable healing life force of their own. Your touch is far more honest than your callous tone or the acidity of your words."

His long fingers curled over the tops of her shoulders and stretched toward her breasts. The gentle, rhythmic pressure of his fingertips sent steadily brighter bolts of electricity shooting through her body. With an effort, she kept from arching her back and beckoning his marvelous hands to the hardening tips of her breasts.

"Touch is perhaps the most versatile of our senses," he said.

The top button on her blouse slipped free.

"Where, how, and when gives it power."

The husky tone sent a tingling through Emily. The second button opened, and the tingling intensified.

"Are your eyes closed?"

"Mm-hmm." The relaxing motion of his fingers along her ribs and the sides of her breasts heightened her awareness of him. If he made love with the same intoxicating devotion as he soothed her sore muscles—

"Do you trust me?"

The seductive whisper almost evoked an automatic affirmative. Emily smiled a dreamy smile. "Should I?"

"No," Royle answered with a chuckle. "Not at the moment."

"What do you want from me?" She arched her head back until she could see the face leaning over her. A savage hunger darkened his blue eyes.

"What every man wants from a woman." All traces of mirth fled the intense expression chiseled on his face. His mouth lowered just far enough for her to feel his heated breath.

"Sex?" she whispered breathlessly.

He hesitated a moment before his hand closed on her breast. "I want to be inside you."

Before she could respond, his mouth captured hers. In a frenzy of motion, Emily felt herself gliding through the water, turning, then hauled hard against the wall of muscle. The restrained hunger of his kiss deepened when her breasts pressed against his chest and his throbbing erection burrowed into her belly.

An unreasonable need to get closer sent her arms entwining around his neck and her body writhing against him. The only way to be any closer was to remove their clothing and allow him inside her. She broke the heady kiss, then stared at him, openmouthed and stunned.

"Emily."

The ragged sound of her name tugged at something inside her. Sex was the ultimate intimacy. She wasn't ready to share *that* much of her newfound self, though heaven help her, she wanted to. Denying herself and him, she shook her head. "We can't."

"Why not? You want me."

Yes, she wanted him with an intensity that nearly consumed her. A small moan of anguish escaped Emily as Royle ran his hands down her ribs, into the valley of her waist, then over the flare of her buttocks and hips. With a flat palm, he pressed against the small of her back, pushing her against the undeniable desire his body expressed.

Fighting herself harder than Royle, she mustered a shred of reason. "There's a little more to life than what I want at any particular moment." The flame of desire burned white-hot. She ached to wrap her legs around him as tightly as his arms held her against him.

"I know," he sighed, resigned, as he laid a heated trail of little kisses along her temple, over her ear to her jaw, then back.

"Royle. . . ." The heat of his hand exploring the naked flesh of her back robbed her of breath.

"I approve of your brief corset." After a momentary fumble, the hook on her bra gave up the last barrier.

His hands shaped her breasts. "There are ways of finding pleasure without my taking you fully."

Emily bit off a cry as his thumb and forefinger closed on her hardened nipple. Exquisite desire tortured every nerve ending in her body. "No facades here, Royle. This is real."

For a moment, his hand stilled and his brow furrowed in contemplation. "The last thing I want is to hurt you. The only way I can protect you is to leave. Now. And I don't want to."

Emily relaxed. His defenses were down. His words

dripped honesty and mirrored the concern in his eyes. "You can't hurt me unless I let you." The sudden tightness in her chest allowed just enough air to make her voice earthy, almost breathless. The impact of his masculinity flowed through her like a dark, compelling tide.

He unwound her arms from his neck, then eased her shirt from her shoulders. "You go right on believing that, Emily, because I will never love you. I can never marry you."

She let him remove the bra, all the while watching him struggle with something beyond her comprehension. "I didn't ask or expect either, nor did I offer it." A small voice in the back of her mind whispered a warning that went unheeded.

Yet even as he claimed her mouth and released the fastening on her jeans, she craved his affection. For now, she would settle for his body, in a limited sense.

The way he plundered her mouth left no recess secret from his voracious appetite. Like a raptor intent on consuming his prey, he devoured her senses while stripping the remaining barriers from her flesh.

The last semblance of control slipped from Emily's grasp. Each touch, each erotic titillation spoke to her heart as well as her body. She was as helpless in separating the two as she was in denying the magical power of his touch.

Exactly when she had submerged her hands into the warm mineral water, she didn't know. The raw nerve endings in her bruised and battered fingers registered every curve, mound, and valley contoured into his back and shoulders. Emily savored each texture and nuance.

For a moment, the pool churned as though alive. Water flew from his trousers as he tossed them onto the ledge behind them. In the wake of ripples bouncing against the stone sides, Royle held her hips and drew her against his naked body.

Emily gasped in delight. She stared up into knowing blue eyes and an expectant smile. In that instant, she realized that she was in deeper than the water lapping at the undersides of her breasts.

"You look frightened," Royle murmured, cupping her cheek and running his thumb over her kiss-reddened lips.

Frightened barely described the sudden emotion shooting through her head like fireworks. It seemed she had stepped into a role for which there were no barriers. What was she doing? This was real. This was uncharted ground. The only roles she knew for making love came from the silver screen or the safety of her living room television. Although her mind was experienced with lovemaking, her body wasn't. Discovering who she was with her clothes on took bravery, but with them off . . . For the space of a long breath, Emily closed her eyes.

"Don't be afraid, Emily, I won't hurt you," Royle whispered, lifting her onto the stone. "Nor will I take you."

Before panic set in, Royle pressed against her and kissed her with a restraint that made him tremble. *Follow your heart,* echoed a voice from childhood. *That is the road leading to happiness.* In a glittering burst of sensation, the currents of passion drew her into the heat of his embrace.

Lost, she moved with the mounting crescendo of desire as though she were the tide and Royle the moon luring her higher and closer with each foray or touch. She met his kiss without restraint, greedy for more, taking as well as giving, drawing him into her heart and exploring the dark treasures he offered willingly.

"You're more beautiful than I suspected," he marveled, cupping her breasts in his hands. With deliberate slowness, he captured each nipple between his thumbs and forefingers, then caressed and tugged.

Emily cried out in ecstasy and startlement, then gasped, arching when he drew a nipple between his teeth.

In the moments when he alternately worshipped and ravished her, the ache growing in her lower abdomen blossomed. Unwillingly, she sank into the water.

Her chest heaved when his head lifted. She didn't know which she wanted more, his mouth and hands on her breasts or the mounting ache in her loins to cease. How could anything that felt so good bring such torment?

Staring into the clear blue pools of Royle's eyes, realization dawned. Regardless of what she had read, witnessed, or seen in films, nothing had prepared her for the actuality of primal need. In the past, she had known desire and perhaps even understood lust. What she felt for Royle gave a new meaning to both. Until this moment, all the yearnings she had experienced in the past could have fit into the space of a single raindrop; Royle created a hurricane.

Of their own volition, her fingertips trailed down the whorls of chest hair plastered to his flesh. "You are beautiful. And hard."

He brushed the errant streamers of hair from her face with both hands. "I don't know about beautiful, but I'm damn hard."

She let her fingers follow the contours of his sides below the water. Then curiosity got the better of her. With a sudden boldness, she ran her fingertips over the length of his erection. A satisfied smile lifted the corners of her mouth when his entire body stiffened with a harsh inhalation. She took her time exploring his erection with her hypersensitive fingers and memorizing each change of texture and pulse.

"You're not playing fair." The warning in his glittering eyes spoke louder than the softly spoken words uttered between rapid breaths.

"Then tell me what you consider fair," she breathed, lost in the marvelous sensation of delights racking her being. The water lapped at her shoulders and upper chest as she settled onto her heels.

Instead of answering, he bent and picked her up by the thighs, then set her down straddling him. Her initial cry of surprise evolved into laughter. She clung to him, realizing the beads of moisture on his face were perspiration, not water.

Laughter caught in her throat. Her gaze flew to his at the first touch of his fingertips on the pearl normally hidden snugly in the thatch between her legs. Mounted on his thighs, she lay open, exposed, and inviting whatever he might do.

The tendrils of need coiled tighter in her lower abdomen. She responded in kind. The remnants of her smile faded when she found the head of his erection. The last traces of laughter melted from Royle's sensual lips, inviting a kiss. She slanted her mouth over his and became lost in a carnal maelstrom incited by his mouth and hands. He seemed to be touching every part of her, her mouth, her breasts, her exciting woman's heart.

In turn, she filled her hands with his erection and followed the rhythm he dictated and her body pulsed. Just when she thought she would fly out of her skin, he inserted a finger inside her. She cried out against his mouth, but his free hand held her locked in the kiss, his tongue filling her mouth.

She craved more, feeling ecstasy a breath away, and cried out again. When a second finger slipped into her, he broke the kiss with a raspy echo of her name. Powerless to do anything but let the bliss breaking over her mind, heart, and body carry her away, she soared into the pleasure high he created. Dimly, she heard him groan, then felt the rapid surge of his body finding release.

She basked in the solid peace of his embrace for a long time as their breathing steadied and the thrum of their pounding hearts slowed. She laid her head on his shoulder and relished the movement of his strong hands along her back, buttocks, and thighs as he worked out the muscle kinks lingering from her ordeal in the tunnel.

"Why didn't you tell me?" he whispered into her ear.

"Tell you what?" She started to lift her head, but he held her in place.

"You're a virgin."

"Would that have changed anything?"

She waited for a long time before Royle answered. "No."

"At least you're honest about that." She was willing to pay the price of being a participant in forging her destiny—to a point.

His soft chuckle made her smile. "Why not? Though you seem to have a cavalier attitude about virginity for one who has held on to it for so long. It is not replaceable," he said, then kissed her shoulder.

"If I decided on a cure for my virginity, I wouldn't want it replaced."

"I won't be your cure, Emily."

She heard the regret in his voice and wondered at the resolve in his words. "You mean you don't want to be my cure."

Head shaking, he kissed the crook of her shoulder and neck. "I mean, I *will not* be. Save it for a man you love, one who will marry you. I'm not that man."

Confused, she drew a deep breath, then slowly released it. "You're the only one speaking of marriage, Royle. For the record, whether you can't or won't or don't want to marry me doesn't make any difference. It seems to me you're the one with the hang-up."

"Hang-up?" He sat a little straighter forcing her to stiffen.

"Problem. Obsession. Preoccupation. Whatever you want to call it." She captured his face in both painful hands. "Furthermore, don't go telling me what to do with my body or my emotions. They're mine. I won't abdicate them or who I am again." Denying him the opportunity to answer, she took possession of his mouth.

Now that she knew what to expect, she vowed to have more control over the next pleasuring.

Chapter 9

ROYLE WATCHED EMILY as she sat in a circle of light on the floor of the tunnel. His eyes reflected the diligence of a hawk guarding a fledgling chick. If he was not careful, his entire future would unravel beyond repair. Lately, he felt as though two men lived in his skin. One controlled his body and the unreasonable, possessive desires raging in Emily's direction. The other lived in his mind and whispered of duty, obligation, necessity, and posterity. While his body held forth with the demon set on destroying his future, his mind clung tenaciously to the goal he had sweated, sacrificed, and slaved toward every day since returning from England as a lad of sixteen.

During the two weeks since their sensual water play, he burned for her more each time she neared. He had hoped his desire would ebb after the brief taste of her body. Instead, it had become a raging wildfire. His traitorous body responded to her presence with a violent rush that continuously amazed him. Never had he allowed lust to control him. It rankled him more that *she* was the source of the heat rippling through him and the throbbing in his loins. No longer would just any woman satisfy his needs. It was Emily he craved. She filled his dreams, waking and sleeping.

He lost count of the times he berated himself for following her into the water. Until then, he had managed to cling to the pretense that she was not what she seemed. In truth, she was more. Far more.

"Are you going to sit there all afternoon and pick fly-specks of gold out of the dirt?" Damn, he could not leave her alone, nor could he tolerate being this close to her without touching her. Soon, her hands would heal enough for her to use the sluice box to separate the gold from the rubble. Open sunlight and fresh air might help him keep a clear head when he was around her.

"Every one of these little specks represents a few pennies toward Teigue's retirement."

Guilt made him look away when she glanced up at him. "Teigue can retire anytime, anywhere, and any way he wants."

"Easy for you to say. You're young and healthy. There's no Social Security or company-matching 401k for Teigue. He has to provide his own security. I aim to see that he has at least this much of a cushion."

"What the hell are you talking about?" Just when she started sounding rational, she spoke of things he had never heard of. He decided against pursuing his question. "Never mind. If you want to stay here and pick through the rubble, that's your choice. I have other things to do."

"No one asked you to stay. I don't see chains and manacles holding you to the wall. Go. Leave me in peace. Please." She adjusted the lantern and continued painstakingly sifting through the fine-rock piles scattered across the floor.

He started down the tunnel, then returned and checked the shoring he and Teigue had put in place before allowing her inside.

"It won't fall down, Royle. I suspect the entire mountain will collapse before those supports give way."

With a casual shrug that shifted and coiled the muscles beneath his close-fitting shirt, he turned away.

"Royle?"

The sound of his name stopped him in his tracks. Maybe she wanted him to stay. It was only natural to want company in the tunnel that had entombed her for nearly two days. Hell, he knew strong men who had mined for years who never ventured underground after surviving a collapse. She had guts. More guts than she had sense.

"Yeah?"

"Thanks for offering to stay, but I'm fine alone. Really."

"Sure." He kept walking. She might be fine alone. Hell, she was safer alone. For that matter, so was he. Away from her, the perpetual arousal stretching his pants might have a chance of softening. Lately, it seemed the only way he could urinate was by leaning against a tree and aiming in the general direction of the ground.

"Another week," he mumbled.

"Another week of what?" Teigue asked, shoveling a load of ore into the cart.

Royle pulled on his gloves and snagged the pick. "Until we go to Silverton and get rid of our star boarder and cook."

"I'm not leaving her alone there."

Royle mentally heaved a sigh of relief. He had not realized the depths of his dread for turning Emily loose in Silverton. So much could happen to her. For an intelligent woman, she seemed oblivious to the dangers around her. Hell, she'd be easy prey for a reptile like John Galloway. The smooth-talking saloon owner had a penchant for luring inexperienced women to his bed. When their novelty wore thin, they became saloon decorations with no way of supporting themselves other than by pleasing the customers.

"You want to bring her back here?" Royle swung the

pick over his shoulder, then brought it around, perfectly splitting the silver ore from the surrounding rock.

"Yes. I plan on keeping her as long as she'll stay. I've grown fond of her. Having Emily around is sort of like having a daughter or a niece." Teigue loaded another shovelful into the cart.

"Is that what you plan telling the folks in Silverton? Emily is your niece?"

Teigue shrugged and pushed the shovel into the crumbling pile. "Why not? They all know you're my nephew. I'm just a regular family man."

"Tell them whatever you like, just tell Emily and me first so we can keep the stories straight."

"You don't seem as upset that I'm going to keep her with me as I thought you'd be."

Royle swung the pick harder than usual. Rock splintered in all directions. "I'm not upset. She is a nuisance and an inconvenience, but she can cook. You could do worse. Besides, I don't run your life anymore than you run mine."

" 'Course, having her with me is for your benefit, too."

Royle shot a glance at Teigue, then scowled at the mischievous light dancing in his brown eyes. "How so?"

"When you come to your senses, you're going to see what I see."

Royle kicked away a large rock and hoisted the pick. "What is it you see?"

Teigue chuckled and held his silence.

Royle swung the pick and worried it into bringing down a large chunk of the wall. "Are you going to answer me?"

"No."

Royle stared at the broken rocks that represented his life. "It isn't like I have a choice in this, Teigue."

"You do have a choice, son. But I guess you'll have to learn that for yourself. Just don't wait too long before you come to your senses, or it'll be too late for all of us."

Royle vented his irritation into the power behind the

pick. Teigue and Emily spoke in riddles and unexplained statements that they expected him to accept as facts.

Teigue set down the shovel, pulled off his gloves and picked up a lantern. "If we're going to eat tonight, somebody had better start cooking. Guess it's my night."

"Yeah," Royle said absently, wishing that he and Emily were in the hot spring creating even more heat. The woman had an unbridled physical appetite he ached to sate along with his own.

Three days later, Emily secured the last of the gold particles from the sluice box into a soft leather pouch. Pleased with the day's efforts, she stuffed the pouch into her backpack, then wiped her cold, wet hands on her pants.

"It will be dark soon," Royle said from behind her.

"I'm ready to go home." She reached for her jacket, but Royle snatched it away. He held it while she slipped her arms through.

Slivers of excitement pierced her shoulders as his fingers curled around them. Emily remained motionless, unwilling to relinquish the exhilaration of his touch. Neither had spoken of their intimacy at the mineral spring. Yet more than the door of erotic curiosity had opened that afternoon. Since then, Royle had become quieter, less acidic in his challenges and the barbs he flung in her direction.

"Emily," he started, then grew as silent as the stone around them. The sinuous pulse of his fingers said what he failed to find the words to express.

She longed to lean against the inviting warmth of his chest and give herself over to the hunger heating the chilled evening air surrounding them. Instead, she stiffened and dipped her cheek against the back of his hand in a gesture of reluctant parting. "I'm ready."

"For what?"

The brush of his lips against her neck sent her head arching farther to expose more of her sensitive flesh. Desire roared through her and drowned all sensible thought. During the small hours of the night, she had awakened with an ache in her lower abdomen. Royle's image burned as a lingering memory of an erotic dream. In the heart-pounding aftermath, she knew her attraction had exceeded the physical pull between them. Alone on her pallet, she sifted and sorted the realities nightly.

The warning that he would never love her posed no deterrent for the tender emotions flourishing in her heart. She hesitated to call it love, for she had never been in love. And what she felt for Royle was very different from the affection growing between her and Teigue. Then again, Teigue was an easy man to love. He returned her affection with an honesty void of games or guile.

"You're a dangerous man," she whispered.

He crossed his arms over her collarbone and drew her closer. The ridge of his desire pressed through the layers of her jacket and sweatshirt at the small of her back.

"To whom? Not you, Emily. You want me as badly as I want you." He trailed small kisses up the column of her neck, along her jaw, then across her temple.

If he had not been holding her tightly, her wobbly knees might have buckled. Despite the distance she had maintained during the days since the pool, she knew she had betrayed the desire burning without cessation inside her.

"There is so much I could show you . . . teach you . . . please you with while you please me." He nibbled on the edge of her earlobe.

Relishing the promise of fulfillment, Emily closed her eyes and relaxed against him.

"Yes, you want it too, don't you?"

Emily whispered an affirmative, then turned slowly in his arms. Gazing up at the dark angel, doubt lanced her anticipation.

As though sensing her hesitation, Royle captured her mouth in a delicate, tantalizing kiss.

With the brilliance of a lightning strike, her conflict vanished. Emily twined her arms around his neck and stretched on tiptoes. Each responsive move fed her appetite for greater intimacy. The heat radiating from Royle warmed her all the way to the ends of her tender fingers.

The tip of his tongue gliding over her lower lip dictated the slow movement of her head. Her parted lips savored the teasing promise of more.

Royle brushed errant wisps of hair from her cheek with the pad of his thumb. "I want you."

"Why?" Eyes closed, she savored his warm breath against her face.

For an instant he stilled, then exhaled softly. "You're here."

The response rattled the little sensibility remaining in her addled brain. She dropped off her toes to a flat-footed stance that put distance between her traitorous lips and his.

She could accept that he could never feel affection for her. Life had taught her how unlovable she was. However, she had more pride in her own newly found self-worth than to conveniently accommodate him and give in to her desires. As she realized that he viewed her simply as an advantageous outlet for his lust, humiliation stung her cheeks with color. Reluctantly, she withdrew her arms from around his neck.

"Excuse me." She pushed a trembling hand against his chest.

"No," he whispered, his blue eyes narrowing with a mixture of confusion and anger. "It's my turn to ask why."

For a long, heart-pounding moment, Emily met his probing stare with a steely resolve. All her years of blending, melding, and conforming to her surroundings flashed through her memory.

"Because . . . because I don't have to please you." The tumult of triumph and disappointment forced her to look away.

"No, you don't." The tender caress of the back of his curled fingers along her cheek caused her breath to catch in her throat. "Let me please you."

Not trusting her voice, Emily locked her jaw and shook

her head. Letting him pleasure her meant pleasuring him. Even now she tingled in anticipation of roaming the robust masculinity she had explored in the mineral spring.

"What is it, Emily? Why did you suddenly change your mind?"

She pulled away from his loose grasp and stepped back, her shoulders against the sluice box frame. "I won't let you use me like a foam cup just because you're thirsty and I'm all that's available."

"What the hell is a foam cup?"

Emily waved off his diversion. "It doesn't matter. You get my meaning. I think more of myself than that."

"Use you." The statement reeked of disdain.

Emily sidled away and fetched her backpack. "You have no idea of how gratifying it is to feel that I'm not only the last resort, I'm the only option. God forbid you should endure any sexual hunger for more than the time necessary to find the only female in fifteen miles to ease your discomfort."

She slung the heavy pack over her shoulder. "I didn't ask you for love, or commitment, or any promises, nor have you given any. What you have given me is honesty. Thank you."

"What the hell are you talking about?"

He moved so quickly that her heart skipped a beat, then hammered in her chest when she saw the volatility blazing in his eyes and the deepened lines of rage at his temples.

"You can't intimidate me by glowering, Royle. I'm not willing to let you do that, either." She met his icy blue glare with her chin lifted in defiance. Only with the shield of outrage could she deflect the weak side of her nature begging for submission to his touch.

"I apologize for the careless phrasing of my thoughts. I meant no offense, Emily." The formal demeanor she recognized as a facade encased him as he straightened. All emotion fled his features as he made them as blank as his placid gaze. "However, it is true. I don't know why I want you, and I wish to hell that I didn't. You could become a bad habit difficult to cast aside. But, I would do so." He abruptly turned away, then extended his arm in a gesture for her to go ahead of him.

Together, they navigated the slope from the mine. Emily kept her eyes trained ahead. In a matter of minutes she had gone from being a convenient sex object to a bad habit he had acquired easily and refused to keep. Her indignation melted into the long, dark shadows cast by thick pines flanking the switchback path between the cabin and mine. The breeze whispered in the treetops.

"What drives you?" Emily finally asked, breaking the uncomfortable silence.

"What do you mean?" The softly spoken question denied the anger he had shown moments earlier.

"You're a driven man. You must have a powerful or important goal. Teigue said you've worked one mine after another since you were sixteen." From experience she understood the need to succeed at something. In her case, she had striven for the personal freedom her mother prized and the financial success her father idolized.

She risked a glance at him. The way his eyes glowed in the fading light gave him an ethereal quality.

"I don't know that you could call me driven. I know what is expected of me . . . what I have to do . . . and I intend to accomplish it."

"Come hell or high water?"

A scowl that stopped short of his unblinking eyes curled the corners of his mouth. "Yes. I was born to it."

With the intensity of a bulldog, she carefully plumbed the depth of his vague answer. "Born to what? Hell or high water?" Was his goal deceptively simple or hopelessly complex? She suspected the latter. Nothing about Royle Tremaine embodied simplicity.

"Neither. Tremaines fought in the Revolutionary War. Tremaines died at Breed's Hill defending Boston."

"Do you mean Bunker Hill?"

"No. They were supposed to go to Bunker Hill, but they became confused in the dark and dug the fortifications on Breed's Hill. They only had one night to construct the ramparts. In the morning, they faced the British."

Emily nodded, conceding the point. Details of the Revolutionary War were not her forte.

"Tremaines died in half a dozen battles in the War for Independence. My ancestors fought for their freedom and their principles with blood, sweat, and suffering. We have been a part of the making of this country since the early 1700s." Royle gripped her elbow and steadied her on the slipperiest part of the final slope.

"Tremaines helped forge this country into what it is now. We're part of the backbone and the future." He paused, halting them both, then turned his head and gazed directly at her. "I'm the last Tremaine of our line."

The finality of his last statement sent a chill through her. "I thought Teigue was your uncle."

"He is. Teigue is my mother's brother. He is one of the few of my relatives who survived the Great War between the North and South. Teigue and my father fought together at Gettysburg. Two days later, my father died of his injuries, and Teigue buried him. My older brother, Henry, died in a Northern prison.

"My parents sent me to live with relatives in England shortly before full-scale war broke out and the blockades started. Henry was nineteen and seemed ancient at the time. My sister, Flavia, was fourteen."

"What did you do in England? Where did you stay?" She imagined Royle as a child sailing alone to a strange country and an unknown future.

"We had relatives in London." She felt him stiffen as though the memories fought against revelation. "They made sure I received an education reserved for the privileged class. I excelled and made damn sure I never caused a bit of trouble for them. I wanted to make my father proud. Maybe he was. I don't know if he received any of the letters I sent." He started toward the cabin, adding, "It no longer matters."

"It matters," Emily murmured. "He loved you, and you

loved him. That always matters, Royle. It must have been very hard for your parents to send you away."

Royle opened the gate to the animal shelter. "That was a long time ago," he said as much to himself as to her. "We Tremaines have always known what we had to do. I will see my part through."

The resignation lacing his tone sent dread slithering up her spine. "What is your part, Royle?" Emily asked as she rationed hay and oats for the mules and horses.

"I'll carry forth as my father, his father, his father's father, and the Tremaine men before them have done. The war and the carpetbaggers have made it more difficult, but not impossible."

She met his eyes reflecting the last rays of light coloring the sky. "What does that mean?" she asked, suspecting she would not like the answer.

"It means buying back Tremaine House and our lands from a blackhearted carpetbagger and re-establishing the Tremaine line through a prosperous marriage. Having sons. As many as Rebecca is willing to have."

"Rebecca?" It had never occurred to her that he might have a woman waiting for him.

"Rebecca Weston, the woman I'm marrying in December . . . in Virginia."

Suddenly, his profession of never loving her, never marrying her, made complete sense. The avowal had gnawed on her nerves for the last two weeks. Under the circumstances, any relationship beyond casual friendship was out of the question. "I see," Emily whispered, holding perfectly still. "You must love Rebecca very much to work so hard for what the two of you want."

Royle shifted uncomfortably, then lowered his head and avoided her gaze. "Love? Love has nothing to do with marrying well and perpetuating the Tremaine line. Marriage is about position. Social standing. Connections. And, of course, money."

Stunned, she wondered how she could have misassessed Royle so completely. "Are you telling me that you're marrying her for her money?"

A hollow chortle filled the distance between them as they headed toward the cabin. "No. It is more like she is marrying me for mine. Or as Teigue would prefer, her father is selling her and his connections for what in other countries is considered a bride price."

Emily's stomach churned and growled. The aftereffect left a queasy roil reaching for her throat. A ball of outrage came from her toes and gathered strength with each inch it traveled upwards. "Do you even know this woman?"

"We have exchanged a few letters. She is educated. She will do as a wife."

"She'll *do*?" The ball of emotion gathered steam. "Do I understand this correctly? You've worked all these years so you can return to Virginia and buy a house someone else may or may not want to sell—"

Resolute determination hardened his voice. "If the price is right, they will sell. The owner is a carpetbagger and cares only about money. The price will be right. Count on it."

Emily forced her tone into a dangerous calm when she continued. "All right. You're going to buy the house and land, then marry someone you don't love and fill the shrine of your past with children to build your future. All for the sake of a name you think should be perpetuated?"

"You have missed the point, Emily."

"Explain it to me."

"Ensuring the survival of the Tremaine lineage and the position we have always held in government and society was the reason my parents sent me to England. As long as a single Tremaine breathed, there was a chance of carrying on the line, regardless of what happened with the war."

"I think it is you who misunderstood, Royle. Your parents sent an eleven-year-old boy to the safety of relatives because he was too young to fight and survive, and too old to escape the disaster they had foreseen. Not for a name. They wanted *you* to survive, not a name. You can't realistically expect to return to the old family home and make it what it once was. It can't be. Building a monument to your family won't bring them back, and I doubt that's what they would have wanted."

His head whipped around. Anger danced in his eyes and tensed his entire body. "You didn't know my family."

"No. I did not." She paused at the porch. "Did you?"

"Of course."

"And you loved them?" Tenderness softened the strain in her voice.

Royle looked away, not dignifying the question with an answer.

"If you loved them, how can you dishonor them by believing they would condemn you—"

"This conversation is over, Emily."

Mouth open, she studied him and felt the anger unwind. Slowly, understanding filled her awareness. "You feel guilty as sin for being alive, don't you? You have to do something to atone for every breath you take. Deep inside, you believe you might have been able to do something if you had stayed . . . maybe prevented a death or hardship with your own life or sacrifice."

Blocking his path into the cabin, she bit back the sting of sorrow and frustration. "Welcome to the real world, Royle. It doesn't work that way. What you have is an untreated, full-blown case of survivor's guilt. Other than dying, the only way to cure it is to forgive yourself for living, for doing what those who loved you wanted you to do—keep on living and making the most of the time you have. Some of us hide. Some rebel in anger and outrage at the injustice of it all. Some spend our lives trying to prevent or find cures for the reasons responsible for our being left behind. All of us hurt, Royle, until we forgive ourselves for surviving. Count your blessings. You had a whole family who loved you. You had Teigue when you returned home. That's a hell of a lot more than most of us get. Don't mess it up by building a box no one wants for you, but you. Don't throw away one more precious minute building a mausoleum no one will visit be-

cause there's no one buried there. And for your sake,
don't marry anyone you don't love. Life is lonely enough
without pursuing that much misery."

Anger burst through his silence as she started to turn
away. He grabbed her arm and spun her around. "Who
the hell are you to judge what I have to do?"

"No one who matters, Royle. Just someone who has already walked that road and who gives a damn about you.
That's all."

He released her arm when she tugged at his grip.

"Who did you lose?" he asked coldly.

"My mother." The memories rushed through the broken
dam of the past in a torrent. "She didn't die in a war. Nor
from a disease I could devote my life to finding a cure for.
She died protecting me from a wild boar. He tore her to
shreds while I watched from the safety of a tree limb. I
couldn't have saved her, but reason is a poor absolution
for guilt when you're a kid, isn't it? Have you ever seen
what a wild boar does to his kill?"

Shaken by the memory of her mother's violent death,
she yearned to flee the horrific visions flashing through
her mind. She had not intended to open those doors, but
only to make Royle realize the errant source of his motives.

She brushed past him and entered the cabin. Immediately, Teigue caught her by the shoulders, then wrapped
her in an embrace. "As long as I draw breath, you have
someone who loves you, Sunshine," Teigue said in a
voice that sounded older than the mountains surrounding
them.

She sniffed, comforted by the presence of his strong
arms holding her like a loving father. "Thank you. I love
you, too."

Emily gazed into Teigue's sorrowful brown eyes. "Oh,
Teigue, is there no way to make him understand? Surely
his family wanted to save *him*, not the Tremaine name."

"That is true, but he refuses to see it."

Royle stomped inside and tossed his jacket and pack
onto his bed. "You two deserve each other. Blind senti-

mentalists. Neither one of you has an iota of appreciation for duty or heritage."

Emily shook her head against Teigue's chest, knowing well who was blind and why. No one could remove the veil from Royle's eyes, except Royle.

Chapter 10

THE WEATHER TURNED unreasonably warm the second morning of the three-day trek into Silverton. Convoluted, winding trails, some barely wide enough to accommodate the span of the wagon wheels, appeared and disappeared in the rocky ground. The terrain posed hazards that awed Emily and heightened her respect for the skills Royle and Teigue displayed with the animals and the land. Transporting the heavy loads of high-grade ore forced them along a route nearly twice the distance of the fifteen miles covered by a more direct, hazardous trail. The steepest pass consumed most of the second day and required frequent rest for the animals.

Emily conceded both men had been right. Finding her way through the wild, unforgiving mountains even with a compass and a detailed map would have been chancy at best. In camp, she redoubled her efforts to ease the endless tasks the men met from dawn until after dark. Once the heat started building, she worked tirelessly to make sure that men and animals had sufficient water. During the evening meal, she cooked enough for the following day.

A delicate truce kept the camp peaceful. An undercurrent of desire-laced tension wove through every conversation Royle and Emily shared. By unspoken agreement, she kept her opinions concerning his plans to herself, and he kept his distance by refraining from touching her except when necessary. The armistice provided no safeguard from his torrid stares that warmed her skin. Nor did it insulate her from the frequent, embarrassing moments when he caught her watching him with carnal fantasies rippling through her daydreams.

Late the third morning, a quiet excitement surrounded the men.

"You'll see Silverton when we climb this next rise," Teigue said with a hint of amusement in his voice.

Anxious, Emily stood on tiptoes and shielded her eyes as though it would allow her to see farther.

"Get on my horse, Emily. You've given him more rest than you can afford." Royle slapped the reins in the traces and urged the mules up the final incline.

Excited by a plethora of emotions that defied sorting, Emily swung atop Royle's horse. As though sensing an end to the arduous journey, the horse trotted up the crest of the rise.

Across the valley, long fingers of bare rock stretched from the timberline to the valley floor. Avalanches and landslides had cleared streaks through the verdant timber. Clusters of wrecked, decaying trees, broken like matchsticks amid the boulders, lay heaped at the base of the mountain.

Wind gusted up from the swift waters of Río de las Animas. Emily inhaled the summer scent of pine and grasses. The clean air banished the cobwebs of comfort from her mind.

The town drew her attention. The stark reality of her time change swept over her with a ripple of gooseflesh. Fear and excitement surged from her stomach and halted her breathing in mid-exhalation.

It had been one thing to accept that the entire world had changed while she dwelled in the insulated realm of the cabin and mine. Staring down, knowing what sleepy Silverton would become in a little over a century, intensified the change.

Approximately four to five hundred buildings dotted the sharply walled valley. Houses, shacks, businesses, and a church lined the heart of the main streets. The majority of the houses had steeply pitched roofs to keep heavy snowfall from accumulating.

"Are you all right?"

Someone was speaking from a distance. She tried to hear the words. The relentless surges of change and acceptance created a ringing in her ears. The full impact of an era void of the support utilities she had taken for granted staggered her. Never again would she drive to an airport and cross the country in a matter of hours for a meeting with a client. Mary and Gil would keep the business going. Relief that she had taken steps to make the company employee-owned in the event of her death swept through her. Her death. Did anyone notice the death of someone who hadn't lived outside the shadows of other people's expectation?

Absurdly, she wondered: What would happen to her house? Her furniture? Her clothing? Would someone who needed her clothes get them?

Her mind leap-frogged.

Staring down at Silverton, she imagined it with power lines and paved streets. The image faded immediately. No sirens screamed in the night here. Heaven help those in need of a trauma center. The primitive remoteness denied them so much as a hospital. In this time, people died of preventable, curable things: smallpox, pneumonia, infections, appendicitis. A deep certainty that she would die in this time crept through the haze.

This wasn't what she had in mind when she wished for a simpler life and time. No, this was downright dangerous. Men walked around with guns strapped to their hips. Women had no rights.

Panic seized her.

She tore her stare from the town sprawling across the heart of the valley. Her instinct to flee sent her searching for direction.

There was none, save the trail ahead leading into the heart of the unknown. The convenient roles of her past that had protected her from exposing herself to the ridicule and censure of the rest of the world no longer existed. In the world below, everything was new, uncharted. Nothing was safe.

As much as the realization terrified her, it also exhilarated her. She had wanted to discover who she was and the depth of her mettle. Now, the opportunity lay at hand. No reprieve. No retreat.

Her heart hammered in her chest so hard that it hurt. *Be careful what you wish. You might get it.* The words from the past that was yet to be born haunted her like ghosts whispering in her ear.

"Emily!"

At the sound of her name, she forced a look in Teigue's direction. Her mouth opened, but no sound emerged.

Teigue braked the wagon at the crest of the rise, then scrambled from the seat. Unable to move, she watched him approach. Worry deepened the lines around his brown eyes. The compassion in his touch thawed her frozen muscles. With his help, she dismounted, and held the reins in a death grip.

"What is it, Sunshine?"

The soothing timbre of Teigue's baritone skimmed the top layer from her tumult. The chaos engendered by the irrevocable change pulled her in a hundred directions.

"I'm afraid," she whispered so softly that only Teigue heard.

Teigue wrapped an arm around her shoulders. Seeking more comfort, she embraced him at the waist. Giving her fear a voice brought it to the surface. Tremors ran their course, shaking her against him, then faded.

"Is it that different? The future you came from and now?"

Not trusting herself, she nodded against his dusty shirt.

The smell of the trail, sweat, and mules filled her nostrils. The arm holding her close felt like safety.

She gathered strength from Teigue's patience and love. She had faced a succession of new worlds. What was one more? Silverton was different. But so was Catholic school after thirteen years of commune living. *I can do this. I have to stand on my own and move forward, just like before.*

The great differences between the past and the present dimmed in the face of her resolve. The turbulence inside her coalesced and changed direction. Fear and panic evaporated, leaving only a trail of wispy agitation in a corner of her mind.

"It's better here," she said, gathering the inner strength that had fortified her during every difficulty she had ever faced. Strong, sure arms gave Teigue's waist a squeeze. "I have a friend." She lifted her head and met his worry. "I never had a real friend before. That makes me rich in ways all my money couldn't buy there."

"Always a welcome sight, isn't it?" Royle removed his gloves as he approached.

"I think you have more than one friend," Teigue murmured, then winked with a smile.

Emily wasn't as sure. She released an arm from around Teigue's waist and straightened beside him.

Smoke trails rose from chimneys and disappeared into the breeze. She recalled her first view of Silverton from the car, then smiled. Deliberately, she cast the image aside. Below lay the future. "Silverton is a sight," she agreed with Royle.

"I was referring to the hotel. Hot water. Clean clothes. Good food. Fine whiskey. Female. . . ."

Head cocked, she glanced up at him when his voice trailed. "Female—what? Companionship? Conversation? Connubial bliss without the impediment of a wife or obligation?"

Royle shrugged and regarded her with a frown. "You will need to curb your bluntness in town or you might be mistaken for something you would rather not be associated with." The harsh line of his mouth softened in slow appraisal. "Dressed as you are, I doubt that you need to worry about being confused with high society, but you do want the miners to regard you as a lady of quality."

"As opposed to a lady of the evening?" she asked, wishing her heart felt as light as her forced smile. "We know I'm not that, nor do I have any wish to be." The smile faded, as did his reproof when their gazes locked. She fervently hoped she hid her desire for him better than he hid the rapacious hunger radiating from his blue depths.

"That's why you stay close to us, Sunshine." Teigue's mellow voice barely penetrated the current arcing between Emily and Royle.

Emily turned, an act that forced her gaze from the mesmerizing temptation of untold pleasure Royle promised without a word. Tonight, he would sate his lust with a stranger and be just as glad for it.

Her heart twisted at the thought of Royle's skilled, callused hands skimming another woman's flesh. That woman wouldn't care if Royle used her to assuage his lust, nor would it matter that he preferred to marry a stranger before the end of the year. No, she would enjoy the moment, then take her money and move on.

For a split second, Emily wished that she could know the full pleasure of making love with him. Just as quickly, she dismissed the notion as folly. She could never just move on. Already she cared too much for him. The physical lure merely compounded the problem. No, she could not don the role of lady of the evening, not even once. Instead of coin, all she'd earn was a broken heart.

"Let's get into town, then. I wouldn't want to keep you from your plans a moment longer." Emily's left eyebrow drew down in question when Teigue squeezed her shoulder just before releasing her.

Emily reached for the saddle horn and hiked her left foot into the stirrup. Strong, familiar hands closed around her waist and lifted her. She knew from the instant heat in her body that Royle had lent the assistance both knew she did not need.

Surprised, she turned in the saddle. The hunger in his

gaze softened with a knowing half-smile that seemed more forlorn than satisfied. An impulse to touch his unshaven cheek allowed her hand to cover half the distance before she realized it.

"Thank you," she murmured, then gathered the reins.

"My pleasure."

She watched him walk toward his waiting wagon and climb into the driver's box.

Before she could dwell on what kind of pleasure he might derive from lifting her onto the horse, Teigue called out, "I'd like some of your gold."

"Take whatever you want." She reined the horse toward the wagons.

"Do you have any idea what you've got in those pouches?" Royle asked over his shoulder.

Emily shook her head. "I hope there is enough to set up a good retirement fund for Teigue. That's all I'm concerned about."

"Retirement fund?"

The croak in Royle's voice drew her attention. From the distance of twenty feet, she couldn't quite make out his expression. "Yes. And I'd suggest that you set up one for yourself when you get to Virginia, if not before."

Teigue chuckled as he slapped the reins in their traces. His lighthearted scolding sent the mules into motion. Emily took her place between the two wagons. The slow going and favorable wind direction held the dust to a minimum. She concentrated on the trail into Silverton as a means of ignoring Royle's heated gaze. Although ineffectual, the effort kept her from glancing his way. With mixed emotions, she consoled herself that a night in the saloons and brothels should appease him. For a while. As for herself, the only pleasure she hoped to realize was the hot bath Royle mentioned.

At the Silverton Hotel, Emily secured the door lock inside her room. A steaming tub of hot water beckoned to every dirt-encrusted pore and tender muscle in her body. Her head still whirled from watching Royle negotiate at the

Greene & Company smelter. He possessed the shrewd tenacity of a Wall Street broker squeezing every dime out of a tax deduction.

Eyeing the tub, she laid out her last clean clothes and unwrapped the floral-scented soap Teigue had given her at the door. Sniffing the heady fragrance, she wondered where he got it. Had he carried it all the way from the cabin?

"He must have," she mused, removing her shoes. Teigue's thoughtfulness made her smile. Amid the strange surroundings and the uncertainty of her future, Teigue remained a warm, bright ray of sunshine in a cloud-riddled sky. Royle was more like the clouds: moody, roiling, angry, and inexorably moving in an easterly direction far from the source of serenity.

Relaxed in the delicious warmth of the tub, Emily recalled hundreds of scenes from Western movies. Eyes closed, the stories flowed across her mind like an old Movietone newsreel.

Hollywood's version of the Old West had discreetly omitted a lot of reality. For one thing, every drop of water in Silverton was hauled from the single spring, owned by Mr. Luesley. In haggling over the cost of an entire tub full of hot water, she found herself bargaining with the water carrier, Frank Schneider. She had waited in the hotel lobby while Mr. Schneider led his burro-drawn water cart up to the side door. Teigue had remained with her and seemed to regard the hot water more precious than the silver they had left at the smelter.

Languishing in the bath, Emily directed the movie footage in her head toward countless clips of men washing the trail dust from their bodies in the questionable privacy of barbershop baths. The water took on a perceptible heat as she envisioned Royle stripping away the layers hiding his magnificent build honed by years of grueling physical work. Her fingers tingled with the memory of following the contours of his chest and powerful arms sculpted of muscle and sinew. She ached for the tickle of the silken whorls of black chest hair against her palms. A shiver danced up her

arms and lodged in her breasts. As her nipples hardened in
expectation, she opened her eyes and heaved a sigh.

Fruitless daydreams, she chided herself, then set about
washing her hair.

All the pragmatism she mustered failed to banish Royle's
image. Like an airborne virus, he pervaded every breath.
Fighting the aftereffects, she scrubbed until her skin
glowed pink. Once out of the tub, she carefully rinsed her
hair with a pitcher of lukewarm water.

She dressed, then sorted the tangles from her hair and
worked the damp segments into a braid that ran down her
back. Just as she prepared to leave in search of Teigue,
someone rapped on her door.

"Teigue?" She unlocked the door and drew it open.

"No, *Señorita,*" said a young Mexican woman not much
older than herself. "The gentleman from the store asked
you be delivered this."

Surprised, Emily accepted the bundle of packages from
the woman. "Wait a moment. I'll pay you for the delivery."
What did one tip a delivery person these days?

"No, no, *Señorita.* He pay me to bring this already. You
no pay me." She paused, then brightened. "He say you wait
here until they come for you."

Emily nodded and assured the woman that she would do
so. "Bless his heart," she murmured, setting the stack on
the bed. She opened the top package.

"Do you need help dressing?" the woman asked timidly.

Emily hesitated, wondering why she asked. Curious, she
laid out the packages on the bed and quickly opened them.
One by one, she held up the garments. "The dear, sweet
man. He thought of everything." When she came to the
corset, she held it out and blinked back her surprise. She
glanced over her shoulder at the woman waiting in the
doorway.

"There is a distinct probability I'll need help with this."
She ushered the woman inside and closed the door. "Would
you mind?"

"Oh, no, *Señorita.* He buy you such nice things, I would

love to see them on you. He must think you very special. Ah, but perhaps you are his wife?"

Emily laughed at the notion of being married to Teigue. "No, I am no man's wife, nor do I intend to be."

"Oh."

Emily caught the knowing look stealing the mirth from the woman's face. "I'm no man's mistress, either, so relax."

Without hesitation, she stripped off her jeans and shirt. "What is your name?"

"Lupe. I helped him pick these pretties for you."

"And a fine job you did, too, Lupe. By the way, my name is Emily." It took a little imagination and Lupe's guidance, but she managed to get into the black satteen corset. Lupe tugged on the laces until Emily objected.

"But, *Señorita*, you must have it tight. It is the fashion."

"I don't care about fashion. Let's see if the dress fits over it. If so, it's tight enough. How do women move around in these body casts?" she grumbled, recalling how restrictive she found panty hose.

The corset had been the strangest and most difficult piece of clothing. In contrast, the hose and foulard petticoat were simple.

With trepidation, she tried on the shoes. The high back, squat heels, and long tongue with a bow reminded her of the yearly fashion shows. The ultrathin models wore clothes no sane woman would appear in public wearing. And the shoes . . . Emily slipped a foot inside, then straightened, amazed by the comfortable fit. She glanced at her beleaguered Nikes and laughed. How Teigue got the size right was beyond her comprehension.

Next came the dress. Fortunately, the dress allowed enough room for her to loosen the corset laces enough for comfort. The pleated sapphire-blue lampas skirt terminated in points at her feet. Like the similar points at the end of her sleeves, a lighter blue satin peeked out from beneath. A soft frill of guipure lace hung at her throat and extended down the front of the tailored bodice to just below the waist.

Never in Emily's life had new clothing excited her—

until she saw the dress. The feel of the rich fabric bespoke
opulence. It felt beautiful. She felt beautiful wearing it.
Even more important, she felt *right* in the garb. Belatedly,
she hoped Teigue had not spent all his gold on the dress
and trappings. If so, she would chisel more from the pocket
in the room of what she called "the isolation chamber."

"Sit here, *Señorita*, and I will style your hair." Lupe
folded her hands in prayer under her chin. Her dark eyes
twinkled. "You are the only woman in Silverton who could
do that dress justice. Your man, he knows. You cannot
leave this room without him, or he will have to fight his
way to your side."

Emily laughed with Lupe, enjoying the fantasy Lupe preferred and not willing to shatter the moment. She sat with
her back to the mirror and allowed Lupe full freedom with
her hair. Lupe rummaged through the wrapping paper until
she found a small packet, which she tore open.

Emily watched in fascination as one pin after another
disappeared from her hand. Then Lupe retreated, her big
brown eyes sparkling with approval.

"Am I done?" Emily rose to face the mirror. Surprise
widened the green eyes of the woman looking back. "Oh,
my. You've done wonders without so much as a bottle of
hair spray." Emily's long, dark brown tresses formed a
crown of rolls and plaits. The upsweep reflected the elegance created by the dress and was enhanced by the sophistication of Emily's even features. The style bore an aching
similarity to the one she had worn as maid of honor at
Laura's wedding.

"*Sí*, I believe the *Señor* will be pleased." Lupe adjusted a
piece of lace at Emily's throat.

"He is without a doubt one of the finest, kindest men I've
ever known." She examined her profile and smiled with
satisfaction.

Lupe gathered the wrappings and bundled them under
her arm. "I go now."

Emily searched her backpack until finding the pouch
with her wages from Royle. Mentally translating the dollar

value to current times, she withdrew a couple silver dollars, which she pressed into Lupe's hand.

"You give me too much," Lupe protested.

Emily curled Lupe's fingers around the coins. "I could never have fixed my hair the way you've done. It's marvelous. But most of all, thanks for helping with the corset."

"*Gracias, Señorita.*" Lupe clutched the coins in her fist to her breast.

Before Lupe could change her mind, Emily ushered her to the door. "I'll see you soon for some practical clothing."

"*Gracias.*" Lupe scurried out the door, then paused and beamed yet another thank-you.

Emily pressed the door closed, then returned to the mirror and fought the temptation to take down her hair and analyze the steps Lupe used to pin it up. The forceful rap on the door lit her face with a smile. Eager to show Teigue the results of his careful shopping, she opened the door.

Chapter 11

ROYLE WAITED IMPATIENTLY in the carpeted hall-way. The formal black suit, crisp white shirt, and black bro-cade vest with complementary tie he kept at the hotel fit well. He glanced up when the door opened.

The woman who had spent countless hours with him in the mine, in the shelter tending the animals, and in the cabin had undergone a drastic change. In a dress that ex-posed only her face and callused hands, her feminine allure shone. The familiar physical reaction in his groin prodded his addled wits.

"Miss Fergeson, you look . . . lovely."

Her welcoming smile flickered, then sparked into life. "What happened to calling me Emily?"

"It might be best if we observed formalities while in town." With effort, he tore his gaze from eyes so green he nearly lost himself in their depths.

"I see. In that case, you may address me as Miss Ferge-son and I'll call you Cousin Royle."

Cousin Royle. He swallowed hard. The charade Teigue had concocted was ludicrous. Even falling-down drunk, he would never think of her as Cousin Emily.

Royle cleared his throat. "You persist in making it difficult to be a gentleman around you. My concern is for you and your reputation here in town."

She had the grace to lower her impish gaze. "I appreciate your concern, Royle. You don't need to worry about me. I've been navigating social minefields for years. Quite successfully, I might add." The hint of a smile curled the corners of her mouth. "Though I thank you for considering my welfare." She squared her shoulders. The movement thrust her breasts toward him like an invitation under glass.

A slight dip of her head conveyed an acquiescence he found hard to believe.

"I'm sure you know best, Royle, but I've never known of cousins living in the same house who called each other Mister and Miss. However, I shall endeavor to hold forth with what you deem socially apropos." She peered up at him through her lashes. "Seriously, don't you think we would be more convincing if I called you Cousin Royle?"

Royle heaved a sigh. The woman would call him whatever she wanted, and there was not a damned thing he could do about it. If he had learned anything about Emily over the last five weeks, it was not to push her head-on. She would buck him relentlessly. "If you wish . . . Cousin Emily."

The slight twitch of her left eyebrow made him wonder if she had as much difficulty envisioning them as cousins as he. Calling her Cousin did nothing to quell the onslaught of salacious fantasies filling his mind whenever he looked at her. It was far more palatable to imagine himself naked with her delicious body heaving against him.

He offered his arm. "Shall we go to dinner?"

Emily glanced up and down the hall. "What about Teigue?"

"He had some business to finish. He'll meet us at the Animas."

"The Animas?"

He covered her hand resting on his arm. "Remember the good food I mentioned?"

"Yes. Wasn't that right before the female—"

"The Animas serves the finest cuisine in Silverton."

He escorted her down the stairs and through the hotel lobby. The long shadows created by the tall mountains hiding the sun dulled the rough edges of the buildings. The open stares of miners who removed their hats and made room on the boardwalk tightened Royle's possession of her hand. Oblivious to the predatory interest of their slow assessments, she smiled at each and took in the surroundings as though she had never seen a town before.

"Tell me about Silverton's history," she requested, her eyes wide and curious.

Royle shrugged. "There isn't much to tell. Twenty years ago not more than fifty people lived here. Miners came for the silver. The town grew. It will grow even more when the railroad arrives."

"I'll bet winter is brutal here."

"It is. Most people leave. The snow keeps the miners who remain holed up near their mines. Business isn't good enough to keep most of the establishments open year round."

"Will the railroad change that?"

"I doubt it. It snows on the railroad tracks, too."

The skeptical glance she darted at him forced a spontaneous smile.

"Lots of snow, Emily. A few years back, we had easily twenty feet of snow. It didn't melt until spring. Teigue and I were eating pretty lean by the end of March. These mountains are unforgiving. So is the weather." He squeezed her hand to draw her attention. "So are some of the people who live here. Not one of the men who stepped out of the way for us to pass is as good-hearted as Teigue. Most of them would give their last nickel to get under your skirt."

"Present company excluded, I'm sure."

Although the teasing lilt of her voice kept the mood light, he doubted that he was much different during a weak moment. Lately, those weak moments were adding up to

long hours. "Present company would not insult you by offering money and insinuating that you were a lady of the
evening, as I believe you termed the profession."

Her hand flew to her throat in mock gratitude. "I feel so
much safer with an honorable champion of my virtue and
well-being at my side."

"Don't mock me, Emily. You damn well know I'm no
sainted champion."

"No. You're a martyr wanna-be determined to sacrifice
yourself on the altar of survival guilt."

She paused without so much as a cringe at the fury of his
glare.

"Isn't this the restaurant?"

Royle bit back the angry retort on the tip of his tongue.
Fuming, he opened the door for her. Neither spoke until
they were seated, their orders were taken, and Royle had
accepted a bottle of wine.

Emily touched his hand resting on the table. She winced
when he pinned her with a warning look. "I'm sorry, Royle.
That was uncalled-for. We were having a pleasant time and
I spoiled it. What you do with your life is of no consequence to me. I appreciate your consideration on my behalf, and I promise, I'll try harder to keep my opinions to
myself."

"What are you going to do, Emily? Will you remain with
Teigue?" His anger ebbed into edgy curiosity. While her
future and his were unrelated, he cared what happened to
her. The thought of her being mistreated was as abhorrent
as envisioning her in another man's arms, her pupils dilated
with desire, her breasts heaving, her tantalizing lips parted,
inviting—

"You're hurting me, Royle," she whispered, her brow
knit and her bright eyes searching for a reason.

He released her immediately, unsure how her hand had
found a way into his. "Sorry." He shook his head lightly
and glanced first at her, then toward the window. "We seem
to hurt or irritate one another on a regular basis."

"I know. Maybe we want too much for and from each
other."

"What do you want from me, Emily?"

She took so long to answer that he abandoned the window view and searched her face. The struggle evident in her transparent features unsettled him. "Is my question so difficult to answer?"

"No. It's just that I don't seem to be able to put it into words." Confusion lingered in the tiny frown turning her mouth into a pout.

He lowered his head and spoke in a near-whisper. "Let me make it easy for you. You want me damn near as much as I want you. But we both know there are risks neither of us is willing to take."

Although she remained silent, he read the answer in her eyes. Even when she averted her gaze for a moment of composure, the ghost of the truth lingered.

"You don't have to say a word. I can see it. I can feel it. It's a damn good thing one of us has the good sense to keep a distance."

Teigue pulled a chair out from the table and joined them. "Good evening, Emily. Royle. Have I joined you at an inopportune moment?"

"No," Emily gushed, color rushing to her cheeks.

"Of course not," Royle said at the same time, releasing his final hold on Emily's wrist.

"You appeared engaged in a private conversation. I don't want to interrupt."

For a man bent on allowing them privacy in a public place, Teigue seemed to take delight in calling attention to the intensity of their exchange. Then, perhaps that was his point, Royle conceded.

Royle filled each wineglass. "Did you finish your business?" he asked Teigue.

"Yes. Before I tell you what I've done, let me say that you are the most beautiful woman in all of Colorado, Emily."

"Thank you, Teigue. It's the dress. What a thoughtful thing to do. I'm amazed that everything fit."

Royle caught Teigue's startled gaze and gave a slight shake of his head. Under the circumstances, it might be best if Emily thought Teigue had sent the clothing. He could not look at her without imagining her lush curves encased in the black satteen corset. Imagining her without it sent a rush of heat through his loins. He shifted and lifted his wine-glass.

"I have something else for you." Teigue reached inside his coat. "The gold you gave me before we came into town bought you half of my share of the mine."

The bottom dropped out of Royle's stomach. Surely, he had misunderstood Teigue. That single pouch of gold represented a pebble next to a mountain if she compared it to owning a quarter of the mine. The old man had lost his mind completely over the vixen beside him.

"Teigue—"

"What you do with your half is your business, Royle. What I do with mine won't concern you after you leave for Virginia."

The resoluteness of Teigue's expression quelled further protest. Royle swallowed the epithet begging for expression and looked away.

Teigue was right. Nothing about either one of them concerned him after he boarded the train in Denver. The framework of his destiny had been sealed in the fiery aftermath of war. He had until summer's end to pull out as much silver from the mine as possible, then sell it and leave. The goal for which he had labored most of his life lay within his grasp. Why did it suddenly seem like a burden whose weight increased daily?

"I'm touched beyond words by your generosity, Teigue. However, I can't accept it." In her distress, she glanced at Royle for help.

He averted his gaze. Did she have to be contrary to every damn thing put in front of her?

"Why the hell not?" Royle snapped.

"Well . . . I just can't. It isn't fair and . . . and I didn't work for it. I'd feel like a . . . a supervisor who came in at the last minute to steal the credit from those who worked for it."

"You're right about that. You didn't work for it," Royle grumbled.

Teigue leaned toward Emily. "You're my partner. My friend. Come what may, we're going to build a house we can both live in, just like we talked about."

"But Teigue—"

Teigue waved off her protest with his left hand. "Hell, Emily, there's going to come a time when you find a man you want to marry and father your babies. I know that. Even if he takes you off to California or up to Oregon, you and I will still be family by choice." Teigue cocked his head and pleaded with his soulful brown eyes. "Not many of us get to choose our family members."

Emily kept her full attention on Teigue. "I know you and I are fortunate in that respect. But Teigue, I don't want your money or any share of the mine. I'm young and strong, and I can work. Besides, I'm your friend, and we're family, regardless of this piece of paper. You've worked hard all your life. I couldn't take a dime of what you've got. I'd feel like I was stealing your retirement."

Emily's apparent anguish over Teigue's future, a concern that should have been his, broke Royle's agitated silence. "Tell her. Or I will."

"Tell me what?" Emily glanced away from Teigue for a second before returning to him.

"When we leave Silverton, you won't have to think about working at anything you don't want to do. We may look like rock-poor miners, but we aren't," Teigue said softly. "Sign this. Please." He nudged the paper and a pen in front of her.

Head shaking, Emily picked up the document and read the entire page. Royle recognized the legal deed giving her full partnership in Teigue's half of the mine.

He wished money motivated her. How much simpler his predicament would be. He could pay her, explore the breadth of her passion at leisure, then walk away without a qualm. Too bad she held different values dear.

"I'm sorry, Teigue. I can't sign this." She set the paper on the white tablecloth and pushed it at Teigue.

"The hell you can't," Royle said. "Sign it. Make him happy. Make yourself happy. Goddamn, somebody at this table should get what they want. Why not Teigue?"

Emily folded her hands on the edge of the table. "I don't think you realize exactly what this document says. Thank you, Teigue, but I can't let you do this."

Royle snatched up the paper and read the fine print. A clause at the bottom reflected the full extent of Teigue's commitment. When Emily signed her name, she also became the owner of half of Teigue's total wealth and his heir. It was a gold-digging woman's dream presented on a gleaming silver platter. All she had to do was sign her name.

The day she showed up at the cabin, Royle had believed this was the sort of devious, conniving plan she had in mind. Over the days that had blended into weeks, one defensive shroud after another had dissolved from the myriad scenarios he had constructed around her and her secret motives. She worked harder than most men. From the onset, she had been more concerned with giving than taking anything, where Teigue was concerned.

Still, he hadn't forgotten her impossible story about leading a hundred and fifty horses through the mountains alone, then losing them in an avalanche. At best, the woman was hiding something; at worst, she was an accomplished liar. Either way, Teigue had made his decision. As he had in years past, Royle supported Teigue, whether he agreed with him or not. Besides, even if Teigue lost half his wealth, the remainder allowed him to live in style indefinitely.

Royle shoved the paper in front of Emily. Her chin rose in open defiance of his determination.

"You have nothing to say in this matter, Royle. This is between me and Teigue."

"But I have," he assured her in a low, lethal voice. "Sign the damn paper or I'll get another one that says you're mentally infirm and need institutionalizing. Most of the people in Silverton would agree."

Disbelief raised her brows in a comical arch. "Who would believe—"

"Anyone who knew you refused to sign this," Royle seethed.

"No one," Teigue assured her at the same time.

Royle felt Teigue's disapproval for the heavy-handed tactic. Further discussion waited while a waiter arranged their meal on the table.

Each wrestled with different aspects of the thorny predicament during the slowly eaten, silent dinner. By the time the waiter took the last dish from the table, Royle had decided on a new tactic. Hell, he didn't care whether she owned a quarter of the mine. What rankled him was that she refused it. Teigue wanted her to have it, and he owed Teigue.

"Cousin Emily," he began with a smile at her wary astonishment over his use of the informality, "tell me something."

Her inquisitive gaze darted to Teigue, then back. "If I can."

"Do you recall what you said when I found you crawling out of the hole you hacked in the collapsed tunnel?" He glanced at her hands. Two of the fingernails ripped away during her frantic digging were growing back. Even now, it gave him chills to think of her walled in the pitch-black cavern and stumbling to pull one rock after another out of the way.

She appeared uneasy, as though ready for him to spring a trap she could not see. "No. It's a bit fuzzy."

Royle nodded. "Even though you were exhausted, you insisted on telling me about the gold you found . . . for Teigue. You thought he had nothing outside of what you saw at the cabin, didn't you?"

A delicate pink blush colored her cheeks with admission.

"You were willing to give him what you damn near died finding, but you won't accept a reciprocal gesture from him. Are you so much more noble than he is that your gift is worthy of acceptance and his is not?"

Flustered, she straightened, her gaze darting between Teigue and Royle. "It—it's not the same thing."

"You're right. It isn't. Your gift was greater. Sleep on it,

Emily." He doubted that she would make the comparison of gifts in the same light in which he and Teigue saw it. It annoyed him that she had unselfishly offered the source of her newfound wealth when she had nothing. Her rejection of Teigue's gift made it impossible to think of her as a money-grubbing gold digger.

"Why does it matter to you, Royle?"

The sincerity lighting her face made him uncomfortable. "It doesn't."

"Then why are you badgering me?"

A slow smile as insincere as she was earnest crept across his mouth. "Am I badgering you?"

For a long, silent moment he regarded her with grudging but growing admiration. Not fainthearted, she held her ground while refusing his game.

In a flash, all the question in her features brightened to sugary cheerfulness. "Cousin Royle, while I appreciate your concern and value your insight and opinion, I consider this matter relevant only to Teigue and me. Unless your plans have changed and you'll be sharing the house we're planning, we would all be best served if you put your questions and concerns about this matter where the sun never shines."

Nonplussed, he watched her stand when Teigue took her chair. Heat boiled up from his throat as he nearly choked for a response. The little vixen had the audacity to diplomatically tell him to shove his opinion up his—

"Cousin Emily," he seethed, then glared at her when she afforded a tolerant glance over her shoulder.

"Yes?"

"We'll be leaving in a day. Be ready."

"I assure you, I will be ready."

He forced a thin smile, void of any merriment, to his lips. He watched her wind through the tables on Teigue's arm. The strength of restraint radiated from her composure. She had not heard the last of this. In the morning, he would collect her and turn her loose at the dry goods store. Whether she accepted Teigue's offer or not, she would get every cent of what she hacked out of the mine by summer's end.

Royle tossed enough silver on the table to cover the dinner fare and a healthy tip. Hands in pockets, he left the Animas and headed in the opposite direction from the hotel. What he needed was a loud saloon, drinkable whiskey, and a woman willing to relieve the horrendous ache in his loins.

"You were very quiet before dinner," Emily said to Teigue as they approached the hotel.

"Royle was doing such a good job of speaking my mind, I hated to interrupt." A wink accompanied his grin and made her smile.

"Why do I get the feeling you enjoy lighting the cat's tail on fire then standing back while Royle and I conduct a Chinese fire drill."

Teigue held the hotel door for her to enter the lobby. "I'm not sure what a Chinese fire drill is, but I think I get your meaning."

"And?" she prodded, lifting the front of her skirt as she reached the stairs.

"It's the most entertainment I've had in decades. You've reached inside him and rattled his bones, Sunshine. They sorely need it. With a little luck, he'll get smart enough to forget this foolishness in Virginia by the end of summer."

Emily shook her head. The stubborn streak in Royle was heat-tempered with honor. The alloy would not snap without breaking him. "I doubt he'll change his mind."

"Yeah, you're probably right. I keep hoping he'll wake up one morning with a clear notion of what he's doing."

"It doesn't work that way. We can talk. He can't help but listen to some of it. But until he puts it together for himself, it's all hot air blowing in the summer breeze. I doubt that even a support group could help him."

"A support group?" Teigue's eyebrows rose.

"People who share tragedies, affliction, or any number of difficulties discuss their feelings and how to deal with their problems in a support group. They are there for each other in times of crisis and help one another cope."

"Royle wouldn't go there," Teigue said flatly.

"No, I don't suppose he would."

She slid her hand down his arm to lace their fingers. "I didn't get a chance to thank you for the beautiful clothes you sent over with Lupe. That was so thoughtful of you, Teigue. I hadn't considered shopping for more than a few things to wear at the mine." She grinned and glanced at her hands. "Including a couple of pairs of good gloves."

Teigue squeezed her hands and shook his head. "I didn't think about you needing a dress, either."

"Then . . . Royle?"

"Royle. He isn't as impervious to you as you might think. No, Sunshine, you've got him running in circles inside his head."

"But he let me believe that you . . ." Why did he attempt to hide his thoughtfulness?

"It suited him to do so. He probably won't like my telling you otherwise. Could be that he was looking out for your welfare."

"Or he didn't want to go to dinner with me in my Levi's," she mused without conviction.

Teigue chuckled softly. "He isn't an easy man to know."

"No, he's not. I doubt I'll ever understand him."

"We've got the rest of the summer."

His pensive expression made her question whether Teigue had a secret agenda. She regarded him closely, wondering what he had in mind. "For what?"

Teigue grinned, bent and placed a kiss on her upturned forehead. "For nature to take its course, Sunshine." Teigue paused at the door to her room. "Lock yourself in your room until Royle or I come for you in the morning. You can't be wandering these streets without one of us. It isn't safe."

"Teigue . . ."

"I've got business with Royle over at the Crystal Palace Saloon."

Emily unlocked the door and pushed it open. "Ah, yes. He should be down to the last item on his list." Why did Royle's spending a few hours with a lamplight lady irritate her so? "I'm sure he's suffering from near-terminal DSB and ready to explode."

"DSB?"

Dreaded Sperm Buildup. She caught herself before giving an explanation. "Never mind. Maybe a little recreation will put him in a more pleasant frame of mind tomorrow." Even as she spoke, the words mingled with the acrid vision in her mind.

Teigue held the door. "Good night, Emily. Lock the door."

"Good night, Teigue." She closed the door and turned the key, then tossed it on the dresser.

"Good night, Royle," she hissed. "I hope you have indigestion so bad it hurts to move."

The woman in the mirror gazed back at her with disapproval. When had she sunk to wishing anyone unpleasantness?

Chapter 12

"I FIGURED YOU'D be upstairs by now working off some of what's been plaguing you." Teigue pulled a chair away from the table Royle occupied, then sat.

Royle poured two drinks and handed one to Teigue. "In good time." The fare of available ladies at the Crystal Palace had already paraded past his table. Although all expressed interest in relieving the ache between his legs, none possessed the spark necessary to assuage the lust created by the vixen packaged in a blue dress.

"Why, Teigue?" He met his uncle's mellow expression with a growing dread. "Why half of your share of the mine and half of everything else you own?"

Teigue settled comfortably in the chair and stretched his long legs. "I'm fifty-two years old, son. I can't live forever. What the hell am I going to do with all the wealth we've carved from one mountain after another? "I'm not sure I did you a favor by sticking around and helping you all these years." Teigue sipped his drink and placed it gently on the table. "No, as I think about it, I know I didn't."

"Is that what you were doing? A favor?" Teigue's motives had never come into question. It had been the two of them since the day Royle returned from England. Who else did they have? Cousin Patty, afraid of her own shadow and the widow of a Southerner who fought for Ulysses Grant?

"Don't know what I was doing. I never gave serious thought to it, at least not more than enough to make myself feel better. I should have."

"What the hell do you mean, make yourself feel better?" The longer that woman stayed with them, the stranger Teigue acted. Thinking about the changes in Teigue was more comfortable than examining those in his own behavior.

Teigue toyed with the fresh drink he had poured. "I've been with you most of your life, Royle. I never knew you to be obstinate with the exception of what you're planning to do at the end of this summer."

Teigue shook his head, conveying a soul-weary sadness Royle recognized. He had seen the expression a few times and remembered each occurrence. Rather than launch into old arguments, he let Teigue continue at a halting pace.

"I should have boxed your ears the first time you mentioned returning to Virginia. Now . . . now, you're hell-bent on going and I can't stop you. I'll miss you, Royle. Madeline told me that when one door closes, another opens. You're leaving. Emily's staying. She isn't tied to me by blood or heritage or even obligation. And it's likely some man will snag her heart and carry her away from me. Until that time, I've got the daughter Maddy and I wanted to go along with the son who grew up swinging a pick at my side." Teigue drained the glass and poured another drink. "I hope to give her better advice than I gave you. But, at least I don't have to worry about her loving whoever she marries. Her heart can't be bought."

Royle snorted. "So she turned down your offer to make her wealthy. Maybe she wants *everything* you've got. Has that notion crossed your mind?" Royle filled his glass and took a healthy pull of the stinging liquor. "You find it very easy to overlook her lies. She still hasn't explained how she found us or how she lost a hundred and fifty horses in an avalanche. Don't try to tell me she was traveling alone. We've seen her ride. She's not good enough in the saddle to handle a pack horse, let alone a string that size."

A slow grin spread over Teigue's face and lit his eyes. "Is that all that's bothering you about her?"

"No, but I would like to know the truth."

"Would you?" Teigue topped off both glasses. "Seems to me you want more than that from her."

Royle turned his head. He did not want to argue with Teigue. "If you keep pouring like that, we'll be drunk within the hour." Even so, Royle lifted his own glass. With enough liquor, one of the saloon girls might become appealing.

"That's what I came here for." Teigue folded his hands around his glass.

Royle shook his head. "That isn't why you came here. You came for the ladies. You always do, just like I do."

"Not tonight."

Royle studied his uncle. There was something changed about him. A chill turned the mellow liquor in his gut to ice. "You're not thinking of . . ." The possibility so confounded him that the question shriveled in his throat.

As though reading his thoughts, Teigue chuckled. "Emily? The Jackson side of the family wasn't big on frigging their kin, either natural or by adoption. Tonight, I'm reminded of the difference between making love with a woman who owns your heart and sweating over one who wants your coin."

"There's a difference?" Royle taunted with a droll smile. Over the years, Teigue had expounded upon that difference on numerous occasions. Tonight, like the other times, Teigue would wax nostalgic over the past, then escort a woman upstairs to sweat over her.

"Yep. One I doubt you'll ever know." Teigue emptied his glass and poured another. "For that, I'm sorry I failed in your education."

A dark cloud rolled over Royle's heart. He had never seen Teigue in the sort of mood he reflected now. It was almost as if his old friend was determined to come to terms with their parting and close the door with a finality Royle found abhorrent.

"How the hell could you fail at my education? You were never responsible for it."

"I failed in teaching you what counts. I don't know whose doorstep I can lay that on, other than mine. Not my sister, Josie's. Not your father's. They married for love. It didn't matter to them if Virginia society turned on its ear when he broke his engagement and ran off with Josie."

Royle closed his eyes and let the dreamy numbness of the liquor blot out the surrounding din. The specter of memory carried him back into the grand opulence of the study in the ancestral Tremaine home. The years receded until he was a child of ten. He recalled his father speaking to Henry, eight years Royle's senior. Royle hadn't meant to eavesdrop, but once he heard the severe tone of Gerald Tremaine's lecture, Royle had frozen in the big chair facing the window overlooking the expansive gardens.

"You are a Tremaine. Everything you do reflects upon the name. As the eldest, it is your responsibility to uphold our good standing. Next month, you will attend the College of William and Mary. After your studies are complete, you will marry into society and ensure the tradition of the Tremaine line.

"In time, you will be head of the Tremaines and responsible for our relatives. This house will be your home until the day you die. It is mine. It was my father's and his father's before.

"The ways of the present link the past to the future, Henry. It is not an easy path, nor is it for the faint-spirited. But it is the only way to ensure a future that embodies the Tremaine values."

"Tradition and duty at any cost?" Henry had mumbled.

"Yes. No leadership comes without a heavy burden. As the eldest, it is yours to carry. It is both your birthright and your destiny."

As the sole surviving Tremaine male, his burden was even more cumbersome than the one Henry had borne. He alone must reconstruct the foundations of a solid future for the dynasty begun in the early 1700s. The luxury of choice belonged to others. He had none.

"My path is clear. I have no other choice," Royle whispered. The specters of the three ladies he had loved as much as life illuminated the inside of his eyelids. He wouldn't disappoint them.

He opened his eyes. Noise, smoke, and the malaise of hard liquor and bodies that had gone too long without soap battered his senses into the present.

"You have a choice, Royle." Teigue finished his drink and brought the glass onto the table with a bang. "Let go of the past."

"Like you did?" The bitter challenge hung in the air between them.

"I let go of it the day we left Virginia. If you're referring to Madeline, well . . . a woman can live in your heart long after her body is beyond your reach. You need to have loved one with all that's in you before you understand."

Teigue pushed to his feet and shoved his hands into his trouser pockets. "You might delude yourself into believing you'll fall in love with Rebecca. In time, you might even find things about her you can call lovable. But the truth is, you don't get to pick who you fall in love with any more than who your relatives are the day you're born."

Royle watched Teigue leave the saloon. He had expected Teigue to take a lady upstairs, but he had not. For the life of him, Royle didn't understand why.

He lost track of time while mulling over Teigue's odd behavior. As he poured the last drop of whiskey from the bottle, a sultry blonde sashayed into the chair Teigue had vacated.

"Hello, Royle. It's been a while." She glanced at the bar, where a tall man in an impeccably tailored charcoal suit lit a cigar.

Royle glanced at the saloonkeeper, then shrugged. He was not in the mood to talk with Mavis. Nor was he in the mood to sit in John Galloway's Crystal Palace, even if it was the best saloon in Silverton.

"I told Mr. Galloway I'd be spending the rest of the evening with you." Mavis set a fresh bottle of whiskey on the table.

During any other of his visits to Silverton over the past five years, he would have felt as special as Mavis wanted him to feel. Not tonight.

As he lifted his glass, he noted the smudge lines of her kohl eyeliner against the heavy layer of powder and rouge. In the warm liquor haze lightening his head, he saw Emily's pink face after she scrubbed in cold water each morning. In contrast, Mavis's kohl seemed a little darker, the powder a little whiter, the rouge on her cheeks garish.

A tingling danced along his lips at the memory of kissing Emily. Eager. Sweet. Honest and uninhibited in her carnal response.

The only natural color in Mavis's face was her eyes. Sad, green eyes, old beyond her years.

Royle fished a handful of money from his pocket and dropped it on the table, then downed his drink. The only bed he wanted to share tonight was at the Silverton Hotel in Emily Fergeson's room. Maybe it was the liquor. Maybe the conversation with Teigue. Regardless, the desire straining his pants for the last five weeks evaporated as surely as the smoke from a burned-out candle.

"I've had too much to drink to show either one of us a good time, Mavis. Maybe tomorrow night." He pushed the money toward her and stood. The room swayed a bit, then steadied.

"Sure, Royle. Don't forget me."

There was something forlorn in her voice and the way she eyed him as she scooped up the money. In his intoxicated state, he couldn't define it, so he dismissed it and headed for the door.

A chilly night wind accompanied him to the hotel. In his room, he plopped onto the bed and stared at the undulating ceiling. He kept his eyes open for a long time before succumbing to the ceaseless vision of Emily in the hot spring. Relentless yearning clutched at his groin.

"I thought Teigue was going to accompany me," Emily said. The Fourth of July was less than a month away, but Royle's red, white, and blue eyes were brighter than any flag. She winced, her eyes squinting in empathy.

"He banged on my door half an hour ago and said he had business to attend. Have you had breakfast?"

"No. Why don't we get a gallon of coffee for you?"

"Do I look that bad?"

Emily slung her backpack over her shoulder and grabbed the room key from the dresser top. "Uh-huh. I hope you feel better than you look."

"I will when I get something from Fleming's Drug Store. He has a headache powder. Salicylic something."

Emily locked the door. "Salicylic acid, from willow bark. It's the basis for aspirin. I hope you have a cast-iron stomach."

"My stomach is fine. It has been a few years since I killed most of a bottle of whiskey by myself."

"If you're going to mingle in high society, Mr. Tremaine, you had better build your tolerance or learn how to pace yourself. It's my experience that they put it away in prodigious amounts. The higher the quality of the booze, the greater the consumption. There is probably a scientific ratio for it somewhere."

"How would you know?"

"I know. Be nice, or I'll sing a rock song at the top of my lungs and blow your head off."

"I'm nice." He led them down the stairs. "Why would you sing to rocks?"

Emily chuckled. How easily her real nature slipped out in his presence. "Because they'll listen?"

Royle gave a half-nod, then stiffened. "I suppose that makes sense. I understand rocks are tone-deaf."

"Which way to the drug store?"

"Down here, next to the Crystal Palace." He held the door for her. "Where is your dress?"

"Upstairs. We're just going shopping for supplies, aren't we?" The gown seemed much too fine to wear among barrels of bacon and salted beef, tins of baking powder, and bags of flour. Hopefully, Lupe would be available to help her pick out more casual clothing and the items she needed for working in the mine.

"Ladies dress before appearing on the street," Royle grumbled, his eyes narrowing to a thin squint in the bright sunlight.

"I'm a miner. I don't want to pretend I'm anything else. I'll dress like the miners do. To humor you, I'll wear the gown when we go to dinner. Is that compromise acceptable?"

"It sounds like it has to be."

Emily laughed softly. "You mean I have the advantage? You're not in a mood to argue?"

"On the contrary. I do my best arguing when I have an aching head."

"I didn't think you the sort of man who required an incentive." Last night's activities had not helped his disposition. She wondered if he got drunk before or after his tryst with the female companionship he had sought.

Emily pushed through the door of Fleming's Drug Store. "Walgreens it isn't," she muttered, quickly scanning the shelves and drug counter. Jars and bottles lined the walls.

A middle-aged man rounded the counter and wiped his palms on a crisp white apron. "May I help you?"

"We need some salicylic acid." She glanced up at Royle's neon eyes. "A large quantity, please."

From the disdain creeping across the druggist's face, she sensed that she might as well have asked for heroin and a needle. With a curt nod, he set about getting her order.

The bell on the door tinkled. "Tremaine," came a voice from the doorway.

"Galloway," Royle acknowledged.

The false politeness of Royle's greeting piqued Emily's senses. She replaced the canister of talc she had been examining.

Galloway wore a finely tailored suit and black shoes that

gleamed despite the perpetual dust stirred from wagon wheels and horses' hooves on the dry street. The gold pocket watch and chain he straightened against his vest gleamed in the bright sunlight streaming through the front windows.

"Is this the enchanting young lady I saw you with at the Animas last evening?" Galloway smiled at Emily.

Instinctively, she bristled. The neatly combed blond hair and cultivated smile that made him handsome did nothing to alleviate the sense of unease he evoked.

Royle moved closer to Emily, but remained silent.

"You disappointed Mavis last night," Galloway said to Royle without a flicker in the hungry eyes devouring Emily.

"She was well compensated."

Sickened by the lascivious scrutiny and the topic of conversation, Emily turned away. They spoke of the woman like meat.

"Mavis fancies you, you know. Your open rejection humiliated her and hurt her reputation." Galloway edged closer to Emily. "Here Mavis had set aside the best part of the evening for you and you walked out on her. The poor woman was near tears."

"I'm sure she was. You probably had her next customer take her upstairs for a dose of comfort before I reached the door. What the hell do you want, Galloway?"

Galloway angled near Emily, who marked his approach with growing revulsion. She had never met a pimp and preferred to keep it that way.

"Mavis is sought after by every man who seeks companionship at the Crystal Palace. She's got a soft spot for you. I guess being bright when it comes to men isn't her strong suit."

"She's with *you*," Royle said evenly.

Galloway pretended not to hear. "I thought about you and that silver sniffing uncle of yours for a long time after you devastated poor Mavis. This is the first time in my memory you two haven't gone upstairs when you came into town. I wondered why. It didn't take long to figure out that you two have something else keeping you happy. But I couldn't figure it out. The woman I saw at dinner with you was much too refined. Or so I thought." He reached a curled finger toward Emily.

"Touch me, and I promise that you will regret it," she warned softly.

Galloway drew back, startled, then laughed. "My, you are a feisty one."

"One what?" Emily demanded, every sense alert.

"Tell you what, Tremaine. I know you're pulling out at the end of summer. Why not let me sample her for a night. I'll tell you what I think she's worth, then—"

Emily never saw the crashing blow that slammed Galloway into the wall beside the door. One minute he stood inches from her, the next he was flying across the room. Awed, she stared up at Royle, but he paid no attention.

"You touch her, and I'll kill you. She is not a whore and you are damn sure not going to make her one." A storm of conviction billowed through the ensuing silence. Neither man doubted that Royle meant his promise.

Blood streamed from Galloway's nose and the corner of his mouth. Dazed, sprawled half-sitting, half-lying against the wall, he merely blinked.

Royle slapped a coin on the counter and pulled the packet of salicylic acid from the druggist's hands. "Let's go."

Emily found her feet and her voice at the same time. "Whatever you say, Cousin Royle."

Galloway groaned. "Cousin my—"

In a flash, Royle hoisted Galloway several inches by the lapels. "Finish it, and you'll never get off this floor by yourself."

"You'll pay for this, Tremaine," Galloway hissed, wiping the blood from his nose with the back of his hand.

Shaken by the swiftness of Royle's reflexes and the depth of his defenses where she was concerned, Emily quickly left the store. Before she had taken two steps on the boardwalk, Royle's hand closed around her upper arm.

"Let's get something to eat. I'm starved."

Emily stared at Royle as he propelled them toward the nearest restaurant.

"Good grief. You enjoyed hitting him." The realization was out before she had time to consider it.

"Damn right I did. Don't you understand what he was implying?"

The entire encounter had taken place so fast that she was still digesting that Royle had not bedded someone named Mavis. Given his intent when they arrived, she did not understand what had stopped him. Of course, the number of saloons and brothels lining the Silverton streets offered plenty of variety. Perhaps he had found what he sought in one of them.

"I, uh, gather he wanted my *companionship* for the night as a test run." The scene rushed to the forefront of her memory. A shiver of revulsion rode her spine. "Of course, I would have refused. I have no tolerance for two-legged slime."

Royle stopped in his tracks.

Emily took an extra step. His hold on her arm dragged her back. The dark angel had fire in his eyes and judgment etched into his scowl.

"You would have refused." It was a statement, a command so softly spoken that it summoned the shiver back to her spine.

Emily nodded. "I'm a nonviolent person. I believe in physical confrontation only as a last resort."

"Are you complaining because I hit him? He wants to buy you, Emily. Like a mule or a horse. When he's done riding you, he'll rent you out." The urgency of his conviction tightened his hold on her upper arm.

"You didn't let me finish."

"Finish."

"I was glad you hit him, and I don't know what to think about that. I know exactly what he wanted . . . what he implied about you and Teigue and me. Teigue would never . . . I mean, he's like my father. A real father." Lost in the maelstrom of explaining what defied words at the moment, she lowered her head.

"That makes me your cousin," he spat.

She could not look at him and lie. Head shaking, she flexed her arm and felt his fingers loosen. "Would you rather be my brother?"

Royle swore under his breath and started for the restaurant. "You stay with me or Teigue. Galloway fancies you. Nothing good comes to anyone he draws around him."

"Like Mavis?" The question popped out of nowhere. Her curiosity gnawed at the fringes of reason and good taste.

Royle shrugged. "Mavis started working for him when she was seventeen. That was three years ago. They've been hard years. She'd be better off marrying a miner and swinging a pick. Her heart isn't in the saloon."

"Is that why you didn't, well, you know."

"My motives and activities are none of your business. You're Teigue's partner. Not mine."

Emily entered a restaurant filled with miners. A sudden lull in the level of conversation broke when they sat at a table.

She wasn't Royle's partner. The trouble was, she wanted to be in ways that could only result in pain. Here and in the confines of the cabin, Royle was a man apart from the rest of the occupants. Sadly, Emily bowed to his need for distance as insulation.

"Thank you," she murmured, daring to meet his intense gaze rife with swirling conflict.

"For what?"

"Coming to my defense. Since my mother's death, you're the first person who has intervened on my behalf."

They gazed at each other for a long moment before Royle turned away. "You're welcome. I would have done it for any woman. Galloway is scum."

A slow smile curled Emily's mouth. "I know. Will he seek revenge? I'm sure you broke his nose."

"Without a doubt, but against me, not you, which is the way I want it. Besides, I don't plan on staying in town long enough for his henchmen to come after me."

Lost in the battle of ideals raging inside, Emily stared at him. Recalling the swiftness with which Royle had deliv-

ered the smashing blow that sent John Galloway sprawling
created a giddy sensation bordering on light-headedness.
While Royle professed that he'd defend any woman from
John Galloway, she wondered if he'd do so with such zeal.
Maybe not. Maybe, just maybe, he considered her a little
more special.

Conversely, the ferocity of Royle's actions should be re-
pugnant. She detested violence. Didn't she? Of course, but
she couldn't muster the disapproval to dampen the thrill of
having him defend her that made her want to laugh and hug
the whole world.

Reluctantly, she admitted that the realities of her present
world challenged the opinions and views formed in a very
different and more benign circumstances. The resulting di-
chotomy wasn't nearly as threatening as her tender emotions for Royle. She gathered the tattered edges of a
protective cloak around her heart. If the winds of love kept
still, she might survive the summer and Royle's departure
without her heart shattering.

She didn't believe it.

Chapter 13

Emily GRIPPED THE saddle horn and glanced over her shoulder. A sigh of relief escaped her when Silverton disappeared beyond the mountain. Two days in town had heightened her appreciation of the open expanses and high mountain vistas.

She rode beside the wagons where the road width permitted. The wind whispered of freedom in the tall peaks. The cadence of wagon wheels, harnesses, and snorting mules forged a hypnotic effect.

As usual, her thoughts strayed to Royle. She pondered his fate once he realized the false promise of the dream he pursued relentlessly. Or was it false? Could it be that he was the one who saw things clearly?

On one hand, she commended his determination to regain his ancestral home and lands. On the other, she believed the title of the old Thomas Wolfe novel, *You Can't Go Home Again.* Not after seventeen years. Not after a war that had shredded the fabric of the past. Not after all those who made the past worth remembering were dead.

None of that mattered to Royle. His loyalty commingled with a peculiar kind of survivor's guilt. The combination forced him to try to resuscitate the proud Tremaine traditions claimed by a war that had nearly destroyed the country. It was his way of justifying his existence and honoring his family.

Under different circumstances she would not fight as hard against the tide of emotion sweeping through her. Head bowed, she longed for the detachment that had come easily in her old life. Countless times she had stood alone in a crowded room and honed those defenses against involvement. She affected no one and no one affected her. By being whatever the moment called for, she owned her emotions and controlled the level of involvement that might put her at risk. In this time and place, everything seemed at risk—most of all, her heart. Yet even knowing Royle would not bend, she could not keep herself from caring.

A shot rang out. Emily straightened in the saddle. The sharp crack reverberated against the mountains.

Her gaze darted from Royle on the lead wagon to Teigue driving the second one. Both fought the mules to a standstill and shouted conflicting orders. A second shot roared from the slope on her right. The bullet splintered the top board of the second ore wagon.

The horse danced nervously under her. Emily gained control, then let him run a short distance toward a snag of deadfall. She leaped from the saddle and wrapped the reins around a skeletal branch.

Frightened, she scrambled out of the horse's stomping range and found shelter amid a snarl of weathered gray-white trunks. Only then did she search for Teigue and Royle.

Rifle in hand, Teigue darted toward her. The barrel of his rifle flashed each time his hand pumped the lever, sending another round into the cartridge chamber. The boom of each report blasted her ears.

Teigue dropped down beside her. "Are you all right, Sunshine?"

"What's happening? What's going on? Why are people firing guns at us?"

A big hand covered her head and pushed her below the weathered snarl of trees. "Keep down. Goddamn bushwhackers'll shoot you if you don't."

"Bushwhackers?" *Bushwhackers? Like in a movie?* Another shot sent rocks splintering over her head. Not like in a movie or book. "Why? What do they want?"

"Beats the hell out of me. We're not carrying silver. Just supplies."

Horrified, she peeked between her arms and saw Teigue take aim, then fire. The rifle report sent her hands over her ears. Her entire body cringed in revulsion and fear. A barrage of shots filled the air. Emily shrank into a smaller and smaller ball wedged against the protection of the tree trunks. Much as she wanted to deny someone was trying to kill them, she hoped Teigue's marksmanship proved better. The crashing reality of being targeted by an invisible enemy filled her with an almost paralyzing fear.

A sudden, absolute silence descended. Nothing but the echoes of rifle fire filled her head. Slowly, Emily removed her fists from her ears and lifted her head.

Teigue scanned the slope above from the top of his rifle. His fingers busily loaded cartridges into the chamber.

"Keep your head down. I'm moving up a piece for a better look."

"Oh, please, Teigue, stay here where they can't shoot you."

"I don't plan on them shooting me. I'm going to shoot those bushwhacking vermin."

In a panic Emily lunged for him, but he was already moving away.

Half a dozen shots rang out, sending her cowering into the protective niche of the deadfall.

"Teigue!"

A groan leaked through the terror enveloping her.

Teigue.

Forcing herself into motion, she stretched her neck high
enough for a view of the jumble of rocks piled among
bleached, broken tree limbs. Six feet beyond the safety of
her deadfall, Teigue lay sprawled at an odd angle. His
hands groped for the rifle near his head. A dark circle grew
on the thigh of his heavy trousers.

"Teigue," she breathed, horrified, angry. "Dear God in
heaven, I've got to get him before they start shooting
again."

Without thought of the danger, Emily surged from the
safety of the deadfall and scrambled toward Teigue.

A bullet splintered a limb two feet away. She caught
Teigue under the arms. With a desperate strength, she
dragged him to shelter. Instinctively, she reached out and
snagged his rifle by the barrel.

"Don't you die on me," she seethed, pulling him against
the base of the old tree.

"I'm not going to die from a bullet in the leg." He gathered his hands behind him and tried to push up. Each movement sent a fresh surge of blood welling onto his trousers.
The overflow seeped into the thirsty rocks. "Gimme my
rifle and quit crying."

"I'm not crying." But she was. Tears flowed down her
cheeks like sheets of rain. She brushed them aside and
turned the rifle around.

From high on the slope came another barrage of rifle
fire. This time, none of the bullets struck close.

"Help me sit up. I can't protect us from down here."

Not knowing what else to do, Emily propped him against
a branch. Fists clenched in denial, she stared at his leg for a
long moment. When she lifted her eyes, perspiration dampened his shirt at the arms and neck. A flash of sheer terror
burst through her.

Nausea welled up from her stomach. The bullet had
ripped through the fleshy part of Teigue's right thigh.

She pulled off her sweatshirt, removed her tee shirt, then
pulled the sweatshirt on again. The soft cotton tee shirt
made the perfect bandage. She wrapped it around his thigh

and tied it in place. Within minutes the white dressing had turned blood-red.

What little she knew about first aid promised that the bullet had not struck a major artery. She would be able to tell, wouldn't she? Blood would be spurting with his every heartbeat.

"We have to get you back to town. You're losing too much blood."

"I'll go. Soon as Royle gets here."

"When? When will he get here?" Frantic, she scanned their surroundings. Royle was nowhere in sight. Teigue might bleed to death if she couldn't stanch the flow. Determined to keep him alive, she retied the bandage and tucked the knot against the upper part of the wound. Helpless in more ways than she thought possible, her trembling hands curled against her thighs.

"He'll join us after he takes care of what's up there."

"Oh, God! He went up there? With men firing down . . ." She couldn't finish. Eyes closed, she envisioned a hundred guns trained on Royle and blazing at point-blank range. The pacifist in her cried out for reason. Her stomach heaved with nausea.

"C-can't we just surrender or negotiate? Call a truce and give them what they want?"

"Maybe where you come from, but not here." Teigue swayed, then squeezed his eyes closed and shook his head. "You can't surrender. They'll take all we have, kill me and Royle, rape you until they're tired, then kill you, too."

The absoluteness of their fate struck her with the force of a physical blow. It couldn't end like this? Could it?

"If they get Royle . . ." His voice trailed as the barrel of his rifle dipped.

"Teigue. Stay with me." If he slipped into unconsciousness, she'd never get him into the wagon or on Royle's horse.

"Yeah. I'm here. Stay alive, Sunshine. No matter what you have to do." The rifle slipped from his hands. Like a fish out of water, he groped for the weapon in all the wrong places.

Emily's heart plummeted to her toes. Teigue had passed out. She was alone.

Three shots rang out in the tall trees.

"Please stay safe, Royle," she whispered. "Please, dear God, don't let us die out here." She sniffed and wiped her tears on her sleeves.

A fierce resolve seized her. She couldn't wait for Royle to save them. He might not come, or at least not in time. Gazing at Teigue, she felt the urgent, frightening responsibility of protecting him. Dry-eyed and determined, she picked up Teigue's rifle. The cool steel and polished wooden stock felt oddly reassuring. She positioned the weapon in the same manner Teigue had earlier. Closing her left eye, she aligned the sights and slid her finger over the trigger.

She waited, watching the bushes beyond the deadfall for the smallest movement. What felt like hours crawled by. Anxious, helpless, she checked on Teigue frequently. The lines around his mouth and eyes deepened with the absence of color. His slack lips pressed together in a grim line framed by a white ring. Twice, he roused, mumbled something incomprehensible, then slipped into the fretful place that allowed neither rest nor wakefulness.

Gradually the mountains resumed the patterns of life and sound. The mules grew restive in their traces. The clank of harnesses emphasized their unease. Birds bickered over territory in the trees. All the while, Emily watched and listened for the telltale sound of her unseen enemy to punctuate Teigue's steady breathing.

When the brush moved, a wave of perspiration broke her skin. Her heart slowed to a near-stop. No one would get to Teigue. No one.

She raised the rifle and aligned the sights on the spot where the bushes had moved. The well-oiled trigger responded easily under the pressure of her finger. The kick of the rifle slammed into her shoulder, nearly toppling her. The bullet struck high and to the right of her target. Rock splintered in all directions.

"Damnit, Teigue!"

She concentrated on sending another round into the chamber.

"It's me. Royle."

It didn't sound like Royle.

She took aim at the movement in the bushes and held her position. "Show yourself."

The bushes parted. Royle sideslipped down the loose rock toward her. Everything in her froze. Royle. Alive. Uninjured. She closed her eyes with a silent prayer of thanks.

Once within reach, she felt the rifle wrenched from her hands.

"Are you trying to kill me?"

Any response caught in her dry throat. Relief blended with worry, but no time existed to indulge either. She focused on Teigue and ignored Royle's vehement curses.

Teigue reached out. She caught his hand and clutched it to her breast. "I'm here, Teigue."

"Madeline." The name exhaled with a whisper.

"Not yet, Teigue. Not yet. Stay with me." The plaintive entreaty coaxed his eyes open.

Royle hunkered down beside them. "Scoot out of the way and watch his head."

Obediently, she complied.

Royle lifted Teigue. "Bring the rifles."

Again, she obeyed. The insulation mechanism switched on. Like a welcome blanket, the familiar state detached her reason from the encumbrance of emotion. Whatever Royle ordered in his clipped, harsh voice, she did without question.

Finally, she climbed into the back of the ore wagon and made Teigue as comfortable as possible.

Royle paced at the foot of Teigue's bed at the Silverton Hotel. Neither Emily nor Teigue had moved since she had positioned a chair beside the bed and enfolded Teigue's hand in her bloodstained fingers. With all the animation of a statue, she focused her concentration on Teigue. Her love for him lay bare for the world to see.

Royle turned away. Would any woman ever love him so completely? He doubted it.

Unbidden, his gaze traced the lines in Teigue's pallid face. Eighteen years Royle's senior, Teigue emanated a serenity Royle envied. Royle doubted that he would ever know such peace and acceptance. Too much anger smoldered in his heart.

At the end of his pacing run, he turned and paused. Emily appeared to be an extension of Teigue. Certainly the bond between them cemented their destiny. Teigue might believe Emily would marry and follow her husband wherever he went. But, watching her, feeling the palpable depths of her grief expand until it filled the entire room, Royle knew whoever she married would have to accept Teigue as part of their lives. She wouldn't leave her adopted father.

The realization saddened and satisfied him in ways that defied comprehension. He closed his eyes and imagined Emily and Teigue aging with the passage of time. If she never married, what would she do when Teigue joined Madeline?

Selfishly, Royle hoped she remained single. The thought of any man unlocking her heart and receiving the reward of her affection and devotion filled him with angst. Guilt fell heavily on his shoulders. What a selfish man he was. Just because he wanted her and couldn't have her didn't justify isolating her. The passion he had tasted at the spring deserved the joy of fulfillment. A woman who responded so eagerly should have a man. And children. *Children*. . . . The air in the room grew thick and made breathing difficult.

The door opened. Royle glanced over at Dr. Allan Bird, a golden-haired man who viewed the world through wire-rimmed glasses perched on a straight nose.

"The laudanum will make him sleep for the rest of the day. You won't be taking him home for a couple of weeks, though." Dr. Bird lifted the blanket and checked the dressing on Teigue's thigh.

Despite Dr. Bird's assurances that Teigue would recover, Royle worried.

"Sheriff Thorniley wants to talk with you," Dr. Bird told Royle.

"I'm not leaving." He glanced at Emily. Although physically present, she seemed more distant than England. "I don't want them alone. Emily . . . needs someone here. She's been through a terrible scare."

Dr. Bird lowered his voice and raised his hand toward the statue-still woman in the chair. "She worries me more than your uncle. I can treat the body with a high degree of certainty, but there isn't anything wrong with her body."

Royle shook his head. Hearing Dr. Bird express the worry ravaging his mind gave it a bleak validity.

Emily abhorred guns. She had never missed an opportunity to castigate his love of them. Yet she had armed herself in defense of Teigue. Sadly, Royle knew she would not have considered aiming a rifle at anyone in her defense. What had the act of defying her convictions cost her? "Thorniley will have to come here."

Dr. Bird straightened the blanket and jerked his head toward the door. "That's what I told him. He's waiting outside. Go. I'll stay with them while you two talk."

Royle nodded his appreciation, then went into the hall to speak with the lawman. In cryptic brevity, he described where they had been bushwhacked and the location of the three men he shot in the timberline.

"You're lucky they didn't ambush you when you came into town," Thorniley mused.

Royle spoke with John Thorniley for a few minutes before receiving assurances that Thorniley's men would bring the second ore wagon into town.

The night was old enough for a semblance of quiet to descend upon the town when Royle quit pacing and dragged a chair beside Emily's. He wiped dried tear traces, dirt smudges, and blood from her face with a tepid, damp cloth. The warmth of her skin defied the detachment in her eyes.

He cupped her chin and drew her face away from Teigue. "He'll be all right, Emily. The laudanum is making him sleep."

As if the words sparked something inside her, a great sorrow seeped into her vacant expression. The glimpse into the pit of her grief sent a wave of tenderness through him.

As quickly as the emotion shone in her eyes, it vanished. She turned her head back to watch Teigue sleep.

Frustrated, he cupped her chin again and held it until she looked up at him. "Talk to me, Emily. Tell me what happened."

Her mouth opened, then closed. Turmoil clouded her eyes and twisted his heart. Again, she lifted her chin free. This time she lowered her head and stared at her blood-smudged hands. Dried, rusty brown patches flaked off the back of her hand when she moved her thumb over Teigue's clean knuckles.

"They shot him. I didn't know what to do, except bring him into my hiding place." She lifted a blood-flaked hand. "I'm such a coward." Fingers splayed, she turned her palm up, then over. "This is Teigue's blood."

"A coward would not have risked pulling him to safety. Those outlaws would have shot him again if you had cowered in the logs. Maybe killed him outright."

She remained silent. The tremor of revilement that shook her reached into the core of him.

"It took a great deal of courage to do what you did, Emily." He caressed her cheek and ran his thumb along the faint shadow beneath her left eye. "It took even more to pick up the rifle and defend him."

Almost imperceptibly, her head shook. "I couldn't even do that right. I tried to kill you."

"Not very hard, or I would have been dead at that range." Her entire body trembled, then stilled.

Royle cursed himself as six kinds of a fool. He wasn't good at this sort of thing. She needed reassurance and soft words of understanding foreign to the harsh life of a miner.

At a loss, he watched her examine her hand.

"I picked up his gun and waited. And waited. At first, I was so scared. Then it went away. I wasn't afraid anymore. I just waited for a sign. With every fiber in me, I wanted to kill whatever moved because they'd shot Teigue. I wasn't going to let them do it again."

Royle felt his throat go dry. Damn, if she had had any idea of how to use a rifle, he *would* be dead. He knew the feeling she described. Too well.

"They won't shoot at us again," he promised in a whisper.

"Did you kill them?"

"Yes." Braced for a tirade condemning violence, he tensed. When she continued staring at her hands without comment, his worry heightened. This was not like Emily. Where was her spirited argument? Her condemnation? The lecture about violence begetting violence?

"Emily?"

"Hmmmm?"

"I killed them. All three of them are dead."

"I heard you." Her dirty fingers gripped her thighs above her knees. "Teigue said they would kill us. I believed him."

"They would have."

She nodded. "Then there wasn't a choice, was there?"

"No." Her unnatural calm reminded him of the center of a great storm. Not for a moment did he believe she had achieved as deep a level of acceptance as she exuded.

He cupped her face and forced her to look at him. "Teigue is going to be fine. Dr. Bird said it isn't unusual for people who lose as much blood as he did to pass out."

"Shock."

"Shock?"

"That's what it is called. He was perspiring but his skin was cool . . . too cool. The shock could have killed him, Royle. Not just the bullet."

He wanted to ask how she knew that and did not doubt she spoke the truth. The authority of her soft explanation added to the mystery surrounding her.

He set his curiosity aside. Now was not the time. "Let me wash you up."

"Do you know how short life is?" Her head tilted in the cradle of his hands.

A ripple of dread coursed down his arms. "Shorter for some than others."

"And when you die, you lose the final chance of changing anything. I've made so many changes lately. I'm tired of them. . . ." Her voice trailed. Long lashes swept over her eyes that now appeared hazel instead of green. "I don't even know what to change, or how, anymore." She tugged at his wrist and freed her face to gaze upon Teigue. "Teigue knows. Other than my mother, he's the only person who's accepted me for me. I don't have to be anything . . . anyone . . . I can love him without fear I won't measure up . . . I don't have to earn it. It's the greatest gift I've ever received."

Royle didn't move a muscle. Never had he seen so far or so clearly into another soul. In truth, he doubted he knew his own that well. He braced his foot against the mattress support. "Come here, Emily."

She continued watching the steady rise and fall of Teigue's chest and did not move.

Royle gathered her by the shoulders and turned her until her back rested against his chest. "I love him, too. We'll watch over him together."

As though he had uttered magic words, he felt some of the tension ease from her. She relaxed against him and laced her fingers through his when his arms came around her. "You're not alone," he whispered in her ear.

Emily heaved a sigh.

Her fragile show of trust tugged at Royle. He felt the blend of sorrow, loss, and joy vie for recognition.

Together, they waited for Teigue to awaken.

Chapter 14

"IT HURTS LIKE hell, and it isn't going to stop for a day or so," Teigue told Emily the next afternoon. "You've been here too long. And you look as bad as I feel with this laudanum haze in my head. Take Royle and go eat something. Order a hot bath."

Emily's fragile emotions had no idea of where to find shelter. Since waking early this morning, Teigue rallied hourly. The hearty breakfast she had insisted he eat had vanished without a protest. Although glad Teigue sounded like his robust self, she couldn't help feeling rejected. "I'll stick around. You might need something."

"I do. Privacy and a chamber pot."

"Oh." Emily stood. The long bedside vigil had allowed tension to settle in her legs. She stretched, then bent and placed a kiss on Teigue's whisker-stubbled cheek. "I'll go. But I'll be back soon."

"Doc Bird will be by around two o'clock." Royle

moved the chairs away from the bedside. "No walking around until he gets here."

"Right. Meanwhile, I want you to make her eat and rest." Teigue's commanding tone sounded stronger than he appeared.

"Sure. I'll drag her to the café and tie her to a chair."

"Do that if you have to."

Emily's stomach lurched with the tenderness of Teigue's brown eyes watching her every move. "Don't worry. I can—"

"Take care of myself," Teigue finished. "I know you can, Sunshine, but I'd feel a hell of a lot better if you let Royle do that for now. Those bushwhackers may have had friends in town."

Royle opened the top drawer of the bureau and withdrew a pistol. After checking the load, he handed it to Teigue. "You're right."

Dread sent Emily's heart racing. "We shouldn't leave you alone. What if someone comes? What if—"

"He'll be fine." Royle caught her by the shoulders, forcing her to look up into his patient blue eyes. "What could you do if they did?"

"I . . . something . . ." What could she do? Nothing. Scream?

"Would you shoot them?"

"I . . ." She swallowed hard as the truth burst into her mind with rare clarity. The sharp edge of mortality honed itself on the strop of her fear of losing Teigue or Royle to a nameless enemy. "Yes," she whispered. "I wouldn't let anyone hurt him."

"I believe you. We'll buy a gun for you after we eat. When we get home, I'll teach you to shoot."

Although he made it sound cut and dried, the sorrow in his smile acknowledged the loss of innocence stripped from her in the mountain pass. Silently, she bowed to yet another change in her character. For the moment, she wouldn't think about that. Later, when she was alone, she would sort out how the rigors of this time challenged each of the tenets she had embraced so readily in another age. Already, the insulating layers had dissolved.

"Royle, you take her home tomorrow. I'll be fine here." Teigue slipped the pistol under the quilts.

"But I can't leave you while you're hurt. Who will take care of you. Who will—"

"I'll get along fine. I'll stay with Allan and let his sister Nelda dote on me."

Emily crumbled inside.

Teigue patted a space on the bed, then offered his hand. A meaningful look at Royle sent the younger man from the room.

Dejected, Emily sat beside Teigue. Without thinking, she entwined his hand in both of hers. "Why do you want to send me away? I'd really like to stay and help until you're on your feet."

"If you stay, Royle will stay. If Royle stays, there will be trouble."

"What kind of trouble?"

"Trouble that revolves around you, Sunshine. Royle knows that Galloway isn't a man who gives up on what he wants easily. He made it pretty clear the other day that he wants you. Royle also made it pretty clear the answer is no. That won't stop Galloway. He's likely to see it as a challenge. I doubt he'll let Royle throw the first punch next time, either.

"It is best for the two of you to leave. Give me a few weeks, say until around Independence Day. Silverton will be jumping. The railroad might be through or close enough to celebrate. Some of these miners will kick their heels up for anything and do it twice if they can."

She understood Galloway and the potential for trouble better than Teigue realized. Considering the way Royle had defended her honor at the pharmacy, she had no doubt that he'd do it again. Recalling the incident, the speed of his wrath still amazed her.

"But you—"

"Will be fine, Sunshine. Nelda Bird runs a boarding house and caters to us birds with broken wings."

In spite of herself, Emily smiled. She knew defeat when it stared her in the eye. "We'll do it your way. If I stayed, you and Royle would be miserable, wouldn't you?"

"Yeah. I'd feel more helpless than I do now if something happened between Royle and Galloway."

"I understand Galloway's type. That's why I'll bow to your wishes, Teigue. Men like him don't get mad, they get even."

Teigue nodded and wrapped his free hand around hers. "You have the way of it, Emily. We aren't going to be here much longer, and Royle won't walk away from a fight. Maybe we can prevent it."

"You mean by me leaving tomorrow morning without a fuss." A genuine smile accompanied the shake of her head. "Teigue, I've been manipulated by the best. You're as transparent as window glass."

Teigue's chest puffed up. "Everything I said is true."

"It's what you haven't said that I'm interested in."

The flash of indignation melted into a grin. "I figure when you come back to Silverton, you two will either be fast friends or bitter enemies. I'm counting on the first. Royle needs a friend."

"Royle needs more than a friend." So did she. She needed Royle in a way that defied understanding. Worse, she wanted him physically and emotionally. The lethal combination promised disaster.

Keeping her distance would be nearly impossible with just the two of them at the cabin and in the mine. Could she do it? "I don't know, Teigue."

The squeeze on her hand forced her out of her speculation. "I think you do, Sunshine."

The weight of the supplies in the ore wagon did little to soften the bumpy ride. Riding beside Royle, Emily felt every rock and rut vibrate from the wooden seat to her backside. Royle had insisted upon tethering the horse to the wagon. Should any other mishap occur, he wanted Emily within protective reach.

Lost in the mire of events and the changes reshaping

her ideals, Emily stared at the rhythmic motion of the mules.

The vegetarian she had been since childhood had disappeared in a pot of venison stew. The convenience of grocery stores and restaurants allowed for preferences and choices. Here, the reality of eating the available fare had not only altered her diet, but her outlook on hunting. The irony smarted. The numerous causes she had supported for years would miss her contributions.

A muffled sound of resignation escaped her.

Two months earlier she had supported banning all guns from the public. Now, she owned a rifle and a pistol. Reconciling the needs of two very different times brought her up short. In the wild mountains of Colorado, there were no prisons to reform criminals or economic safety nets for the disadvantaged. Self-reliance reigned supreme.

"There is no such thing as a simple life," she mused.

"Were you looking for a simple life?"

Shrugging, she shook her head. "I guess you have to change with the times or they'll roll over you. That is about as simple as it gets."

Lost in speculation of the snowballing changes, Emily barely noticed Royle's return to the silence they had shared since leaving Teigue at Nelda Bird's boarding house. Her speculative mood held until they reached the cabin. The journey home required a fraction of the time with near-empty wagons on a more direct, yet hazardous trail.

The long shadows of evening chilled the air. Royle unloaded the supplies while Emily released the mules from their harnesses. Together, they groomed each mule. Even the role the animals filled commanded a fresh respect. Had she not seen it, she would never have believed the mules capable of hauling so much heavy ore such a distance.

She slapped the last mule on the rump and sent him into the pasture. After a routine cold-water cleanup on the porch, she entered the cabin.

Royle had started a fire, put on a pot of coffee, and

fetched water before helping her with the mules. The familiar aromas snapped the last of her introspection. Teigue's absence permeated the familiar room.

"Coffee?"

Startled, she whirled on her heel. In the glow of the lanterns, Royle's presence crashed on her with the force of a hurricane. The flickering shadows of the fire made his blue eyes gleam like sapphires. The elemental power he emanated reached into the core of her and ignited the pressurized fuel of desire.

What she wouldn't give for him to return the tender feelings she battled daily. Gazing into the enigmatic depths of his eyes, she abandoned the fight against the inevitable. She loved him. No amount of denial, distance, or defense supplanted her feelings. Long after he married Rebecca Weston in Virginia, he would hold a piece of her heart in the palm of his hand.

Acceptance loosened one shackle and clamped a second in place. Whether she loved him or not, he was engaged to another woman and would never be hers. To pursue him would cast her in the role of *the other woman* and him as a philanderer. She detested the analogy. Leo Kramer was a philanderer. Royle hardly fit the description. In his way, he fought the attraction as valiantly as she.

"I, ah, guess we ought to eat. . . ." Her voice trailed and her heart began hammering.

Royle closed the distance and gathered her against his chest. "Shhhh."

Emily rested her cheek against the soft flannel covering his chest. The pressure of his embrace felt like a cloak that shut out the world and all fickle measures of time. The rhythmic cadence of his heart against her ear beat out a promise of tenderness. In response, her love for him blossomed. He tried so hard to hold her at a distance, yet seemed to sense when she was struggling within herself. Unquestioning, he extended himself and offered what she needed.

For the moment, she ignored the *whys* and *wherefore*s. The last few days had warped enough of her life's structure. Content with the solace he offered, her arms locked loosely around his waist. The serenity seeping through her conjured the image of embracing the entire world.

She closed her eyes and reveled in the slow, side-to-side motion of his gentle rocking. Soon, the line where she left off and he began disappeared. Their heartbeats matched the sinuous sway that felt like a slow dance.

The soft stroke of his hand flowed along the side of her head and down the braid trapped by his arm. Without thinking, Emily kissed his chest, then nuzzled her cheek against his worn shirt covering a wall of muscle.

His jaw came to rest atop her head. "Sometimes you remind me of your Bambi."

Emily smiled, her arms tightening. "In that case, I'm glad you don't have your rifle in your hands."

He chuckled softly. "I'm afraid what I have in my hands is more dangerous than a rifle." As though to make a point, his fingers splayed, and his hands roamed her shoulders and down her back.

"Only for me." Eyes closed, she rubbed her cheek up and down, letting the peace settle into her soul and the simmering desire bubble through her veins.

"Emily," he breathed, summoning her.

Instinctively, she opened her eyes and lifted her face. The gentle brush of his lips on her forehead warmed her down to her toes. The simple kiss unleashed the hunger for the taste of his mouth and the excitement of his intimate touch everywhere on her body.

The measured pattern of lip brushes and kisses he bestowed lit miniature fires that raced downward and pooled in her breasts and lower abdomen. With a will of their own, her hands roamed the broad expanse of his back. Each foray fed her voracity.

"Why now?" he breathed.

Her lips parted as he traced them with the tip of his tongue.

"Why you?"

Before an answer formed, his mouth covered hers. The tension in his shoulders bespoke the tremendous control he exerted over his desire. The prodding of his rigid manhood against her belly answered her unspoken plea. Like an appetizer for her passion, his tongue swept into her mouth, deepening the kiss and feeding her desire. She savored the taste of him and encouraged more.

She stood on tiptoes and curled her fingers over the top of his shoulders. Stretched the full length of her body, she drew them closer. The reflexive thrust of his hips pressed his manhood urgently against her belly. A small sound of pleasure escaped her throat.

The kiss took on a purpose more essential than sunlight. The tide of passion churned the sands of need. Her love welcomed each wave. The rightness of being with him filled her body with hunger and excitement, and her heart with music.

The glide of his thumbs along the full sides of her breasts turned her nipples into pebbles burrowing into his chest. The erotic memories that had haunted her dreams since the intimacy they had shared at the spring promised a pleasure she craved. In the heated moments separate from the rest of the world, his body whispered the longings his mouth would never utter. Now, she listened with her heart in a place where truth refused silence.

His hands slid down her ribs and over her hips. The firm pulse of his fingers around her bottom matched the throb of his erection. She yielded to the relentless force evoking a response that built with the swelling tide of passion.

Unexpectedly, his big hands closed around her thighs and lifted her. The motion broke the kiss. A couple of steps brought them to the edge of the table, where he gently set her down. Still he held her legs around him. Her loins throbbed against his erection.

Astonished by the heated, almost violent hunger etching his granite face, Emily slipped her hands from around his shoulders. Watching him with a blend of love and awe for the wondrous sensations he created, she released a button on his shirt. With the tips of her fingers and short nails, she combed and explored the black, silken thatch peeking through the opening.

Pressing her lips against his chest, Emily inhaled the scent of his skin. Seeking more, she tasted him with the tip of her tongue all the while freeing one button after another until she reached the waistband of his pants. Undeterred, she released the trapped fabric and continued baring his torso.

The heat flowing from his flesh grew hotter than the radiant warmth of the fire. Caught up in the freedom of exploring him, she felt him tremble when she broadened the range of her wandering mouth across the hard nub of his nipple. Delighted, she gently closed her teeth and brushed the small bud with the tip of her tongue.

His sharp intake of breath conveyed his pleasure. For a moment longer, he allowed her to play. Emily let her love flow in each touch and caress. The language their bodies spoke transcended the barriers of mind and consequence.

As though he could stand no more, he caught her hands in his and placed them on his shoulders. Emily's face lifted with the expectant smile of a woman who enjoyed exploring the man she loved.

"Turnabout is fair play," he murmured, cupping her face in his palms. "First, kiss me."

The aching plea sent her arching against his naked chest, her mouth rising eagerly to unite them. Again, tension knotted the muscles in his shoulders. The gentle way he cherished her lips and the soft inside of her mouth belied the toll she felt his hunger extort. With effort, she tempered the demands screaming through her nerves. Her hands took on a will of their own. She could not stop touching him, moving deliberately along the contours of warm skin over muscle, sinew, and bone. The long, languid kiss whetted her appetite into a razor edge.

Just when he opened the buttons on her shirt, she had no idea. For an instant his finesse disappeared as he fumbled to open the front clasp on her bra.

He caressed her shoulders and eased her away. A small moan of disappointment rose in the back of Emily's throat. Even the scant separation seemed a deprivation of monumental proportion.

The callused pads of his fingertips traced the ledges of her collarbones with the lightness of a hummingbird's wing. Waves of gooseflesh stemming from his touch rippled down her body.

"Are you cold?"

Emily swallowed and shook her head.

A deep satisfaction softened the harsh lines need etched into his face. "You're beautiful, Emily. The most beautiful woman I've known. Not only your body." His right hand dipped over the top of her breast. "Here. In your heart. Watching you with Teigue, it seems you've been saving up all your love until you found someone worthy."

Emily's heart skipped a beat. How close to the mark his words hit. Yet, how wrong. Oh, she loved Teigue in a way she would never love anyone else. He was the father who wanted her, the one she had wanted all her life. But the woman's love blossoming inside belonged to Royle, whether he wanted it or not. Choice had never entered into it. She could no more choose not to love him than she could choose not to breathe.

"I envy the man who wins your heart and wish like hell it could be me."

Reality crashed on Emily like a bucket of water from an ice-melt spring. "You don't want my heart, do you?" The question, spoken with flat authority, stilled his hands.

"What I want and what I have to do are two different things."

Royle shook his head as his hands closed around her shoulders. Emily took his cue and drew back. "Only because you make them so." Her euphoric mood shattered. She unlocked her legs from around him and began fastening her clothing. All the while, she watched his eyes. Passion became anger, then disappointment and finally resignation. A distance that separated him from the rest of the world rose between them. Seeing the transformation saddened more than it angered her.

Royle picked his shirt up from the floor and pulled it on, not bothering to button it. "You didn't answer me."

"What?"

"Coffee?"

How could he shut himself off so easily? A sharp retort hung on the tip of her tongue. She drew a calming breath and slid off the edge of the table. "Yes, please, half a cup."

"Half?"

She snatched a bottle of whiskey from the shelf. "Yes. I have plans for the other half."

"Keep it handy. I'll join you, though I didn't know you imbibed harsh spirits."

"I'm a master at holding my share of liquor. Hostessing societal functions that bore me to tears has made me one." She opened the bottle and sat at the table.

"Do you want to eat with this?"

"No. Food will slow the effect I hope to achieve."

"Which is?"

"Royle, haven't you ever been so overwhelmed by events that you just wanted to get drunk and forget everything except the joy of getting rid of the hangover?"

Grinning, he nodded and sat across the table from her. "Look, what just happened . . . that wasn't fair of me." He shifted, trying to get comfortable. "If it's any consolation, I'll be paying for it for a while yet."

She filled her cup with whiskey and pushed the bottle toward him. "And I won't?"

"I could apologize." He tipped the bottle and topped off his coffee.

Emily drank half the cup of coffee-laced whiskey. "You wouldn't mean it, and it wouldn't matter to either one of us, except you'd have another lie to chalk up on your karma board."

"My what?"

Emily propped her elbow on the table and dropped her chin into her palm. "Never mind." With her free hand, she added more whiskey to her cup.

"You're right. I would be lying if I apologized for anything except stopping."

"Drop it." She needed no discussion to remind her how easily he could banish every qualm she possessed. All he had to do was take her in his arms and kiss her senseless. As long as he did not remind her, nothing mattered in the those moments. Not the consequences of not having any birth control. Not the fact that he was engaged to another woman. For those stolen moments of eternity, she could love him freely and accept his gift of tender passion that felt like love.

For a while, neither spoke. Royle brought the coffeepot and splashed flavor into each cup. They were halfway through the whiskey bottle before Emily's eyes lit with a triumphant gleam.

"Did your parents always do everything you expected them to do?"

Royle cocked his head and leaned back in his chair. His shirt slithered across his ribs. "No. They were my parents. They did what they thought was right."

"For whom?"

Royle shrugged. "For whomever they were concerned with at the time. Did yours always do what you expected?"

A serene smile lit her face and set her eyes twinkling. "Yes. Absolutely. One hundred percent of the time. My mother was a free spirit who did exactly what she wanted, when she wanted, where she wanted, and at any time she wanted. I never expected to come first, even though I know she loved me."

"I see," he drawled, reaching for his cup.

"You probably don't."

"And your father?"

Emily laughed and took another drink. "Ron never disappointed me. If you don't expect anything, you can't be disappointed. Unlike my mother, my father didn't love me and never made any pretense of emotion. He expected loyalty and duty, which I gave. However, if I had gone back, I'm sure I would have disappointed him."

"How?"

"He wanted me to marry a friend of his. Craig is about your age. He's been married four times, and would have been an advantageous business ally for my father. Craig found my financial assets far more interesting than my company." She poured more whiskey. "I made sure he didn't swoon over my scintillating wit and sophisticated banter. He made my skin itch with a burning desire for his absence."

"Where the hell are you from anyway? And what are you doing here?"

Emily started laughing into the cup braced on her lower lip. Although she could not resist Royle, he might find her as attractive as Typhoid Mary if he knew the truth. "You won't believe me if I tell you. You lack Teigue's ability to see people as they really are and trust your instincts. Logic makes a distorted mirror for viewing the world."

"So do lies."

"I've never lied to you, Royle, and I never will. I don't have room for it in the chaos I call a life."

"No? What about the hundred and fifty horses you claimed to—"

Emily's empty cup hit the table at the same time that her laughter erupted. "Chalk that up to a lack of knowledge of how to calculate engine horsepower. The speedometer went up to a hundred and fifty." Still laughing, she recalled her quick calculations. "I figured the horsepower was equivalent to the notches on the speedometer. Actually, I'd never driven it faster than a hundred out on the desert, so I don't know if my car could go a hundred and fifty miles an hour."

"You're drunk."

"Not yet, but soon. I hope." She poured more whiskey, then motioned the coffeepot away when he reached for it. "Where do I come from? A place just a little south of San Francisco. How did I get here? I haven't a clue."

"But you don't want to go back?"

The question sobered her. For all the changes swirling around her life, she wanted to stay. "To what? No, Royle." The sting of tears burned her eyes. "I've found something here I wouldn't trade for anything. When you go, Teigue and I will have each other. After you're gone, you're going to learn the definition of loneliness. Stubborn tenacity holds it at bay only so long. Your only hope is for you and Rebecca to fall madly in love and find happiness with one another. I wish that for you, Royle, with all my heart. I hope you find happiness in your marriage."

Royle folded his arms across his chest and rested his elbows on the table. "Would it matter?"

Not trusting her voice, Emily nodded.

"Why?"

She swallowed the lump in her throat with another swig of whiskey. "I like you, Royle. If you let yourself, I believe you have a great deal to offer a wife and family. I'd like to remember you as happy as opposed to, shall we say, an underachiever at marital bliss."

Royle chuckled. "An underachiever? Marital bliss? Isn't marital bliss an oxymoron in most cases?"

"Was it with your parents?"

"No," he admitted, "but their marriage was the exception. What about yours?"

Emily shrugged her left shoulder. "My parents spent a summer of free love in Golden Gate Park. They neither married nor saw one another again."

The mirth fled Royle's expression. After a moment, he leaned forward over the table. "I'm not drunk and neither are you. Yet. The things you say add up only to a point, then they don't make sense."

"That's because you're missing a critical fact."

"Which is?"

"I told you there was no future living in the past. Those words came from a country-western song. You don't know about country-western because it doesn't exist yet.

"Get that second bottle, Royle. I'm going to tell you who I am and where I come from. You'll either believe it or not. Your inability to accept it won't change what is, though it will undoubtedly change the way you look at me."

Emily watched him open the second bottle of whiskey. When she finished the story and the last drop of whiskey, she would not have to worry about keeping Royle at a distance. He would do it himself.

Chapter 15

SHE WAS WRONG.

Each time Royle buried the pick in the silver vein, his pounding head pleaded for mercy. Through the hammering, the tale Emily had spun last night echoed with abysmal clarity. Over a second bottle of whiskey, she had woven a story as intriguing and far-fetched as *Gulliver's Travels.*

He had listened as she matched him drink for drink. The longer she talked, the more convincing she sounded, and the faster he drank. She ended her outrageous tale at about the same time they polished off the second bottle. He hadn't said a word, hadn't known what to say. Long after she retired, he sat at the table staring at the empty bottles and wondering how he had come to share his cabin with a demented woman.

His instincts had been right the day she arrived. She was dangerous. Crazy. What more proof did he need beyond her fantastic tale of being from the future? Only a madwoman claimed such absurdity as truth.

Adding injury to the insult, she had been disgustingly bright-eyed and chipper all day. Much as he hated admitting it, Emily had drunk him under the table last night and held her liquor better than any man he knew.

She was an enigma. At times, she conveyed a sophistication that made him marvel. The scant insight she afforded into her life before she arrived at the cabin had intrigued him, though he would not ask her to elaborate. Not now. She swore she had never lied to him, then related a whopping fabrication too outrageous for credence even in his inebriated state.

She responded to his touch and kiss with the hunger of an experienced woman anticipating the ecstasy sure to accompany their joining. How did a woman who had never made love know so much? Not once had he sensed fear or the inhibition he associated with a virgin.

Even though Royle did not believe her story, he knew Emily believed every word she had spoken. And he believed that Teigue had accepted her story as gospel and never questioned the validity or wisdom it defied. What he could not fathom was why. Teigue was a discerning man and an excellent judge of character. Either she had duped him or . . .

Royle shook his aching head. Although none of her explanations of the life she had once led deserved credence, he could not bring himself to completely disbelieve her. If he considered her actions and reactions in context with her story . . . He could almost believe she came from another time. Hadn't she gawked at Silverton as though she had never seen a mining town? Hadn't she watched people like a hawk, then mimicked their actions? Why hadn't she known how improper it was for her to appear on the streets in her trousers instead of the dress he bought? And why was she always talking about things he hadn't heard of, like "IRAs" and "retirement funds" for Teigue?

He tossed chunks of ore into the cart.

Money.

She had coerced an exorbitant wage from him, with Teigue's help. Only after reading the collection of newspapers had she tried modifying their deal. The woman had a conscience. At least about money. Not about lying. Or was she lying?

Her heart did not lie. She loved Teigue like a father, perhaps as much as he loved Teigue. The difference was that she would remain with Teigue. Her devotion defied question. When she had thought they were grubbing for a living, she had offered the gold strike.

To some, giving up that much gold to ensure a man's last years were free of financial worry might seem crazy. Not to Royle. The magnitude of her generosity had corkscrewed her deeper into his affections. That lay at the root of his trouble. He craved a woman he had no business caring for, in ways that defied definition. Offensive suspicion had not provided the safe distance he needed for protection. She had proven too open and good-hearted. Silence had failed. Her ways of challenging him into a response with some outlandish statement saw to that.

Royle grabbed the pick and swung it hard. Rock splintered in all directions. A shard grazed his throbbing temple. The sting blended into his headache.

"You're bleeding," Emily said, offering him the canteen.

He kept working. It was his headache, his blood, and he was going to enjoy every throb and drop. He had earned it. Deserved it for trying to match the self-professed time-traveling socialite drink for drink.

"Are you going to teach me to shoot this afternoon?"

His entire body shuddered. The pick wobbled at the top of his swing. Was she out of her mind?

Of course she was. She thought she was from the future and painted an elaborate tale he denied more easily than she could prove.

"Tomorrow." Tomorrow, he would teach her to shoot. Today the noise would kill him, if she didn't with a misfire.

He stole a glance at her.

She appeared so normal. She had fooled him for over six weeks.

The notion of putting a rifle or pistol in her hands gave him pause. Which was worse? Arming a crazy woman or leaving her vulnerable to the intruder who had wandered outside the cabin while she bathed?

Life had been simple before Emily's arrival. Now, even suffering the effects of too much whiskey in peace eluded him.

"Why are you suddenly eager to learn how to use a gun?"

"For the obvious reasons. Protection." She hung the canteen on the corner timber of the ore cart. "Besides, once you're satisfied I can protect myself, we'll both have a little more freedom."

"Freedom. That's very important to you."

"Yes," she answered softly, checking a rock in the lantern light. "More so all the time."

"And if you had all the freedom you wanted, what would you do?"

"At the moment?" Crouched to sort through the rocks piled at Royle's feet, she glanced up. Her eyes sparkled in the lantern light and banished Royle's headache for several heartbeats. Peering into their depths, he saw a truth that contorted his logic and rendered his defenses useless.

"At the moment," he agreed.

The same hunger for the joy of making love to her that had nearly consumed them last evening flashed through Royle. Seeing it reflected in her eyes, he tightened his fingers on the pick handle to keep from reaching for her.

Emily lowered her head and resumed the task of sorting ore. "I'd return to the cabin and finish putting things away while dinner cooked. Meanwhile, you could go soak in the hot spring. It would do your head good."

Sympathy replaced the desire he had seen earlier when she glanced up again.

"Forget dinner. We'll both go to the hot spring." Royle leaned the pick against the wall before realizing the consequences of being in the warm pool with her. Unbidden, images of their last watery encounter rippled through his mind. The physical anticipation of holding her smooth, naked body against him incited a throbbing that had nothing in common with his headache. His fingers tingled with the memory of molding her breasts in his hands and the delight of her nipples hardening in his fingertips.

"Tempting, but not a good idea, Royle. Tonight, we need to eat, not drink." Quickly, she stood and dropped her booty of rocks into the cart.

Royle wrapped an arm around her waist and drew her hard against him. Desire burned unmercifully in his loins. Her fingers trembled as she grasped his shoulders. The crush of her breasts against his abdomen evoked a wild pleasure. He thrust his knee between her legs. The heat of her rode up his thigh as he drew her into a tight embrace.

"Which—which one of us is crazier?" she asked in a hushed whisper.

He cradled the back of her head in his hand and drew her against his shoulder. "Did you tell me that story last night so I would think you were crazy and pretend we didn't want each other?"

"No. I told you because it's true. I had to tell you who I am and where I come from." Her fingers dug into his shoulders.

"You believe you're from the future?"

"I am, Royle. Just as you know your future doesn't include anything outside of reestablishing the Tremaine dynasty in Virginia."

Royle's good sense flooded him with reality. Damn. With so much at stake, he had to use his head. Maybe he was crazy for wanting her more than he had thought it possible to want a woman. What the hell was he doing? It was one thing to make love with her when he thought her in full control of her faculties. It was quite another to indulge his passion with a woman who lacked a firm grasp on reality.

He released her. An emptiness of need, deeper than the physical, washed through him. "Right now, it's a bit difficult to decide which one of us is more deranged."

Visibly shaken, Emily straightened, keeping her eyes averted. "Let's finish up and go home. A decent meal might return some clarity to your head."

Oddly, his headache had vanished. Considering the state of his body burning with need and the strange sense of loss permeating his mind, he preferred the anesthesia of the headache.

He tucked a finger under her chin. "That, I believe."

"You have a natural marksmanship ability." Royle loaded the pistol. He had doubted that he could teach her to shoot the rifle without touching her. Part of him had hoped she needed close instruction. That part found disappointment in her quick learning and sharp eye.

"I still despise guns. I've merely accepted that they are necessary here." She opened the breech of the carbine and checked the chamber. Satisfied it was empty, she exchanged the empty rifle for the loaded pistol.

The Colt felt like compact death. Royle's explanation of the lethal abilities of each weapon promised that the rifle was the more dangerous of the two.

"A pistol is personal," she mused, reflecting the range of each weapon.

"All guns are personal." Royle examined the rifle and set it aside. "Killing of any kind is personal."

"In this era, that's probably true most of the time." She faced the target area, gripped the pistol in both hands and took aim. She drew back the hammer. "It seemed less true in my time."

The first shot went high and to the left.

"Relax. Put the target in your sight and caress the trigger until it fires. A Colt is less forgiving than a rifle."

"Relax, the man says. I've a gun in my hand and you want me to relax. I seriously don't think so." She aimed at the second target and tightened her hand until the trigger moved. She repeated the process four more times, hitting two targets.

"You're a natural," Royle admitted with admiration in his voice.

Agitated, Emily opened the cylinder and let the shell casings fall into the box Royle had set aside for them. "No, I'm not, and I consider it an insult that you would think so. Killing is not natural. Neither is practicing the art of putting a bullet into a small target when that target may someday be a living, breathing human being."

"But you could do it?"

Emily's shoulders slumped. "Yes," she whispered, wishing she had not learned that dark truth about herself. When she had hovered over Teigue in the mountain pass and helplessly watched him bleed, she knew she would not have hesitated if her enemy had appeared. A small voice had whispered a summons on the breeze, daring him to show, eager to assuage her helplessness, fear, and anger.

In that, she felt like the fraud Royle perceived when she spoke of her past. How many ideals had she accepted without question because it was safer, easier than a challenge? She would not be so blind in the future.

"I'll set up the targets while you reload."

Emily stared with distaste at the box of cartridges and the six empty chambers in the cylinder. "How many times do I have to do this?"

"As many as it takes for you to get comfortable with the Colt and hit the targets, too," he answered from a distance.

"There aren't that many bullets in all of Colorado," she muttered, reaching for half a dozen bullets.

After loading, she pointed the gun at the ground as Royle had instructed, for safety purposes. At the beginning of their lesson, both of them had been nervous. The way he avoided touching her conveyed the effectiveness of her revelation.

She smiled sadly. Either Royle had a cast-iron commitment to making sure she could fend for herself, or he was a fool. He had willingly put a gun in the hand of a woman he thought a liar at best or mentally unbalanced at worst. The way he watched her the first hour, she suspected he doubted the wisdom of his actions. But he had given his word. He would persevere regardless of the consequence.

Mentally, Emily dubbed him *Loyal Royle*. The man would prevail in the face of adversity and reality. Neither logic nor common sense thwarted the fulfillment of an obligation involving his honor.

Did Rebecca Weston have any idea of the prize she was

getting in Royle Tremaine? Did she see beyond his hard-earned wealth?

Recalling Laura's wedding to Leo Kramer and the nearly primitive, yet sophisticated manner in which Howard and Lucy Sawyer had bartered their daughter for social standing, every muscle in Emily's body tightened. Including the hand holding the Colt. One round discharged into the ground beside her right foot.

"What the hell—"

Shaken, Emily kept the barrel pointed at the ground. "That was an oops."

"That's a loaded revolver. There is no 'oops' when you squeeze the trigger. Damn it, Emily! You could have shot your foot off."

"Or your head, if I hadn't had it pointed at the ground."

Color drained from Royle's tanned face. "Damn right. Then how would you have gotten back to Silverton to tell Teigue you killed me?"

"The gun wasn't pointed at you, Royle." The tremble in her voice betrayed her scare and the surge of relief that the bullet had not struck either of them. Determined not to allow him the complete upper hand, she pressed the mental blade she had begun honing this morning. "Besides, don't you consider arguing with a demented woman holding a gun a bit risky?"

"I don't believe you're demented any more than I believe your fairy tale about being from the future. You're too damn normal."

"And you would have seen through me otherwise?"

"Yes." The curt answer narrowed his unblinking gaze.

"What do you see when you look at me, Royle?" Her heart hammered in her throat while she awaited an answer.

He closed the scant distance between them. The intensity of his gaze grew more menacing with each step. The late-afternoon breeze sweeping down the steep mountain slopes sent his black hair on a restless caress around his face.

He bent slightly and wrapped his hand around the Colt. "Trouble."

After a deliberate appraisal of his features, Emily's

breath caught. The fire glowing in his eyes pinned her in place. She released the revolver into his hand. "Trouble? Is that all?"

"That's enough."

A sudden bravado lifted her chin in defiance. "Trouble for whom? Teigue?"

"Not directly." Still watching her, he unloaded the Colt. "I think we've had enough practice today. Stick with the rifle. Carry it with you until being without it is the equivalent to being naked in a blizzard."

"I've never been in a blizzard." The temptation to touch his firmly set jaw sent her fingertips dancing against the palms of her closed fists.

"Use that vivid imagination of yours."

Her imagination worked overtime on Royle Tremaine. Regardless of how hard she fought the attraction, his image defied banishment. It impugned her good sense. With an opportunity to drive the wedge between them deeper, she stared back at him. "The only thing worse than an overactive imagination is the lack of one. Yours stopped functioning years ago. All you can imagine is your ancestors without consideration for how their visions might have changed with the aftermath of the Civil War."

"Were I to believe your fairy tale, I would have to believe that you know nothing about loyalty and duty. A dutiful daughter loyal to her family would not have protested marrying the man her father selected."

Anger surged through her. "Wrong again, Royle. In my time, women make their own choices about who they marry. I have worth, value, even if only to myself. Neither duty nor loyalty without love have a right to make demands on my heart. They do not have a claim on my soul or the right to cast me into misery not of my making. I have a responsibility to find my own happiness, even if it turns out badly. My family, such as it is, or was, had a duty and loyalty to me, too. My father married who and when he wanted. I'm entitled to the same."

"No, you are not. You are his daughter. Obedience is

your only course. Go home, Emily. Before . . ." His voice trailed as though he'd said too much.

"I can't go home. There is no road through time, no map to show the way. I'm here. My father is not, nor will he be born for decades. You think living in a past I had only read about or seen pictures of is easy to accept?" A hollow laugh rose from her toes. "I'm the queen of acceptance, and I still wake up wondering how and why it happened.

"You, on the other hand, accept no changes in your life after 1865. It is so much easier to sculpt your life based on someone else's guidelines. You don't have to make decisions, nor do you have to deal with the questions or consequences. You just blindly follow a path that disappeared before Lee's surrender at Appomattox."

His deep intake of breath caused her to sink her teeth into the inside of her lips to keep from further taunting him. Already, she had said more than she intended.

"You are an ungrateful daughter."

"I'm sure Ron Warner has agreed with you on that score a dozen times since I failed to show up." She exhaled sharply and dragged her gaze from his. "Love commands loyalty. Your family had a great deal of love."

"If you cared for your father the way you do for Teigue, how could he not love you?"

"Because I was a breathing reminder of a mistake. Ron detested mistakes, especially his own. If they were around, you could confirm that with any one of his four ex-wives." She put her back to Royle. "And you're right. I didn't love Ron. I quit trying to see him as lovable years ago. Rejection is a sure killer of that kind of emotion, and there is no substitute, Royle. God knows, I've tried them all. Maybe God took pity on me and gave me Teigue. For that, I thank Him every night."

The fight in her evaporated. She had Teigue as a loving, caring father figure. The powers molding her destiny had been generous indeed. Having Royle's love was asking for too much. She could give him her love and have his body for what remained of the summer. But that was all he would give her, besides a broken heart and a child if she

was not careful. A child. . . . In this time, society ostracized
bastard children.

Shuddering at the thought, she picked up the rifle, loaded
it, then headed for the cabin. Why was not having a chance
to seek happiness with the man she loved so hard to accept?

Chapter 16

Eᴍɪʟʏ ʟɪsᴛᴇɴᴇᴅ ꜰᴏʀ the sound of Royle's deep breathing to assure herself that he slept soundly. For the last three weeks her sleep had been sporadic at best. Dreams of a future denied roused her, then lingered as taunting reminders of her impossible heart's desire.

Reason demanded she accept that the sweetly disturbing dreams belonged in the fairy-tale realm Royle believed she embraced. The futility of trying to earn her father's affection had taught her a valuable, albeit painful, lesson. Nothing could make Royle love her; nor could she stop herself from loving him.

Stocking-footed, she eased down the ladder. Outside the cabin, she stepped into her boots. With her backpack hoisted over her left shoulder, she balanced the rifle in her right hand.

A full moon shone overhead. The warm glow bathed the grasses swaying in the mountain meadow. The soft light guided her way with the quiet grace of a guardian

angel. Calls from the mountain creatures prowling the
shadows and soaring across the starry sky became music
in the invigorating night air.

Lighthearted, she waded through the meadow. She
wended her way through the trees, then climbed the
jagged slope to her destination.

At the hot spring, she rummaged through her pack for a
candle. In her excitement for the midnight adventure, she
dropped it, then caught it before it landed in the water.

Once it was lit, she had enough light to find the driest
surface for her clothing. Within minutes she had undressed, and sank into the steamy water with a long, loud
sigh of pure delight. More than anything, she relished the
solace from the persistent tension between her and Royle.
Three weeks of verbal sparring punctuated by long, stony
silences had frayed her nerves raw. The only outlet came
during target practice. The echoes of gunfire vented the
shouts of frustration locked inside her.

Submerged to her earlobes, Emily arched her neck and
shook her long tresses until the mass shimmied free in the
water. Wishing to banish all stressful thoughts, she
hummed an old tune from childhood.

Steam haloed the candlelight against the rock swelter-
ing above the ledge. Cooled drops of condensation
dripped from the arched ceiling. She caught one on her
tongue, then laughed.

With leisurely abandon, Emily washed, swam, and
played in the warm spring. As she prepared to leave the
pool, she heard the sound of hard soles crunching fine,
damp pebbles. Wide-eyed, she watched the entrance and
sidled toward her rifle. Whoever lurked in the night shadows lacked Royle's stealth. He seldom made a sound.

Royle woke fighting against a nightmare that had coiled
him into a fetal position. He forced his legs straight and
unclenched his white-knuckled fists. The recurring dream
had plagued him since the first target practice with Emily.
Something in her diatribe had struck an invisible, elusive
chord. Even after awakening from the vivid dream, he had

no idea what had sparked the incessant vision or whether it signified anything meaningful.

It was a dream—a disturbing dream—in which he lay suspended above the ground. Tethers fastened his arms and legs to four strong horses ready to draw and quarter him. Nameless ancestors of all ages prodded the nervous horses as money changed hands in wagers for the victor who got the largest share of his remains. At three of the corners, his mother, his Aunt Madeline, and his sister, Flavia, whispered calming words to the horses. Like the many times they had intruded on his dreams over the years, they seemed to be waiting. For what, he did not know.

Running his cramped fingers through his hair, he swung his legs over the side of his bed, then listened.

An eerie silence filled the cabin. He was alone.

Emily.

Anxious, he donned his pants on the way to the ladder leading to the loft. A quick glimpse of her pallet confirmed her absence. He glanced at the gun rack. Her rifle was gone.

Cursing her lack of caution, he haphazardly pulled on his clothes. On the way out the cabin door, he snatched up his rifle and gun belt.

The woman may as well have descended straight from the moon for all the sense she showed. Wandering the mountains at night was the stupidest thing she had done thus far. At least she had the foresight to take her rifle.

Bent against the chilly wind, Royle crossed the meadow at a brisk pace. There was only one place Emily would go in the middle of the night.

Cougars and wolves lurked in the darkness. So did two-legged mammals. Although he had seen no sign of an intruder, his experience in the Dakotas had taught him that a careful man left none. The more dangers he imagined, the faster he walked.

Water burbled over the stone lip at the edge of the hot spring and raced into the creek meandering through the

meadow. Nearby, two horses stood in the shadows below
the rocky face harboring the hot spring.

Royle faltered. His worst fears confirmed, he loped
through the trees, his approach acknowledged by the saddle horse. The pack horse snorted, but otherwise gave no
sign of alarm.

How long had she been here? A backward glance at the
horses gave no hint of how long they had been waiting.
Ugly visions of the heinous deeds a man could commit
against a woman swam in the back of his mind.

Royle skirted the loose rock at the mouth of the ele-
vated grotto. Caution tempered the unreasonable urgency
compelling him upward. He hoped like hell Emily would
not try talking whoever owned the horses into boredom
before realizing she had to shoot him. While he had faith
in her ability to defend Teigue, or perhaps himself, he
doubted her willingness to pull the trigger when she was
the only one at risk.

Once clear of the entrance, Royle shouldered his rifle
and scrambled along the boulders forming the outside wall
of the cave. Halfway up the side, he brought the rifle
down and exhaled to compress his ribs. Rock scraped his
chest as he slithered through the narrow, twisting fissure.

He emerged ten feet above the steaming pool. From his
vantage point at the back of the cavern, he made out
Emily's faint outline in the rocks along the left side of the
spring. Relief flooded him. She was all right. So far.

Across the narrow expanse and near a sputtering candle,
a man stood with his hands raised slightly from his hips.
Steam billowed lazily over the water. Though he appeared
familiar, Royle could not see him well enough in the scant
light to pin a name on him.

"I don't mean you no harm, little lady. I jest figured
you and me could, well, ya know, make each other
happy."

Royle peered through the mist, his rifle sighted on the
intruder. Hearing the vile intent directed at Emily, his finger curled around the trigger. Then froze.

So many of her strange beliefs had undergone change in

the short time she had been in the mountains. He had to know whether she would defend herself. He refused to examine why it mattered for him to know, though he recognized the importance of her finding her limits.

Reluctant to rob her of the test she faced, he held his hand still, but ready.

"Which part of *no* don't you understand?" Emily demanded.

She deserved credit. Not a trace of nervousness sounded in her voice. In her place, he would have already shot the bastard and dragged his carcass outside. Ruefully, he acknowledged his survival instincts were barbaric by her standards.

"But ya haven't even seen what I'm offerin'." He lowered his hands to his belt buckle.

"You have nothing I want to see. Now, get out and don't come back."

The thick air muffled the sound of the stranger's buckle unfastening.

A shot rang out, nearly deafening Royle. He flinched. Without changing his aim, his gaze darted at the shadows hiding Emily, then to the intruder. The cretin was still standing. Damn, she hadn't put a bullet in him after all.

"Goddamn, lady. Ya like ta have took my ear off." The stranger touched his left ear. In amazement, he drew back his fingers and stared at them as though expecting part of his ear to dangle from the tips.

"No, I didn't. If I had wanted it gone, it would be." Emily retreated further. The thick shadows hid her completely. "Let's see . . . as a prospector, you need your arms. A bullet in the shoulder would shatter the joint or shoulder blade and render that arm useless. I guess you also need your legs for riding and climbing."

"What're ya gettin' at?"

"If you don't leave, I'm going to have to shoot you. I'm deciding where. Seems to me that thing you were so eager to show me got you into this predicament. You don't need it to make a living, do you?"

Royle kept his eye on the stranger, not trusting the sudden stillness of the man. Mentally, he complimented Emily on her steely nerves. She knew exactly where a man's greatest pride and vulnerability rested. No man would ignore the threat she issued with a casualness only a woman was capable of delivering.

"I seen you in town, then before that when you was sashaying around Teigue's and Royle's cabin a while back. Now, old Teigue, he's laid up for a spell. Ya been lettin' yer cousin poke ya. Why not me?"

Cold revulsion swept through Royle. The bastard would never get close enough to lay a hand on Emily. Royle drew a bead on the stranger's heart.

"Oh, so you're the prurient voyeur who was trying to watch me at the cabin?" Anger clipped Emily's words. The distinctive sound of another round entering the firing chamber of her rifle cracked in the mist.

"I seen ya in the water here with Royle. I also seen ya sneak outta his cabin tonight. He don't even know yer gone, does he?"

"My next shot will strike flesh."

"Gettin' nervous or changing yer mind? I'll treat you good. I'll even let ya be on top, like Royle done in that pool there."

Royle stopped breathing. The stranger had called Emily's bluff by holding his ground. With great restraint, Royle remained silent in the darkness. Why the hell didn't she shoot the vermin and be done with it? Why was she putting herself at risk?

"I'd suggest that you start thinking with something above your belt, because I'm running out of patience."

About damn time, Royle seethed, perspiration running down his whiskered cheeks.

"Ya ain't gonna shoot me, so let's you and me have some fun fer as long as it lasts." Head shaking, he started around the pool presenting a clean profile in the glow of the candle.

Emily fired again.

The stranger bolted, screaming, grabbing his buttocks

and twisting as though he could stretch his head around far enough to examine his injury.

"Now get the hell out of my hot tub." Emily's shout vented a fury that made the fine hair on Royle's neck rise. "I don't have much that I prize, but my privacy is right at the top of the list. Get out!"

"Goddamn you, whore! You shot me!"

"I'll shoot you again if you don't get out. Now."

"I'm going! I'm going, you bitch!"

Teeth gritted, Royle watched the stranger hobble toward the entrance. All his instincts compelled him to follow and make sure the lecher never returned to bother Emily again.

"You ain't seen the last of me," the stranger growled.

The anger festering inside Royle made his finger itch to pull the trigger on his rifle. "If you so much as speak to her again, I'll kill you," Royle said with all the menace he felt.

The stranger halted in his tracks, his back stiffening. A sudden silence rode the tension curling amid the steam. "I hear ya, Tremaine. She's your cousin ta poke. I ain't stupid enough ta give her another try. She had her chance with me."

"Keep riding until you're clear of my mountains."

The stranger waved a bloody hand in disgust, then limped toward the entrance.

Royle listened, gauging the direction and distance. "I'll be back," he said softly to Emily.

He wormed through the fissure and emerged in time to see the prospector painfully mount his horse. The man cursed everything in and under the sky in the process. It would be weeks before he sat in a saddle comfortably.

Royle marked the intruder's progress from the heights, resisting the urge to run to Emily before he ensured that the stranger was well on his way. Anger pervaded every fiber of his being as he tried to push away images of what *could* have happened. And the lingering remnants of a feeling Royle couldn't quite name tugged at his heart as he swore to kill the man if he ever saw him near Emily again.

Emily let the rifle slide through her sweaty hands. Using the barrel as a cane, she sagged against the damp stone wall. The quaking in her knees reverberated all the way up to her teeth. Doubled over, leaning on the rifle for support, she concentrated on breathing. The spinning in her head taunted the nausea roiling in her stomach.

She had shot a man.

Intentionally.

Wounded him severely enough to draw blood.

She wanted to vomit. Her empty stomach cramped. Disbelief, horror, realization—all swirled through her with disgust. Desperately, she sought detachment.

The last shreds of bravado melted away with the strength from her bones. She sank onto her heels and wrapped her arms around her legs. She drew a heavy breath in an attempt to clear the revilement for her actions. When it remained, she rested her forehead on her knees in resignation.

"You pulled the trigger and shot him. Accept it," she whispered, reverently setting aside the rifle. "Accept it. It can't be changed or undone. Nothing died." Except a little piece of an identity she struggled to maintain. What kind of person was she?

He would have raped you, a small voice raged at her. *Would you have been content being his victim?*

"No. I won't be a victim." The vehemence of her reflection sent her rocking from side to side. Out of habit, she alternately rubbed and patted her arms to comfort herself as she had done during countless crises faced alone. "Let it flow through you. Let it settle," she whispered in a voice she might use to soothe an agitated child. "Accept it . . . then let it go. Shoulder the consequences."

The old ritual she practiced since early childhood imparted scant consolation. Wondering if she would have mortally wounded him had the flesh injury not stopped him, she drew a sobering breath.

Eyes closed, she leaned her head against the rock and replayed the incident in vivid detail. Casting herself in the role of an impartial third person fostered an objectivity that dulled the sharper edges of her remorse.

The choice had been his more than hers. At any time he could have turned and left. She, on the other hand, had no way out except past him.

"He's gone."

The soft rumble of Royle's voice opened her eyes. In the flickering radiance of the dying candle, anger glowed around him like a dark angel's halo. She lowered her head to her knees and braced herself for the onslaught of fury he was sure to unleash.

Royle dropped her pack beside her, then laid her loose clothing on top. "Put your clothes on. We're going home. I'll wait outside."

She dressed methodically, shouldered her pack, and picked up her rifle. The candle sputtered and winked out as she walked by it. A moonbeam pointed the way outside. Shoulders squared, she left the steamy atmosphere with a fresh resolve. She had acted in the most humane manner possible to ensure her safety.

Emily climbed partway down the rubble in front of the entrance, then paused to listen to an owl calling from the trees below. Moonlight glistened off the creek wandering aimlessly through the meadow. A faint wisp of smoke rose from the chimney of the cabin. The last bits of snow clinging to the high peaks cast a pearlescent definition to the frigid caps.

"Beautiful, isn't it?" Royle gave voice to her thoughts.

"Breathtaking. It's a shame to have to leave it at the end of the summer." Expecting him to yell at her at any moment, she let Royle guide her down the last portion of loose rocks.

"I suspect Teigue has a place picked out that rivals the beauty of this one."

They navigated through the trees and walked slowly across the meadow in silence. Emily waited until they entered the cabin and both had put their guns aside before speaking. "Go ahead and lecture."

"You scared the hell out of me." Royle filled the coffeepot.

Emily added kindling and stoked the fire. "How long were you watching from the ledge?"

"Long enough to know he was not listening to reason and for you to realize the only way to get his attention was to shoot him." He measured freshly ground coffee from the grinder. "You were convincing. I wasn't sure you would defend yourself."

At the time, she had not known what she would do—until he started around the pool. "So you watched and waited." Restless, she roamed the cabin. "If I had not shot him . . ."

"I would have." The hard edge in his voice left no doubt. "In answer to your next question, I always shoot to kill."

Her dark angel had been her guardian angel from his lofty perch. Had she not deterred the intruder with a flesh wound, Royle would have delivered death with a single bullet. She drew a deep breath, and felt better about her handling of the situation.

Royle set the coffeepot on the fire grate. "I considered going after him. I don't want him coming back to try again. We might not be so lucky next time."

"We?" The question emerged on a shrill note.

He caught her arm and turned her to face him. "We, Emily. You. Me. And Teigue. Do you honestly think if he had laid a finger on you that all three of us wouldn't feel it? Do you think I wouldn't track the bastard down and make him suffer before I killed him?"

She bit her lip, appalled by the conviction he radiated. "I . . ." Stunned by his readiness to protect and avenge her against the predators who would harm her, she stared at him.

"You what?"

"Why?"

"How can you ask why? Do you think I would let anyone hurt you and get away with it?"

"I don't understand why you would bother. I mean, I'm not really a part of your life."

The scowl deepened, as did the angry, sapphire glint boring into her.

Undaunted, she asked, "I mean . . . why?"

He took his time before answering, "So Teigue wouldn't get himself killed doing something I can do better."

"And just who would you be avenging? Me? Teigue?" A new understanding of the violent streak he let rise unguarded dawned on her. She studied him. In the firelight dancing in the hearth behind him, his wind-tousled hair was as black as his mood. The tension of his tightly coiled body seemed ready to shatter with his next move. "Or a past you can't change and an anger with no other outlet?"

He blinked. A hard-won battle for composure ended and erased the danger from his eyes. "This has nothing to do with anyone but you, Emily. Don't go looking for fairy-tale motives." A tight upward curve at the corner of his mouth passed for a warning. "When I found you gone, you scared the hell out of me. Tonight could have turned out a lot worse. Do you think he would have let you live to tell me or Teigue if he had raped you?"

"Were you worried that he'd take what you want me to give you?" The barely audible whisper escaped her thoughts and hung in the space between them.

"Make no mistake, Emily. I want you in my bed so badly I walk around hurting with it. What makes it more difficult is that you want me, too." His gaze dropped to her lips as she wetted them.

"This isn't about whether I want to hop into bed with you, Royle." All the dangerous, delicious sensations that haunted her erotic dreams burst through her senses.

"Isn't it?"

Without warning, his hand snaked around the back of her head and wound through her thick, damp tresses. She felt the pressure increase until she tilted her face, and his

mouth captured hers. She tasted and felt the anger in his
bruising kiss. Even so, the need suffusing her veins commanded a response. Her lips parted in eager acceptance of
his hungry tongue.

His hand slithered down her back and through her hair,
caressing, drawing her into a crushing embrace. Caught up
in desire, she wound her arms around him, holding him so
tightly that she thought she could fuse his heart to hers.
The peaks of her breasts hardened against the heat of his
chest.

The kiss gentled into a seductive exploration that
robbed her of reason and burned her to the marrow of her
bones. He drew her away from him, evoking a small
protest from deep in her throat. The spread of his palm
over her breast summoned yet another sound, this one of
pleasure. Heat blossomed in her loins.

She curled her fingers behind his neck and pressed her
hips against the ridge of his desire. Slowly, awash in a tide
of marvelous sensations, she raised and lowered her leg,
running her inner thigh along his outer leg and hip.

His hands worked the buttons of her shirt, then freed
the front fastener on her bra. Cool air caressed her heated
skin. His hands on her naked skin were a brand, pleasuring and heating her until nothing else mattered.

Abruptly, he enveloped her in a tight embrace and
broke the kiss. "Damn it, Emily. This is suicide."

As disappointment stole the fog from her reason, Emily
relished the last delicious sensations of his powerful leg
and lowered her foot to the floor. Yet he did not release
her. Instead, he bowed his head into the crook of her neck
and shoulder and kissed the soft hollow.

"You proved your point," she murmured against his
chest. She tilted her head and tasted the hot, bare skin in
the hollow of his throat. The thunder of his pulse against
the tip of her tongue matched her own. She felt the vibration of his groan, then opened her mouth to fully kiss his
throat.

Gently, he cradled her head in his big hands and drew

her away as his mouth abandoned her neck. "Emily." His coarse whisper reflected her aching frustration.

She released him, her gaze meeting his torment. Slowly, she curled her fingers around his wrists and removed his hands from the sides of her head. She lowered her gaze and his hands, then quietly walked to the ladder and climbed onto her pallet. In that moment, she knew whether they made love or not, she would love Royle until she drew her last breath.

Chapter 17

SILVERTON OVERFLOWED WITH Fourth of July
revelers eager to celebrate. Although it would be six days
before the arrival of the Denver & Rio Grande Railroad at
Blair and Twelfth Streets, it made little difference to those
who had ventured into town from the rugged mountains.
With the sixth anniversary of Colorado statehood a scant
four weeks away, many added it to the reasons for an extra
bottle of whiskey.

Festivity charged the late-afternoon air. Red, white, and
blue banners hung from rooftops and spanned Greene
Street. Officials from the Denver & Rio Grande Railroad
strutted along the boardwalk. Their prim, dark suits distinguished them as harbingers of the most important event in
Silverton's history since silver captured the interests of the
gold prospectors roaming the San Juan Mountains years
earlier.

Emily required no reminder to stay close as she and
Royle made their way from Carlyle's Stable in the upper

part of town. Through the throng of townsfolk, she spied Teigue leaning on a cane in front of the Silverton Hotel. She quickened their pace, bidding Royle to hurry. When he moved too slowly, she broke away and darted between half a dozen pedestrians. Laughing with delight, she rushed into Teigue's open arms.

"Ah, Sunshine, how I've missed you." Teigue embraced her hard and kissed her forehead.

Joy for his good health and rapid recovery brought tears to her eyes. Enfolded by Teigue's strong embrace, she felt loved with a depth beyond her dreams. "I've missed you, too," she breathed, giving him an extra squeeze before dropping her hand holding the rifle. "How is your leg?"

Teigue kept an arm around her and extended a hand to Royle.

Royle clasped the offered hand. "I'm damned glad to see you getting around."

"The leg is practically as good as new." Teigue grinned down at Emily. "Maybe even good enough for a waltz tonight with the most beautiful lady in Silverton."

Emily melted into a radiant smile. "In that case, I'll wear the blue dress and put red and white ribbons in my hair."

"You'll be the belle of the ball." Teigue's brown eyes twinkled his enjoyment. "Royle will have to help keep an eye on you, Sunshine. Every man in town will be asking for a turn around the floor with you."

Reflexively, Emily stiffened. Her smile dimmed as she glanced at Royle in time to see his grin wilt. "I'd love to dance with you, Teigue." Heeding Royle's raised brow, she quickly added, "And Royle, if he knows how."

"I may surprise you." Royle shifted the heavy pack on his left shoulder.

Emily tightened the arm lingering around Teigue's waist. "Is he going to tell me he dances as well as he shoots?"

Teigue shrugged. "I don't know. I've never danced with him."

Delight lit Emily's face as she gave Teigue a one-armed hug.

"Let's claim our rooms, then find something to eat," Royle suggested.

Emily started toward the hotel lobby. Before she took a second step, she stopped cold. Several miners held their hats and grinned at her. Further down the boardwalk, Galloway leaned against a porch post and spoke with the same man she had shot at the hot spring. "Teigue, who is the man talking with Mr. Galloway?"

"Bull Stinson. You don't want to know him." Teigue guided her into the hotel. "He's as mean as they come."

Royle's massive chest blocked her view of Stinson. "He won't be bothering you."

She glanced up. The set of Royle's jaw kept her silent.

Once inside the hotel, she dismissed her uneasiness concerning Galloway and Stinson. Visitors demanding rooms cramped the normally sedate lobby. Flanked by Teigue and Royle, she felt completely at ease. Her fingers caressed the Winchester. The rifle had become as much a part of her attire as her faded denims.

A wooden platform constructed for the train station at Blair and Twelfth Streets served as the dance floor. The air vibrated with music from an assortment of players who sounded better than they looked.

A warm smile lit Emily's face as Teigue led her around the dance floor. His grace belied his injury.

"Thank you for coming to my rescue," Emily said.

"You were limping more than I do after the last three buffoons. If they'd cut in on each other any more, you could have sat down and they'd never have missed you," he teased with a wink.

Emily's laughter reflected her high spirits. "Oh, Teigue, where have you been all my life?"

"Mining these mountains with Royle and waiting for you."

Her past flashed between them with silent understanding. "I got here as soon as I could."

"Soon enough for Royle?"

Her smile lost some of its brilliance. "Are my feelings for him so transparent?"

"They are to me, Sunshine. If it's any consolation, you've got him chasing his tail."

"Funny. There have been times when I had the distinct impression we were chasing each other's, as well as our own."

Teigue's deep laugh slowed their dancing. "Have you told Royle where you're from?"

Emily nodded. "He thinks I'm crazy, which might be a good thing."

"Why?"

Embarrassment colored her cheeks. Speaking openly about anything so personal was a new experience. "Let's just say it helps us keep our clothes on."

"I see. Is that why you told him?"

"You see too much, Teigue."

He chuckled. "I would have loved being a fly on the wall and seeing his face."

"You would have been stuck on that wall a long time. It took two bottles of whiskey."

"Two bottles?" Teigue stopped dancing. "Damn, you must have had a hangover as big as Colorado the next morning."

"*He* did." She winced, then grinned, recalling Royle's surly mood the next morning.

Teigue laughed, his head shaking in sympathy as he led her to the sidelines.

"I believe this is my dance," Galloway announced with a stately bow.

Emily shook her head, denying any show of the revulsion she felt for the man and his request. "Thank you, but I've promised the next dance to Royle. It is getting late, and we've had a long day."

Galloway's bemused expression ignored her rebuff. "Perhaps he's had his fill and is tired . . . of the dancing."

The protective cloak of Teigue's arm around her waist bolstered her. "I'm sure he has been momentarily detained. I shall wait for him."

"Ah, there you are," Royle said from behind her. "Have you worn Teigue into a rocking chair?"

"I believe it is the other way around," Emily answered with a forced smile. "If you would like to claim the dance I promised, we'd best be about it. The day's activity has begun taking its toll."

The flicker of an eyebrow was the only surprise Royle showed. "Shall we?" He offered his arm.

With the regal poise of the debutante she had been, Emily accompanied Royle onto the dance floor.

"Mr. Galloway makes my skin crawl," she muttered as Royle took her in his arms. The very proper dance position put what seemed like miles between their bodies.

"He has that effect on a number of people." A sudden grin revealed a flash of white teeth.

Emily followed his movements around the dance floor with abandonment. His expert turns never missed a step as he guided her from one whirling sequence to the next.

Gazing into the banked passion in his eyes charged her with excitement. She arched her neck and laughed with her eyes closed. The dizzying sensations electrifying her blood reminded her of Scarlett O'Hara whirling around the ballroom in Rhett Butler's arms.

She opened her eyes, her laughter gone.

In a couple of months, Royle would belong to Rebecca Weston. The only similarity to *Gone with the Wind* was the dismal plight faced by the Southerners in postwar Virginia.

In a couple of months, Royle would be a memory haunting her for the rest of her life.

"Is something wrong?"

Emily shook her head and forced a smile while trying to recapture the mood. "You dance better than you shoot."

"You follow much better than you shoot, which is damn good."

Emily's smile became genuine. She was content in the circle of his arms and wished they were alone and naked. "Have you ever lived for the moment, Royle?"

"Philosophy questions? I don't dance nearly as well as I had hoped."

"Be serious."

All traces of gaiety faded, leaving the shadow of a battle fought, but not resolved. "Every time I become serious around you it means I'm not going to sleep for a long time." He led her toward Teigue when the music ended. "If I lived for the moment, neither of us would have left the cabin these last two weeks. We would have made love every way I can think of and found a few more in the meantime. I suspect that fertile imagination of yours would have come into play, too."

Emily pondered his softly spoken avowal as they accompanied Teigue to Nelda Bird's boarding house and told him good night. She and Royle dawdled on the way back to the hotel, both reluctant to end the evening, neither speaking.

At the hotel, Royle escorted her to her room on the second floor. With each step, Emily's heart pounded faster. The daring idea wiggling through her mind since their dance bolstered her courage. At the door of her room, she pressed the key into his palm and waited until he opened the lock. "If there were no consequences, no strings or ties, no expectations, would you live for the moment?"

"It is never that way."

"You didn't answer my question." Head lowered to hide the color staining her cheeks, she slipped inside her room.

Royle followed, carefully leaving the door open. He struck a match and lit the lamp on the bureau. "What are you asking me, Emily?"

She drew a quick breath and lifted her head. Inwardly, she shook like a leaf in a windstorm. How foolish. She had made the decision and needed his answer.

Beside the lamp, her dark angel radiated a hunger she felt in the pit of her soul. Desire mustered her courage into a surge of bravado. With slow deliberateness, she closed the door. "I'm asking you to give us the moment, Royle. No strings. No promises. You and me. Let's end the tension between us."

Head tilted, his glittering blue eyes met hers with desire, hope, and doubt. "Are you seducing me?"

Heat suffused her neck and flamed across her cheeks. "I

don't believe in seduction." She locked her knees in place. More than she wanted her next breath, she wanted him in her arms, holding her, kissing her, making love with her. How else could she express the love stretching her heart to the bursting point? Giving was the only form she knew. Giving herself to the man she loved without hope of more was the most selfish and unselfish act she had ever contemplated.

"What do you believe in?" A couple of steps took him to the door.

Emily's heart lurched with dismay. He was leaving. "Closure," she whispered.

Royle pushed the key into the lock. The sound of the bolt sliding into place sang in a brief lull of the noisy revelers celebrating in the street below. As he turned around, he tossed the key on the bureau.

"I won't stop this time." The warning hung between them as a reminder of past denials both had paid for during long, empty hours of aching, unfulfilled desire. The controlled violence of his promise bordered on a threat.

"Nor will I, Royle." She extended a trembling hand.

Royle accepted her offer and lifted her fingers to his lips. The gentle glide of his thumb over the tender skin at the inside of her wrist alternately melted and froze her in place. How easily he ignited every nerve in her body.

"You may hate me tomorrow," he murmured, reaching for the guipure lace at her throat.

"There is no tomorrow. Only now. This moment." With trembling fingertips, she traced the arch of his eyebrow and the hairline along his temple.

"Would that it was true, Emily."

Neither could deny themselves a taste of the other. Their lips met with a rapacious hunger that reached into her soul. His kiss, deep and demanding, evoked a cry of gladness.

His tongue invaded the moist, eager recesses of her mouth with a voracious appetite that reflected her own.

As though sensing the depth of her need, he tempered the kiss and drew her tongue into the heat of his mouth. Emily strained on tiptoes, seeking, exploring, savoring the glori-

ous delights washing through her like storm-tossed waves
against a solid shore.

Royle caressed her shoulders, then drew her back until
she reluctantly ended the kiss. He stared at her pink, parted
lips for a long moment, during which Emily feared he
might change his mind.

He shook his head as though reading her thoughts and
denying her fears. A slow tracing of his finger along the
side of her neck led him to the pearly buttons hidden by the
lace at her throat.

The confines of their closeness intoxicated her. Through
the lingering aftershave the barber had applied earlier, she
inhaled the distinct male scent of him. She closed her eyes,
memorizing the tiny detail for future dreams. She had
promised herself not to think about what came with the
dawn when he again belonged to another woman. Tonight,
he belonged to her and filled her world with passion and
love.

With a painfully slow deliberateness, he released the numerous buttons on the front, then the back of her gown. Not
once did his gaze wander from hers. The depth of the passion in his eyes consumed her. She held him locked in a
mute soliloquy professing the love overflowing her heart.
Of their own accord, her fingers released the buttons on his
coat, vest, and shirt. The heat of his body lingering in the
soft fabric quickened her breath. When she could stand it
no longer, she flattened her palms on his bare chest and
flexed her fingers. The muscles beneath flinched in response to the heat building between them.

She spread her hands and cleared the obstacles away
from his shoulders. Continuing on, she followed the contour of his upper arms, pushing the layers of his clothing
until they fell away.

Braced against his shoulders, she leaned forward and
kissed the hollow of his breastbone. Silken black chest hair
tickled her nose and cheeks. She turned her head to the side
and nuzzled his chest with her cheek.

"You're ahead of me." He cradled her head against him

and began plucking pins and ribbons from her hair. Section by section her hair unwound and cascaded down her back.

"I have ached to touch you like this . . . and more . . . so very much more." Her palms slid around his ribs, caressing, pressing with each small movement up his back. In this world of flesh, Royle was her king. Her magician who cast a spell as potent as any magic man in legends. For this enchantment was real. She reveled in the supple movement of his flesh as he returned the stroking along her shoulders. The tension coiled in his body warned that his tolerance for her exploration was nearing an end. Longing for the press of his naked flesh against hers, she lowered her arms and straightened in his embrace.

The dance of disrobing continued with Royle taking the lead. He stroked her throat, coaxing her neck into an arch and parting the prim lace.

"The treasures you offer can melt a man made of stone."

She felt the vibration of his lips at her throat all the way to her toes. The fiery trail of kisses and nibbles he laid across the hollow of her throat and along the ledge of her collarbone opened the lace at the front of her dress. The left side of the dress slithered down her arm and caught at her elbow. She let it fall, then twined her fingers in his thick hair.

He leisurely made his way to the clothed shoulder. The sparks of electricity he created with his mouth scorched the strength in her body. Her breasts ripened with anticipation.

She buried her face in the crook of his neck and shoulder. Breathless, she kissed him repeatedly, tasting his skin with the delicate greediness of a starving lady at a banquet.

In a whoosh, her dress and petticoats fell around her feet.

Royle caught her hard against him and straightened. One hand gripped her buttocks, pressing her pubic bone against the throbbing ridge of his erection.

A small cry escaped Emily as she clung to him, her feet dangling and her shoes falling into the disarray. Her hips ground against him in a shared rhythm.

Royle kicked the clothing aside. The motion sent her clutching at him. Her legs reflexively wrapped around his

waist and drew his erection into the valley of her femininity.

Royle muttered a curse. His hands slipped beneath her
bottom, holding her, rocking them in a sinuous motion that
promised heaven.

He placed a knee on the bed and brought them down on
the comforter. The solidity of the mattress allowed her to
loosen her arms from his neck. She gazed up into eyes so
blue they were nearly black and glittering recklessly with
something she barely understood.

"You have so much fire in you. So much passion," he
breathed, slanting his mouth over hers.

Emily returned his kiss with every ounce of the desire
surging through her. His possessive touch on her breast became the sun from the sky burning the source of life into
her flesh. All the while his erection rocked against the
swollen, sensitive nub of her clitoris.

Breathing raggedly, Royle ended the kiss. "You have too
many clothes on," he exhaled, pulling the ties on her corset.

"So do you." She wormed her hands between them, forcing him to rise on his knees. With anxious, shaky fingers,
she opened the stubborn buttons on his pants. She cried out,
and he flinched when his erection filled her hand.

"I want you inside me," she rasped, caressing him with
both hands, alternately stroking and squeezing the marvelous manifestation of his desire for her.

"Have no doubt that I'll be there—too soon, if you don't
let go of me." He pried off one boot with the toe of the
other, then worried off the second. Each hit the floor with a
distinctive thud. "Help me get rid of my trousers."

Reluctantly, she released him and pushed his trousers
over his tight buttocks. Everywhere she touched, she discovered fresh delights.

Naked, Royle drew his knees up under her thighs. The
intense way he studied her incited a tinge of fear and even
more excitement. A sheen of perspiration coated his shoulders and chest.

"Is it warm in here?" She extended a forefinger toward
the bead of moisture forming on the tip of his erection.

He caught her wrist, then grinned and raised her knuckles to his lips. "It is about to get warmer."

In rapt fascination and anticipation, she remained motionless while he unlaced the corset binding her breasts and laid it open. Her heart raced at his intense concentration. His hands hovered over her breasts. Ever so lightly, his palms descended. Rough calluses grazed the tops of her nipples. Reflexively, she arched, thrusting her breasts into his open hands.

Thick, black lashes rode over his eyes at half-mast. "I've had a hundred dreams of touching you like this."

Her heart cried out in agreement. The reality of his naked flesh was far more exciting than anything her feeble imagination had conjured.

The feather-light circles his fingers trailed around the globes of her breasts sent her squirming. The circles narrowed around her nipples. The tightness in her chest coiled with anticipation. All she wanted was to feel his passion and her love mingling in the pleasure of his touch.

His head bowed. His mouth closed on one of her turgid nipples as his fingers plucked the other. Emily cried out and captured his head against her breast, wanting her love to nourish him as it burst through her with a desire beyond imagination. The delicious heat consumed her and sent her hips writhing for a similar coupling that would free the odd tension winding tighter and tighter inside her. A desperate longing to cherish him with every part of her body burned through her. A hot ache ran from her breasts to her loins. He built upon it by worshipping her breasts. The lifting, molding, and taunting nips and kisses pulsed through her blood at a feverish tempo.

Without warning, he grasped her drawers and tore them from her hips. Yet his head never lifted as he blazed a new trail across her abdomen and down to the cluster of curls over her mons.

The sensation of the tip of Royle's tongue on her clitoris was Emily's undoing. Her teeth sank into her lip to keep the cry of ecstatic delirium from escaping. Her knees rose, pressing into his shoulders. His fingers slid inside her,

pushing, exploring, making her gasp and tremble with pleasure. The fierce spiral expanding inside her sent her head
tossing and her fingers gripping the comforter to hold her
earthbound.

The delicious, agonizing rhythm he created intensified,
sending her up a blissful vortex with wild abandon. She
cried out his name.

And he was there, gazing down at her with a nearly violent ardor. "Em—"

Her eyes and mouth flew open. Sweet ecstasy became
the pain of penetration. She clutched at him, reaching for a
sensation beyond his physical presence. Her hips curved up
against him, and kept him from withdrawing. She wanted
him to share the anguish of her paradise. Then it didn't
matter. Her body shuddered in the glory of love.

When she came to her senses, Royle held her so tightly,
she thought he would melt into her. And she loved it, and
drew him closer.

The sinuous motion of his erection at the threshold of
womanhood tantalized her. She kissed his shoulder and
tasted the salt in his perspiration.

Royle pushed up on his elbows. The storm clouds of desire rode heavily on his expression. "Are you all right?"

She nodded and ran her tongue over her lower lip. The
pain of losing her maidenhead had vanished into the pleasure of the beautiful climax. "Are you?"

"I will be. Soon. Too soon," he whispered, slanting his
mouth over hers.

She tasted his need and felt it vibrate in him like a caged
wild thing raging for freedom. She ran the arches of her
feet along his legs, pushing against his thighs to deepen the
penetration he denied. His hunger touched something in her
and fueled the subdued blaze into a conflagration.

In the oneness of their lovemaking, her love bound Royle
to her heart forever. The last floodgate of defense crumbled. She met each thrust with an abandoned desperation
that carried them both to a piece of heaven where fantasies
beyond mere mortals became reality.

When Emily opened her eyes, Royle watched from a few

inches away. "It seems that living for the moment cured your virginity." He kissed her nose, then grasped the comforter and rolled onto his back with Emily on top of him.

Now she needed a cure for the cure. She smiled at him, amazed by the magic lingering in the air. Her hair spilled over her shoulders and across his. "Thank you," she whispered, then snuggled against his shoulder and tried to stretch the moment into infinity.

"Both the honor and the pleasure are mine."

Chapter 18

WHEN ROYLE ACCEPTED Emily's challenge to live for the moment, he expected relief from his unreasonable need for her. He'd considered sex a purely physical act—until tonight, when it became akin to a religious experience. Countless times, he had suspected that making love with her might be vastly different from the release he found with the ladies of the evening, as Emily called them. What he had not expected was the rapture glowing in every part of his body. He marveled at the serenity their lovemaking forged over his troubled heart. She gave herself without demand or expectation. Through submission to the raging demon-desire, she had emerged the stronger.

Given a choice, he would have held her in his arms until their bones turned brittle with age. Gazing into her eyes filled with wonder and a deeper emotion he could not identify, he thought her the most beautiful, desirable woman born. He stroked her back and ribs, his thumbs lingering over the delicious swell of her breasts, then eased down her thighs folded against his ribs. Her body reflected her enigmatic personality: strong and soft, rigid yet yielding. She reminded him of a crystal prism held to the brilliance of the sun and radiating a myriad of colors blending and changing the world around her. If he spent a hundred years with her, he would never tire of the scintillating facets she exposed at every turn.

They did not have a hundred years, or even a hundred hours, in which to explore the depth of their passion. They had the moment. Nothing more.

The thundering reality gripped him in talons of regret. It could not be otherwise. An odd sense of loss stole the edge from the euphoria of their lovemaking.

"Emily, sweet Emily," he whispered sadly as he stroked the center of her back down to the rise of her bottom. "Why did we wait so long?"

The soft kiss she brushed across his lips teased a reaction from his manhood. Her head lifted with a questioning light in her eyes. "Timing is everything. The moment wasn't right until tonight."

"The moment is not over yet," he murmured, drawing her mouth to his. "Let's stretch it until sunrise."

He covered her parted lips with lingering kisses and traced the outline with the tip of his tongue. The quickening of her breath on his face and her heartbeat against his chest matched his.

Desire stirred his erection in her tight, moist passage. His hands slid down her sides to her hips, guiding her, suspending her while he tested the depth of her. Her desire rose around him. When he was certain he could bury himself in the heated vise pleasuring him beyond reason, he caught her mouth in a rapacious kiss and pushed her bottom down to his trusting hips.

The small moans and cries of passion she could not withhold fired his need. Their slow, measured rhythm burned into the core of his soul. The desire to pleasure her as he pleasured himself became obsessive. She radiated an inner light that lit the darkest corners of his heart. Joining with her made him complete. He felt capable of moving the tallest mountain, should she ask for it.

At the brink of ecstasy, he rolled on top of her. The bed did not stretch to accommodate his ardor. Tangled among the comforter and sheets, they slid down the side and landed on the floor. Emily's reflexive embrace around his neck held her upright.

Braced against the side of the bed, Royle grinned at her startled expression. "Not exactly what I had had in mind," he apologized, adjusting her among the tangles of bedding entwined around them.

"You thought about doing this?" Emily laughed softly in disbelief as her hands slid across his shoulders like fiery butterflies.

The sprightliness dancing in eyes the color of the pines summoned a wave of tenderness. He whispered her name and drew her tantalizing mouth to his.

Desire crashed on them with the force of a winter avalanche. It careened down the mountain and cleared every obstacle in the way. Their ragged breathing broke the kiss. Gazing into her passion-darkened eyes, Royle yielded to the force beyond the physical pleasure they shared.

The first pulses of her climax banished any thought of denial for either of them. Gripping her hips, he gave them the magic that carried them to their special paradise. Through the haze of euphoria, he saw her arch her head back, her eyes closed in blissful surrender. The graceful curve of her neck and back thrust her delicious breasts against him.

When he could move, he gathered her against him in a crushing embrace. He never wanted to release her. He buried his face in the cascade of tresses streaming through the crook of her neck and shoulder. Gradually, the sounds of celebrants firing guns and fireworks in the streets below leaked through his awareness.

"Very erotic, Tremaine," came a sugary voice from inside the room.

The intrusion snapped the lingering euphoria. He squinted in disbelief.

Galloway stood beside the opened door. He flipped a key into the air and caught it.

Protectively, Royle tightened an arm around Emily and drew the disheveled bedclothes around her as a shield from prying eyes. Outrage supplanted his elation. He reached for Emily's rifle propped beside the bed. The son of a bitch had found a way to get back at him.

"Don't bother, Tremaine. She's everything I suspected. Small wonder she refused Bull Stinson's offer for company. If he only knew . . ." Galloway's smug, malevolent smile accompanied a casual shrug of his shoulders. "I can see Miss Fergeson is not receiving visitors." Galloway pushed the door open wider. "I'm sorry, ladies. We seem to have called at an inconvenient time."

Royle brought the rifle to bear on Galloway and kept the impulse to pull the trigger a hair's breadth from reality. He held Emily's protesting head against his shoulder. His gaze darted to the two horrified women waiting in the hall.

"Get out before I kill all three of you." The steely anger in his voice sent the shocked women into motion.

Galloway ambled toward the doorway, paused, then sniffed the air. "My favorite perfume. You must wear it with me, Miss Fergeson."

Royle pointed the barrel at Galloway's heart and tightened his finger on the trigger.

Galloway strolled into the hall and closed the door behind him.

For a long time, Royle held Emily in a death grip with the rifle aimed at the door. Anger, outrage, and a soul-wrenching desire for retribution incinerated the safe harbor he had luxuriated in with Emily's passion.

"Royle?"

"I will kill him for this." He had never considered killing a man in cold blood. However, Galloway resembled a reptile more than a man. The bastard had deliberately set out to ruin Emily and succeeded, with the unwitting help of two of Silverton's most prominent ladies.

"Why bother?" Pushing against the lopsided mattress,

she lifted her head. The mass of bedclothes tumbled around her waist.

Incredulous, he tore his gaze from the door. The serene innocence of her gentle expression belied the sage wisdom lighting her eyes.

"Do you realize what just happened, Emily? What sort of ramifications are involved for you?"

His astonishment deepened, as did his anger, when she nodded. "What does it matter? People talk and speculate all the time. I don't care what they say or think. I care what you think, Royle. I'm not ashamed of making love with you." A cloud furrowed her brow. "But you are, aren't you?"

How could she not care? How could she not understand the far-reaching consequences of viper tongues and the conniving menace of John Galloway? "Emily, sweet Emily." Searching her face, he thumbed a stray hair from her cheek. "Shame is probably the only vile thing I am not feeling at the moment. What we shared is beyond anything I thought possible. I will not allow Galloway to make it tawdry gossip."

"How can you silence him? By putting a bullet in his heart?" A palpable sorrow melted the glow of their love-making from her countenance. "If you're worrying about my reputation—don't. Anything you do to Galloway hurts both of us."

Emily raised her hands as though reading an invisible newspaper. "I can see it now. 'Man Shoots Love Nest Intruder.' If you think we've given the gossip mills fodder now, what do you think will happen should you actually shoot Galloway?"

"You don't understand—"

"But I do, Royle. I've known many men like John Galloway. They wear different faces and clothing, but they share a black heart that cannot help but try to corrupt the world around them. Galloway isn't unique." A grim half-smile curled her lip. "Galloway reminds me of Craig Lyman, the man my father wanted me to marry. They are brothers under the skin. Perhaps that's why I found Galloway so revolting." The other side of her mouth lifted in a genuine attempt at a smile. "Apart from his charming personality and his offer of a personal evaluation at the drug store, of course."

Picturing Emily among men of Galloway's ilk filled Royle with revulsion. Any father who tried to marry off his daughter to a man who shared Galloway's reprehensible bent for corruption deserved a horsewhipping before being tortured.

"The only way you can thwart him is not to do what he wants."

"I doubt he wants me to kill him."

"No. He wants you to try. He's ready for you. When the smoke clears . . . you'll be dead." She flowed across his torso and embraced him in a ferocious grip that all but grafted her to his body.

"What makes you think—"

"I know, Royle. Believe me, I know the feel of a trap from someone like Galloway. Like my father," she whispered. "All that matters is what they want. No one and nothing else. It becomes an obsession. The irony is that the very obsession becomes more important than the initial object. Galloway picked me. I don't know why. The truth be known, maybe he doesn't either. Maybe it has something to do with you, and I'm merely an excuse to bait you. Clearly, he does not like you."

Her insight amazed him. He had not met many reasonable women. The rational path she drew him down quelled the roil of vengeance churning his emotions. "Galloway has despised me for years. I knew him when Teigue and I were mining in the Dakotas. I took a girl away from him. Carney was barely sixteen when her father died in a mining accident. Galloway offered to let her work in his saloon. Had she gone into that hellhole, I doubt that she would have seen seventeen. I put her on a stagecoach and sent her back to her sister in Baltimore." He heaved a sigh and leaned his head against the mattress.

Emily straightened slightly. The gentle tracing of her finger along his cheek penetrated another layer of his turmoil.

"Ah, you committed the most lethal crime of all— undermining his omnipotent power. No wonder he is baiting you. He hasn't gotten even with you for taking something he wanted. The question is, do you want to give him what he wants now, or stay with me for the rest of the night?"

"You cannot be serious. The best thing I can do for you is escape without being seen." The woman had the oddest sense of choices.

"But we were seen by the most reputable ladies in town. Galloway never has to say a word. They'll spread the word for him. Accept it. Nothing will change it."

"You accept too easily."

Emily's neck arched as she laughed. "Years of practice. I was queen of acceptance, until the weekend I woke up." Green eyes shot with hazel rays regarded him with a hint of seriousness. "That was the weekend I met you and Teigue. The best and worst all rolled into one."

Royle propped the rifle against the wall. Carefully, he lifted Emily from his lap, then helped her to her feet as he stood.

"Now what?" she asked softly.

The way her eyes searched his face made him uncomfortable. "Now, I get dressed and find a way to outwit Galloway's trap without springing it."

"Would you stay if I asked you?"

He studied the swirl of emotion flickering in her eyes. For reasons he could not fathom, he did not want to disappoint her in any way. Conversely, he felt obliged to defend and avenge the condemnation sure to arrive with the dawn. "Would you ask me to abandon your honor and stay?"

"Oh, Royle, there is no honor in railing against the truth. Only false pride. You would serve honor more valiantly if you pushed the bureau against the door and remained the rest of the night with me. They will talk regardless. If the price must be paid, why not make our time together last as long as we can? What more can they say?"

The feathery sweep of her fingers across his lips kept him silent.

"I said no strings. No commitments. I meant it. I have no right to ask anything of you, nor will I."

The reiteration of freedom bound him more surely than tears or pleas. She had made her position clear and left his fate in his hands. Yet, it did not feel as though he held the smallest bit of control.

His head bowed in defeat that felt more like victory. He set the lamp on the floor, then heaved the bureau in front of the door as an answer.

"You go nowhere in this town without me, Emily," he ordered, brooking no resistance.

"I would gladly accommodate your request." Smiling a secret smile, she placed the lamp on the bureau and lowered the wick until a golden glow bathed the room. "I am going back to bed." She extended her hand toward him. "Coming with me?"

"At least once more," he answered, taking her hand, his anger melting into desire.

The repercussions of Galloway's visit with the society ladies became evident the moment Royle and Emily entered the lobby the next morning.

Royle tried to tell himself it was his imagination that focused the hungry eyes of the miners camping in the lobby on Emily. Glancing down, his heart skipped a beat at her radiant smile. She did not have the good sense to act contrite or aloof. In her prim white blouse, puffed-sleeved jacket and plain skirt, she radiated the aura of a queen descending to the adoration of her court. The rifle in her hand might as well have been a scepter.

Royle swore under his breath and tightened his grip on Emily and his rifle. The first man who approached her with anything other than respect would regret it.

"Your *uncle* left word that he'd meet you two at Mary's," the desk clerk sneered.

Royle lost the ravenous appetite that had coerced them from the haven of Emily's bed. The implications of claiming Emily as his cousin practically shouted damnation in the clerk's reference to Teigue.

"Oh, thank you," Emily said with a smile. "I never dreamed when my great-aunt Bessie married Royle's fourth cousin Sherm that I'd have a distant uncle as kind and thoughtful as Teigue."

Royle was still trying to figure out the lineage of cousins as he opened the lobby door for her. "That was quick thinking."

"That's the trouble with lies. They demand it." She beamed up at him. "With a little time, it should dissipate the incest gossip."

Surveying the sparsely populated street, Royle credited her wisdom of defending herself through innuendo and allowing the ripple effect to solve the speculation. Perhaps he had underestimated her comprehension of what she faced today.

They found Teigue reading the newspaper at a table in the corner of the café. The speculative look Teigue gave them both and the years of living with him assured Royle that the town's hottest news was not in the paper. Word had already reached Teigue.

Countless reasons why he should not have made love with Emily made themselves clear in the morning light. Yet, he could not bring himself to regret a moment spent with her in his arms.

Teigue closed the paper and set it aside as they joined him. "Royle, you look like hell. Emily, you look radiant. So, the gossip is true."

"Yes, it is," Emily said brightly. "And the sun rose even though Emily Fergeson made love with Royle Tremaine."

Royle choked, then coughed and tried to catch his breath.

Teigue winked at Emily. "Sunshine, you are sunshine and a breath of fresh air all in one."

Royle wondered how the two of them could make light of the stigma now attached to Emily. "What the hell is wrong with you two?" he rasped, then coughed and finally breathed easily.

"Why, not a Goddamn thing a wedding wouldn't cure," Teigue answered softly.

"No wedding. No coercion," Emily protested. "Royle and I are consenting adults who make our own decisions."

Thoughts of the wedding waiting for him in Virginia crashed down on Royle. After the summer ended, Emily would be a haunting memory. He fervently hoped Rebecca Weston possessed a fraction of Emily's passion. She would never have Emily's ability to reach inside him and soothe his heart in troubled times.

What did it matter? He had never intended to marry for love, nor did he think he would know love if it knocked him down. The goals demanded by his destiny lay clear. "No wedding, Teigue."

Teigue leaned across the table, all trace of warmth gone from his harsh features suddenly lined with age. "All right. No wedding—unless Emily here comes down with a serious dose of motherhood. If that's the case, you'll find a rifle in your back and a preacher in your face."

"Fair warning served and noted," Royle answered through gritted teeth. What the hell had he been thinking with last night? Dismayed, Royle stared out the window. He had been thinking with the same part of his anatomy that had controlled his fantasies the last couple of months. To make matters worse, the next two months stretched before him with an agonizing realization. If wanting Emily had tied him in knots before, having plumbed the depths of her passion and sweetness, he would be a raving lunatic long before he caught a train to Virginia.

"Fine. We all understand how it going to be. Let's eat, load up, and go home." Teigue signaled Mary, who arrived with coffee and an interested glance at Royle and Emily.

Watching Emily ride beside Teigue in the wagon ahead heightened the sense of isolation enveloping Royle. A bite he recognized as jealousy for the easy way she and Teigue conversed about the simplest things pricked his ire. Old memories stirred. He had felt like an outsider looking in all the while he was in England. This time, he knew the reasons and could do nothing to change them. Though he wanted Emily in ways he struggled to understand, he could not abandon his duty to have her.

Marriage to anyone outside the circles of Virginia society denied him access. In so doing, it denied his children the right and responsibility of carrying on the Tremaine tradition.

The choice of marrying for love or position had died with his brother in a Yankee prison. As the last male in the Tremaine line, generations of Tremaines depended upon him to carry forth and do his part in placing the family name in a position of leadership and prominence.

They returned home shortly after dusk. By then, Royle thought he had found the borders of hell. Although barely fifteen hours since he had relinquished Emily's bed, an almost violent need for the press of her soft flesh seized him.

Presently, the flesh he stroked belonged to the mules.

"I reckon you have some decisions to make over the next couple of months." Teigue picked up a brush and started grooming the next mule.

"All my decisions were made years ago. There's no changing anything."

"Your decisions are based on hogwash. You found it easier to accept them than to tear down the shrine in your mind. They've become the mileposts of years. Never changing. Constant. Comfortable. These mules allow themselves more freedom than you."

"They are animals without responsibility. Of course they have more freedom." Royle turned the mule out and reached for the next one, tethered to the fence post. "I have a duty, Teigue. I'm sorry you don't see it that way. It would make it a lot easier if you did."

"On who? You?"

"You. You would understand why I cannot break off with the Westons and go with you and Emily, wherever it is you want to go."

"Emily and I are going to a place I bought above Colorado Springs. Remember that little valley with the stream and thick grass fit for raising horses?"

Royle recalled the place. "She will like it."

"Yep, I'm sure she will, providing we get a house built fit enough to live in come winter. I've been ordering what we need and making arrangements to get us started. We're pulling out in a month, Royle. You're welcome to travel with us."

"Have you told her you're leaving early?"

"Nope. I figure it's best. It's only a matter of time before you two wind up in bed together again. If she is not carrying your child now, I doubt you would want her in a family way. Such things tend to haunt a man marrying a woman for her position, even if she is marrying him for his money."

"I would marry Emily if she is carrying my child." Oddly, the words imparted a strange relief. And hope.

"Nope. She wouldn't have you."

"What the hell do you mean, she wouldn't have me? She damn well had me. . . ."

Teigue chuckled. "Don't know much about women, do you, Royle?"

The mule tossed his head in protest over Royle's quick, hard strokes with the brush.

"That little piece of sunshine cooking our dinner won't have any man who doesn't love her. Most women are that way. Sex isn't the same after you've known love."

"Sex is sex."

"Is it?"

Teigue pushed the mule away and tossed the brush into the tack box. "Funny, I don't recall you ever spending an entire night with a whore."

Royle set the mule free and threw the brush over his shoulder. "Damnit, Teigue," he seethed, cursing himself rather than his uncle. The last thing he needed was to hear the truth spoken aloud.

Chapter 19

THREE WEEKS OF enduring Royle's polite, distant behavior dimmed Emily's flagging optimism. He had become more withdrawn after her assurance that she did not have a case of motherhood. Like clockwork, her monthly had appeared when expected.

At the ore dump, she found a flat rock and settled down with a sigh. She went about sorting the ore from the slag with a hammer and chisel. Teigue had insisted that the final load hauled into Silverton be of the purest quality.

In a week or so, the three of them would make their last trek down the mountain together. Teigue had planned to depart from Silverton as soon as they booked passage on the train.

Royle remained committed to mining the rest of the summer, then selling the mine. Representatives from two large mining endeavors had already registered bids that provided a favorable percentage of the profits for the next ten years. The wealth Royle had pursued for most of his life was assured.

Emily did not care about the money. She sorted rocks and swung her hammer out of habit. Memories of her mother flitted though her mind. Lately, she'd discovered a new insight to Lorena. One of the great mysteries Emily had never solved had centered on how two such different people as her mother and father had found enough in common to indulge in the intimacy of sex. For years, Emily had thought it was because of her mother's promiscuity. Free love. They were both at the right place at the right time. Chemistry. Or maybe reveling in newfound freedom had seemed an exciting way to spend a summer.

Recalling the tender way her mother spoke of Ron Warner, she doubted their union had been rooted in such superficial motives. Since her night with Royle, she had begun viewing her mother in a different light. Now, she recognized the source of the tenderness Lorena had emoted when she spoke about Ron.

"She loved him," Emily muttered, then brought the hammer down on the chisel and cleaved a chunk of excess rock from a piece of high grade ore. Lorena had cautioned her to never have a child with a man she did not love.

The hammer stilled.

Lorena had loved Ron and let him go. Forever.

Had Ron loved Lorena?

She swung the hammer. Both had been different people during their summer of freedom. Even so, it was impossible to imagine Ron Warner in love with anything or anyone who did not enhance his position or wealth. Yet, perhaps he had loved Lorena. Briefly.

Emily glanced up and saw Royle striding toward her. She ignored him and continued working.

Without a word, Royle joined her and busied himself with the same task.

Unable to help herself, she stole glimpses of him during the next hour. Her hammer slowed. Memories of his strong, callused hands gliding across her body, pleasuring her, carrying her to the brink of ecstasy, then holding her there until she nearly went out of her mind with needing him inside her, changed the tempo.

"I will never love you." The vow he had made in the hot spring intruded on her memory. He may not love her, but he felt some tender emotions concerning her. Of that, she was certain. Words of denial contradicted his actions to protect and defend her. No man made love with such reverence and a passion that ran the spectrum of tender to nearly violent without deep emotions.

Had Ron spoken those words to Lorena?

Absently, she touched the acrylic pendant hanging around her neck. Lorena had treasured the gift from Ron.

"What is that?"

Startled, she glanced up. "What?"

"The thing you wear around your neck."

"It's a pendant my father gave my mother before I was born. Their initials are on the leaves of the rose. The acrylic oval lets the flower float freely, like my mother's spirit. I suppose it also protects it from damage. He gave it to her in a little ceremony near the Golden Gate Bridge."

"Never heard of it," he mused, tossing a hunk onto the ore pile.

"The Golden Gate Bridge was finished in 1937, nearly five years before the bombing of Pearl Harbor that started World War II in the Pacific."

Royle sat very still for a long moment.

"My parents met near the bridge while protesting yet another war called Vietnam. About five years later, Saigon fell. That was in 1975. By then, Mom and I lived in a commune deep in the Santa Cruz Mountains and my father had graduated from Stanford with a master's in business administration." She kept working, not caring whether he believed her.

"My mother left a will. Ron got me and I got the necklace. When I turned eighteen, I inherited 9.8 million dollars of Fergeson money and entered my father's alma mater with a fine social pedigree. It turns out that Mom, like you, was the last of an old line. I guess that makes me the last Fergeson." Emily smiled slowly. "The very last, since in my time I'm probably listed as missing or dead."

"You expect me to believe you inherited that much money?"

"I don't expect you to believe anything, Royle. Your mind is closed tighter than a collapsed mine tunnel." A sharp laugh escaped. "You know, 9.8 million is worth a lot more in this time, but it still buys the same amount of happiness. Zilch."

She had lost Royle as surely as Lorena had lost Ron. The realization made her wonder if the Fergeson women had a genetic defect when it came to men and love.

In the bright light of day, their night of lovemaking seemed a distant dream. She let her mind drift and relive each spectacular moment.

"Emily."

The softly spoken entreaty lifted her head. A shiver rode her spine when she met the misery in his eyes before he masked it. "What?"

"It might be a good idea if you decided which pile is good ore and which is secondary."

Emily glanced down at the mixed piles around her feet. Methodically, she began sorting. "Guess my mind was elsewhere. This isn't exactly mentally taxing work."

"Where was your mind?"

A sudden stillness enveloped the rock pile. Emily lifted her head slightly, then met his inquisitive gaze. "You don't want to know." A breeze whispered in the treetops as agreement.

"Were you thinking of the past?" A slight twitch at the corner of his mouth conveyed his reflective mood.

"Everything before this moment is the past, Royle. So, yes. I guess I was. The past is just that. Past reliving. Past changing." Much as she wanted to drag her gaze from his, he held it in a hypnotic grasp.

"Would you change it?"

"Change which part?"

"Silverton?"

Emily swallowed the sudden lump in her throat. "Never," she whispered. "What I would change is the distance you keep from me since. It makes me feel as though you have regrets."

"I do."

A crushing weight pressed her entire body into the flat stone upon which she sat.

"I regret that we had only the one night. I regret that night could not stretch to consume all the empty ones since, and those ahead. Most of all, I regret that I am not free to follow what I desire. Those are my regrets, Emily."

She would fly to his arms now if he gave the slightest sign of welcome. Yet, as rigidly as he held his body, she knew he fought the potent need flourishing between them. Perhaps she could seduce him and give them both what their bodies and her heart cried out for. But even if she did, nothing would change. Watching his controlled demeanor, her heart grew heavy. Whether they shared another moment of bliss or not, his destiny lay as clear to him as the sun shining overhead in a cloudless sky.

"I share those regrets, Royle."

"Regret alters nothing. Unfortunately. We both accept life as it is. It has to be this way. The paths of our destinies lead us in different directions. Mine goes east." He stood. The sun behind him cast a halo around his head. The breeze fluttered through his black hair and tipped it with golden rays.

Emily said nothing, merely watched as he walked away. She conceded the rightness of his assertion that regret was useless. It was the acceptance part she struggled with. For some reason, it refused her summons.

Gradually, the horrible reason of his visit dawned on her. In his way, Royle had said good-bye.

Heavy-hearted, Emily stood beside Teigue on the station platform. Her gaze scoured the steep slopes of the mountains and the jumbled architecture aligned in perfect rows of planned streets. Sadly, she knew the town would always fight the elements for survival. What the weather did not challenge, world events and politics would. She drank in

the scene and tucked it into her treasure trove of memories.
The Silverton Hotel would always be her fondest.

"He's not coming," Teigue apologized.

Royle had not uttered more than a few sentences in her
direction since the day on the ore pile. He'd moved into the
animal shelter the day after their return from Silverton. She
seldom saw him after the evening meal.

Sadly, she wondered how great a toll the war he waged
within himself was taking. "He'll be here," Emily said with
more conviction than she felt.

"I expected more of him," Teigue grumbled.

A hiss of steam gushed around the wheels of the engine.
The conductor called for boarding. Still, neither Teigue nor
Emily diverted their attention from the street.

"Teigue. Emily."

Emily whirled around at the familiar sound of her name.
A lopsided smile pained Royle's expression.

"About damn time you got here. We're leaving now."
The thickness in Teigue's gruff voice heightened the dole-
ful mood enveloping them.

"Take care of each other." Royle extended a hand to
Teigue, who brushed it aside and caught him in a bear hug
as powerful as the affection behind it.

Seeing her dark angel for a final time shattered the careful reserve damming the acknowledgment of loss and
heartache. Drawing on her last shred of practiced composure, Emily cried without shedding a tear. Her chest heaved
with unshed tears for their parting. Her feet locked in place
on the boards and stubbornly refused to walk away from
him. No amount of preparation diminished the agony of
losing Royle.

Then he was standing in front of her, his gentle blue eyes
darkened by sorrow. Resolve set his jaw in a determination
Emily knew well.

"I can't accept this." The words may as well have been
spoken by a stranger for all the control Emily had over
them.

"You have no choice, Emily. This is the way it has to
be." Tentatively, he extended a hand, then opened his arms.

She flew to him, catching him around the neck so tightly that her arms felt fused. The delicious vise of his embrace crushing the air from her lungs brought her as close to his heart as was humanly possible while clothed. She wanted to feel the impression of his body on hers as strongly as it was imprinted on her mind. With all her might, she let her love for him surge in the silence they shared, the words unsaid, the tears unshed.

Too soon, his lips brushed her forehead and his hands slid along her arms entwined around his neck. "Catch your train, Emily. The railroad does not wait for good-byes."

Swallowing hard, she gathered the last tendrils of her dignity and lowered her arms, then folded them beneath her breasts to keep from reaching for him again. "With all my heart, I wish you happiness, Royle."

"Not success?"

His attempt at diversion failed miserably. Torment shone brightly in his eyes and his strained features.

"Success is getting what you want. Happiness is wanting what you've got, or so it is said. I've known a lot of successful people, but not many happy ones." She let Teigue guide her toward the step stool at the railway car.

Seated by the window, she stared at Royle standing on the platform with his hands in his pockets. He stood apart from everyone else.

Her gaze locked on his. Memories flooded her. Royle showing her how to worry gold from the rocks. Royle crooning to the mules at night, then insulting them into hauling the heavy ore wagon up a slope. Royle kissing her with tenderness, then a passion so fierce that it consumed her.

The whistle sounded and the train inched forward. All the while, she held the link of his gaze that seemed as lost as she felt. Abruptly, the spell was broken.

Galloway grabbed Royle's arm and spun him around.

Emily let out a cry.

Royle glanced her way, then unleashed a violent fist directly at Galloway's jaw.

The station house blocked her view. Instinctively, she

stood, ready to run back. Teigue grasped her arm and pulled her down to her seat.

"He'll be fine. He's just itching to hit something. Good thing it's Galloway. That bastard deserves what Royle will do to him."

Unbelievably, the faint trace of a smile touched Teigue's mouth.

"What about Galloway's cronies? Who's going to watch Royle's back? We need to help him."

Teigue shook his head. "We've done all we can. Haven't we?"

"Have we?" In her sobbing, breaking heart, she knew of nothing she might have done to change Royle's mind. He commanded his destiny. She knew too well how long a fall lay ahead of him once he began realizing that nothing he did could breathe life into a past dead and buried. Survivor's guilt was one of the most punishing forms of guilt she knew. Given Royle's commitment to fulfilling the destiny he believed was his, she wondered if never coming to terms with it might be kinder in the long run.

She and Teigue spoke little during the long trek to Colorado Springs. Although they seldom strayed out of sight from one another, the privacy of their deep emotions demanded a distance both observed.

The second day in Colorado Springs, they rode into the mountains above the town. Teigue trailed a pack horse and led the way. When Emily looked down on the valley Teigue had offered as her spot in the world, she knew she had found home.

"This is perfect. It's even more beautiful than the land around the cabin." The sweeping mountains rose around them like walls to a fortress.

"See the creek?"

"It looks almost like a river," she marveled, watching the late-afternoon sun dance like diamonds on the surface.

"It sure as hell does in the spring when the snow melts. We'll build well above the floodplain." Teigue kneed his horse down the slope and across the valley.

The spot he had selected suited Emily. They had camp

set up and a good fire going by sunset. Perched side-by-side on a piece of deadfall they had rolled near the fire, they watched the changing colors in the sky.

"You seem a mite cheerier today, Sunshine."

Emily shrugged. "I've stopped grieving for Royle." She poked a stick in the fire and watched the end ignite.

"Smart trick. Tell me how you did it. You love him, but if you aren't grieving because he's gone his own way, you're a better man than I, Emily."

She bounced her shoulder into his upper arm and looked up. "No, sir. I am not. I've decided to live in denial."

"That's a constructive decision. What are you going to do? Live in this valley for the rest of your life and wait for him to come?"

"I'm not that strong." She waved the glowing end of the stick in the air. The problem of what to do about her inability to accept Royle's loss had plagued her relentlessly. "I'm not that stupid, either."

She stood and tossed the stick into the fire, then slowly surveyed what little topography she could make out in the near-darkness. "This valley is beautiful, Teigue. I'll live here the rest of my life. We'll make it a happy place. We'll build the house we planned, and buy the stock and raise the horses." She glanced down at Teigue who watched her with open curiosity. "I'll even read a few books and learn about the various breeds."

"You're leading up to something. What is it?"

"I don't really know what to do about Royle. I just know I can't let it be."

"What happened to living in denial?"

"Denial." Restless, she dug her toe into the dirt. "Well, it almost worked for a few hours. I don't know what to do, Teigue. I feel so . . . so . . . I don't know. I want to scream. Hit something. I've never felt so out of control. I just can't walk away—or let him walk either. But I can't stop him."

"I heard you tell him you couldn't accept him staying in the mountains. What happened? Did you finally run out of acceptance?"

Emily sighed in resignation. "It seems so. Maybe I'd find

it if I believed he felt nothing for me. Lord knows, he warned me that he'd never love me—even if he didn't think I was crazy. He said he would leave me. I heard the words and believed them. But I also felt his touch and something I can't begin to explain."

"The damn fool is in love with you and won't admit it even to himself. That's what you feel. If he gave you half a chance, you'd be able to convince him you're not crazy. I think he's got doubts about that, too."

"What makes you say that?"

"He quit leaving when you and I talked about how the world changed and started listening. Hell, he even asked a few questions."

"Yeah, he did," she mused, wondering if it meant anything.

"So what do you want to do about him?"

"I don't know yet. Something." She found another stick and poked it in the embers. "I've never really fought for anything I wanted before. Nothing was ever important enough to put myself at risk."

She glanced at Teigue, who watched her with a silent intensity. "Appeasement was all I cared about. At least it was until I got so sick of it that I choked."

"Are you talking about your friend's wedding?"

"Yes and no. It started before then. The wedding was just the straw that broke the camel's back." She poked the fire hard. Embers rose into the dark sky. "I got angry at Laura because she went into it with her eyes wide open. She was weak and refused to fight for herself. I was angry at myself for not knowing how to help her. The truth is, I was afraid that would be me in a little while. If I let it."

She stabbed the stick into the ground and hung her head. The sorrow filling her leaked into the night with a mirthless laugh. "When I left Durango, I was determined not to let my father pressure me into marrying a man I didn't love. Then I met Royle and fell in love. At the time, it never occurred to me that he'd be as determined to marry someone he didn't love as I was not to do the same."

"He isn't married yet," Teigue grumbled.

"He may as well be," she sighed, lifting her head and picking up the stick again. "I don't know how to fight for him, Teigue. That's my fault."

"Nothing about this is your fault."

She did not believe him, but appreciated the sentiment. "He'll write us after the marriage," she mused. The image of Royle pledging his fidelity to another woman sent her further into the abyss of hopelessness.

"That's one marriage I'm glad I'm not seeing," Teigue said, taking the stick from her hand, then giving the fire a hard poke.

Emily watched the embers rise in the flames. "Maybe we should." The thought rose from her hopelessness like a phoenix rising from the ashes.

"I'm not going to Virginia," Teigue said flatly. "I've got a house to build before the first snows fly."

"I could go." The sudden race of her heart charged her with energy. "Out of sight, out of mind, Teigue. Suppose I didn't stay out of his sight long enough for him to . . ." Her voice trailed. "Stupid idea."

"Not necessarily," Teigue mused, handing the stick back to her. "You? Go east? Seduce him into marrying you? It'd be easier there, if that's what you have in mind."

Emily stared into the fire as the answer formed. "I won't trap him. I want him on fair terms. Here. Not Virginia."

"I see." Teigue stretched his long arms, then hunched over and reached for the coffeepot. "Seems to me that between the two of us we ought to be able to figure a way to make him see what's in his heart."

"It isn't that simple."

"Yeah, it is, Sunshine. Disillusion is right around the bend and waiting for him. He remembers the grandeur of the Tremaines from a time that's come and gone. He saw it with the eyes of a child. And he saw the aftermath through the eyes of a grief-stricken, angry young man when he returned from England. Hardest thing I ever had to do was tell that boy his entire family was dead. His land belonged to a carpetbagger. His bank account was gone along with even the smallest memento of his proud Tremaine heritage.

All he had was what he brought from England, and me. He wouldn't go west until I took him back to Tremaine House. He wanted to visit his mother's, Madeline's, and his sister's graves. I gave in. I took him."

Emily imagined Royle as a sixteen-year-old racked with grief and loss seeking closure at his mother's grave. The image forced her to sit as the strength rushed from her knees.

Teigue handed a cup of coffee to her. "It was bad, Emily. We had to sneak into the graveyard at dawn. We had barely found the graves, which were poorly marked, when the blackhearted carpetbagger owner came after us with a whip. A couple of his hands leveled shotguns at us. When Royle beseeched him for a moment, just a Goddamn minute at his mother's grave, the bastard took the whip to him.

"That's the only man I ever regretted not killing, and I'd had a bellyful of killing, seeing men suffering and dying with no help either way."

"Is that when Royle decided to make his fortune and restore the Tremaine name to Virginia society?"

"Probably. It wasn't like a decision. It was more like a conviction. A religion. And Tremaine House is the Holy Grail."

The roots of Royle's destiny ran deep in Virginia soil and even deeper in his soul. "He has the money to buy anything he wants, including Tremaine House."

"That he does. He's made damn sure of it." Teigue met Emily's troubled eyes. "But there isn't enough money anywhere to restore Virginia to what it once was. Money can't do it. I've been there. Trouble is, most of those folks refuse to believe it's gone, so they languish in old traditions and shabby illusions. The longer they cling to what can never be again, the more they hurt themselves by not joining the rest of the world."

"Reconstruction went on for years," Emily mused. "The South always tried to preserve an aura of regal dignity about their circumstances." She stared into the fire. "I wish I had read more post–Civil War history."

"The real test for Royle is whether he sees it for what it is when he settles in. I told you before, he's his own worst enemy."

"Most of us are, Teigue."

"True enough."

"So how do we become his allies in Virginia?"

"*We* don't. You do. You go there. Think you can step into what passes as high society there?"

Curious, she swiveled around on the log. "Of course. Old habits die hard. You have a plan?"

"Yep. But it isn't done cooking yet."

She grinned, hopeful. "Well, turn up the oven temperature. I don't want a half-baked idea. I want this to work."

"Hell, we're dealing with Royle. There's no guarantee. He's a stubborn man and you might wind up with more heartache than you have now."

A wellspring of optimism bubbled inside Emily.

Chapter 20

MEMORIES OF EMILY seeped from the moist walls of the mineral spring. If not for its healing properties, Royle would have avoided the place. The water caressed him with the velvet nimbleness of her exploring fingers.

The worst of the deep bruises marking his body had faded to a pale yellow-green. The somewhat regular soakings had alleviated the lesser injuries Galloway's men had inflicted with their rifle butts. Every lingering ache and pain had been worth pounding that foulmouthed reptile into the ground.

Letting Emily board the train to Colorado Springs had been more difficult than anything he had done in his life. Watching the train pull away from the station, he had been in the mood to hit something. Galloway had been unlucky enough to pick that moment to lay hands on him.

For the past month, everything about his surroundings, even the mules, had reminded him of Emily. She haunted him with the tenacity of the three ghosts in his dreams of

Tremaine House. Even the recurring dream of being drawn
and quartered by four nervous horses cheered on by face-
less ancestors held Emily's image. Last night, he dreamed
she had descended from the cloudy heavens and severed his
bonds. When she did, his mother, Madeline, and Flavia had
disappeared. The melodious sound of Emily's voice lingered as she called, summoning him, elevating him from
the ground, and drawing him to the warmth of her breast
and a freedom he craved.

He reminded himself that she was demented—no one
traveled through time because of an earthquake. But it did
no good. Her memory dominated his thoughts.

He had begun questioning his own sanity when her de-
scriptive accounts of a world over a century in the future
had begun making sense. The things she had spoken of in
great detail made his head spin—medicines that prevented
disease; tiny, powerful lights that cut skin and cured disfig-
urement; and injections that prevented death. He tried to
imagine a machine that showed his bones without pain or
bloodshed. The more she talked and Teigue asked questions, the more believable she had become.

What bothered him most was her relentlessness. If her
claim of being from the future wasn't true, why had she expanded their view into her dementia? In all other areas,
Emily had proven intelligent, sensible, and quick at adapting to any situation.

The concrete things that defied explanation or dismissal
baffled him. The worn-out shoes she had left behind were
like nothing he'd seen. And that strange thing she called a
bra . . . If she was from the future, men had a far easier path
to pleasure than the one constricted by a corset.

None of it mattered now. Emily Fergeson was out of his
life. The chances of seeing her anytime in the near future, if
ever, were nonexistent.

Water sluiced down his lean body as he exited from the
pool. Once dressed, he gathered his belongings, cast a final
glance over his shoulder, then strode into the cool dawn
staining the eastern sky. Today, he'd leave the serene valley and embark on the long journey to Virginia.

An hour later, he had all the mules in harness. The circuitous route he chose took five hard days. He considered the additional time worth the edge his unpredictability afforded. Alone, he represented an invitation to Bull Stinson and any of Galloway's men seeking retribution.

He spent less than a day at the smelter and the bank. Satisfied with the purchase agreement for the mine, he signed the documents. The following morning he boarded the train without incident.

In Colorado Springs, he remained in his seat when his fellow passengers availed themselves of the amenities of the station. His appetite had suffered a malaise since Emily and Teigue's departure.

Staring at the mountains rising like sentries behind the town, he wondered about their progress on the grand house they had planned with meticulous detail. Knowing their tenacity, he figured they would be far enough along to comfortably survive the winter before the first snow flew.

He turned away from the window.

Memories of Emily's easy laughter and Teigue's quick wit filled his mind. He closed his eyes and tried to relax. The images persisted. He abandoned the fight and let them flow. He knew the details of the house. He had made suggestions they accepted with an eagerness that twisted inside him.

The temptation to get off the train and join them in the high valley proved so strong that he had to grip the armrest beside the window. He had come too far, worked too hard, to abandon the future demanded by his father and the countless Tremaines who had come before.

Emily was lost to him. Her claims of not belonging in the world from which she came may be true. But there was no room for her in his future either. The closely defined circles of Virginia society accepted few outsiders. He had been fortunate to find a way to re-enter it with Rebecca Weston.

When the train pulled out of Colorado Springs, Royle forcibly relaxed his knotted muscles. He had thought the hardest part over when he bid them farewell in Silverton. The urge to join them had nearly undone the raw calluses

forming over a tender place he had not thought he possessed.

The sophistication of Denver in comparison with his last
visit six years earlier distracted Royle. The long train ride
had provided ample opportunity to consider what he needed
for the final leg of the journey. He found it strange that the
saloons and drinking palaces held no appeal. What he
wanted in the way of female companionship lived in a high
mountain valley above Colorado Springs.

The day of his departure from Denver, he concentrated
on recapturing the zeal that had once marked every action
leading to the journey ahead. He managed an entire hour
without thinking of Emily and considered it a triumph.

His life had changed, yet remained the same. With effort,
he shed the years of hard living and rough mannerisms. He
relegated them to the West where he had acquired them.
The demeanor of gentlemanly conduct drilled into him as a
child and reinforced in London was a distant skill he summoned with relative ease.

At the Denver train station, he noticed a cadre of men
surrounding a young woman in a silver-gray traveling
dress. Beside her, a second woman in her mid-forties, probably her companion or a relative, oversaw the propriety of
the men's attentions.

He would have to become accustomed to having his
every move watched when in the company of a young lady,
particularly Rebecca. A hint of impropriety or a whisper of
scandal would ruin him. Ignorance was worse than an in-
tentional infraction of the courting etiquette.

Royle checked his watch. With a few minutes before
boarding time, he sidled closer. He intended to eavesdrop
and sharpen his rusty social skills.

"Why, I thank you so very much for your insightful suggestion, Mr. Mayhew," the young woman said in a soft accent. Through the delicate trace of a Virginia inflection, the
tone struck his heart like a lance. He cursed quietly. How
long before all women stopped sounding like Emily?

"Mrs. Preston and I will take your excellent advice and

think most kindly of you while we dine," the young woman concluded.

"I would consider it an honor and a privilege if you and Mrs. Preston shared a table in the dining car with me," came a humbled baritone in response.

Royle's head whipped around in time to see Teigue approach. He blinked. Damn, Teigue and Emily. Here. His heart leaped with joy, then plunged into the depths of agony.

Too late, he noticed Teigue rounding the group and heading in his direction. The shock of seeing them shot through Royle with mind-numbing conflict.

"I didn't expect you to reach Denver for another week or so," Teigue said. Excitement lit his face with a grin that made his brown eyes shine as though feasting upon what he saw.

Without thought, Royle clasped Teigue's hand. "Neither had I. Why are you here?"

Teigue shrugged, then tilted his head toward the cluster of men behind him. "Emily is going east to take care of some business for me and buy the furnishings for the house."

"You aren't going with her?" The lilt of Emily's laughter drew Royle's gaze. All he could see was her pert hat with a feather. One of the men shifted and obliterated even that view.

"No. I'll finish the house. The snow might come early this year. We need to be ready. What a great stroke of luck you'll be on the train with her. She attracts men like a bear brings flies. Will you help Mrs. Preston watch over her a bit?"

"Watch over Emily?" The notion was ludicrous. All the hard-won resolution he had built over the last month evaporated like a drop of water on a desert at high noon.

"Thanks, Royle. I don't know what I'd do if anything happened to my Sunshine. But then, you know what she means to me." Teigue clapped him on the shoulder.

"Yes," Royle answered, still trying to catch a glimpse of her and fighting the instinct to walk away at the same time.

"Come on. Let's surprise her."

Royle squared his shoulders, not knowing what to expect. Although unintentionally, he had hurt Emily by maintaining the distance between them. He doubted that she understood. One more night like the one they shared in the Silverton Hotel would destroy him. He would abandon his course for the soft loving of a woman. Once he traded his future for the bliss of the present, he became less of a man than she deserved. Worse, forsaking his destiny meant losing himself. He would become a failure, a man without honor, void of loyalty to those who deserved it most.

She posed the greatest test of his character. She was a treasure he could never claim without sacrificing his beliefs.

The cluster of men parted as Teigue led Royle through them. Royle lifted his gaze.

The brilliant smile lighting her face flickered, then softened. For an instant, Royle recognized a tender emotion in her eyes. It fled in the sweep of her eyelashes.

Lord, but she was lovely in the fashionable traveling suit that looked as soft as he knew her skin felt. He yearned to snatch her up and run to the nearest place with a locked door where he could worship her with all the need clamoring inside him. Instead, he drank in the light of her presence like a bittersweet opium more addictive than sunlight.

Emily locked her knees to keep them from buckling. It was too soon. She wasn't ready. According to the plan she and Teigue had made, she would see Royle in Williamsburg, on her terms. The queasy, exciting sensations quivering in her stomach helped her regain a modicum of control. Even so, seeing him now unleashed the turmoil she had carefully tamped into a logic-lined compartment of her mind.

Her eyes feasted on him. Through sudden waves of vertigo, Royle appeared thinner. She had worried about the altercation with Galloway until receiving word from Dr. Bird that Royle had not sustained any life-threatening injuries.

"Mr. Tremaine," she crooned, thankful her chameleon nature remained strong enough to hide the chaos ravaging her serenity. "It is a delight to see you again. I had thought you still in Silverton."

Royle took her offered gloved hand and pressed it to his lips. The fabric lent no protection against the potency of his touch or the warmth of his lips. An involuntary flinch of her fingers gave him pause. The way he inhaled during the brief caress of his lips on her fingers filled her with longing. She gathered the streamers of her wild emotions and reined them in sharply. Today, she practiced a role, one she knew well, with a few twists and an accent she had learned from a college friend.

"May I present my companion, Mrs. Preston. She has graciously agreed to accompany me on my journey." *And throw a net over me if I lose my mind and so much as think of doing something stupid where you are concerned.*

Emily concluded the introductions just as the conductor sounded, "All aboard!"

"Perhaps I'll see you on the train, Mr. Tremaine?" She kept her voice feather-light and projected the image of the socialite epitomized in the etiquette books she had devoured over the past week in Denver.

"It may be unavoidable," Royle answered as though dreading another encounter.

She bid a hasty yet polite farewell to the swains gathered around her. They had been good practice for what awaited her in Virginia. Emily had appreciated their presence. Then she was alone with Teigue, who held her upper arms in a fatherly embrace. "So it begins a little sooner than we anticipated."

"Too soon, Teigue. I don't know if I'm ready. Seeing him so unexpectedly nearly took my breath away."

"You contained your surprise admirably. But if you aren't ready or you want to call it off, I'll escort you down the platform, and we'll go home."

"I will not get another chance like this. I have to be ready." Mustering her courage, she smiled brightly at the concern in Teigue's expression. "I can't give up until the fat lady sings and I know we've lost. I'm not throwing in the towel because the game took an unexpected twist."

Teigue squeezed her hands. "Good girl. Remember, his crossroads lie at Tremaine House."

"And with Rebecca Weston."

Teigue dismissed her concern with a shake of his head. "He has Jackson blood in him, too, Sunshine. We're notoriously single-minded when it comes to women we love." Teigue kissed her forehead.

Impulsively, Emily hugged Teigue, not caring whether it was proper or not. She relished the strong support of his love before embarking on the subtle battle for the man they both loved.

"I will be home before winter," she promised.

"Bring Mrs. Preston with you."

Emily raised a speculative eyebrow. "Camilla?"

"It might be interesting spending a winter with her around." Teigue's knowing wink made her laugh despite her situation.

"I'll do that." She took his arm and joined Camilla Preston.

As the train rumbled out of Denver, Emily and Camilla followed the conductor to their stateroom. Two sleeping berths converted into a comfortable velvet-upholstered sofa. A lamp table jutted from beneath the window draped by a fringed and scalloped shade.

The conductor assured them that their travel luggage was tucked into the small closet. A porter would bring them warm water and anything else they desired.

Neither woman spoke until they were inside. "So, the brawny giant dressed in black is the one," Camilla said under her breath as they seated themselves. "He appears to be in mourning."

Emily had interviewed a dozen women who answered her solicitation for a companion. Two minutes with Camilla had ended the search. The forty-four-year-old widow possessed a healthy portion of her own chameleon abilities and would adapt in any circumstance.

"He is the one," Emily sighed, glad for the privacy where she could let down her guard. "It shook me down to my toes when he showed up on the platform. I thought I had a little more time to get this role perfected."

"You say the strangest things, Emily." Camilla removed her gloves and hat. "But I can see why you are smitten. Mr. Tremaine exudes a very masculine charisma, nearly as much as his uncle."

Emily faltered in removing her hat. Apparently, Teigue wasn't the only one whose interest had been sparked during the week the three of them had prepared for the journey.

"Your Mr. Tremaine is also a very troubled man," Camilla concluded.

Emily rummaged through her traveling case and withdrew a deck of cards. "He will always be troubled unless he makes peace with himself."

"Few men do." Camilla stashed their hats and gloves, then resumed her place. "No poker, Emily. Whist. It is the card game most played in the society parlors."

Determined to succeed in her role as a desirable socialite of the 1880s, Emily settled into serious study of a variation of a card game that eventually became bridge. Under Camilla's expert tutelage, Emily mastered the trick of counting the cards and the order of each suit. She doubted luck had as much to do with winning as did the theory of number probability and learning the nature of her opponents. The lesson lasted a strenuous two hours, during which Emily's concentration tried to run away in speculation of where Royle was on the train.

As though sensing her preoccupation, Camilla put the cards away. "Shall we freshen up and stroll the train for some exercise? Perhaps we should seek out the refreshment car and have a glass of lemonade."

"You mean do I want to go look for Royle?" Emily liked the way Camilla's mind worked.

"Please, Emily." Camilla lowered her dusty blond head in feigned disapproval. "It is inappropriate for a woman to chase a man."

"I'm not chasing him . . . just not letting him forget me." She adjusted her hat. Maybe she *was* chasing him. In this game, she had more practice at escaping than capturing.

Until Royle, no man had fired her heart with such a tide of anguish and love. He was worth the effort, and the cost if she failed. Belatedly, she realized the tenet of free love was false. Love always demanded a price and paid dividends. Sometimes, as in her love for Royle, the risk factors compounded the dear cost to her heart.

"Let us make your presence known." Camilla tilted her fine jaw with an imperious air. Her gray eyes held a hint of mischief. "If we encounter him, of course, it is mandatory for you to acknowledge him. After all, he is Mr. Jackson's nephew."

Emily gained confidence from the intrepid widow who had become a fast friend in the short time they had known each other. The high stakes Emily played for meant that the next time she rode the train to Denver, either Royle would choose to accompany her or she would find the acceptance of his loss that eluded her as nothing else in her life had.

A muttered comment from behind drew Royle from the scenery moving outside the window in the refreshment car. The contrast between the miner who worked the ore piles and the sophisticated lady gliding toward him seemed impossible. Until he met her gaze. Regardless of dress or demeanor, Emily shone like a polished golden nugget on a pile of coal.

The startlement of seeing her earlier prepared him for this encounter. Unfortunately, it also revived the physical discomfort that had plagued him all summer. The only reprieve had been the silent, spirit-dampening month of separation.

When she paused to speak with a man he recognized from the station platform as the dashing Mr. Mayhew, his mood darkened. Seeing her laugh and talk with another man ignited an unreasonable fury.

He brooded and furtively watched her settle into a seat near Mayhew. Briefly, he wondered if anyone besides Emily would notice if Mayhew disappeared from the train when he left the refreshment car.

What the hell was he thinking? He could not toss every

man Emily spoke with from the train. He held no claim on her, nor she on him.

Royle finished his coffee and tried to relax. Each time he heard the laughter that had brightened even his darkest days at the mine, he tensed. He wanted to find fault with her faint Virginia accent, and could not. It was perfect and as phony to her character as a three-dollar bill.

What game did she play?

Royle rose and turned away from where Emily beguiled the smitten Mayhew. He headed for the smoking car, where women did not venture. He needed to clear his head. At least the cigar smoke would not cloud his thinking.

Royle stared at the newspaper he held in front of him like a steel curtain until late in the dinner hour. The smoking car became an island of neutrality.

The longer he thought about it, the stronger became his certainty that Teigue and Emily were up to something. Why else would she have left Teigue and traveled east? He wondered about her final destination and decided to ask.

The years of rough living rolled aside. Rules of etiquette instilled by his mother and honed under the auspices of his English cousins took on fresh meaning. If Miss Emily Fergeson wasn't the socialite she had proclaimed, her actions would give her away. Her ability to mimic those around her would carry her only so far. When she slipped, he'd have one more layer of armor shielding him from her potent effect on his heart. He sorely needed some kind of defense because at the moment, he didn't care where she thought she came from; he wanted her with an illogical urgency. All he had to do was abandon his familial duty to have her.

The desolated faces of the three women haunting his dreams rose in his mind.

He couldn't abandon them or the Tremaine heritage, regardless of the personal cost.

When he entered the crowded dining car he saw Emily with Mrs. Preston. The lack of empty tables made him smile. Without waiting for a formal seating arrangement, he strode directly to Emily's table. As he took a place opposite her, he gestured at the porter.

"Why, Mr. Tremaine, I do not recall inviting you to dine with us. However, you are most welcome," Emily said with remarkable aplomb.

"I would hope so, since we're practically family. Cousin." He flashed a warning grin, then ordered dinner.

When the porter left, Emily responded. "I am hardly your cousin. I thought that tidbit of misinformation had been put straight in Silverton."

The softly spoken rebuff reminded him painfully of the circumstances that had made the correction necessary. For a frozen moment, he met her gaze and knew she remembered the rapacious need and tender lovemaking of their magical night. The air became unbearably warm. The erection growing in his trousers ached for the warm, moist softness a few feet away under the table. His heart cried out for the soul-soothing balm of her touch and the delicate absolution of her kiss after she had shared the bliss he had found nowhere else. Nor did he believe he would find it again. Not without Emily.

The woman was wearing him down with the tenacity of water flowing over a slab of granite. With enough time, the rough edges smoothed and the rock molded into the shape created by the resilient caress of the water. The drought of her absence had toughened him, yet made him thirstier than ever for the nectar of her passion.

"Will you be going on to Boston or New York?" Royle leaned his forearms against the edge of the table and folded his hands.

"We have not decided," Emily answered casually. "Teigue requested that I attend to a few matters for him in Williamsburg."

Williamsburg. He had half-expected it because it was the only place he hoped she would avoid. She pushed the remainder of her food around the plate, but had stopped eating.

"Teigue never mentioned any business there to me." What business could Teigue have in Williamsburg? "Why did he send you? He could have asked me to handle anything he wanted done. Or gone himself."

"We both know how he feels about returning. Let's not pretend otherwise, Royle. As for you, perhaps he did not wish to encumber you or pose an impediment to your plans. Two months is not much time for you to establish your own household before you wed Miss Weston. I, on the other hand, am of little use in building the ranch and can afford the time for the trip. Besides, I'm rather enjoying the sights. And it is an excellent opportunity to meet some very interesting people."

"Like your Mr. Mayhew?" The acerbic accusation was out before he thought about it. Damn, he sounded like a jealous lover. Which, to his chagrin, was exactly what he was.

"Yes," Emily answered softly.

"Mr. Mayhew hails from Boston. A fine, upstanding family with business interests in Denver," Camilla chimed in. "From the little Mr. Jackson revealed about you, Mr. Tremaine, I should think you would applaud the expansion of Miss Fergeson's social sphere. I understand it was rather limited before her departure from Silverton."

"She didn't seem to mind," Royle grumbled. The facade of manners disintegrated. Somewhere along the line, the tables had turned. The women across from him used words with the same precision with which a sharpshooter used bullets to make a pattern in a piece of wood. Only he was not wood. At the moment, he would give anything, even his destiny, to be in the mountain pool with Emily. Naked. No pretense. No barriers.

As though she read his prurient thoughts, color crept over her high collar and stained her cheeks a bright pink.

To his relief, Royle's meal arrived. Although it was artfully arranged and steaming, his appetite fled.

"If you're finished, Camilla, I'm ready to retire. It has been a long day. Mr. Mayhew will be expecting us for breakfast and I would like to look rested."

"If you'll excuse us, Mr. Tremaine, we'll take our leave." Camilla nodded at Emily. "I'm certain we shall all run into each other often until we reach Williamsburg."

Royle deemed the mild statement a calculated prediction.

Short of living in his stateroom or the smoking car, he had no way to avoid them.

Royle drank in the lithe, graceful motions of Emily's departure from the chair. Every muscle in his body ached for the press of her sweet, soft flesh against his.

"Have a pleasant evening, ladies, and sleep well," he said in a formal voice that yielded none of the desire hammering him to pulp inside.

Emily paused, then gave him a heart-stopping smile. "The same to you, Royle." Her voice dropped as her head dipped. "May all your dreams be of me."

Dry-mouthed, Royle watched her navigate the tables with the sway of the train on the tracks. Damn her to hell. His dreams were rife with her.

As she disappeared through the dining-car door, he wondered which one of them had won this bout. It felt like it belonged to Emily. The next one had to be his.

Chapter 21

"GOOD EVENING, MISS Fergeson, Mrs. Preston," Royle said, rising as the porter seated her and Camilla. "I've carried out Teigue's wishes and taken steps to ensure that your meals will be uninterrupted by our fellow travelers."

"Excuse me?" Emily arranged her skirts, her hazel eyes narrowing as her mind raced.

"I explained our close family relationship to the conductor. From now on, unless you take your meals in your stateroom, you'll be dining at my table."

He looked so proud of the coup, she nearly lost her appetite. "And if I choose not to dine with you, Mr. Tremaine?"

He set his fork down and looked straight at her. Emily stared back, concealing her churning emotions as well as he hid his.

"Why would you do that?"

"Why indeed," she retorted, drawing her napkin onto her

lap with a bit more flare than necessary. "Are you in any way suggesting that my conduct requires supervision, or that Mrs. Preston is negligent in her duties as my companion?"

Taken aback, his hands lifted in protest. "No, not at all. I am merely sharing the burden, as Teigue requested, of seeing that your reputation suffers no ill effects by overzealous suitors."

"I have no suitors."

"I beg to differ with you, Emily. Mr. Mayhew pays you far too much attention for his interest to be that of a casual traveling companion. At breakfast this morning, I saw him take your hand." Royle's head shook in disapproval.

The pique of Royle dictating her dining companions heightened. "I did not permit any liberties. And if I had, it is no business of yours."

"Teigue—"

"Don't tell me Teigue asked you to watch every move I make. What is your real reason?" She hoped it was because the sight of another man with her forced him to see a future without her as unbearable.

"Your reputation reflects on Teigue. And me. It has a way of following wherever you go, even Williamsburg. I'm looking out for all of our interests."

"I see," Emily said with a tight, formal smile that strained her patience. "You can rest assured that I will not mention anything that might be perceived as the slightest peccadillo when we reach our destination."

The flash of irritation that made him scowl kept his gaze averted. "That would be wise."

Dinner arrived and Camilla ate heartily. Her comments about the fare and their fellow travelers built a modicum of ease in the scant conversation.

Inwardly, Emily quailed. What had started as a reminder of her presence had turned into a battle of wits. She doubted that maintaining her good name had as much to do with limiting her dinner companions as he pretended. Yet his demeanor implied little else.

She bided her time until the last dish disappeared from

the table, and Royle took the back of her chair. When she was so close to him that the lingering scent of aftershave filled her nostrils, she looked into his eyes and whispered, "Have I your permission to remember, in great detail, all the so-called stains on my reputation? The Silverton Hotel is my favorite."

She had the satisfaction of seeing the color drain from his face before leaving the dining car.

Damn, but she was good. She had thwarted him at every turn. This was becoming the longest train ride any man could survive. Having Emily so close was proving more difficult than her last month at the cabin, when he'd slept in the animal shelter. The strain of taking each meal with her increased with the obvious pleasure she took in sharing the table with him.

The way she struck up conversations and formed easy alliances among their fellow travelers amazed him. Not until the third time he found himself amid a small group of strangers in the refreshment car did he discover her secret. The way she asked questions created an aura of genuine interest. Then, she listened and asked more questions. The natural enjoyment people found in talking about themselves, to someone who listened as intently as Emily, endeared her to them.

On the other hand, Emily offered little insight about herself. Her adroit manipulation always shifted the focus to others. The expertise she demonstrated had to come from years of practice. He began to believe she was all she said she was. Wryly, he mused that it figured he'd conquer every conceivable obstacle only to have a woman travel through time and make him question everything and disrupt his life. Of one thing he felt certain: there would never be another like Emily Fergeson.

Torn between the demands of honor and the direction of his heart, Royle grappled with his conscience. Either way, he lost.

Their arrival in Virginia came on a day as gray as his mood. Despite the relentless conflict she sparked, he would miss the luxury of seeing her at every turn.

"We will go our separate ways soon. I hope my conduct has not given you any reason to regret my presence in Williamsburg," Emily said.

He reached in front of her and Camilla to open the door leading to the stateroom car. A rush of air caught Emily off balance. He grabbed at her to keep her from falling. The feel of her in his arms had him turning her and lowering his mouth before she pulled away.

"Don't tempt me, unless you mean it," she breathed.

"Isn't that what you have been doing this entire journey? Tempting me?" Irritation at himself and at her for calling him on the impulse bolstered his defenses. He released her, all the while feeling Mrs. Preston's scrutiny.

"No, not really." Emily followed Camilla through the connection passage and into the stateroom car. The buzz of people preparing for departure hummed through the narrow corridor.

"What would you call it, Emily?" Whatever name she gave her actions, they had been damned effective. Sometime during the long journey, he had discovered the poison of wanting her in bed had become secondary to needing her in his life. The multiple facets of her moods uplifted his spirits and kept him sharp.

"I'd call it visibility. I won't fade into the woodwork around you, nor will I allow you to consign me there." She slipped into her stateroom.

Royle stared at the closed door for a long time. Like so many other doors in his life, it was not in his power to open it and claim the prize he craved within. His sense of familial duty precluded that option. He was a dutiful son. As such, honor demanded that he walk away.

By the time Emily reached Williamsburg, sheer obstinacy had bolstered her determination to remain near Royle. Regardless of how hard she tried, acceptance of his marriage with Rebecca Weston eluded her.

Camilla hired a coach at the train station to take them to the home of Teigue's cousin, Patty Conklin. Emily stared out at the ravages of a war over for almost eighteen years. Lost in thought of what lay ahead, she spoke little.

The strains of past opulence peeked from the three dormers in the steep, sloping roof of Patty Conklin's home. Despite the need of a paintbrush, the house appeared inviting.

A jack-o'-lantern fence with missing pickets that had once been white defined a yard around the house. The lower gardens reflected an elegance and care the taller shrubs and trees lacked. Early autumn chrysanthemums, asters, and late-blooming roses cheered the house.

A short woman with silver hair and rosy cheeks that dominated her round face hurried across the worn porch. As she neared, Emily recognized the gemlike quality of the brown eyes she realized were a Jackson family trait.

Emily introduced herself and Camilla to the stout woman.

"My, you have made such a long trip. You are certainly brave to travel so far alone. Just the two of you. Across strange country."

Emily knew that no one here had any idea of how strange the endless countryside had become. Devoid of freeways and interstates, the terrain felt empty. It seemed naked without signs, telephone poles, and the giant, high-tension scaffold towers tying the nation into power grids. From the train window, the entire world beyond the tracks had turned out the lights when the sun set. Even the towns, too small for her to call them cities, had seemed too quiet when the train stopped.

Years ago, she had tuned out the hum of incessant traffic and screaming sirens. Now, their conspicuous absence made the new sounds of horses, wagons, and jangling harnesses crisp.

What she missed most was a telephone to call Teigue to share her experiences. It seemed ironic that now she had someone worth calling and no telephone.

Emily shook off the reverie of the journey that had taken days instead of hours on a commercial airliner. A secret smile lit her eyes. The train ride with Royle had offered time she wouldn't trade for all the convenience of an airport.

With a surprising efficiency, Patty issued instructions for the luggage to the coachmen. All the while, she ushered Emily and Camilla into the house.

Crossing the threshold of the Conklin home was like entering another dimension. Briefly, Emily wondered what Patty had done with the money Teigue had sent over the years. Now she knew. It was on the inside of the house. Thick carpets on highly polished oak floors caressed her feet. Silver candlesticks and ornate stained-glass lamps decorated every piece of exquisite furniture. The decor reminded Emily of a private San Francisco antique showroom.

"Oh, do come into the parlor and meet my friends. You needn't stay long. Certainly you are weary from your long journey. It will only take a moment," Patty entreated. "And a cup of tea might be just the refreshment you need."

Eager to please their hostess and learn more about the relationships and people Royle wished to cultivate, Emily agreed.

The parlor reflected a stately richness embraced by the very wealthy, stemming from old, inherited money. Two women on a brocade sofa sipped tea and smiled in welcome as she entered. They rose in greeting. The similarity of their features and flawless ivory skin proclaimed them mother and daughter. The stunning beauty of the daughter's raven hair and shocking green eyes outshone the older version, but not by much. Both possessed sensuous lips and a fine, straight nose. In comparison to the younger woman, Emily felt like an aging hag. Consequently, she smiled at the mother.

"This is my Cousin Teigue's ward, Miss Emily Fergeson," Patty said by way of introductions. "And her companion, Mrs. Camilla Preston." Patty clasped her hands at her waist and beamed. "I am so delighted that you came. We get so few visitors outside of Williamsburg these days."

"We're honored that you opened your home to us for a visit," Emily assured Patty. The elderly woman had the hyper disposition of someone who had consumed too many chocolate-covered coffee beans. Teigue had not elaborated on Patty's high-strung nature.

"May I present my dearest friend, Mrs. Sarina Weston, and her daughter, Rebecca, whom I've known since her birth. She and Mr. Tremaine will be married in two months. We're all so excited. I haven't seen Royle since he was a little boy. Before the dreadful war."

Emily's eyes locked on the young paragon of loveliness. The future Mrs. Royle Tremaine. The woman destined to share his bed. His life. Carry his children. Grow old and laugh with him.

Envy stabbed Emily's heart. The sharp edge cut deeper in the presence of Rebecca Weston's classic beauty. The urge to walk out and not stop until she reached Colorado Springs dimmed the smile frozen on her mouth.

"Thank you for taking the time to receive us with Mrs. Conklin," Camilla said warmly. "Southern hospitality is certainly proving to be all we heard about in the West."

Emily summoned the lifesaving insulation responsible for shielding her from the most callused aspects of life. She released the breath lodged in her windpipe. The familiar rush of anesthesia dulled the razor edge of her tumult. A brilliant smile lit her face as she extended a friendly hand toward Rebecca. "Mr. Tremaine and Mr. Jackson have spoken of you often, Miss Weston." With a supreme effort, she addressed the older woman. "Mrs. Weston. A pleasure. I'm sure you're pleased about the coming wedding."

"Oh, we are indeed," Sarina beamed.

"I'm dreading it," Rebecca murmured. She cast a guilty glance from her mother to Emily, then picked up her teacup as she settled back onto the sofa.

"It's only natural for a bride to be a bit nervous before her wedding," Sarina Weston chided. She gestured to a pair of plush upholstered chairs and resumed her seat beside her daughter.

"Do you know him well, Miss Fergeson?" Rebecca's curious green eyes darted from her mother to Emily.

"I know him," Emily admitted. "Please, call me Emily."

"Thank you, Emily. What kind of man is he?"

"Rebecca," Sarina interrupted. "It isn't proper to interrogate anyone you've just met about another person. Heavens. You'll meet Mr. Tremaine soon enough and learn what you need to know. Once you're married, you will have years to discover his nature."

"Of course, Mother. I'm sure you're right. However, I would prefer to have a bit of insight prior to the years you mentioned." Rebecca offered a brave smile to Emily. "I apologize for my poor manners. You have just arrived and must be fatigued from your journey."

Emily thought of Laura. Watching the emotion flare in Rebecca's eyes, she thought this woman possessed more backbone. The willful streak she sensed might have benefited her as a woman of the 1990s. However, the plight of women in the 1880s allowed no tolerance for defying a family's wishes concerning marriage.

Teigue was right. Rebecca's father had virtually sold her to Royle. The girl had no idea of how fortunate she was. Suppose Royle had the character of that reptile Galloway? Emily stiffened at the thought.

"I can empathize with your curiosity over the nature of a man you're to marry without much time to get to know one another, Rebecca. Rest assured, Royle Tremaine is a man of honor," Emily offered, accepting a cup of tea from Patty. The jealousy rising in her craw made the tea bitter.

"Thank you for understanding. It is just that he is so old," Rebecca mused, obviously not reassured.

Emily laughed. "He's only thirty-four."

"That's nearly twice my age. I'm only twenty. He's almost old enough to be my father."

"Rebecca . . ." Sarina warned over Emily and Camilla's laughter.

"That might be stretching it a bit, but I see your point. Don't worry. He's not exactly offensive to the eyes." Why, oh why was she trying to ease Rebecca's fears? Why not let her find out about Royle for herself? A part of Emily's mind admitted that she couldn't help defending the man she loved.

Sarina took her daughter's hand and patted it. "The wedding will take place as planned. Your father has assured us that all is in readiness. With Mr. Tremaine due any day, we can get on with the final preparations." She kissed her daughter's cheek. "You need not worry, Rebecca. I'll not allow any wedding to take place if I disapprove of the intended groom. Your happiness is important."

The news left Emily with mixed emotions. Royle Tremaine represented every mother's dream of a son-in-law, especially if she looked beyond the financial aspects. Royle's real value lay in his character.

"Your first public appearance with your fiancé will be at the Autumn Ball." Sarina tilted her head. "You will come, won't you Miss Fergeson? You too, Mrs. Preston. It is the most celebrated event of the year. Absolutely all of Williamsburg society attends."

"I wouldn't dream of missing it," Emily heard herself say.

"I will personally make sure you both receive invitations. I suppose you are like family to Royle, being Mr. Jackson's ward for how long?"

"Long enough to consider him an excellent father I dearly love, Mrs. Weston."

"I had thought you a much younger woman, possibly younger than Rebecca, since Mr. Jackson claims you as his ward. I am surprised he has not arranged a suitable marriage for you." She had the grace to blush.

Emily's left eyebrow flickered a warning to the older woman. "Given our different circumstances and philosophies, that is unlikely."

"What circumstances and philosophical differences might those be?" Sarina asked cautiously.

Emily leveled a cool gaze at Sarina. "My age, for starters. I'm what you might call a late bloomer. I'm not married because I don't choose to marry. Teigue Jackson would never suggest otherwise. He believes a woman should choose who she marries with the same equality as a man."

"Ah, yes, that sounds like Cousin Teigue. He and Madeline were so much in love. He worshiped her. It broke his heart when she died," Patty said in a rush. "I don't believe he ever remarried."

"He has not," Emily confirmed. "However, he and Maddy always wanted children. In some ways, I guess Royle and I became those surrogates." She smiled patiently at Sarina Weston. "Perhaps you might know where I might buy some furniture. I have an entire house to furnish and decorate."

"Oh? Will you be settling here?" Sarina asked.

"No. Like Teigue, my life is west of the Mississippi." Her warm smile melted some of Sarina Weston's reserve. "Though Virginia is beautiful, it is not my home."

The conversation turned to furniture, a topic Patty and Sarina loved and spoke on at length. The welcoming tea party lasted into the late afternoon.

Later, in the privacy of her upstairs bedroom, Emily settled on the edge of the bed. The layers of anesthesia fell away. Like an overfilled dam cracking under the strain, the emotions she had shuttled away from the conversation crashed down on her.

"Are you all right?" Camilla asked as she entered the room.

Emily lifted her pale face and looked around wildly for a basin.

"Oh, heavens," Camilla muttered and grabbed the basin from the washstand beside the door. She thrust it onto Emily's lap just in time.

Emily cradled the basin until the last of the tea she had consumed was gone. "I'm miserable."

"I hadn't noticed. Are you through?"

Emily nodded and yielded the basin. She accepted a handkerchief from Camilla and sat with her head hanging until Camilla returned with a damp cloth and a fresh basin.

"I wondered if you were paying a price for the sangfroid you exhibited." She sat beside Emily on the bed and pressed the cool cloth against Emily's cheeks.

"I always pay a price. But never this bad. What the hell am I doing here? I don't have a prayer."

"Now is not the time to doubt yourself. From what I saw on the train, it is Mr. Tremaine who requires prayers."

Emily let herself sag into Camilla's comforting arms. Together, they rocked on the edge of the bed while Camilla patted her hot face with the cool, damp cloth. "Oh, Emily, women have been doing things for love they'd never do for any other reason since the beginning of time. The worst of the shocks is over."

"Is it?" With every fiber of her being, she hoped Camilla was right. Each time she closed her eyes she saw Royle with the lovely, young Rebecca. How could any man resist those green eyes and ivory skin?

Royle parted the curtains in his rented second-floor room. The shabbiness of the homes and buildings reflected his forlorn spirit. Teigue had been right about nothing being the same after so many years. While he had not expected all traces of the war to disappear, he had anticipated a return of the prosperity that had distinguished the town.

He suspected it required more than Western resilience and an infusion of capital to restore Williamsburg to its former position. The deep wounds of the war lingered over the run-down buildings.

With the resignation of a man marching to meet his fate, Royle left his room and strolled the cobblestone street to Agustus Weston's office. The directions had been concise. Landmarks remembered from childhood guided him to the old brick building.

Agustus Weston projected the refined image of a Southern gentleman. A short, portly man with sad brown eyes and snow-white hair, he shook Royle's hand with his left hand. The coat sleeve of his right arm was tucked and pinned at the elbow.

"You are a man bent on punctuality, Mr. Tremaine. You wrote that you would arrive the third week of September and managed to do so. I commend your planning abilities. The trains are not always so accommodating." Weston gestured to a chair facing the desk he settled behind.

"So I understand." Royle studied the man who would be

his father-in-law in a couple of very short months. Pride marked his demeanor. Yet the sadness in his eyes said more than words or actions. "Have you the papers?"

"Of course." Weston removed a sheaf from the side drawer of his desk. "In all fairness, I must tell you that Rebecca is not as eager to wed as I had hoped."

"Perhaps she will change her mind once we have an opportunity to know one another. The unknown is always more frightening for a young woman than the known. I suspect that may be especially true when it comes to marriage." Royle picked up the papers and thumbed through them.

Weston pulled a second sheaf from the drawer. "As you requested, I have looked into Tremaine House. Thorndyke's representative has agreed to sell it to you."

The news lifted Royle's head and spirits. "Good."

"I must caution you, Mr. Tremaine, the current owner made many modifications. It is barely recognizable as the home of your father. It is also in need of heavy repair."

A smirk curled the left corner of Weston's thin lips. "Even some of the carpetbaggers ran on hard times. You might say that the spoils of war spoiled over time."

"I anticipated that it required work." He had expected a total renovation to remove the stench of the carpetbagger's occupation. The sting of a bullwhip on his back and the instant hatred he had felt at the time remained strong in his memory.

Royle came to the last page of the marriage agreement. At a glance, he saw that it embodied all the conditions they had agreed upon through correspondence. "You have not signed this."

"No. I have not."

"Is there a reason for reluctance?" Royle placed the signatory page atop the papers on the desk.

Weston studied him for a long moment before lowering his gaze to the papers in question. "During our correspondence in arranging these matters, I confess my enthusiasm was high. Perhaps an old man's indulgence of his daughter has addled my reasoning. She is my only daughter, my only child. Of late, she has been most anxious. I have never seen her so unhappy." Weston exhaled a sigh. "I could not bear to see her remain so, even though she would lack for nothing married to you. I knew your father. I knew your entire family. Their word was their bond. Even though you have been away most of your life, I believe the apple does not fall far from the tree. In my head, I am convinced you would be an exemplary husband for my Rebecca."

"Are you voiding our contract, Mr. Weston?" The softly spoken question belied the irritation rising inside Royle.

"No. No," Weston assured him. "I am asking for your patience. Soothe her fears. I would like to see her smile when I walk her down the aisle and place her in your keeping."

As Royle considered the request, an odd relief calmed him. "I have a number of business details to tend. I perceive no harm in a delay in finalizing our agreement for a week or two."

"Two weeks," Weston mused. "Thank you for indulging an old man. Considering the limited time at our disposal, I suggest we make the most of it. Will you accompany me home to dinner? The sooner you meet Rebecca, the more quickly you might allay her concerns."

Royle accepted the invitation and the rationale. His earlier irritation faded into an inexplicable relief.

With the subject of the marriage shelved for the evening, Royle posed queries about the business prospects of Williamsburg. Before reaching the Weston home, he had decided they were bleak, but not impossible.

The Weston home reflected a slightly higher standard than the rest of Williamsburg. The interior contained several pieces of quality furniture. The housekeeping conveyed a meticulous pride characteristic of the South Royle knew from childhood.

Sarina Weston proved a gracious, if somewhat calculating, hostess. Royle overlooked her reserve and considered that she, too, shared a concern for Rebecca's future happiness. After all, he was practically a stranger. They knew

nothing about the way he had lived and little concerning
how he had acquired his wealth.

He chatted with the Westons in the parlor about the up-
coming Autumn Ball. The years among saloon women had
not required small talk, merely coin and a bottle of
whiskey. Even the polish of his youth failed to quell his
growing unease.

When Rebecca joined them, Agustus Weston performed
the introductions. Royle studied his prospective bride during the brief formalities. Three things struck him immediately. Damn, but she was young. Her pale face betrayed
trepidation so great that he nearly checked the room for an
intruder. Most striking were her eyes. They were the same
deep green as Emily's in the throes of passion.

Emily.

The woman gave him no peace. Everywhere he turned,
her visage reminded him of what could never be his.

Through dinner, he did his utmost to charm Rebecca and
put her concerns at rest. He was not the most polished gentleman in Williamsburg. With time, he'd remedy that.
However, he was the most wealthy and as such would provide anything his bride desired.

After dinner, he returned to the parlor. Agustus excused
himself, leaving Royle with the women. Sarina sat in a
chair slightly removed from the sofa and chair Rebecca and
Royle occupied. The awareness of her presence hovered
over the room. Royle decided he did not care much for the
courting rituals, but would conform as society decreed.

"You have seen a great deal of the world, Mr. Tremaine,
have you not? Is it all so different from Williamsburg?" Rebecca asked. Her fingers twisted into white-knuckled knots
in the folds of her dress.

"Some of it, yes." Needing to fill the void, he described
London, New York, and Denver. Expounding on faraway
places offered little insight to Rebecca, but seemed to put
her at ease.

"What interests you, Rebecca?"

She met his question with her Emily-in-passion green

eyes. "I have few interests beyond the domestic arts. However, I have always wanted to travel to Atlanta."

"I've never been there. What intrigues you about the city?"

"Rebecca, I'm sure Mr. Tremaine has no interest in your fantasies," warned Sarina Weston.

Royle witnessed the exchange of glances, then saw a tinge of embarrassment creep across Rebecca's ivory cheeks. "To the contrary, I'm very interested." More so now than before, he decided.

Rebecca averted her gaze. "So much of the war happened in Atlanta."

Royle accepted the explanation, sure that had not been the reason for her desire to visit Atlanta. Instincts honed from making split-second decisions about men and situations warned that something was amiss. What, he had no idea.

"Rebecca?"

She turned her head toward him in response.

"Are you afraid of me?" he asked so softly that only she heard. Searching for truth, he watched her shake her head.

"Not as much as I was before tonight."

He believed her.

Chapter 22

PATTY CONKLIN SHARED her knowledge of furniture with an exuberance that wearied Emily. Patty's energy never flagged, nor did her concern over the smallest detail.

Emily discovered that she had only to mention a subject and Patty would launch into an explanation more complete than an encyclopedia. Emily decided to find out how generous Patty Conklin was with her knowledge a week after her arrival. Before visiting the artisan Patty insisted she meet, Emily instructed the coach driver to detour past Tremaine House.

From the road, the disrepair of the once-grand manor ripped at Emily's heart. She asked the driver to pause and stared at a shutter dangling from the second-floor window like the teardrop from a smudged eye. A veranda skirted the front side of the house. It sagged where some of the fluted columns had been removed. Even through the broken line of trees framing the rutted drive, Emily saw that weather had taken a harsh toll on the majestic front doors.

"Tell me about Tremaine House," she implored Patty.

Patty remained silent for so long that finally Emily diverted her attention from the relic echoing past glory.

Patty stared at the floor of the coach. "It is a house of lost men and dead women. Some say the ghosts of Josie, Maddy, and Flavia haunt it. Mr. Thorndyke, a carpetbagger from Pennsylvania, owns it. He has not lived there for nearly two years. His wife went mad. He took her north with their son. Rumor has it that she killed herself, but no one knows for sure.

"Once in a while, someone looks at it, but no one buys it. Sarina said a lawyer in Philadelphia has refused all offers on the house and lands. No one knows why. According to Sarina, Agustus thinks that the solicitor is waiting for the right buyer." Patty's gaze darted at the house. "Perhaps for Royle."

An eerie sensation rode the fine hairs rising along the nape of Emily's neck. "Royle will buy it."

"He should not have to," Patty murmured, her voice growing faint. "Tremaine House belongs to him. Delia says the spirits of Josie, Flavia, and Madeline are uneasy."

"You mean, they haunt the house?" Emily mused, wondering who Delia was.

"Delia says the whole world is haunted, that there are spirits all around us. If they are at peace, we remain unaware of their presence."

"Has anyone seen the spirits of the Tremaine women and Madeline?" Emily squinted, trying to peer into the heart of the antebellum mansion.

"Not that I know of, except maybe Delia, who won't say, and Mrs. Thorndyke, who may have joined them. I have never spoken with Sarina concerning Tremaine House. She would worry for Rebecca. Teigue wrote that Royle would return and attempt to restore it to its former greatness. If there are spirits lingering among the halls, perhaps they will remain quiet for Royle and Rebecca." Patty settled into the back of the carriage seat and wrung her hands. "Royle has had so much taken from him by the war. I could not bring myself to jeopardize his dreams of living in Tremaine

House with Rebecca. She is such a sensible, dutiful girl. I did not want to add to her tribulations of marrying a man she does not know."

Distressed by Patty's sudden ashen pallor, Emily bade the driver to continue onward.

"Who is Delia?" Emily asked when they were underway and Patty's color resumed a lifelike pink hue.

"She was a slave. Even after Gerald freed her, she remained at Tremaine House until Mr. Thorndyke threw her out. She lives in the cottage behind my house. Since the end of the war, Teigue has seen to our welfare." Patty lowered her eyes. "You may find it odd, but other than Sarina, Delia is my dearest friend."

"I would like to meet her."

"She said you would," Patty murmured. "Perhaps after dinner, after Royle leaves, you could visit."

"Royle is coming to dinner tonight?"

Patty nodded solemnly. "He indicated that he wishes to speak with you."

Surprised, Emily studied Patty. The strain of the unexpected detour to Tremaine House lingered in the fine web of laugh lines around Patty's eyes. Emily decided to drop the subject for the moment and rebuild the flagging enthusiasm for the outing.

The craftsman she spent most of the day with helped her finish the designs for several tables and dressers. Buying furniture had been an excuse for the trip. The sophisticated stores in Denver offered anything she or Teigue wanted. Upon seeing the plight of the Williamsburg residents, she decided to give them the business. Emily spent a tidy sum on the pieces she commissioned, and a bit more than practical, considering the shipping.

Throughout the day, thoughts of Delia and Tremaine House haunted her. When Royle arrived for dinner, Emily was eager to speak with him privately. With Camilla's assistance, the opportunity arose shortly after they left the dining room.

"I went to see Tremaine House today." Emily tucked the heavy shawl Patty kept near the door around her shoulders.

The evening air warned of autumn. Soon, the few bright leaves swirling around their feet would outnumber those clinging to the branches of the stately trees marking the Conklin property.

"Why?"

"Curiosity. Patty talks about everything with the thoroughness of a local historian." She glanced up at Royle's contemplative expression. "She does not speak at length about Tremaine House."

"Delia says it may be haunted. Do you believe in such things?"

Delia. He had spoken with her and learned the secret Patty had not shared until today. "Yes. Considering all that has happened to me, how could I not?" She regarded him closely. "Do you?"

"I don't know. Right now, I have no time to be concerned one way or another. Buying Tremaine House entails wading through a sea of bureaucracy. I have to go to Richmond for a few days." Royle pushed his hands into his trouser pockets. "I need to make sure Tremaine House is completely mine when I pay for it." He smiled wistfully. "There is more to it than the convoluted conditions of mining silver in the San Juans. Teigue would find it laughable, if not ludicrous."

Emily gazed down the road leading to Williamsburg. "Teigue would find it sad. Although the South will never rise again, Williamsburg will, but not for a long, long time. I visited this place eleven years ago at Christmas with a school friend. All of Williamsburg had been restored by then. Not just the way it was before the Civil War, but to colonial times. It was magic. People came from all over the world for the lighting of the Christmas lights. Candles and electric Christmas lights burned in every window. Everyone dressed in period costumes."

"Electric lights," he mused. "You spoke of them so much at the cabin, I almost understand what they are. Still, it is difficult to imagine an entire city as bright as day from little globes attached to wires."

Lost in memory, she leaned on the fence. "The pictures

in the museums didn't do the devastation justice. They didn't capture the ambiance of crumbling pride. It makes me want to cry for the years of struggle these people faced. I'm glad it was restored for those in my time to appreciate."

Royle stood close enough for her to feel the heat radiating from his body. "I did not believe you. In the cabin," he started haltingly. "But you keep talking and talking. You're like a mountain spring wearing me down. You know so damn much, and so little."

"I haven't lied to you, Royle." Mentally, she held her breath, fearing he would call her crazy and walk away again. "I never will."

"I'll be damned if I understand why, but I believe you."

At that moment she loved him more than she thought it possible for any woman to love a man. His leap of faith was beyond anything she had hoped. His admission alone was a miracle. The joy expanding her chest denied speech.

"Why are you here, Emily?"

A steely calm quickly replaced the delight swelling her heart to the bursting point.

"Please do not tell me you came to Williamsburg to buy furniture. You could have ordered anything you want in Denver. What is your business here?"

"Patty Conklin. Teigue has been sending her money all the years you two were mining. He wanted to know her situation. She has been rather secretive about her standing in the community. He doesn't want her final years spent in discomfort."

"She has weathered the worst of the storm and survived admirably," Royle said, gazing down the road leading away from town. "Being married to a man who died fighting for the North is about the worst thing that could have happened to her. Unless he had survived and returned home. No one would have hailed the conquering hero."

"Did you know Teigue has been supporting her all these years?"

"No, though I suspected it when he discouraged me from doing so. I read her letters. She never mentioned it, either."

A breeze rustled the leaves clinging to the trees. A spray

drifted from the high branches and swept across them. A leaf caught briefly in the flutter of Royle's hair, then rose with the breeze and continued its journey.

Emily longed to touch him. Her fingers tightened in denial on the weathered pickets.

Royle turned slightly and pinned her with his probing gaze. "Why are you here? Besides Patty."

She swallowed, then licked her lips. Her heart beat a little faster in anticipation of his reaction. "I didn't want you to forget me."

"Forget you?" Royle shook his head. A pained smile twisted his mouth. "Lady, I'll never forget you. God knows, I've tried. You're like a canker on my nose. Always there. Never out of sight."

"A canker?"

"Right. A canker. The only cure is amputation."

"So the solution is to cut off your nose to spite your face?" In disbelief, Emily began to laugh. *A canker?*

Royle did not join in her levity. He waited until it ran its course before speaking. "Do us all a favor and leave before the wedding."

The laughter died in her throat. The wedding. How could she have forgotten so easily? "You mean, do you a favor and leave, and don't come back, don't you?"

The slow bob of Royle's head answered her question.

"I'll go when you look me in the eye and honestly say you don't want me in your life or even in your bed." The battle of wills stretched Emily almost to the breaking point.

"What I want and what will be are two different things."

"Do you love me, Royle?" The picket filling her right hand bit into her flesh.

"I'm not sure I know what love is."

"Do you love me?" she ventured again in a breathy whisper. She felt perched on top of a lofty precipice with nowhere to go but down, yet she could not stop the words tumbling from her heart.

"It would be kinder to both of us if we did not see each other after I marry Rebecca. I wish to be fair to her. I would be less of a man if I succumbed to infidelity after the marriage. You are my downfall, Emily. Even now, it takes great effort not to touch you. That will not go away once Rebecca is my wife. Time and distance from you are the only hopes I have for making her happy."

"When you make love with her, will you pretend she is me?" Emily's heart became a stone in her chest. Nothing would make him see the emptiness ahead, regardless of how wonderful Rebecca was as a wife.

He did not answer her bold question, but merely looked at her with a hunger she shared.

"How can you marry one woman while loving another?"

"I did not say I loved you."

"You don't have to say it. We both know you do. That's why I'm here, Royle. As much as you want me to let it go and accept what you intend to do, I can't. I've come across time to find you, and you want me to go away. Tell me, where do I go to escape what I feel? How do I make it go away? I can't change it, and I can't deny it. What do I do with all the love I have for you?"

"I have no answers for you. I can't even find any for myself. All I have is a duty to my family. Go, and let me carry on with what I must do."

"I see." Unfortunately, she did see. Regardless of his heart, he would hold fast. "Give my best to your bride when you see her."

"Emily—"

"I happen to like Rebecca. It isn't her fault she's being coerced into a marriage she doesn't want. That's the trouble with this whole situation. There aren't any bad guys, no Galloways to blame or lash out at. It's just life." She turned away. "Just . . . life." For a fleeting instant she regretted being a participant instead of a spectator. When she glanced over her shoulder and saw Royle outlined against the last rays of sunset streaking across a cloud-riddled sky, the regret vanished.

Royle walked through the gate and headed for town. When he was even with her on the other side of the fence, he paused. "Good night, Emily."

She marveled that she could hurt so much inside without

bleeding all over the ground. "Good night, Royle. Dream of me."

She thought he smiled.

Unable to face Patty's exuberance, Emily tucked the shawl over her shoulders and walked around the house. She spotted Delia's cottage through the trees casting their bountiful leaves to the evening breeze.

The squeak of a worn floorboard on the porch drew Emily's attention. A small, leathery, brown woman rocked in an oversized rocking chair. Her wizened brown eyes reflected the light streaming from a lamp in the window. "Come on up, child. I've been waitin' for you."

"For me?" Emily climbed the stairs and studied the old woman. "Why would you be waiting for me?"

" 'Cuz I know you come a long way looking for answers. I ain't got none for some of your questions, but I'll help any way I can. That's how Mr. Teigue helped me and my family. So did Mr. Gerald, when he's alive, God rest his soul."

Emily leaned against the porch railing. The house blocked the bite of the wind. "Can you tell me why Royle feels compelled to revive an era that has come and gone?"

"Nope, but I can tell ya about the Tremaines and maybe you'll understand a little." Delia tamped tobacco into a pipe, then lit it before continuing. "They's not all dead, ya know."

Emily sat a little straighter. "No, I didn't. I thought Royle was the last of his line."

"Oh, he is. He is. He just don't know it in the proper sense. But he will." Delia rocked a little faster as she chuckled. A plume of smoke roiled around her head and blended with the gray in her black hair.

"I'm listening and grateful for any insight you can provide, Delia." Emily had a feeling it would be more than she had bargained for.

"Good evening, sir. Allow me to introduce myself." The dapper young man matching stride with Royle extended his hand. "I'm Harvey Baxter. Perhaps you recognize me from the bank?"

Royle did recognize the young man, but was in no mood for banter. He shook the man's hand only because it was the polite thing to do. "Is there something you want from me?"

"Yes, sir. I'd like an introduction to your uncle's ward. I realize you may have been besieged by men such as I who wish to court her. However, my intentions are strictly with marriage in mind. I have an excellent position at the bank and a nest egg sufficient to purchase a comfortable home."

Royle's impulse to tell the young man to call on Emily and make his own arrangements refused voice. Not only didn't he want any man within fifty feet of her, he damn sure did not want her marrying anyone and settling in Williamsburg. If a worse hell existed, he had yet to imagine it.

"I'll consider it after I see a dossier on you and your family, your bank statements, and references from at least three people I consider trustworthy judges of a man's potential and character."

Harvey Baxter missed a step, but hurriedly regained his stride. "I will meet all your requirements, I assure you. Have you any objections to introducing us at the Autumn Ball?"

"Not at the moment. One dance. That's all. I won't have her be subjected to gossip or speculation because you fancy her."

"Mr. Tremaine, I have no wish to incur your wrath in the matter, only your cooperation."

"Fine. Good night, Mr. Baxter." Wishing he had a pick in his hand and a streak of silver to free from a mountain, Royle turned down the street toward the Weston home.

Baxter was the third man in as many days to seek approval for courting Emily. Each request deepened his irritation.

As he approached the Weston home, a man slammed the front gate. The glow of the street lamp illuminated a rage in the man's eyes that reflected the ire rankling him. Their gazes locked and both slowed their step.

A palpable hatred charged the air between them, though Royle didn't know why. Neither spoke. When they passed on the street, both continued staring.

Royle opened the gate and glanced at the broad shoulders of the back retreating into the darkness. After straightening his clothes, he knocked on the door and did his best to set aside the evening's turmoil.

To his surprise, Agustus Weston answered the door. Royle had expected the maid to greet him. Weston appeared nervous as he peered into the street.

Royle glanced behind him at the man disappearing into the night. "Is something amiss?"

"No. Nothing at all," Weston assured him, then opened the door wider as an invitation.

Royle knew he was lying. However, any problems Weston might have had with the hate-filled man on the walk were not his concern. He allowed that Weston was entitled to withhold household or business confidences.

"I'm afraid Rebecca is a bit under the weather this evening," Weston apologized. He led Royle into the parlor.

"I hope she regains her favorable disposition before the ball." Royle shook his head when offered a seat. "I stopped by to let you know I will be leaving for Richmond in the morning. I'll return for the ball."

Ashen, Sarina joined them in the parlor. The forced smile belied the clenching and unclenching of her restless hands.

"I would not dream of upsetting Mrs. Weston's plans for the evening. Patty tells me you have worked on organizing the affair for months." Royle started toward Sarina, then paused. The puffiness around her eyes indicated that whatever had transpired in the moments before his arrival had carried a severe impact.

"We appreciate you adjusting your schedule to accommodate the Autumn Ball, Mr. Tremaine," Sarina said in a throaty voice that reminded him of tears.

Growing more uncomfortable by the second, Royle took

his leave as quickly as possible. He hoped their troubles were resolved during his absence. Involvement on yet another front would stretch him too thin.

In his room, he passed the night staring at the ceiling. Achieving his goal lay within sight. Events had favored him, as though paving the way to fulfilling his destiny with great ease. Once assured of a clear title void of the stiff penalties imposed by the Reconstruction bureaucrats, he would sign the papers and release the funds that made Tremaine House his again.

Rebecca's trepidation concerning his character had lessened. Though they shared little common ground, he supposed that would change after the marriage.

Marriage. The rest of his life with Rebecca as his helpmate. He had trouble envisioning her as anything other than fragile and dependent.

The question Emily had posed burst forth with a storm of guilt. *"When you make love, will you pretend she is me?"*

The unspoken answer shamed him.

Before Emily, lust came and went, like the women who assuaged it. Since her arrival in the San Juan Mountains, he had wanted no other woman.

While Rebecca was a beauty by any man's standards, she wasn't Emily. Pretending she was Emily was the only hope Royle had of carrying off a wedding night. Perhaps afterward, they might develop a mutual desire for one another.

Royle doubted it.

He gave up trying to sleep and packed his bag for Richmond. Before dawn, he walked to the coach house. He arrived at the same time as the proprietor. Over a pot of coffee, he listened to the old man's political opinions.

Later, Royle settled into the coach and looked out the window. The morning sun stung his eyes, which were sensitive from a lack of sleep. When the coach pulled out, he saw the man from in front of the Westons' the previous evening. He recognized the rage in his gaze and felt it bore into him. Was the stranger's presence a coincidence, or was he watching for nefarious reasons? If the latter, Agustus Weston had some explaining to do.

When he returned from Richmond, he'd make it his business to learn all he could about the stranger. Anyone emanating that much menace had to be an enemy. Royle liked to know his enemies, especially their weaknesses.

Chapter 23

FOR THE FIRST time in eighteen years, Royle stood upon Tremaine land. The rewards for the long days and countless dangers of extracting gold and silver from the reluctant mountains sat beyond the broken rows of trees lining the rutted, weed-infested drive. His efforts in Richmond had removed the final impediment for returning the land to the Tremaine name, where it rightfully belonged.

As he drew nearer to the house, he felt compelled to hurry. Up close, the shabby condition caused by years of neglect struck him like a thunderbolt. A torrent of loss as fresh as the day Teigue informed him of the deaths of his family followed.

The old magnolia he had climbed as a child was gone. A jagged trunk poked through the weeds where it had once majestically perfumed the summer air. Snarls of wild honeysuckle dragged down the corner of the veranda. The tendrils prodded the loosened boards from the house with a steady, relentless tug.

He tied the horse to a weathered column, then climbed the veranda stairs. The painted wood underfoot was peeling and gray.

The key from the land agent fit the rusty lock in the front door. He pushed hard against the warped jamb. The door swung open on squeaky hinges.

The interior had fared better. The solid construction of the house and windows had stayed the brunt of the elements.

An urge to announce his homecoming and let it boom through the lower rooms and up the staircase summoned memories of childhood. Gazing at the dank light filtering through dirt-streaked windows, he remained quiet. No warm greetings would respond to his announcement.

A patina of dust and grit obscured the finish of the few pieces of scarred furniture. Cobwebs clung to the ceilings and corners. They bled up the wall from the floor like gossamer wallpaper.

Dust swirled around the footprints marking Royle's exploration of the parlor. He closed his eyes and breathed the stale air. Not a trace remained of the fragrant flowers his mother had kept around the room.

He tried surveying the interior with an eye for restoring the house to its former greatness. But his mind wandered. He could almost hear the laughter and voices that had once dominated every corner.

He gazed at an empty spot in the study that had been his father's favorite. His father had been sitting there when the news of Virginia's secession had arrived. War. It seemed too small a word for the enormous consequences it represented.

"The war is over. Go home, son."

"I am home." He turned on his heel, expecting to see his father striding toward him.

A whorl of dust plumed from the carpet too threadbare and dusty to discern a pattern. Staring at the empty walls and hearing the echo of his voice made him feel a bit foolish. Of course no one had spoken. Certainly not his father.

Discomfited, Royle strode across the house to the

kitchen. The big stove his father had installed was gone. Hooks jutted from the hearth once used to cook meals for his ancestors. A single black pot hung from one of the hooks. A small animal had used it for a nesting perch.

Memories of his sixth birthday rushed through him. Flavia and Henry had sneaked him into the kitchen to see the cake Delia had made. Henry had been his idol, his big brother, with a flare for daring enterprise. Although often reckless, he took great pains with Royle's safety when he included him on one of his temerarious endeavors. Henry had loved excitement as much as he detested responsibility beyond that which he chose for himself.

Royle recalled the first time Henry had whisked him out of bed in the middle of a hot summer night. They had ridden bareback, something Royle had never done, and swum naked in the pond. What a glorious night that had been— until they returned home to their waiting father. Royle had escaped punishment. Henry had seen to that. Henry . . .

Lost in bittersweet memory, Royle crossed the kitchen to the passage leading to the back stairs.

A cry jolted his head up.

In a flash, he saw two men beating Aunt Madeline about the head. Their ferocity intended her death. Her screams pierced the silence and blended with another woman's.

Outraged, Royle started forward. A glance down halted him.

On the floor just inches from his boot tips, Flavia screamed at him in silent horror. Terror contorted her delicate features as a phantom backhanded her, ordering her to hold still while he tore away her clothing. The brutality of her rape ripped shouts of protest from Royle's lungs. He wanted to do something, anything to stop the two men ravaging her.

When he could move, he lunged at the images.

They disappeared.

As he lay sprawled on the floor, Royle's heart slammed in his chest. Fury clouded his vision. His breath came in raw gasps.

"Goddamn." Every hair on his body tingled. Revulsion

churned his stomach. He wanted to kill the men in the vision.

But they were gone, as were Madeline and Flavia.

He pushed to his feet and stared at the empty place on the floor and stairs for a long time. He had not known exactly what had happened to Aunt Madeline, only that she had died the night Flavia had cut her own wrists with a piece of glass.

At last, he shook off the morose images. His imagination had become overactive of late. Perhaps he had not seen anything after all, only imagined it. Like his father's voice in the parlor.

"Too many stories," he muttered, recalling the vivid detail of Delia's accounts of his family's demise. But Delia had not mentioned the brutal rapes that had cost Madeline her life and later, Flavia's, out of despair, shame, or God knew what.

His feet moved, not stopping until he reached Flavia's room. A sudden chill in the air peaked his awareness. He glanced around. Dust devils skimmed the floor behind him.

He opened the door half-expecting Flavia to be sitting at her mirror trying a new hairstyle. She had discovered boys before he left for London and decided she liked them.

The room was empty. And cold. Colder than the depths of the mine in winter.

Royle left the door open. The sound of his boot heels on the wooden floor seemed very loud as he continued down the hall.

He paused at his parents' room and glanced inside.

His mouth became a desert; he could not swallow.

His mother lay shimmering on a bed floating in the center of the room. Her once thick, raven hair was snow white and thin. She turned her rheumy eyes on him.

Instinctively, he took a step forward, aching to comfort her and himself.

She lifted a thin hand to stop him.

"It is over. Go home."

Her voice, pleading and frail, filled his head as though she stood beside him and spoke in his ear.

"I *am* home," he whispered again.

Her gaunt face turned away in denial.

Then nothing but an empty room filled his beleaguered gaze.

Shaken, Royle strode down the hall to the main staircase. He needed air and sunlight. His mind raced, unable to digest what had happened.

Outside, he kept walking around the house, no longer aware of the ravages time had taken on the buildings and grounds. His destination was the family graveyard.

He rounded the back of the house and ramshackle carriage house, then stopped short. A stone building sat on the site of the Tremaine graveyard.

In disbelief, he raced around the building. Perhaps he had mistaken the location.

Open land dotted by trees stretched along the gentle slope of a low hummock he had rolled down countless times as a child. A stone building stood in place of the Tremaine cemetery.

He climbed the rise and stared at the remnants of his heritage. A sorrow so great that it squeezed light from his spirit descended. The sting of tears blurred his vision. In the heart of Tremaine land with a sensation of his family surrounding him, Royle began to grieve.

Royle escorted Rebecca to the Autumn Ball at the Governor's Mansion. Her pale-green ball gown complemented her natural beauty. The style reminded him of the gowns worn by visitors to Tremaine House galas years ago.

Caught in the macabre, soul-wrenching events of the day's visit to Tremaine House, Royle was quieter than usual. He was glad for the Westons' company. Sarina's worry over the final details of the festivity filled the void. He made the appropriate responses when asked for an opinion, but ventured nothing else.

The splendor of the year's finest event escaped Royle. He immediately scoured the ballroom for Emily. Although he failed to see her amid the throng, he noticed the angry young man he had seen leaving the Westons' and again as he departed for Richmond. At the moment, he did not care why the man regarded him with murder in his eyes. The crossroads he had traveled late in the afternoon had shifted his outlook. For the first time in eighteen years, his destiny was uncertain. The struggle for new answers to old questions he had avoided consumed him.

"Good evening, Mr. Tremaine, Miss Weston. May I take the liberty of saying you look lovely tonight, Miss Weston," Harvey Baxter said. Excitement fairly danced around the young man.

"I don't see her, Baxter. You'll have to wait until she arrives," Royle grumbled. The last thing he wanted to do was introduce the amorous Baxter to Emily. He wanted her to himself.

"Oh, but she has, sir." Baxter gestured toward a cluster of people at the far end of the room. He withdrew a packet of papers from his inside coat pocket. "Here are the credentials I promised. I trust they will meet with your approval."

Royle doubted it. At least Baxter had upheld his requirements for an introduction, which was more than the slavering swains collecting around Emily could claim. He had a mind to wade through them and knock each one to the floor. What the hell did she think she was doing by flirting with everything in trousers?

"You did not mention that you had business to attend," Rebecca said in an even tone.

Damn, he had forgotten that he was not alone. He summoned his most gentlemanly decorum and a feeble smile. "Not important business. Mr. Baxter wishes an introduction to Miss Fergeson."

"Oh." Rebecca diverted her gaze to Harvey Baxter. "I am sure they will like one another. Harvey is an old friend of the family."

Watching the warm smile Rebecca bestowed on Baxter, Royle wondered if anyone in Williamsburg was not an old family friend. No doubt Rebecca knew all that was necessary about everyone in attendance tonight.

"It seems Miss Fergeson is occupied at the moment,

Baxter. I'm sure a better opportunity will arise for me to speak with her on the matter."

Having no choice, Baxter nodded. He betrayed his disappointment with a glance in Emily's direction before taking his leave.

Flush with excitement, Sarina approached them. "Might I borrow my daughter for a moment?"

Royle watched them depart, glad to be relieved of the responsibility of acting the escort. Standing aside on the stair, he noted the formal gaiety of the people. They existed in a dreamlike quality echoing the past. For an instant he felt eleven years old, peeking through the stair rails. The excitement of a ball made the ladies' smiles more dazzling and the elegant clothing magical.

The moment passed. The age of many of the ball gowns was reflected in the outdated styles reminiscent of before the war. Closer inspection revealed the addition of lace to hide wear and alterations or a makeover for the current wearer.

Two men walked by. One wore evening garb carefully preserved and pressed, yet shiny with wear on the elbows and knees. The fashionable suit tailored for his companion sharpened the contrast. Whether they wore new or worn garb, the partygoers clung to the aura embodied by the old Southern traditions. For one night each year, the North ceased to exist. The hallowed halls of the governor's mansion shut out bleak reality and recaptured the elegant life of the past.

Gradually it dawned on him that they all imbibed the grandeur of an era gone by. They wallowed in the old glories in their dress and attitudes. The aftermath of his visit to Tremaine House sharpened his awareness of the past for which most in the room longed.

He understood that yearning. Yet turning the clock backwards was something only Emily had accomplished.

Emily.

An irrepressible need lured him from his perch. He paused to exchange pleasantries.

The first strains of music subdued the staccato din of the

gathering. On cue, people moved away from the dance
floor, then paired for the first turn around the floor.

"Forgive me for taking so long. Mother had a last-minute
detail that required my help," Rebecca said, her face flush
with exertion or excitement, he did not know which.

"Shall we?" Royle offered his arm. Protocol dictated that
he and Rebecca share the first dance of the evening.

Wooden. The description bolted into Royle's mind. For
the first time that evening, Royle took a long look at Rebecca. She was pretty, beautiful, in fact. Her flawless
complexion and pert shape drew glances from around the
room. Any man would be proud to have her as a wife.
Sweet-natured and docile, she would seldom give her husband a moment of vexation. But . . .

"You are quiet tonight, Mr. Tremaine. Have I done
something to displease you?"

Royle turned them on the floor and cast a speculative
gaze into her green eyes. "Not in the slightest, Rebecca."

"I hope your business in Richmond has not met with a
distressful outcome."

"On the contrary. All is in order. I've only to sign the papers when they arrive from Philadelphia and Tremaine
House and its lands will be ours." He guided her through
the next turn while studying her reaction. She did not seem
the slightest bit perturbed by living in Tremaine House with
him.

"I've heard stories that ghosts haunt the halls," he prodded. "Will you be afraid there?" Who was he kidding? He
had seen and heard the ghosts today. The more he dwelled
on the events, the more certain he became that his imagination had nothing to do with what he'd seen and heard.

"I had not thought about living in Tremaine House."

Her casual answer caught him off guard. "You knew I
was planning to purchase it, did you not?"

"Yes, but until you arrived, I suppose I pretended it was
some other Rebecca who was to be your wife and live in
the relic defiled by the worst carpetbagger in Williamsburg."

"And now?"

"Now is now. You have allayed my fears of marrying an ogre." The lilt of her laugh had a sad note. "In many ways, you were a legend before you returned. I suppose that was one of the reasons I was afraid of you. Living legends are rare here. Most of ours are dead." Rebecca lowered her head to stare at his shirt. "My father believes you can single-handedly restore Williamsburg's economy to what it was a decade before the war."

"I hate to disappoint him, but no amount of wealth can do that, even if I were foolish enough to attempt it."

"I know," she said softly, then lifted her head. "They want what they had before the war. Miss Fergeson and I are the only ones who look forward. The war changed everything except attitudes. The only life I know came after. I suspect, in time, I'll be like everyone else here. Maybe I'll even long for the old days because they seem better than a future steeped in endless Northern reprisals."

The resignation beneath the smile pasted on her face coupled with her words. Together, they left Royle besieged with apprehension. He knew Rebecca would do her utmost to conform to his expectations. But conformity was as poor a substitute for spirit as duty was for passion.

The first dance of what promised to be a long evening ended. Fulfilling his social obligations, he kept his appointment on Sarina's dance card. Her ebullience with what promised to be another successful Autumn Ball removed the burden of conversation. A nod and an occasional monosyllabic response kept Sarina talking. Meanwhile, Royle watched Emily whirl across the dance floor in the arms of a grinning young man. Soon, very soon, she would be in *his* arms.

His turn around the floor with Patty Conklin proved effortless, except when she stepped on his foot.

"I believe this is my dance," Royle told the man offering his arm to Emily.

At a glance, he took in her elegant rosy magnolia satin gown embroidered with beads of a dozen muted colors. A jardinière of variegated roses rode her left shoulder. The colors matched the smaller flowers woven through her hair.

Lord, but she took his breath away. He extended his hand, responding to her warm smile as she excused herself to join him.

He smelled the roses and heard the swish of the beaded satin train of her gown as she accompanied him onto the ballroom floor.

"I missed you," she said, flowing into his arms.

"I missed you, too. You are the most beautiful woman here." Holding her eased the disquiet riding his thoughts.

"Shouldn't you be saving those compliments for your fiancée? Or do you say that to all the women?"

"In your denims with a day's worth of dust covering you from head to toe, you would still be the most beautiful woman here. Or anywhere."

"Careful, Royle. I might get the wrong idea if you don't change the subject."

"I'm not the only man here who thinks so."

When she did not question, he continued. "I've been besieged by potential suitors begging for formal introductions and permission to court you."

"Permission? Excuse me?"

A grin flashed at her surprise. "It is my duty to review suitors for my uncle's ward, as I am his closest male relative."

"I see. And if I do not wish to be courted by any of them?"

"I will tell them so, though it will break their hearts."

"Are you that eager to be rid of me?"

The resignation in her voice tightened his hold on her hand and lifted her face.

"Come with me on an adventure."

She considered a moment while he wished he could hear her thoughts. "All right. When?"

"Tomorrow. I'll bring a horse for you."

"Two horses."

"Mrs. Preston is not coming."

"Then I can't—"

"Don't you trust yourself with me?"

Instead of answering, she lowered her gaze.

"Do you trust *me*?" he asked softly.

A glimmer of amusement flashed in her gaze.

His grin broadened in response.

"Are you trustworthy?"

"At the moment, yes."

Emily laughed. "Aren't you worried about gossip? Staining your reputation—or mine—by gallivanting on horseback unchaperoned?"

The question wiped the grin from his face. "No, I am not." The admission startled him. Since he had returned from Tremaine House, the compulsion to speak at length with Emily had bordered on obsessive. For the life of him, he did not know why. "However, I would not request this if it was not important."

"More important than your need to observe propriety and appearances?"

"Yes," he admitted, suddenly worried she might decline. Considering the constant distance he had struggled to maintain between them, he would not fault her if she did refuse.

"Then it must be very important. Of course I'll go with you. I'll be ready, only don't come to the house. I'll meet you at the southwest corner of the Conklin lands. I walk out there often." The reassuring squeeze of her hand on his shoulder lent comfort. "Now, dance with me as though you're Rhett Butler and I'm Scarlett O'Hara—the way we did in Silverton."

While he did not know who Scarlett or the Butler gentleman was, he understood what she wanted and gave her the benefit of his considerable ability. Holding her, watching her flashing eyes and glowing smile, he stretched the dance into a second and would have gone a third if not for Harvey Baxter's tap on the shoulder. The merriment of the crowd crashed into his awareness.

He watched Emily from the sidelines until Baxter and Emily crossed paths with Rebecca, who was dancing with the young man he had seen twice before. Royle leaned toward a woman accepting a glass of punch from her husband.

"Who is the man dancing with Rebecca?"

"Why that's Jason Harbauch. I wonder why he returned?" The woman glanced up at him, then quickly took her husband's arm and ushered him away.

Royle watched the couple with increasing unease. Any man as angry as Jason Harbauch was dangerous. The least he owed Rebecca was protection. Decisive, he strode across the floor to reclaim his fiancée for the next dance.

To his surprise, she seemed unhappy to relinquish Harbauch's company. The waltz was well underway when he asked, "Who is Jason Harbauch?"

Color infused Rebecca's ivory cheeks. A guilty gaze flickered up at him, then dropped as she missed a step.

"Who is he, Rebecca?"

"He wanted my hand in marriage, but, of course, my father refused," she answered, then added, "His family fought for the North."

"And your father had promised your hand in marriage to me," he mused, eyeing Harbauch watching from across the room.

"Yes. And so it shall be."

Royle said nothing. He and Harbauch shared the same room in hell. Each wanted the wrong woman. The difference was that he had what Harbauch desired.

Chapter 24

Emily barely slept after the ball. The agonizing decision whether to fight for what she wanted or to accept Royle's rejection whipsawed her thinking. Each day the odds against his change of heart grew longer.

According to Delia, unless Royle returned to Tremaine House, he would not find peace. The sincerity the old woman exuded left no doubt that she believed it best for Emily to go home. In retrospect, Emily hadn't known what she expected to learn from Delia, but it wasn't that she return to Teigue and leave Royle in Williamsburg.

"Let Mister Royle do what he came ta do, Miss Emily," Delia had said. "Don't make it no harder on him than what it's gonna be. Go home, child." Delia's parting words echoed like a death knell.

The words might have not carried such a crushing impact if she had been able to dismiss Delia's concern for Royle and her. Speaking with Delia had been a brush with reality. Her soft heart held no malice, only truth.

Bowing to defeat, Emily had let Camilla make train reservations for Denver the next morning. Their scheduled departure lay a short two days away.

Seeing him approach with a second horse in tow sent her heart racing. Now, she tried not to draw any false conclusions from his request for a rendezvous.

Even before she spoke with Delia, Emily's hope had flagged severely. He genuinely wished for her to leave Williamsburg. The duty he perceived came first. It kept him from admitting that he loved her, even to himself.

Knowing well the power of self-repression, she gradually bowed in defeat to his decision. She had erroneously believed he was the reason for her sojourn through time. At last, she had found the family she craved, the love and acceptance denied her for so long. Teigue gave her both. With Royle, she had reached too far. He was not hers. Then again, just knowing the depth with which she could love a man might have been the reason for her presence. The night they shared was worth the trade of any of the creature comforts so plentiful in her former world.

Royle nodded at the clouds churning in the sky and dismounted. "We may not have as much time as I had hoped."

"We'll take as much time as you need," Emily promised. She laced her fingers through his, as though it was the most natural action in the world. "First, there's something you should see."

She led him into the well-tended graveyard. The season's last flowers dotted the headstones of indiscriminate age with color. At the far end of the fenced cemetery, Emily released his hand. Granite markers bearing the Tremaine names Emily had come to know better than those of her own family lined the back fence.

"Patty had them moved here. Your father and brother aren't really beneath the markers." She stared at the gravestones. "Perhaps they are in spirit."

Royle sank to one knee and stared at the markers for a long moment before bowing his head. His forearms crossed on his thigh as his head dipped lower.

Emily waited beside him. Just when her hand came to
rest on his shoulder, she could not say. The instinct to
comfort him, to relieve the dismal pall she felt enshroud-
ing him, was overwhelming.

When he lifted his head and stood, not a hint of emotion
lingered in his eyes. "Thank you," he said, taking her
hand. "Come."

Neither spoke while riding through the woods skirting
Williamsburg. Judging by the somewhat familiar land-
marks, Emily surmised their destination was Tremaine
House. Obviously Royle sought privacy.

They were bound to find it there.

She bit back the questions riding the tip of her tongue. A
tense, unnatural quiet between them put her on edge.

The horses passed a series of broken toothpick stakes
sporadically marking the ground.

"We're on Tremaine land," Royle announced as he
crossed the broken barrier. "This was once tobacco for as
far as you can see."

Considering the significance, Emily expected it to feel
different. It did not. It was land, the same as that on the far
side of the markers.

They continued in silence until the house and outbuildings came into view. Approaching from the rise of the
hummock, Tremaine House appeared very different from
what she had seen with Camilla and Patty from the road.
The size amazed her. It was not a house. It had been a
mansion reminiscent of the antebellum South. The slave
quarters were gone, as were signs of anyone living there
for a long time.

"I won't ask you to go inside," Royle said, leaning heavily on the saddle horn. "I went in yesterday."

When he did not continue, hurt feelings prodded her.
"You don't want me inside your house?"

"That is not what I meant." His head turned away from
the house. Tormented blue eyes sent a chill up her spine.

"Madeline, Flavia, and my mother are still here. At
least, I think some part of them is." His eyes narrowed and
Emily felt the brunt of his scrutiny.

"What do they want?"

Royle straightened. "What do they want? Damned if I know. They showed me how they died. It was . . . awful. I don't want to risk . . . I'd prefer you didn't go inside."

From Delia's account of what took place the night of Madeline's and Flavia's deaths, Emily had an inkling of the gruesome fate each had met. Royle was right. If the women were re-enacting the horror, she did not want to witness it. Delia had cried when finally speaking of Josie's sudden turn for the worse and her death the day following Madeline's and Flavia's deaths.

"I didn't ask any questions," Royle continued, gazing at an upstairs window. "I wasn't sure what I saw and heard . . . was real."

When his voice trailed, she followed his line of sight to a second-story window. She squinted, trying to see what captured his complete attention. All she saw was a window.

"Did you hear that?"

The alarm in his voice whipped her head around. Only distant thunder and the susurration of the wind in the grass and through the autumn leaves riding its wake reached her ears.

"Thunder," she murmured, doubting that was what he meant.

Royle settled in the saddle and sent his horse down the hill. He skirted the stone building, leading them around the side and toward what might have been a blacksmith shed. A rusted anvil awaited the lighting of the charred, crumbling forge.

"In here." Royle dismounted and led the horse inside. He helped Emily down and tethered her mount to the interior support where his horse waited. The first fat drops of rain fell from the angry sky.

Emily rushed inside. When she glanced around, she was amazed to find the interior of the old building relatively clean. "Have you already started restoration?"

"No. I spent time out here thinking yesterday. The

smithy was the one place none of the women ventured near."

"Are you . . . are you afraid of them, Royle?"

Royle gestured to a stone table, then helped her up to sit on the cleaned surface. "I'll admit I experienced more than I thought possible yesterday." A hollow chuckle escaped him. "When I was a kid, any one of those women could put the fear of God in me. Especially my sister, Flavia. She knew ways of threatening me and making me behave that I'm sure my father coveted. She and Henry persuaded me to go to England. I had forgotten that . . . until yesterday."

Emily listened as the storm raged outside and through Royle. He poured out memories of his life at Tremaine House. With it, she recognized the grief for his loss.

She had returned to the peaceful meadow ten years after her mother died violently in the tall grass. It had taken another month after that before the ominous pall of loss faded. But she had grieved from the moment it happened.

According to Teigue, Royle had never mourned. Instead, he became angry, then obsessed with making it right, turning the clock back, and re-creating something that could never be reborn. Restoring Tremaine House had given purpose to his life.

Emily listened without comment as he described a house brimming with love as distant from her comprehension as it was from its present state. The depth of his loss filled her with sadness. By the time he ran out of words, she had nearly run out of tears. The front of her riding jacket was damp from the silent streams flowing down her cheeks.

A finger curled under her chin. "Why are you crying?"

"For—for all you've lost. You had so much of what's important, and you lost it."

His big arms engulfed her in a crushing embrace that pinned her hands between them. "Yes, Emily. I lost it. It's gone. Really gone. The question is what do I do about what remains?"

Finally, she understood. Even by returning, he had only partial closure. Her forehead rocked from side to side on his chest. "I don't know, Royle. I know what you want to do and that choice is yours alone. You have all you sought and the wealth to do whatever you like. You have a sweet, beautiful bride waiting for you at the altar." The image created a painful hitch in her throat. "You have what you wanted. All I know is that I don't belong here. I belong at home in the mountains with Teigue."

"Home," he echoed.

The lone word sounded distant and empty, like her dreams and the fleeting threads of her crumbling hope. "Home," she affirmed, "where I can be myself and not worry about making people love me."

Royle caught her chin in the web of his thumb and forefinger. "Let me love you, Emily."

Her heart cried and leapt in the same beat. Fool that she was, she wanted nothing more than to make love with him. It did not matter that he belonged to Rebecca and would return to her when they left. All that mattered was the moment and this one last chance to share the love burning brightly in her heart.

"Make love with me and nothing will be the same again. I promise," he whispered, lowering his mouth to hers.

The reverence of his kiss seared her soul. The gentle glide of his hand cradling the back of her neck, then sliding along her shoulders and down her arms, belied his physical strength. Barely breathing, she wallowed in the intoxicating play of the tip of his tongue stroking hers.

Royle kissed her nose, then her forehead. "I brought you here to talk."

"There are many ways to communicate," she answered breathlessly, her fingers working the buttons of his shirt. "Sometimes more is said in silence than any words can express."

A wildfire burned brightly in his eyes. The growing storm pelting their shelter paled in comparison to the frisson of need between them. As though starving, he alternately plundered and caressed her with his lips and tongue. The way his arms locked around her back and buttocks, Emily thought he would never release her and prayed she was right.

When his mouth slid along her jaw and across her neck to nibble at her tender earlobe, she moaned.

"How I need you, Emily. I need you," he rasped in a whisper, his breath warm against her ear.

"I'm yours." For now. For tomorrow. Forever, her heart cried. He was what she wanted, what she needed for the rest of her life.

Within moments, she pressed her naked breasts against Royle's bare chest. The pendant hanging above her cleavage warmed with his heat. She fed on his need and revealed hers in a rapacious kiss. The tangible force of his desire vibrated until it engulfed her. The last of her reservations dissolved in the heat of his passion. Her tongue tangled with his as his hands kneaded her buttocks through the folds of her skirt. Each pulse drew her closer to the edge of the table.

Her fingers worried the buttons on his pants free. He stiffened when the proof of his desire filled her hands.

"Too fast," Royle breathed, pushing her skirts above her knees.

"Too long," Emily answered. Every fiber of her being ached for their joining, for the brief suspension of time when heaven belonged only to them.

He agreed by tearing the seam on her drawers, then scooting her to the edge of the stone table.

Emily wrapped her legs around his waist and pulled him close until the head of his throbbing erection nestled firmly in the moist hollow secreting her woman's heart.

Instead of entering her, he closed his hand over her breast. She opened her mouth to cry out and found his lips waiting. His hungry tongue set the rhythm of his hips and the sinuous roll of her nipple in his expert fingers.

As badly as she wanted him inside her, she wanted to savor every magnificent sensation he evoked and the delicious contours of his loving body. Never again would she have the luxurious freedom to explore him as though he belonged to her.

She tasted tears in their kiss and realized they were hers.

Royle ended the kiss. His big palms cradled her fine jaw. "What is it? Why are you crying?"

"I don't know. Maybe because you don't cry or grieve. Maybe because of what has been lost for both of us." She traced the plane of his cheekbone. The maelstrom of conflicting emotions blazed in his eyes, threatening her scant composure.

"Will you also cry for all we have gained?" The softly spoken question carried an attempt at a smile.

"I don't know. Right now, love me, Royle. Make love with me until nothing else matters." Visions of the endless years without him ripped a moan from her plunging spirit.

Cupping her face in his hands, he lowered his head. "Nothing else does."

The promise that for the next little while the world belonged to them sent Emily's heart soaring. With an almost violent desperation, she abandoned everything for Royle's kiss. Long weeks of repressed desire denied restraint. In the sheltered eye of the storm raging outside, Emily shut out the rest of the world. Only Royle and the love she gave him without reservation existed.

Greedy for the heated, hard contour of his flesh, she dug her fingers into his arms. Needing to pull him into her heart where she could cherish him for all of time, her hands flew along his back. Her fingers pressed against the power rippling through him.

Her need churned in the throbbing moistness aching for his possession. The fire leaped as he lifted her from the table and entered her.

The intensity of their joining sent Emily over the edge. With a cry of surprise and ecstasy, she soared into the blissful piece of heaven created by the sharing of their bodies.

When she floated into awareness, she was clinging to Royle. Her bottom rested against the edge of the stone table.

Perspiration beaded his forehead, though the wind blowing through the empty windows felt cool. An enigmatic smile lit his face. Hunger burned in his blue eyes that blinked with each lingering spasm of her climax. He watched her in silence.

"I didn't expect that," she murmured when she could speak.

His smile broadened. "Neither did I. Damn, but you are magnificent. I'd move a mountain with a pick and shovel just to see you look at me the way you did then."

The sinuous stroke of his erection conveyed a demand she understood. Yet, he kept the pace slow, the strokes shallow, fanning the fire glowing in her heart and heating the sensitive places on her body.

"I'll never have enough of you, Emily. Since making love with you, nothing is the same. It never will be."

Mesmerized by the erotic and ever-deepening movement inside her, the words barely registered. The sparks of desire flared when he captured her nipples between his thumbs and forefingers. How well he had learned her body in a single night.

One hand slipped beneath her skirts and found the sensitive pearl riding above his shaft. A moan escaped them both and added a voracious dimension to their kiss.

The long, deep strokes quickened. The rhythm built. Urgency wound around her heart to a nearly crushing intensity. The first contractions of her climax shattered their kiss.

"Mine," Royle rasped, then buried himself in her depths and unleashed a low growl.

Emily rode the wave carrying them to the heights of ecstasy. Love overflowed her heart and turned her world into a fiery ball of rapture. She basked in the searing release, never wanting to let go of the jubilation dancing in her heart.

A lightning flash followed by a deep roll of thunder shook the ground and drew her back to the present. Clinging to one another, their ragged breathing gradually evened. Still, she could not force her arms to release the tight hold pressing her to him, nor did he ease the powerful embrace molding them into a singularity she cherished.

As the moody storm ebbed and built, the air became

chilled. Reluctantly, Emily lifted her head from Royle's shoulder. He released her and helped her dress before donning his shirt and coat, then adjusting his trousers.

"Now what?" she asked, more to herself than to him.

He lifted her down from the table and held her for a moment before answering, "Now, I do what must be done."

Although she had expected nothing more, hearing the decree robbed her of most of the lingering, dreamy euphoria spawned by their intimacy. She held him for the last time, but she could not bring herself to say good-bye.

The late-afternoon sun peeked from between quickly moving clouds promising another deluge. Locked in an embrace, they watched the rain begin again.

Go home, the wind whispered in her ear. She wanted to, but not without Royle. And he was already home.

Sobered by the imminent and permanent parting ahead, Emily tightened her arms, savoring the feel of his body against hers. Then she released him and stepped away.

She followed Royle's gaze to the stately ruins of Tremaine House. Even in disrepair, it projected majesty. The twinge of sorrow for herself turned in his direction.

The intensity of his sudden gaze on her sent a wave of gooseflesh over her body. "What is it, Royle?"

"I need you here. . . . I need you to help me do what has to be done."

Angst and joy warred on the ravaged battleground of her heart. The proclamation made it impossible for her to remain in Williamsburg and more difficult than ever to leave.

Whether by the throes of passion or the calculated design of a man wanting it all, he had claimed her in the most intimate way possible. How many times had she longed to hear him say he wanted her in his life?

Not this way. Not as a mistress. Such an arrangement would destroy them both, and Rebecca as well.

"You love me, Royle," she whispered in a trembling voice. Not trusting herself, she untethered her horse and prepared to mount. "I have to go. Please don't follow me."

"What the hell do you mean don't follow you?" He spun her around, his grip hard on her shoulders.

Emily uttered a cry of surprise. The horse danced nervously beside her. "Just what I said. I need some space." The anguish tormenting her found an angry edge. Her love ran too deep for explanation. The last shreds of her dignity threatened to dissolve and cast her heart to the mercy of the elements.

"If you think I'd let you ride alone through those woods, you're out of your mind. Besides the strangers you might encounter, you've got a pack of slavering men panting after you."

She felt the inferno of his ire and refused to look at him. A remnant of insulation sheltered a modicum of her composure. "They're after a quick fling or a long marriage with the money they think I have."

"They know you're the wealthiest woman in this part of the state."

Emily shook her head.

"You think because you didn't sign the papers Teigue had drawn that you own no part of what he wanted to give you? Damn, you financed this sojourn with your own little cache of gold?"

"So what if I did. It's my folly. My choice."

"Folly is right. Half of Teigue's holdings became yours when he had the papers drawn. Apparently you didn't read the fine print as well as I thought you did."

"I read it. You're wrong." The argument helped her focus. She retreated a step, grateful he did not try to restrain her.

"No, sweet Emily. You're wrong. You don't know Teigue as well as you think. When he wants to do something, consider it done. He is a bulldog when it comes to getting his way. Want it or not, you are a very wealthy woman."

"So what? What does it matter? What does it change?" The storm reflected her mood as some of the fight drained from her.

"Not a damn thing."

"Then what's your point?"

"You don't take your safety seriously. Just because these people wear nicer clothes and speak in a refined manner—"

"I know all about wolves in sheep's clothing," she interrupted. "If you want to accompany me, please save the lectures."

The rain stopped as quickly as it started. Emily took advantage of the lull and mounted the horse. Royle followed. Together, they rode in silence for the next few minutes.

"Why did you run away when I told you I needed you here?"

The misery in his voice mirrored hers. "It was time to go, Royle. We will both be missed soon enough. Gossip dies hard in a close-knit society that has nothing more to occupy the evening hours. Think of Patty. God knows, the woman has already overcome enough by being the wife of a Northern hero people here wouldn't kick out of the road. And what about Rebecca? She's an innocent in this." She afforded a glance in his direction. The strain of resignation etching his features pierced her heart.

Royle released a deep breath. "You are right, of course. I have no wish to hurt her."

A soft, steady rain plastered his hair to his head and dripped from the clustered spikes formed by the fickle breeze skipping through the trees. She ached to brush away the shock of black hair riding low over his brow.

"Don't for a moment believe I would trade what we shared at Tremaine House for anything. I'm not that altruistic."

"Yes, you are," he muttered as the border markers of the Tremaine lands came into sight. "The burden of the ramifications is mine alone. Not yours, Emily. I will make it right."

The deep regret in his voice forced her to glance his way. Despite the determined set of his jaw, she knew that nothing could make it right.

Go home. The command rode the wind blowing from Tremaine House.

A sudden torrent of rain drenched her and washed away the tears streaming down her face.

She crossed the line of markers, knowing she had left Tremaine House and Royle behind.

Chapter 25

"THE WEDDING WILL be the most splendid affair in Williamsburg since before the war," Sarina Weston said at dinner the following evening. Her delight shone in the animation of her expressive eyes that fairly danced among the guests in Patty's dining room.

Reflexively, Emily glanced at Rebecca, who seemed detached, then at Royle. He held her gaze with an air of confidence that dampened her already low spirits.

"I understand you signed the papers for Tremaine House today," Agustus Weston said to Royle.

"I did."

"What will you do with it?" Patty nodded to Delia, who had offered to serve the intimate dinner party.

"Why, restore it, of course," Sarina chided, straightening her napkin. "Now that ownership has been rightfully returned to the Tremaines, surely we will prosper."

"Is that true?" Patty asked Delia, her eyes wide with doubt.

Delia's gaze settled on Royle. "He's gotta do what needs to be done or there won't be no peace for anybody. He's the only one that can put things right." The straight backbone of her slight form betrayed an inner strength.

"How do you know that, Delia?" Camilla asked, taking the platter of fried chicken from her.

"Some things ya just know, Miss Camilla. I been with Tremaines since Mr. Gerald bought me and gave me back my Jacob. He bought our children and let us be a family. He made our hard times better. We stayed after the others left. I couldn't run out on him when his family needed me. 'Sides, there weren't nowhere to go." Delia brought another dish from the sideboard and handed it to Camilla.

"Me and my little girl buried them ladies side by side. But they didn't stay in the ground. They come back. They got ta do somethin' before they move on. So they been waitin'."

"For Royle?" Emily asked, her heart thundering.

"Yes, for him and somethin' else."

"Do you know what that something is, Delia?"

"No, Miss Emily, I don't. They never told me." Delia's knowing gaze settled on Royle. "Mr. Royle, he'll be knowin' in good time."

"Oh, gracious," exclaimed an ashen Sarina. "Do you mean Tremaine House has ghosts? If so, it may not be safe for Rebecca to live there after the marriage."

"No, ma'am. Them ladies ain't enjoyin' the wait." Delia made a final trip to the sideboard for a platter of fresh rolls. "Ain't nobody in danger at Tremaine House, lest they get in the way of what the ladies want. There weren't a mean bone between the three of them."

"Thank you, Delia," Royle said.

"Did you know about, about the, ah, ghosts when you bought Tremaine House?" Rebecca turned an inquisitive gaze on her dinner partner.

"Yes," he answered unperturbed.

"Then, do you know what they want?"

"Yes, I think I do," he said to Emily as though she was

the only other person in the room. "But it will take time to sort it all out."

Emily held her breath. Why in God's name was he so bold? She glanced at Rebecca. The distressed young woman had not appeared to notice the personal exchange. Emily released her breath and took a platter from Camilla.

"Well, since everything is safely in Mr. Tremaine's capable hands, perhaps he will share whatever news he heard in Richmond," Camilla suggested.

Emily could have hugged Camilla for turning the conversation away from Tremaine House. Even so, the dinner lasted longer than most funerals Emily had attended. In fact, it *was* a funeral. In a very private service, the corpse of her dreams would be laid to rest when she caught the train to Denver in the morning.

She and Camilla had confirmed the arrangements for transporting the furniture Emily had consigned. The two women had packed without alerting Patty of their departure. The morning would be time enough to make their farewells.

Constrained by the Westons' watchful eyes, Emily kept a safe distance from Royle and seldom spoke to him directly. The way the Westons scrutinized her every move made her wonder if she and Royle had been seen yesterday. For Rebecca's sake, she fervently hoped they had escaped detection.

As she told them good night with Patty, a sundering finality descended. From the door, she watched Royle see the Westons into their carriage, then offer his arm to Rebecca. The echoes of the horses and jangling of the harnesses faded. She watched Royle and Rebecca stroll toward town until they disappeared in the shadows. Emily Fergeson closed the door on Royle Tremaine.

"Why did you wish to walk?" Rebecca asked.

"It is time we spoke privately." Royle glanced over his shoulder. The lights of the Conklin house flickered into nothingness beyond the skeletal trees shedding the last of their colorful leaves.

"I am surprised my parents allowed us any privacy."

"Convincing them that your reputation would not suffer required a great deal of persuasion on my part."

"Is my reputation safe with you, Mr. Tremaine?"

"Much safer than if you were in the company of Jason Harbauch." He caught her when she stumbled.

"Jason . . ." Her slight shoulders lifted like armor. "I told you, he is not a concern. My parents would not consent to him."

"But you would have."

"Oh, yes," she whispered, her head bowed.

"You love him." The statement required no answer. Royle nodded and tipped his hat to a couple passing on the street. He answered their formal greeting with a friendly response.

"You may as well know that we tried to run north together. His lands and home are in Ohio. My father caught us and forbade him to call again. Consequently, this is the first time I have ventured anywhere unaccompanied by my mother since last Christmas."

"Things begin to make sense. Their restrictions seemed a bit overprotective. I thought them concerned I would ravish you before the wedding."

"I will do my utmost to be a dutiful wife," Rebecca assured him. "My mother did not love my father when they married. But they have grown to admire one another greatly. Perhaps they love each other now."

"Not acceptable," Royle muttered under his breath.

"I will try to love you."

"It doesn't work that way, Rebecca." He exhaled relief. "We are a pair. Both of us love someone else."

"You?" Bright green eyes lifted in hope. "Miss Fergeson?"

He grinned and nodded. "I'll be marrying her, if she'll have me. I hope that doesn't disappoint you too much."

A weak smile formed, then faded. "My parents . . ."

"Yes, your parents. Leave them to me. Meanwhile, get word to Jason Harbauch that I want to meet with him."

"Why would you think I know how to do that?"

She was a poor liar, which endeared her to him. "No games, Rebecca. Tell him I want to see him tomorrow at noon."

"Oh, Mr. Tremaine, I can't do this. My father will be ruined if he does not have your financial backing."

"Some might think he deserves it for trading his daughter's happiness to ensure his comfort." Royle chuckled. "I'm beginning to sound like Teigue. You leave your father to me. Rest assured, I'll give him a generous settlement for breaking his little girl's heart by calling off the engagement."

Rebecca stopped and gazed at him as though he had grown another head.

"You would do that? Why?"

"It is the honorable thing to do. I'm nothing if not honorable." He chuckled. "Besides, it is also the wisest course. All I ask is that you do nothing, say nothing, other than what I request, until I am ready to free us both."

"You have my solemn vow, that of a friend, Mr. Tremaine."

"Thank you." The oppressive weight that had settled upon his shoulders more than half his life ago began to lighten. "We have some plans to make before we reach your house. Let's use the time wisely."

Not trusting the unsteady reins he held on his newfound freedom, Royle avoided Patty Conklin's home for a week. Arranging the convoluted details of his future absorbed his time with the efficiency of a wool shirt in a spring shower.

Agustus Weston had proved difficult. The notion of losing an affluent prospective family member outraged him. Royle had endured his wrath for an hour before dropping the iron that turned Weston a strange shade of purple. The generous settlement he made bought his freedom and that of Rebecca to marry Jason Harbauch.

The bright spot turned out to be Harbauch. He reluctantly agreed not to uproot his precious bride until after the marriage. He further agreed on an open-door policy when it came to the Westons.

Pleased by the resolution of the complexities concerning the Westons, Royle opened the gate to Patty's home. His eagerness to tell Emily of his progress in clearing the way for their marriage added a bounce to his step.

Damn, he had not asked her to marry him. Proposing had been the last rational thought in his mind when they made love in the blacksmith shed. But they had made love before and she had rejected the idea of marriage when Teigue tried to force it in Silverton. Later, Teigue had been certain she wouldn't marry without love.

She loved him and knew he loved her.

He breathed a little easier.

She'd marry him. Wouldn't she?

Anxious to propose and claim Emily forever, he knocked on the front door.

Patty's normally cheerful nervousness was notably absent when she invited him inside. Her pale eyes darted from the flowers in his hand to his face, then to the floor.

"Is Emily home?" Impatient, he glanced around the parlor and hall for a sign of her.

"Oh, dear me, yes. I'm afraid she may be by now." Patty ushered him into the parlor and urged him to sit.

"May I see her?"

"That may be most difficult. She is at home."

On her good days, Patty made little sense. When flustered, she made no sense. "If she is home, I would like to see her. Is she in her room or out walking?"

"Why, I don't know what she might be doing now." A pensive expression stilled Patty's darting gaze for half a minute.

"May I check her room?"

"Oh, that might be most difficult."

Seeing she would be of no help, Royle handed the flowers to her and went upstairs. The room he knew as Emily's was empty. The pristine neatness of it filled him with dread. It was too tidy even for Emily. Not a hint of her occupation showed on the bureau or nightstand.

With mounting dread, he opened the wardrobe.

The bottom fell out of his stomach.

She was gone. Not a trace lingered as a reminder of her presence.

"Emily," he whispered, unable to do anything but stare at the back of the wardrobe.

"She and Mrs. Preston went home."

At last he understood what Patty had been trying to tell him. "When?"

"The morning after my dinner party. I have been so distressed, Royle. She did not inform me they were leaving so quickly. When she did, she implored me not to tell you. She said Teigue would want it that way. Oh, I do certainly hope so. I have been so worried. I have written to Teigue, but of course I have not heard if I did the right thing." She touched his arm, freeing the paralysis that kept him staring at the back of the wardrobe. "Are you angry with me?"

He wanted to rage and break things. Why the hell did she go? Didn't she understand the commitment he'd made when he cherished her and told her that he needed her at his side to finish what needed doing?

She had never said she loved him. She didn't need to say it. She loved him. Him. Royle Tremaine.

So why did she leave?

"Did she say anything? Leave me a note? Anything?"

"Yes. She asked me to wish you happiness in your success. I believe that's what she said. I can't recall exactly."

"That sounds like her," he reflected. Success. Happiness. Hell, he wanted both and had neither without her.

"She was very unhappy, Royle. As unhappy as you appear to be now. What is wrong? Sarina sent word there would be no wedding between you and Rebecca. Is that so?"

"It's true. I broke it off. Sarina will get over it, as will Agustus. In time." Time. He felt as if time was running out.

He closed the wardrobe. "Where did she go? Denver?"

"I don't believe so. She said she was going home. I don't believe she lives in Denver," Patty mused, wringing the handkerchief in her fingers into a thin, white strand.

He left the Conklin home and hurried toward town. His first thought was to book passage for Colorado Springs.

Emily wouldn't linger in Denver. She would go home to Teigue.

Halfway into town, he realized that while he might be free of his marriage with Rebecca, the obligation that had brought him to Williamsburg still bound him. He was the last Tremaine.

He rented a horse and wagon and stocked it with provisions. Without Emily lighting the corners of his dark world shrouded by duty, he had only one direction.

A ghost of a man tied to the roots of his heritage, he belonged with his kind. When he arrived at Tremaine House, he felt as miserable and bereft as the place looked. Striding up the porch, he knew what he had to do, regardless of the cost.

He shoved the sticky front door open and stood in the lofty foyer. "I came back! Where the hell is everyone?"

"It will wait until tomorrow, Sunshine." Teigue removed the paintbrush from Emily's hand. "It's late and Camilla has kept your dinner warm long enough."

"I'm not hungry."

"Maybe not, but that child you're carrying is."

A flame of discovery colored her cheeks. "What makes you think I'm carrying a child?"

"You got the look that means a serious dose of motherhood. I've half a mind to go to Virginia myself and drag that misguided hellion back here by his hair. Barring that, just beat some sense into him."

Sickened by the thought, she wiped her hands on the oiled rag beside the paint. The past seven weeks had felt thirty years long without Royle. "He has no idea, and I forbid you or Camilla to tell him. If I *am* pregnant, this is *my* baby."

"Like hell it is. The day's coming when that little fellow asks about his daddy. What are you going to tell him? What will you tell Royle when he comes to his senses one of these days and knocks on the front door?"

Weary, she waved aside his concern. "I'm not even sure I'm pregnant. Let's deal with one thing at a time. That's all

I'm capable of these days." She retrieved the paintbrush and continued painting the parlor. "I'll eat after I finish this room."

The constant busyness of one task after another filled her days and most of her nights. When she fell into bed, exhaustion shoved her into a sleep rich with memories and dreams as distant as spring in the snow-covered meadow.

She had tried not to consider the significance of missing her period. Regular as she was, it meant exactly what Teigue had surmised. The selfish side of her cheered for the product of the love she and Royle had shared. Having a part of Royle to hold brightened her dismal mood.

But Teigue was right. The child would ask about its father. Her exhilaration plunged.

"Don't buy trouble until it's for sale," she reminded herself for the tenth time that evening.

She finished painting and cleaned up. A slow satisfaction lifted her flagging spirits. Teigue and Camilla had retired for the night. They had married within days of Emily and Camilla's return to Colorado Springs. Both agreed they had little time to waste and much to make up for the years of aloneness.

In the small hours of the morning, Emily bathed and crawled into bed. Sleep claimed her instantly.

In her dreams, she stood on the hummock behind Tremaine House. An eerie glow emanated from deep inside the house. Vicious talons of lightning raked the night sky.

The stone building had been disassembled. The piles of rock reminded her of slag heaps outside the mine. A second cluster of building stone marked the ramshackle smithy. The table upon which she had made love with Royle remained in the midst, like an altar too sacred for desecration.

Flames reached out of the ground and engulfed the carriage house and crumbling tobacco-drying sheds. Moments later, the remaining outbuildings blazed against the black night.

The upper windows in the main house shattered. Horrified, fascinated, she watched the great mansion burst into flame so bright it hurt her eyes. For an instant, the skeleton of the walls shimmered in the pyre. With a groan, the house collapsed on itself.

Sensing she was not alone, Emily slid her eyes to her right, then her left. Three ghostly visages stood beside her. One was clad in a flowing nightgown, the other two in disheveled, tattered dresses. Although she recognized them, not a tinge of fear touched her heart. Like her, they watched the death of Tremaine House.

Royle, bearded and bare-chested, emerged from between two burning buildings. As he approached the hummock, the lower wall of the house fell outward. Sparks and embers rode the gathering wind. When the column of flames settled, Royle had disappeared.

Emily woke with a shout of protest, her legs drawn up to run down the slope and find him. The glow of the embers in the cast-iron stove warming her room imparted just enough light for her to recognize where she was.

She was home. Safe. Far from the terrifying nightmare. Even farther from Royle. The terror of losing him with such finality reduced her to a quivering mass of anguish.

Drenched in perspiration, she hugged her legs. Her breath came in great gasps. It felt as though an invisible claw had carved her heart from her chest. The tears came next. Lord, she cried at the fall of a snowflake lately.

But those were no snowflakes falling from the sky in her nightmare. They were white-hot embers and ash raining across the Virginia landscape and sailing on the wind to who knew where.

In truth, Royle was as dead to her as if he had ceased to breathe. Patty's disjointed letter told of how he had extricated himself from the marriage agreement with the Westons. Alone, she had read the letter a second time. Tears rolled down her cheeks. Happiness that Royle had avoided a loveless marriage ignited the hope of his return home to Colorado.

Reality dashed the glimmer of a dream. Royle had elected to remain at Tremaine House. Alone. He wasn't leaving. No one ventured close. Not even Patty.

Royle wasn't ever leaving Virginia. Bone-crushing despair doubled her over. There weren't enough tears to wash away the anguish seizing her heart. In the end, the only avenue left was resignation for the inevitable. She had misjudged his feelings for her. He didn't love her, didn't want her in his life. If he had, he would have written to her, asked her to join him at Tremaine House.

Emily closed her stinging eyes.

"I need you."

His avowal rang in her head. Why couldn't he have said the words in his heart? He loved her. Enough to prevent a disastrous marriage with Rebecca. Not enough to ask her to be his wife and share his world. Not more than the duty he perceived. Not more than Tremaine House and the perpetuation of the Tremaine heritage.

"I love you, Royle. Wherever you are. Whatever you're doing, I love you," she whispered. "Come home."

She knew he would not. His choice had been Tremaine House. Not her. Even if he did come, she could not endure being second in his affections.

The realization formed on the remnants of the dream steeped in conflicting symbolism. Acceptance finally blossomed. Royle was truly lost to her. Forever.

Chapter 26

*G*O HOME.

The words he had been hearing since returning to Tremaine House became a traveling cadence. The wheels of the train, carrying him across the cold winter countryside, repeated them at every revolution.

Each mile away from the remnants of Tremaine House stripped a layer of weight from his shoulders. The second night on the train, Royle fell into the first restful sleep he had known in months. The dreams that had plagued him in Silverton, then intensified in Williamsburg, had ceased. They had been laid to rest with the freedom of the ghosts at Tremaine House.

Freedom.

From the privacy of his compartment, he watched the Mississippi River flow beneath the bridge. Teigue had been right in his refusal to cross the mighty river. With a certainty born of conviction, Royle knew that he was crossing it for the last time. Once he reached Emily, his roaming

days were done. No more mining the dark tunnels hewn
from the mountains. No more searching for the next silver
lining after a blast.

The woman who had traveled through time to love him
was all he needed. If she'd have him.

The tumult of putting Tremaine House and his family to
rest had nearly driven him mad without her. She had left
him and he did not know why. He had demolished the reminders of a proud heritage stone by stone, board by board,
with his hands. In doing so, he'd grieved and accepted that
the era of the Tremaines had ended with the death of his
family. The casualties of war had been too great to conquer,
regardless of intent and wealth.

Visions of his mother, Flavia, and Madeline dying in the
house lessened with each mile. He would never forget what
they had shown him. They, too, had wanted the house gone.
They had been waiting, knowing he would come, ready to
show him the way to free them all.

Go home.

Home was with Emily. And Teigue. Absently, he patted
the brief letter tucked inside his coat pocket. Teigue had
been direct. *Camilla and I were married. A baby is coming
in the summer.* Teigue never did waste time when he
wanted something badly.

The letter went unanswered and Royle's journey west
unannounced. He would give Emily no more warning of his
arrival than she had given of her departure.

Snow and a damaged section of track delayed him for
three days in Omaha. Royle endured the interruption with
stoic resignation. A restlessness that grew with each passing hour sent him walking one street after another. Come
hell or blizzard, he would reach Colorado Springs before
Christmas.

Another setback in Denver cost him an anxious day,
which he whiled away shopping. Of the hundred things he
wanted to buy for Emily, he settled on one: a wedding ring.

Snow fell in the mountains behind Colorado Springs
when the train pulled into the station. This close to his goal,
wintry elements posed no deterrent.

The great yellow eye of the sun peeked over the horizon the next morning. Like an aged beacon, it burned holes in the clouds and gave Royle direction.

Heavy snow hampered his journey. Undaunted, Royle led his horse and pack mule through the worst drifts. He broke a trail with the mass of his body and sheer determination where the snow collected to a height above his knees.

Heavy gray clouds shrouded the mountains rising to Pike's Peak, the weight of their burden pressed down the slopes. Royle checked the reins in his numb hand. They were still there. The house and barn across the valley beckoned with a force more powerful than nature. Even from a distance, he recognized the chimneys, porches, and turrets from the plans the three of them had spent hours poring over in the cabin.

He batted away the icicles dragging the muffler from his face and urged the reluctant animals down the mountain. His squinting gaze remained on the house, and where it should be when trees hid it from view.

Cold seeped into the marrow of his bones, slowing him. He imagined Emily warm and safe within the Victorian walls of home. Would she be happy to see him? Would she light up with the smile he loved and fill the room with laughter?

When she ventured away from the house, did she carry her rifle in the possessively casual way she had in Silverton?

He yearned to sit beside a warm fire with her and listen to her tales of the impossible world she had known. She had brought him more conflict and peace than he had thought possible for one man to experience in a lifetime.

Without her, he had almost gone mad at Tremaine House. Mad from wanting her, needing her sane voice to ease the doubts and see things in a different light after she had made him angry.

But she had left him. She had revealed the beauty of her love, forced him to acknowledge his love for her, then left him.

"Emily!" The raging shout in his mind barely cleared his icy lips.

He dropped the reins and stumbled up the porch stairs. With frozen fists, he pounded on the beautifully carved front doors. The solidity of the barrier was all that separated him from having her or knowing why she left him.

"What the hell . . ." Teigue practically dragged him into the house.

A rush of warmth on his icy skin sparked the awakening of nerves Royle had forgotten. "Horse," he croaked.

"I'll take care of them after I take care of you. Damn, but you're six ways to a fool." Teigue unwrapped Royle's face and began tugging at the frozen layers of clothing. Snow and ice fell on the tiled foyer and puddled on impact.

"Emily," he managed in a raspy voice.

"It's good to see you, too." Teigue tugged the gloves from Royle's red, icy hands, then started on the coat. "She's a little under the weather, but fine."

As much as his stiff, numb fingers allowed, Royle undressed down to his boots and trousers. He gratefully accepted a quilt from Camilla when she brought it.

The warmth of the room restored feeling to his legs. The burning sensation stretched to his feet. "I have to get my boots off," he muttered, eyeing the massive puddle growing around him.

Teigue fetched a stool from beside the hearth.

Unsteady, Royle accepted Teigue's assistance as he settled onto the low perch. After several minutes, he hobbled to the fire. Staring at the flames, he willed the burning needles piercing his extremities to hurry and run their course. Much as he wanted to see Emily, he did not want her to see him in such a pathetic state.

"Warm your insides, too. It's not hot, merely warm, so you won't burn your lips."

He glanced at the cup of coffee Camilla offered, then at her. Whatever she had found with Teigue put a glow in her eyes and stripped years from her features. He mumbled his thanks, then took the cup in his shaking hands, glad she had the foresight to fill it only half full.

"After you warm up a little more, you can get in the tub. That will help you the most."

He nodded his thanks and glanced toward the doorway. It was empty. The sight of Emily would warm him like nothing else.

An hour later, tired and achy, he headed for the stairs.

"Hold on a minute, Royle. I've been quiet for as long as I can stand it." Teigue barred his way up the stairs with a strong arm.

"Go gently," Camilla said.

"Go gently with a fool who doesn't have the sense to wait out a snowstorm? With a fool who doesn't have the sense God gave a goose in picking a mate for more than the time it takes—"

"Teigue." Camilla spoke softly, though the warning echoed in the foyer.

Teigue ran his callused fingers through his hair.

"A fool who what?" Royle pressed. "You think I'm a fool? Then that's what you think, Teigue. I'm going to see Emily. You had best move out of my way."

"You are not taking her back to Tremaine House." The softly spoken declaration struck the heart of the matter.

Royle shook his head. "She's traveled far enough to find a home. I'm not taking her away from it, Teigue." Royle held fast under the scrutiny of Teigue's glare.

Teigue hesitated, then retreated, leaving the path to Emily clear.

Climbing the stairs loosened his muscles and tightened his joints. The effects of the cold had been worse than he thought. His gaze focused on the top stair.

Emily was up there. Hiding? Angry?

Why had she left him when she knew he loved her?

He opened the door and saw Emily amid the quilts piled on her big bed. Needing the warmth of her smile and the heat of her body against his heart, he entered and closed the door.

He lit a lamp and turned the wick low, reluctant to wake her, despite the demand for understanding clamoring in his head.

In the soft light she appeared pale and frail. Alarm sent a frisson of panic through him. How ill was she? For how long?

Royle watched her sleep for a long time before removing his clothes and slipping into bed beside her. She stirred when he gathered her against him. Her hand opened and closed on his chest hair before settling with a reassuring pat.

Holding her against his heart, he wondered how he had survived for so long without her.

"I love you, Emily," he whispered, then kissed the top of her head. A serenity as elusive as the mother lode quieted the questions in need of answers. She was in his arms, and he would not let her go.

A familiar churning in her stomach awakened Emily. She wanted to ignore it. The dream she had of Royle was too good to relinquish. The physical discomfort increased enough for her to inch toward the edge of the bed. Something blocked her escape. She was not alone.

Her eyes flew open as she drew a breath to scream.

"Good morning, Emily."

Royle. Staring at her with laughing blue eyes.

She had never heard of hallucinations accompanying morning sickness. Needing to bolt, she slapped the vision on the chest to make it disappear.

Her palm stung.

It was not a figment of her imagination beside her. It was Royle. Warm and naked.

The sudden roll of her stomach sent her scrambling over him. As he called her name, she ducked into the bathroom and barely made it to the basin. Any doubt of her pregnancy had vanished with the onset of morning sickness. Initially, the bouts came late in the day. Like her waistline, they shifted. After an early morning bout, her stomach settled for the day.

Heaving stomach acid into the basin allowed no time to think about what awaited in her bed. When the queasiness passed, she washed her face and brushed her teeth with a liberal amount of tooth powder.

She rinsed her mouth, then hung her head. Visions of Royle in her bed took the starch from her knees. As she braced herself on her palms, a movement in the mirror captured her attention.

Clad in his trousers, with only the bottom two buttons fastened, Royle filled the bathroom doorway. The shadow of a two-day-old beard accentuated the anxiety burning in his gaze.

"Royle." She blinked. The potent, masculine image remained. Her stomach fluttered with either another bout of morning sickness or excitement, she was not sure.

"Of all the reactions I anticipated, I had not expected you to vomit at the sight of me."

Emily stared at him in the mirror. The flutters in her stomach congealed into a ball of dread. "Why are you here and not in Virginia?"

"Why did you leave me, Emily?"

"I never went there to stay." The ball of dread evolved into a sorrowful reminder of the loss she had lived with since boarding the train for Denver. "Besides, I thought you were marrying Rebecca. I . . . I couldn't stay. I finally realized I couldn't compete with a lifetime of sacrifice and dedication to perpetuating the Tremaine line and restoring their standing in Williamsburg."

She sagged against the edge of the counter. Before she caught her balance, Royle swept her up and carried her to the bed. With loving hands, he drew the quilts around her, then he lay beside her and propped his head on his left elbow.

"Making love with me, knowing I loved you meant nothing?" he continued as though the interruption had not occurred.

Emily barely heard his words. Impulsively, she traced a fading pink line above his right eyebrow. "You've been hurt."

She lingered at the edge of the injury. The silken fall of his hair across her fingers made her want to cry.

"The hurt I've been living with has nothing to do with scars. Thinking of you, wondering why you left—*that* was pain, Emily. I'll ask you again, did making love in the blacksmith's shed mean nothing to you?"

Emily flattened her hand along the side of his face and searched his eyes for the source of the disquiet radiating from him. "Making love with you is the most beautiful experience I have ever known. I thought you were telling me good-bye, and I wanted that moment of being with you more than anything."

Royle's head followed the direction of her hand trailing along the side of his neck. "I told you I needed you with me."

"I could not be your mistress and destroy us and Rebecca." Heavens, but he felt delicious to her starving fingers.

Royle bolted into a sitting position on the edge of the bed, his forearms resting on his thighs and his head hanging.

Alarmed, Emily stared at the pink scars forming on his back and braced herself against the pillows. "I could not stay, Royle. I could only cause pain by staying. You fully intended to marry Rebecca and live at Tremaine House. I'm sorry. That was something I could not watch. I don't know what prompted you to break off the engagement, but—"

"I love you, Emily. I told you nothing would be the same once we made love in the smithy. I thought you understood that I'd do anything, even walk away from Tremaine House right there and then, had you asked me. Instead, you left. You left, and I damn near went out of my mind."

The anguish in his hunched shoulders became a wall Emily feared she could never tear down. She drew a long breath through her dry mouth. "I thought—"

Like a cat, he pounced, whirling around and pinning her to the pillows. "You thought. What the hell did you think? That I could make love to you, and marry Rebecca? Damn it, you knew I loved you."

The wildness in his eyes as he searched her face for an

answer withered her vocal cords. She nodded, bracing for the onslaught she expected.

Instead, he lowered his shaking head. "Do you perceive me as that callous? That single-minded?" His head dropped lower in protest of an answer he didn't want.

"I—I thought you felt duty-bound to carry forth regardless of how we felt about one another," she managed. "I loved you for your sense of honor and hated you for the same reason. I wanted it all, Royle. Not just a piece. That's what I thought you were offering. I tried everything I knew and invented ways of trying to change your mind. That last night during dinner with the Westons at Patty's, I accepted that I had lost. And lost you."

"I suppose you had every right to think that. I've given you nothing but grief since you came to the cabin. I tried to disbelieve your claim of being from the future, and couldn't. I wanted to believe you were anything, except the loving, intelligent, passionate woman you are. At first, I thought you were dangerous to Teigue." A choked sound that might have been a laugh left a sad smile ghosting the corners of his mouth. "You were dangerous, all right. To me. To yourself. You knew the power of love and wouldn't let me deny it."

A tear slid from the corner of her eye. "I love you, Royle. Leaving, accepting defeat, was the most difficult thing I've ever done."

A sad smile pained Royle's features when he met her eyes again. "Oddly enough, you won, then left. Damn it, woman, I didn't want to love you, but you wouldn't let me hide. Everywhere I turned, you were there to remind me of what I would be throwing away. Your laughter and quick wit ripped away any misconceptions I had about marrying a woman I did not love. There I was, clearing the barriers in the way of making you my wife . . . only to learn you had left Williamsburg. Vanished without a word."

"Maybe we should have talked instead of making love," she offered guiltily. "And maybe if you let go of my wrists, my hands will stop tingling."

Instantly, he released her and mumbled an apology while

stroking her wrists with his thumbs. "That thought has crossed my mind in the last few minutes."

"Which thought? Letting go of my wrists? Talking?" Uncertain, she stared at his mouth and felt her cheeks color at the memory of all the marvelous things he had done to her with that mouth a few inches from hers. "Or making love?"

"Making love with you is always on my mind. However, we had better talk for the moment."

Again, she touched the pink flesh above his eyebrow. "I had a dream, a horrible dream, that you burned Tremaine House. The wall fell on you. Then, you were gone. I couldn't see you anywhere. I woke up feeling you were lost forever. Your mother, Madeline, and Flavia were with me on top of the rise at the back of the house."

The caress of his fingers along her damp temples warned that she was crying again.

"I dismantled the buildings stone by stone. Then I burned everything. Tremaine House no longer exists. I gave the land to Rebecca Harbauch. The legacy of the Tremaines ended with the war." He brushed his lips across hers.

"The healing wounds on your back and face . . ." Her fingers caressed the pink scar forming above his right eyebrow.

"When the house was burning, a wall fell on me. I didn't even feel the scrapes and burns until the next day."

"You're not going back?" Hope leaped in her heart.

"Going back?" Surprise arched his brow. "To Virginia?" Royle chuckled, then laughed with abandon.

Amazed, Emily gaped at him. She had never heard him laugh. Chuckle, yes, but never a full belly-laugh the way he laughed now.

"No. I doubt Williamsburg society, even with a cartful of money in the offering, would welcome me back." All traces of mirth faded. "I'm home, Emily. My ghosts are at peace."

"What do you want for your future now, Royle?" Her heart quickened in hope and dread.

"I want what I found in the San Juans. I want the impossible—the woman who came through time to love me and let me love her. Marry me, Emily. Let me love you for the rest of our days. Have children with me. I promise, I'll spend every day loving you and trying to make us happier than either one of us thought possible. I won't let you regret loving me for a moment."

"Yes. Yes. And I am," she dared, giddy with happiness.

"Yes, you will marry me?"

She nodded, intent on his approaching mouth.

"Yes, you will let me love you for the rest of our days?"

"Yes," she breathed, curling her hand around the back of his neck to draw him closer.

He brushed his mouth across her parted lips. "Yes, you will have children with me?"

"I *am* having a child with you."

Royle froze, his mouth hovering over hers. "We're having a child?"

"Yes," she exhaled, feeling him stiffen.

"You weren't going to tell me?"

"I don't believe in seduction, or coercion. We both made a choice without regard for the consequences when we made love last time. I love you, Royle, but I wouldn't entice you into marriage because I'm carrying your child. I want you here because this is where you want to be—with me and the child we're going to have.

"Tell me, do you want to argue about something that has become a moot point, or make love with me?" she asked. For a moment, she thought he would argue. "We have all winter to talk."

"And make love," he murmured, shucking his trousers.

Thank you, she prayed to the powers that had carried her across time. Without a doubt, she and Royle shared a love that would last forever. Emily lifted the quilts and extended her arms to Royle. "Welcome home."